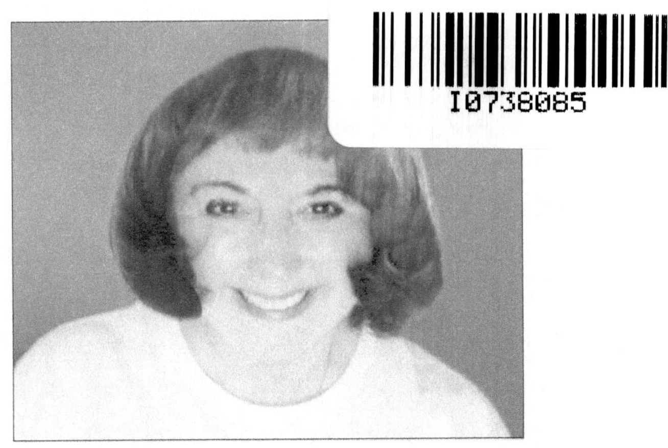

About the Author

MY CHILDHOOD IN TEXAS

My Texas roots are deep in the land, rivers, and trees. As a child I spent my summers on a ranch, just outside Junction, Texas, about 115 miles west of San Antonio. In the late 1950s, Junction was small, with wizened old timers sitting on the walkways outside the few stores on the main street.

Nestled in rocky hill country, the ranch had been a dude ranch for boys run by my aunt and uncle. The ranch was situated up against rocky hills with gnarled cedar trees pushing up between the rocks.

The property had a main ranch house, bunk houses, and a big stone building used for activities. It also had a large mess hall with restaurant sized stoves and refrigerators.

I rode horses with my two cousins on a path alongside the Llano River and on ones that went high up into the hills. We often saw wild turkeys and pheasants.

We swam in and floated on inner tubes on the river. There was a wooden diving board out over the river. On the riverbank were metal stairs secured in concrete that allowed us to exit the river. Standing in the water by the bank, I felt the cool moss on the rocks under my feet.

Early in the mornings, I went fishing with my grandmother and we caught freshwater bass, which we fried for breakfast.

One of my favorite things were the horned toad lizards, which were everywhere silently sunning themselves on the rocks.

I look back fondly on those days, remembering the expanse of the land, the quiet, and a timeless quality of life.

I now live in Santa Monica, California. I have a master's degree in screenwriting from U.C.L.A. I've had three stage plays produced in Los Angeles: *Birds of a Feather Stuck Together, Two Nowhere Men*, and *Sitting on the Edge of the Chair.*

Tessa's Heart: A Texas Story is my first novel.

Praise for Tessa's Heart: *A Texas Story*

"...the book is haunting in its presentation of the protagonist's primal, raw emotions, such as her longing for a loving father, her deep need to be seen and heard, and her complicated feelings surrounding sexuality."

—Kirkus Reviews

Tessa has been born into a family of Texan eccentrics. Her mother, a beautiful woman, craves male attention at any cost. Her grandmother, a religious zealot. In order to survive her environment, Tessa does little dances to express her frustrations. With an imagination akin to Huckleberry Finn's and a streak of contrarianism like Scout in *To Kill a Mockingbird*, Tessa wards off the ghosts of her ancestors, with whom she is in too constant communication. Intelligent and open, she rejects the prejudices foisted upon her by her grandmother and becomes friends with Josey, an eleven-year-old, black ranch hand...

—Jan Shure-Hurwitz, Writer and Educator

I've always preferred to be taken to an earlier time, a time that tells a story of those lives carved out that resonate in today's world. *Tessa's Heart* isn't simply another tale of dreams and aspirations of strong women. I enjoyed watching Tessa, as a nine-year-old girl, assert herself. This story goes into each character's psyche as only Jackie Lewis can. From Tessa's childhood to young adulthood, the narrative drew me toward individuals I felt each-and-every emotion for.

—Jon D'Amore, Author of *The Boss Always Sits in The Back, Deadfellas, The Delivery Man,* and *As Long As I have Lips*

From the very first sentence, Ms. Lewis captures the reader's attention in a cliff-hanger way. Tessa is growing up in the center of the tumultuous relationship between her beautiful mother and religious grandmother. It keeps you holding on, in order to find out more about the life of a matriarchal Southern dysfunctional Texas family. Highly descriptive and most pleasurably a page turner and a reader's delight...A must read.

—**Diane Ward**, Author of *Confessions of a Good Catholic Girl*

In *Tessa's Heart: A Texas Story*, Jackie Lewis paints a Texas that is both familiar and imaginative. The canvas of characters, told through the eyes of the adorable Tessa, mingle between the absurd and supernatural, propelling the reader through a farcical world with unexpected confrontations. A coming of age story set in the 1950s is just as poignant today as we all root for the Tessas of the world.

—**Thomas Minnich**, Writer

TESSA'S HEART
A TEXAS STORY

JACKIE LEWIS

The quotes in *Tessa's Heart* from the Bible are from the version published by:
Division of Christian Education of the National Council of
the Churches in Christ of the United States.
Old Testament Section, Copyright 1952.
New Testament Section, Copyright 1946.

Cover art © Lou Beach
www.loubeachart.com

Published by:
Flying Horse on Fire Books
Santa Monica, California
www.jackielewisauthor.com

jackiewrites3@gmail.com

ISBN: 978-0-578-80964-9 Paperback edition
ISBN: 978-0-578-77299-8 Digital edition

200913-v8

This book is dedicated to:
Barry Cohen,
Brett Shaw,
and
Jim Krusoe
Their encouragement and support made it possible.

CHAPTER ONE

In the spring of 1952, Mom and I drove out by Big Brushy Creek, where she spread out a blanket under an oak tree. We had tuna fish and Miracle Whip sandwiches, followed by Oreo cookies. The bluebonnets covered the land. Their bonnet-shaped petals nodded in the wind as if they were young ladies talking to each other. The bees buzzed their secret language in the lady bonnet's faces. The sun warmed my face while Mom played the guitar. I threw stones in the river and watched the water flow around the smooth rocks, which I was sure spoke some slow rock language I couldn't understand.

No matter where I move or how old I get Yoakum, Texas, is deep inside of me. It was my first home. Yoakum was known for the wildflowers that bloomed every spring and the city folks who would drive out to see them. That was my favorite time of year, and before Gertrude was born, it was just Mom and me.

Yoakum sits south of Highway 10 between San Antonio and Houston. On the map, it looks like a dot that someone had accidentally dropped there. A person has to have a reason to seek it out down that flat empty highway. At the city limits, there is the faded yellow sign that reads: "Yoakum, the Leather Capital of the World."

I still see the faces of Mom, Grandma Bernice, and Great-grandmother Eunice; their voices like cords pulling me back into the past. At nine-years-old, I'd never been outside of Yoakum.

Virginia, my beautiful mother, had high cheekbones, and a perfect nose. She also had large brown eyes and brown hair, but she said brown was a plain color, so she always dyed her hair red.

Mom said I was cute, but I didn't think so because my two front teeth were pushing out my upper lip. But people were always saying my large brown eyes were beautiful. My hair had been blond, but it was now getting dark like Mom's. I often braided it and put bows on the ends. I was tall and slender for my nine years.

That day, when we were out at Big Brushy Creek, besides worrying if I was pretty, I had Mom on my mind. When I was dangling my feet in the water, I noticed that Mom had stopped singing. I turned around and saw that she had tears in her eyes. I went to her and she hugged me, ran her hand through my hair, and kissed the top of my head. "When we are out here, we're away from your grandma. She's a poison mouthed snake. I know she says things about me, to turn you against me. Promise you won't listen to her."

"I'm good at not hearing things," I said.

"I'm sorry about your father. I thought he loved me and would be in our lives and take us away from her. Nothing is working out like I thought it would."

"Won't he come to see me someday?" I asked.

"I hope so."

Mom didn't seem very sure about that. Talking about my father made me feel sad, but I didn't want her to feel bad. "I like it that it's just you and me," I said. I held her close.

"Tessa, you're a fine girl and could be so much."

"I know Mom. Don't worry." I turned my head away because I didn't want her to see my tears.

At home, Grandma Bernice was quick to criticize everything. For years, she said I wasn't a normal child because I had trouble talking. When I opened my mouth, nothing came out. So, I made all sorts of movements with my arms and legs. I had my Chicken Dance with my hands in my armpits, and if I wanted to be fancy, I had my Eagle Dance with my arms outstretched. I also had my Marching Dance.

In my ninth year, something opened in me and words shot out, like bullets. I talked as much as possible to anybody other than Mom or Grandma. But still I moved my arms and legs while talking, to help me find the words.

Everyone knew everyone in Yoakum, and people never tired of talking about Mom's comings and goings. But it was possible to run into strangers at Mrs. Thelma's Five and Dime on Lott Street. The old brick store with white metal awnings had been there for as long as anyone could remember.

One Saturday, Mom left me at the lunch counter sitting on a red plastic stool and ordered me a root beer float. She went next door to the shoe store to order high heels from San Antonio.

Since I rarely saw my father Jeffrey Carter II, the cowboy, who lived with his mother, I took a special interest that day, when a grimy cowboy came in and sat down. I slid over onto the stool next to him. He ordered a cheeseburger and a Coke. When he finally looked at me, I asked "Do you know my father Jeffrey Carter, who has a ranch, The Big Grassland, south of town."

"Can't say I do," he said. He was served his cheeseburger and bit into it. It dripped cheese and he wiped his moustache with the back of his hand.

By now, I was starting to like to hear myself talk and I leaned toward him. "I learned in school that Yoakum was the start of the Chisholm Trail, which made it important in the cattle trade of the Old West." I stood up and did my Eagle Dance, turning around and swooping down.

He looked me up and down and wiped his mouth again. "What are you doing?"

"My Eagle Dance. I used to have trouble talking and this helps me. Things come to me now."

"I can see that. But I'm not much of a talker," he said.

"Bet you didn't know Yoakum was empty flat land until the construction of the San Antonio and Arkansas Pass Railroad in 1887."

"Missy, you're smart for your age and pretty, too." I gave him my prettiest smile.

My earliest memories of home were of Grandma's Victorian house. These remained saved in my heart, like an album filled with old photos.

The house was built in the late 1880s when shops were growing up around the railroad. That brought in the city people, as opposed to the people on the tooth and nail ranches on the outskirts of town.

Grandma's house was on a corner, but set back with a comfortable yard. It stood there stubbornly even though its blue paint was peeling, revealing a layer of white and then the naked wood below, an affront to its Victorian modesty. The downstairs windows had cut leaded glass, which caught the light like jewelry.

Even though Grandma Bernice didn't have the money to fix up the house on the outside, she controlled her domain inside and never let Mom or me forget who was in charge.

Upon entering the front door, a visitor would confront the dark mahogany furniture crowded into the entry hall, living room, and dining room. The furniture was from the big house Grandma Bernice's father Old Man Henry had owned. When he lost his money, he moved his wife, Great-grandmother Eunice, and daughter Bernice here. The rooms were like silent spectators waiting for someone to arrive.

On the surfaces of the tables and cabinets, lace doilies and runners clung like fabric spider webs. If a cloth got bunched up, one of Grandma's white fleshy fingers, would glide over the table to smooth it out. On top of all the doilies were an assortment of serving dishes, pitchers, and trays made of silver plate. There were a few pieces of real silver, a water pitcher, and a small elegant coffee pitcher. They were the captains of this silver army and were out front.

One would think that with all the serving dishes people visited quite often, but that was long ago before Bernice's husband, my grandfather

Floyd, left. That was before I was born and before aggravation came into the house along with the tarnish on the silver. Or maybe the silver just got tired of sitting there and became tarnished hoping that it would be gently touched while being polished.

Grandma Bernice walked through the house with a determined step. She had brown hair with gray woven into it, which rested unevenly on her jaw because she cut it herself to save money. She was chubby with a short Irish turned up nose. Her double chin looked like a fleshy necklace. Her eyes bulged a little like her own mother's eyes. She had an aversion to the sun and wore a hat and gloves. Her skin was paper white, so she had to put rouge on her cheeks to give herself some color.

She ordered clothes from the Sears and Roebuck catalogue. Sometimes she'd have Lilly Mae, our colored maid, sew on some lace around the neck to spruce a dress up. She always wore nylon stockings held up by garters above her knees with her black grandma-style shoes.

Mom said many times, "Your stockings are always bunched up around your ankles, so why don't you wear flats or loafers with socks."

Grandma puffed up. "I'm not like you. I don't want people to see my bare legs. You'd go naked if you could."

"So what? Nobody comes to this house."

"Any day somebody might drop by," Grandma said.

Grandma couldn't tolerate her arms to be empty, so she kept Queen Victoria, a small mop-headed dog, also with bulging eyes, on her right arm. Queen Victoria's lower teeth protruded over her upper teeth. Her mouth looked like a trap for insects. She was obsessive about licking the air to indicate she never got enough to eat. Grandma wouldn't let Queen Victoria bark. But she was allowed to growl and when she bit people Grandma would say, "My sweetie doesn't mean it." Grandma even taught herself to eat and write, rather sloppily, with her left hand so she could keep Queen Victoria on her right arm.

But she could straighten her arm when she sat in her floral high-backed armchair in the living room. One Sunday, Grandma Bernice was sitting tapping her pudgy fingers on the arm of the chair and Queen Victoria was curled in her lap like a fuzzy caterpillar.

Mom was out on the screened-in back-porch smoking, reading movie magazines, and practicing singing with her guitar. Grandma insisted Mom practice on the porch because she didn't want to hear Mom's donkey twang. Mom was only allowed to sing church hymns in the house.

I was in the kitchen sneaking Oreo cookies from the Aunt Jemima cookie jar when I heard, "Tessa come in here." I went into the living room chewing with my mouth open to show Grandma she was disturbing me. "Go and tell your mother to come here."

"She told me she don't want to be disturbed." Some cookie crumbs sprayed from my mouth.

"Where are you getting that bad English? You say, 'She doesn't want to be disturbed.' I don't want people thinking my granddaughter is low-class and keep that big mouth of yours closed when chewing." When Grandma got that pinched look on her face, it meant she had an argument coming on. "Just go and tell her I want to speak to her."

When I told Mom, she said, "Damn, I never get a moment's peace." I pretended to go upstairs, but snuck back down and listened from behind the hallway door. Mom stood in front of Grandma with her face twisted as well. Two faces that didn't like each other.

"Virginia, I can't afford Lilly Mae very often so why don't you make yourself useful and polish the silver."

"I've worked all week. I deserve some relaxation."

"I'm not running a charity house here," Grandma said.

"You're always clucking over that silver like you laid a golden egg. I hate it. It's only silver plate. It's old like everything else. You should get rid of it. We can barely move in here."

I peeked around the corner from the hallway. Grandma was pointing her fleshy index finger as if she was going to shoot a gun. She took a deep breath. "You don't know the value of things, that's why you're divorced with a child. You know people are talking." She pulled her skirt down to cover the garters that were tight above her knees.

When Grandma brought up Mom's being divorced, as she always did, it made me feel something was wrong with me. I didn't know any other children with divorced parents, and it was like there was a crack right down my middle and I was in two halves. I called it my "divorce crack" and it had its own voice, which screamed for everyone to look at the strange girl.

"That was nine years ago and nobody's talking about it anymore," Mom said.

"I don't understand why you didn't get married before you had Tessa."

"Not this again. Jeffrey said he wasn't going to be pushed into anything," Mom said.

"His mother thought she was better than us. I'm a well-respected member of my church and people are still talking about your divorce and now they're having a heyday talking about how you are running around with your, God forgive me, your puss … puss … pussy all over the place." Grandma actually spat into her handkerchief because the word gave her a bad taste in her mouth. Then she raised her hands and glanced up to heaven. "Forgive me Jesus, please," Grandma said. Her body shook a little.

Mom ran her hand through her hair. "Mother, keep your voice down. I don't want Tessa talking like that." She always had so many words right there when she needed them. The reason I found it difficult to talk around her and Grandma was because there was no room for me.

"Bad times call for bad language." Grandma said. She looked to heaven again and continued, "Jesus, it just comes out. I can't help it."

"I'm surprised you remembered that word. You forgot you had one. You said your virginity grew back and you didn't want to lose it again. That's why Dad went out on you," Mom said. She paced back and forth with her arms crossed in front of her.

"Shut up. You can't talk to me like that."

I didn't know what virginity was, but maybe it could grow back like Grandma said. Grandma's skirts always came below her knees so I couldn't look and see if anything was sprouting from her legs. The other girls at school didn't know about this, so I knew more than they did.

Behind the door, I felt I couldn't breathe and I moved my arms. The anger, like arrows, flew back and forth between them.

My mother said, "You drove Dad away. You thought you were the boss. He couldn't do anything without you spewing criticism."

Grandma said, "He was a nasty heathen. Always running after pussy like a chicken with its head cut off."

There was that word again. That's an important word. She wasn't talking about a cat. What did she mean?

"Don't criticize me with your garbage mouth," Grandma said.

"You always have answers for everyone but yourself."

Grandma's face tensed and turned dark. She pulled her shoulders up and pushed her head forward. The wrinkled skin around her neck reminded me of a turtle. I didn't mean it in a bad way, but it was just how I saw her in my mind.

"You didn't know what it was like with your father, Floyd the peacock, all those years," Grandma said.

Mom had her hands on her hips. "I read an article. I can't remember exactly what it said, but there's a new way to understand things. To … to take a look at yourself. That's what it said."

"I already looked in the mirror this morning." Grandma ran her hand over her hair, trying to make it look better.

"Not that way. It's called self-reflection. Don't you see you're always angry and flying off the handle," Mom said.

"Because my daughter is humiliating me. If I wasn't a Christian, I'd box your jaws," Grandma said.

"You're constantly saying the coloreds are going to rise up. You're obsessed with keeping the windows and doors locked. You're afraid of everything. I read about this … this new thing. It's called therapy … uh, psychotherapy. That's it. Now it's possible to talk to someone. I read Marilyn Monroe does this."

"Marilyn Monroe? That whore people are always talking about? Marilyn can stick the therapy up her ass, but she probably already has," Grandma said. She raised her hands and shook them a little as she glanced up to heaven. "Jesus, I'm trying to control myself. I go to church every Sunday. Praise Jesus."

"Please read this article. There're nice people … professional people that you sit and talk to. You talk about your feelings. Then you might not be so angry and afraid all the time."

"Well, whoop-de-do. Is that why you snuck off to Corpus Christi? Was it to see one of those new psycho-mental doctors? I hope you told him to look between your legs. I'd be worried too if my mind was stuck down there."

"Psychotherapy helps people to deal with their emotions."

"Pshaw. Emotions, lotions, potions. It's all the same," Grandma said.

Mom took off her loafers and threw them against the wall. "You're a narrow-minded stubborn old…."

Grandma puffed herself up, pushing her head forward in her turtle posture. She said, "I can't have your temper in my house. Nobody here would pay a person to talk to them about their feelings. Reading those movie magazines, you fancy yourself one of those lazy movie stars sitting around and spreading her legs and doing what'd you call it … psycho-talking … blah, blah … listen to me, blah, blah … make me feel better … blah, blah …. If you want to reflect on something to help your mind, reflect on my ass."

I couldn't stand still and I bumped my arm against the door. There was silence and then I heard, "Tessa, stop listening to adult conversation." Mom came around the door and grabbed my arm.

"You don't want me to know anything, but I heard everything," I said.

"Go to your room now."

"I want to sit around like a movie star doing psycho-talking. And I'll get you a mirror so you can reflect it on her ass," I said.

"Tessa, hush your mouth. Upstairs now," Mom said.

I walked up the stairs, whispering, "One pussy, two pussy, three pussy comes to tea, four pussy is behind the door, five pussy is alive, six pussy picks up sticks …."

CHAPTER TWO

Mom and Grandma Bernice arguing was the only way I found out about my, father, Jeffrey Carter II. There was an unspoken rule not to ask about him. Also, there was some forbidden secret about my great-grandfather, Old Man Henry. I didn't dare mention him. Each man was a disappointment, who left a silent shadow in the emptiness of the house. Old Man Henry had been an important man in town and sometimes I heard other people talking about him.

When I was five, I found a picture of my father, Jeffrey, holding me as a baby. It was stuffed way back in a drawer and from then on, I slept with the picture under my pillow. I also found pictures that I thought were of Great-grandfather Old Man Henry. Every so often I'd find things the men in the house had left, like a small black bag with a razor and shaving lotion, or an old pipe, or some medals. Along with the pictures, I hid these things because I didn't want them thrown out.

I remember my father visited me when I was younger. Now for quite some time, I had only gotten a glimpse of him when he was driving his mother through town in her Cadillac with the silver horse on the hood.

I'd look at him and want to shout, "Look at me. I'm here," but Mom would always drive us in the other direction.

Every once in awhile, we actually ran into my father in town. The last time was at "The Genuine Circle B Barbeque." People came from miles around for their barbeque. It sat on the north side of town on the highway surrounded by oak trees. It was a rectangular building with a covered cement patio attached to it. The barbecue smells were carried on the white smoky fog that billowed from the back where the meat cooked in big drums. Pickup trucks with gun racks were always coming and going in the parking lot, kicking up their dust storms. Usually dry tumbleweeds blew across the highway, their thin branches turned over and over scraping the earth like bony fingers, a lonely reminder of how things come and go. The lowing of cattle on the nearby ranches could be heard.

That day with Mom, I shuffled my feet through the sawdust on the patio floor. We got our sliced brisket sandwiches dripping in barbeque sauce and looked for a table. Mom didn't see my father until we sat facing the back where he was sitting. He had on his cowboy hat, gold belt buckle, and cowboy boots with gold tips which he always wore.

Mom had told me that he didn't do much cowboy work on his mother's ranch. Mom never approached him when he was with his mother. That day he was alone, and Mom took my hand and pulled me over to him. She said, "Hello Jeffrey," as she pushed me toward him. He looked at me and his warm eyes were the color of the sky. His left eye crossed slightly, looking in toward his nose, but it didn't bother me and it felt wonderful when he looked right at me, with his other eye.

"How's my girl?" he asked.

All my new ability to talk left me and I couldn't say anything. He seemed like a stranger. But he was my father. I was supposed to know him.

"I understand if the cat's got your tongue," he said.

I thought about when kids at school said that. "Don't say that. I'm not dumb. I hate it when people say that." My voice sounded angry and he seemed surprised.

"Well, just remember, you're the prettiest girl around these parts and don't let anybody tell you different."

I looked from his normal eye to his crossed eye, but I didn't know what to say.

"Tessa would love for you to come and see her once in awhile," Mom said.

"Daddy, I want to see you. See, I'm a spider." I hunched over, made my hands into claws, and wiggled my fingers like they were spider legs. He took my hands and put them down by the sides of my dress.

He looked at my mother, his eyes like ice. "I reckon I might run into one of my wife's beaus at the house. It might be a right awkward situation."

"I'm your ex-wife," Mom said.

I put my hands in my armpits and flapped my arms.

"You don't have to see me. You can take her out if you want," Mom said.

"Yes, please take me out. See, I'm a chicken. Chickens are good. If you don't want to take me, you can take the chicken out."

Jeffrey smiled. "When I did come to your house, I wasn't exactly made to feel welcome by your mother."

"Always excuses. Spend time with her. Take her to your house," Mom said.

"Daddy, I want you to take me to your house." I moved my arms in my Eagle Flight Dance. "I'll fly to your house," and one of my arms bumped into a man at the other table. Mom took my hand.

My father looked sad. "I'm sorry sweetheart. I don't mean to disappoint you. You'll understand when you're older."

In my heart I wished I really had been a bird that could fly across the empty space that was opening up between him and me. Mom pulled me away and as I looked back, I flapped my free arm. He kept looking at me with his crossed eye and his good eye. Inside, I felt the "divorce crack" getting bigger and I felt split into two pieces. If Mom didn't get me out of there, one piece was going to break off and go back to him hopping on one leg. I turned my face away so he didn't see the moisture on my cheeks. Mom took our sandwiches to the take-out window and had them put in bags and we went home to eat.

That night when I was supposed to be in bed, I squatted outside the kitchen door to hear Grandma and Mom. I got an antsy feeling whenever they talked about my father. I wished they wouldn't talk bad about him. That made my "divorce crack" split open more.

"You have to go back to court and try to get more child support. He's giving you so little. He should take care of his own. He can afford it," Grandma said. I knew she was pointing her fleshy index finger at Mom, the way she always did.

"It's his mother's money. She will fight it. How do we pay a lawyer especially if we don't get any more?"

"I've never seen a more domineering woman," Grandma said.

"I'm familiar with domineering women, puffing up like big hens, throwing their weight around, and taking pleasure in squashing people."

"What's that supposed to mean? You can't blame me for your mistakes. I told you he was a mama's boy and I think that witch of a mother incested him. He has that weird look out of his eyes. I told you he wasn't right, but no, you wouldn't listen to me," Grandma said.

"One of his eyes is crossed from birth. He couldn't help that. That has nothing to with his mother."

I crept back to bed wishing I could be like the other kids. The kids at school thought I was different because I didn't have a father. I wanted him to take me places. Didn't he know I was alone?

CHAPTER THREE

Every morning the sun shone through the leaded glass windows, making light stars on the walls and furniture. The sun, my friend, was trying to bring warmth into the house, but Mom and Grandma's arguments made things cold and dark. Their voices reverberated through the house, clinging to the walls like a pattern of worn flowers on cheap wallpaper. They gave me prickly feelings in my stomach, and then I had to do my dances. My uncontrollable movements irritated Grandma, and when Mom wasn't home, sometimes she'd use a switch on my legs telling me to be still.

When I needed to get away from her, I went into the silence of the living room with the smells of the past woven into the fabrics. The end tables, the brocade couch and chairs, all on mahogany legs, filled the room. They had been sitting in their places for as long as I could remember, mute members of our family. There was a white wooden mantelpiece over the fireplace that was never used. Grandma didn't like mirrors except for the one downstairs across from the mantelpiece, the gold-gilded oval mirror with the carved wooden bows.

Right above the mantelpiece was a sepia portrait of Great-grandmother Eunice in her dress with a high collar and small buttons up the front. Eunice's large protruding brown eyes followed you wherever you went in the room. Many times, I wished I could talk to her. For as long as I could remember, Grandma complained, "People were always talking about my mother, Eunice, and my great aunt Gertie because they said they could see and talk to spirits. People came to their séances out of curiosity. Behind their backs, people said Eunice and Gertie were 'two jigs ahead of a fit'." Grandma continued, "As my mother got crazier, she walked around talking to spirits even in town and many times she didn't hear me speaking."

Then it happened. It was after one of Grandma's and Mom's arguments that I snuck into the living room where I could be alone. I looked at the gold-gilded oval mirror on the wall across from Great-grandmother's picture. At first, I thought it was my imagination but as I got closer to the mirror there seemed to be light coming from it. The wooden frame glowed and the cut crystal bowl below it on the table lit up.

I pulled a chair in front of the mirror and stood on its brocade seat. I looked in the mirror at just the right angle and saw the reflection of Great-grandmother Eunice's picture staring back at me. I couldn't take my eyes off the image. Then I slipped into a different place and the reflection seemed to come alive. Then her face moved and changed into other women's faces flashing before me. I was scared, but I couldn't move. Then I heard women whispering and then their soft voices. I knew these were the women who went before me. I stood straight and felt proud. Then I heard a woman's voice. It sounded far away, "Tessa, I know you can hear me. I've waited so long to be able to talk to one of my relatives. I'm your great-grandmother Eunice."

"You know me?"

"I've been watching over you since you were born," Eunice said. Her voice became clearer.

"You sound just the way I imagined you would," I said.

Eunice's face was in the mirror. She wore her blue dress with the high white collar. "You don't know what it's like to be stuck in this place."

"What place?"

"We're in the spirit world," Eunice said.

"Your face keeps changing into other faces. Who else is there with you?" I asked.

Then I heard, "Move over. Let me look through the mirror." I saw another face in the mirror.

"Why can't I see her?" the other face asked.

"Hold still. Be quiet and maybe you'll see her," Eunice said.

The other face became clearer in the mirror. "Oh, now I see her. Oh, she's wonderful. I hope you see me. I'm Gertie, Eunice's sister. I'm the pretty one." Gertie had pink lips and blond curls framing her face. She wore a white lace collar with a pink cameo.

"I don't know anything about spirits. Everyone says they're not real," I said.

Eunice's face came back. "We've come to guide you. We want to help."

Gertie pushed her face into the mirror. "Eunice, you're not going to have her all to yourself. You never let me talk. I want to feel her world."

"Can't you talk to people where you are?" I asked.

"There're a bunch of dumb spirits here who don't know they can talk. They just stare into space like they did at the old folk's home," Eunice said.

"It's my turn, move over." Gertie's face pushed into the mirror. "Also, there're spirits here who are angry about what happened when they were alive. They say nasty things," Gertie said. The curls around her face shook.

"They were boring in life and they are boring here," Eunice said.

"Do they say the word 'pussy' where you are?" I asked.

"Tessa, you don't talk like that," Eunice said.

"Let her talk the way she wants," Gertie said.

"I'm feeling confused." I wobbled on the chair. "I don't have many friends at school."

"You're not alone. You can talk to us. And we get to feel your world for a few moments. It gives us a feeling of ecstasy," Eunice said.

"Mom and my father Jeffrey are divorced and he doesn't come to see me."

"We're sorry to hear that," Eunice said.

"Do you know why he doesn't come?" I asked.

"No, we didn't know him," Gertie said.

"Can't you do something to get him to come and see me? Don't you have some power?" I asked.

"Dear, I'm sorry. I wish we could help, but other people can't hear us, and he came after our time. We're stuck back in our time. Sometimes we get glimpses of things, but so many things have happened that have passed us by," Gertie said.

"We want you to know you come from a long line of strong women. Nobody can take that away," Eunice said.

"I carried a gun, and I showed my underwear to beaus when I wanted to. I loved it when they got excited," Gertie said and giggled.

"Hush. Right away you start taking about your underwear," Eunice said.

"I can talk about whatever I want to. I found out how to have a big, big … I can't remember the word. It's a big 'O', and you can't stand to hear me say it." Gertie opened her mouth and moaned a little and said, "A big 'OOOO'."

"Shut your crudeness. It was Father who kept you from being run out of town," Eunice said.

"You might have been better off if you could have had one," Gertie said.

"I wasn't mean like you," Eunice said.

I was getting dizzy. "This is really interesting," I said.

Gertie pushed Eunice out of the mirror. "Eunice, stop trying to make me look bad, or I'll slap your face."

Eunice pushed her face back into the mirror. "Move over. Stop talking about yourself. We're here to help Tessa." A splash of light from the mirror fell onto the cut crystal bowl on the table making it glow brightly.

I felt a breeze and tingling as if fingers were touching me all over. "I'm getting mixed up. I'm dizzy."

The next thing I knew I was staring at the carpet. I looked up and the mirror was blank and the voices were gone. The whole room felt lonely.

I noticed Grandma was standing over me, her legs stiff in her old lady shoes. "Tessa, what are you doing on the floor?" she said.

I stood up. "I guess I fell."

Grandma looked at the chair. "Why were you standing on my good chair?"

"I was talking to Great-grandmother Eunice and Great-aunt Gertie."

Grandma's face tensed and she looked scared for a moment. "Don't ever say that again. You weren't talking to them. It's against the Bible. Do you want to become crazy like them and go to hell?"

"Why does your mother have such big eyes?" I asked. Then I did my Marching Dance and I cupped my fingers and put them around my eyes. "Bug eyes like this." I started laughing and couldn't stop. I didn't mean any harm, but Grandma went to the broom closet and got the switch that she always had ready.

"Guess you think my eyes are like that too. My mother had a medical condition." The switch made its swooshing sound as it hit my legs.

After that, I had dreams of Great-grandmother Eunice holding me close. One night, I suddenly awakened feeling warm and I smelled roses. The old wooden floor in the hallway was creaking, and half-asleep I went into the hallway and I saw Eunice and Gertie in long, old-fashioned lace dresses, their hair piled up on their heads, gliding gracefully down the stairway, their white-gloved hands holding onto the railing. When they got to the bottom of the stairs, they turned and looked at me for a moment and then they moved down the hall.

I felt a rush of greatness because they were a part of me. And people hadn't been able to tell them what to do.

CHAPTER FOUR

Often Mom would yell, "You're driving me crazy. I should put my head in the oven and breathe in the gas."

Grandma would yell back, "Suit yourself. I can't do anything."

Then Mom would grab her purse and say, "We're going shopping."

"You just want an excuse to parade around," Grandma said.

Then in Grandma's 1948 maroon Buick we'd drive into town that was four blocks away. The canopy of the sky stretched over Yoakum making the town look as if made of miniature two-story buildings. On Grand Avenue, the main downtown street, the roofs of the brick buildings stood out against the sky, with its sculptured clouds. Sometimes the clouds were like balls strung across the sky, and other times they were all together like thick floating cotton candy masses.

In front of each building were wood or metal awnings jutting out and shading the sidewalk. They were held in place by metal poles attached above the awnings onto the fronts of the old buildings. I liked to imagine the wood-frame storefront windows were the building's eyes and the awnings were their eyelids protecting the windows from the Texas sun.

Above the awnings were the old style second-story windows with three next to each other, like sisters standing together gossiping.

Every time we went to town, we drove past the Green and Wellhousen Building, a heavy stone building on the corner of Grand Avenue and Lott Street. The front entrance faced the corner and above the door it said The Lone Star Bank.

In the next block on the right was the red brick building with white trim and an old metal-covered awning with a sign that read, Mrs. Thelma's Five and Dime. We parked the car in front of the store.

When Mom walked down Grand Avenue, the owners came to the entrances of their stores to watch her. Her long, wavy red hair brushing against her tight-fitting dress flowed down her back. She proudly owned her body, soft and smooth, like an expensive fabric. She swung her hips and had a way of tossing her head that showed her long neck. Usually, she wore red pumps with red toenail polish that matched her fingernails. The polish on her toes was messy at times because she never had the patience to get it on right.

That day, sitting in the passenger seat of Grandma's Buick, I felt I was a part of Mom as if I had been sewn onto her. She was the queen of Yoakum, and I was her princess, the only princess. Actually, she had been Homecoming Queen before I was born. Before she could get out of the car, I hugged her. She said, "Tessa you're my affectionate daughter."

"I love you always, Mama."

We got out of the car and went into Mrs. Thelma's Five and Dime. That day, skinny Mrs. Thelma was behind the counter. Her bright blue eyes had no lashes and stood out above her beaklike nose. She had smile lines, and time lines; in fact, her face was wrapped in lines. She was demonstrating her latest cold crème product, and she insisted Mom watch her rub the white cream into the folds of her neck until they were covered like a bird lathered with Crisco. She smiled and said, "See, this gets rid of the turkey neck."

"But I still see the turkey neck," I said. I put my hands in my armpits and flapped my imaginary wings and clucked.

She put her face close to me and I smelled her breath. "I'm surprised you actually said something." Then she looked close at Mom's face. "Virginia, you don't worry about wrinkles now, but the day will come when your face will look like a prune."

Mrs. Thelma was a gatherer of news, and it clung to her along with the sweet scent of her own five and dime perfume. Her interest in my mother spilled over onto me, and she would run her wrinkled fingers with the polished nails over my head as if she was examining a prize calf. She would invariably say something to irritate Mom. That day she said, "Even though she doesn't talk much, she looks like your grandmother Eunice."

Mom wouldn't let on that she was worried because I was hardly speaking. "That was a long time ago, and I didn't think you were old enough to really know Eunice."

"I was very young but everyone knew Eunice. She was one of the most interesting people to ever come from Yoakum. Nobody ever found out what happened to her husband, your grandfather, Old Man Henry. People talked about the mystery for years," Mrs. Thelma said.

Mother spoke with an edge in her voice. "Well, Tessa isn't at all like Grandmother Eunice. She's smart and doesn't waste words."

"Yes, I'm just like Eunice. I talk to her all the time and nobody told her what to do."

This shocked Mrs. Thelma and she stood there not knowing what to say. Finally, she said, "Well, I'll be. So, are you going to have séances at your house?"

"She's just talking about a child's game." Mom was quick to intervene.

"No, I really talk to her and I see her too," I said. Then I stretched out my arms for my Eagle Dance and bumped into the cold cream jars.

"Don't contradict me," Mom said.

Mrs. Thelma pursed her lips together, her lash-less eyes got bigger, and she stood up straighter. "Well, she makes up for not talking by moving so much. That's not normal."

"I have something to say now. And that is that I know the word 'pussy'. Do you have a pussy or are you too old?"

I waved my hands while saying pussy a few more times to irritate her even more. Mrs. Thelma dropped the nail polish remover into Mom's bag making a clunk.

Mom grabbed my arm hard. "Tessa, hush your mouth."

"What are you teaching that child?" asked Mrs. Thelma. She put the Kleenex and soap into the bag. Mom ignored her.

Then we went to the lunch counter and sat on the red plastic stools. On the counter were ketchup bottles, sugar containers, and salt and pepper shakers next to the small jukeboxes spread along the white Formica lunch counter.

Betty Lynn, Mrs. Thelma's daughter, came out from the back, put her hands on her hips, and stared at us as we sat at the counter. Betty Lynn, a younger version of her mother, was beginning to have the same lines etched onto her face and also lash-less eyes. She wore a beige waitress uniform with a folded down white collar. At first, she gave us a smile, but as she got closer to us it turned into an ugly frown. Her bleached blond hair was piled high on her head with a small comb in the back, which she took out, and scooped up the unruly hairs and then replaced it. She quickly took out a small can of hair spray from under the counter and sprayed the back of her head. The smell stuck in my nostrils. "We just got in some fresh Velveeta. How about some grilled cheese sandwiches?" she asked.

"No, just our usual root beer floats." Then Mom pushed her red hair back over her shoulders and smoothed out her skirt.

The noise from the parakeets in the back filled the store. While waiting for our floats, I punched the red keys on the small jukebox on the counter, but Mom didn't seem interested in music that day. Betty Lynn served us our floats, without saying a word.

We were almost finished with our floats when Larry, a ranch hand, walked through the front door. Larry's worn jeans were tight and held up by a silver belt buckle. He had thick sandy-colored hair parted on one side. His muddy cowboy boots clacked on the floor as he walked confidently toward Mom. Then he took off his cowboy hat, marked with a sweat ring, and set it on the counter. He smelled of horse, sweat, and dirt. His face warmed with a smile. "Hello, my sweet Virginia." He stood close to Mom, resting one arm on the counter, his denim shirt unbuttoned at the top where his chest hair edged out of it. He nodded to Betty Lynn and me, but I wasn't worth any words. Only Mom counted.

Mom sat up straight. "Hello Larry." Mom's red lipstick was all shiny and he ran a hand down her hair and then he put his arm around her and kissed her while he also looked Betty Lynn in the eye.

Bette Lynn said, "Larry, why don't you go someplace else for that?"

"Mind your own business," Larry said.

"Don't be rude with me. I've known you since you were born."

I didn't understand why Mom got so much attention from men and I stood up and did my Eagle Dance, but they ignored me.

"I've called you, but your mother always says you're not home," Larry said.

"She's the censorship committee," Mom answered.

"I just got back from working on Whittaker's. I was gone a couple of months with the round up, branding, and building new fences. Why don't you come outside, and we can talk in my truck?" he asked.

She went outside with Larry and he opened the truck door and she slid across the seat.

This was supposed to be our time together and I hated being left alone. I said loudly to Betty Lynn, "Get me another float."

"You watch your rude mouth with me."

"Nice Betty Lynn, pretty please, get me another float with two scoops of ice cream."

Betty Lynn quickly made the float and went to the front window to watch Mom and Larry. Betty Lynn searched her pockets for her sunglasses and put them on because the sun shining through the window made her squint. I moved to the end of the counter and sat down. All I could see was the back of Betty Lynn's starched uniform.

"Betty Lynn, can I ask you a question?"

"What?" She didn't turn around and moved even closer to the window.

"I don't know how to ask this," I said.

"Well, go on and ask. I don't have all day."

"Does my father Jeffrey come in here?" I asked.

"Sometimes." Then she moved some pots and pans in the window to get a better view.

"What does he talk about with you?" I asked.

"Just ordinary things." She put her hands on her hips and continued staring out the window.

"Does he mention me?" I ran my hand down one of my braids and adjusted the pink bow on the end.

Betty Lynn turned around and pushed her glasses up from the end of her nose. Her lash-less eyes, like her mother's, stared at me. "Tessa, don't you see your daddy?"

I felt embarrassed but I tried not to show it. "I do, but I just wondered what he talks about."

Mrs. Thelma came out from the back and Betty Lynn nodded her head, pointing her beak of a nose toward the window. Mrs. Thelma made a beeline to the front window where she squeezed in between stacked suitcases, towels, and bottles of detergent. She looked over at Betty Lynn a couple of times and widened her eyes.

The awning cast a shadow over the front of the truck, which made it possible to see Mom and Larry's faces. As Mom sat up straight, Larry put his arm around her and kissed her, but then Mom pulled away. They looked like they were yelling at each other. When Mom tried to get out of the truck, he held onto her arm.

It didn't seem to bother her that she was being watched. She pulled away from him, got out, and swung her hips as she came back inside. I sucked loudly on what was left of the float. Standing with her arms crossed in front of her as if she owned all the ice cream in the world, Betty Lynn told Mom I had insisted on another float.

Mom turned to me. "Tessa, you can't eat as much as you want. Do you want to have fat bulging all over? You can't get a husband that way."

"She's only nine-years-old. And what's the point of getting a husband if you can't hold on to him?" Betty Lynn asked Mom, "Do you see much of Jeffrey?" Mom looked down and didn't say anything. Betty Lynn puffed up and said, "Well, we see him. He comes in here sometimes, and I see him driving through town with his mother in her Cadillac. Mighty nice car. Seems like you were set up for awhile," Betty Lynn said.

"Betty Lynn, why would you say all this in front of Tessa?" Then Mom pulled my arm to leave. But on the way out, she saw a girl's purse with the handle standing straight up.

Betty Lynn said, "This is the first time we've carried these purses in the store." Mom bought it and I knew it was because Betty Lynn had mentioned my father.

CHAPTER FIVE

Besides getting me in trouble at school, my uncontrollable urge to do my dances and kick up my legs up was a problem Grandma worried about all the time. Grandma was always telling me, "Imagine your legs are two tree trunks growing next to each other and they can't be moved. You have to keep your legs together for Jesus."

But when things were pinching me from inside, I'd wave my arms and bounce one leg then the other. Then Grandma would run that switch over my legs and say, "If you keep moving your arms and bouncing your legs, you're going to come down with the St. Vitus dance. Men will think you have a disease and won't want to marry you."

I'd say, "But I'm only nine-years-old." That didn't matter because she'd still make me go to my room for hours until I could hold still.

Up to this point, one reason that I didn't talk that much was because Grandma was always correcting me. Sometimes, Grandma held a switch when she corrected my manners, posture, voice, and even my pronunciation. I got tired of having to repeat words correctly so I'd say as little as possible. She even had me walk around with a book on my head.

She'd touch that switch to places on my back where I needed to straighten up. "It will take years of training for you to be ready for marriage. An unmarried woman is like a ship without a rudder on a stormy sea," she'd say.

I thought that I didn't want to have a rudder sticking out of my butt.

She had a serious look on her face, but she looked off into space as if talking to someone else. "You're all I have left. You won't bring shame on me like your mother. You're not going to run around. Mark my word, you'll be a lady and a Christian one way or another." She whacked that switch against her leg for emphasis. She winced. The next time she made sure to hit it against the chair.

Another reason I didn't talk very much was because there weren't any children my age in my neighborhood. Most of the houses on our block had old people sitting on the front porches, stiff like ceramic lawn decorations.

Cathy was the only girl my age who lived close to me. Grandma wouldn't let me play with any dirty boys.

My friendship with Cathy was an on-again-off-again thing because of our mothers. There was an old argument about a boy from high school, and when they were getting along we were allowed to play with each other. But when the old disagreement came up, Cathy's mom would grab her out of our tea parties, leaving me alone again.

But I had Lilly Mae, and I talked to her when I could. Every week Grandma would take some bills out of her money sock. Then she'd have Lilly Mae come in to polish the silver and clean the house. She was a plump colored woman, high cheekbones, a large bosom, and dressed in bright print dresses she'd made herself. Lilly Mae had worked for Great-grandmother Eunice when she was very young, and even though she was old, her hands were still strong enough to cook and clean.

Grandma Bernice was in her element when she was bossing Lilly Mae while she was polishing and cleaning. After Grandma got Lilly Mae started in the kitchen, she would go into the living room and sit in her floral armchair. Lilly Mae would bring her a plate of fresh-baked Toll House cookies. With Queen Victoria in her lap, Grandma would hold a cookie in her mouth and Queen Victoria with her bottom teeth sticking out would nibble on it. Grandma didn't see the look on Lilly Mae's face when Queen Victoria put her tongue in Grandma's mouth.

While sitting in her armchair, she always had a full porcelain teacup in its saucer next to her. She called it her "daytime coffee" but it was really wine. She had a different teacup and saucer for her "nighttime coffee" which was also wine.

In the kitchen, Lilly Mae went about her work talking to herself for hours because nobody else talked to her. I'd overhear her saying, "Lordy, how does this silver get so dirty just sittin' here. It's like some evil spirits is comin' in here and tarnishin' this here silver jest to make my life hard. If Jesus hisself came down to Yoakum and walked along Grand Avenue, Miss Bernice would be sayin', 'You can't leave this house until you finish the polishin'. She wouldn't care if I missed the whole end of the world and the Judgin' Day. She's surely goin' to miss it herself cause she can't lift all this silver to take it wit her."

A couple of days later in the afternoon, the sunlight came through the dining room window, reflecting orange off the silver and warming everything. Lilly Mae, alone in the kitchen, was polishing the silver and I didn't want her to feel lonely, so I went in to show her something.

I'd found a faded photo in an old suitcase in the unused bedroom in the back. There was the date 1895 on the back of it. It was of a man wearing a suit with a vest, a cowboy hat and boots, and next to him a dark-skinned woman in a lacy dress, hat, and gloves. I wondered whether this was my great-grandfather Old Man Henry, who no one would talk about? And who was the pretty dark woman standing next to him?

In the kitchen, Lilly Mae had the silver stacked up by the sink. She had taken a break and was sitting at the old wooden kitchen table drinking some sweet tea.

"I found this picture. This has to be my great-grandfather, Old Man Henry. I don't have any relatives, so I must be a related to this woman. And she looks part Indian. So that means I'm part Indian," I said.

"Tessa, you're not part Indian. That's your great-grandfather all right, but that ain't no relative of yours. You put that picture back. Your grandma will get real upset if she sees you wit that," Lilly Mae said.

"I like this picture. Why won't Grandma or Mom talk about Great-grandfather Old Man Henry? If she's not a relative, who's this pretty lady?"

"That weren't no lady," Lilly Mae said.

"Tell me about her, please."

"She not supposed to be mentioned in this house. Your grandma will have a hissy fit if she finds out I told you," Lilly Mae said.

"Please tell me." But Lilly Mae hesitated. "I have to know."

"While your great-grandfather, Old Man Henry, was married to Eunice, she was his fancy woman," Lilly Mae said.

"A fancy woman. That sounds nice. But her skin is dark."

"She's colored," Lilly Mae said.

"Really? Did he live with her?"

"No, he was married to Eunice, but he built her a house on the other side of town. Give me that." She reached for the photo.

"No, it's mine," I said, backing away.

"You better hide that picture real good. And never mentions what I told you," Lilly Mae said.

"But Lilly Mae, look how dark my eyes are. I must be part Indian. I like Indians."

"Tessa, I told you to quit saying that. People get upset at the thought of white folks marrying injuns." Lilly Mae got up and went back to the sink and started polishing the coffee pitcher, rubbing the curved spout.

I had to tell her something, but I didn't know how to start. I did my Marching Dance, moving my arms up and down like I was in a parade.

"Tessa, I know you has somethin' on your mind, but stop that moving and tell me," Lilly Mae said.

"I have a secret. If I tell you, you won't tell Grandma, will you?" I did my Eagle Dance with my arms outstretched.

"I tell your grandma as little as possible." Lilly Mae rubbed the belly of the pitcher.

The words came quickly. "I see them. I really see their faces in the mirror and they talk to me." I marched around the room.

Lilly Mae held up the pitcher to see if she'd gotten all the tarnish off. "Child, slow down. I cain't make heads or tails 'bout what you're saying. What's that your seeing?" she asked. She put the pitcher on the counter next to the polished serving dishes.

"When I look really hard in the mirror in the living room. Then their faces come to me, Great-grandmother Eunice and her sister Gertie. Their faces flash right before me. Then I hear their voices whispering to me." It felt good to finally tell someone, and I moved my arms in my Eagle Dance.

Lilly Mae was taking the good silver out of the drawer to be polished, but she put it down and turned, wiping her hands on her apron and putting her hands on her hips. She looked frightened. "Now, you jest stop that. You don't want to go meddling with the dead spirits. Leave them be. I suppose you got that from your great-grandmother Eunice. She had the power and her sister had it too. The power ain't good for no white girls or white women. They can't handle it. Colored women can handle it. The spirits git in the white women's heads and makes 'em do things, crazy things. For you own good don't tell anybody 'bout this and stop doin' it."

I'd never seen her so serious.

"Is that what's wrong with Grandma? Does she have spirits in her?" I asked.

"Don't you ever let her hear you say that."

"Most of the kids at school don't talk to me and I need someone to talk to." I felt the "divorce crack" right down the front of me.

"You better listen to me. Don't stare in no mirrors and don't try to see things. They will be goin' away if you stop tryin' to talk to them."

I loved Lilly Mae, so I promised I wouldn't talk to them anymore, but I knew I would.

CHAPTER SIX

After Queen Victoria and the silver, my grandma's most prized possession was her antique doll collection. She had dolls of all sizes that belonged to her mother, her aunt, and others. Each one was carefully laid on small blankets and pillows in decorated boxes, cedar boxes, and hatboxes. These boxes were like miniature coffins holding dead children with curly ringlets, small stiff hands, and open, staring eyes. Their eyes were as clear as the day they were made, even though their dresses were yellowed. They were stacked in the musty closet, permanent silent guests like little people with secrets.

Also, the closet was full of Grandma's clothes from years ago, hanging shadows of her former selves. She had linen dresses with long skirts, padded shoulders, and wide belts completely different from the loose dresses she wore now. She couldn't fit into them anymore. Every once in awhile, Grandma would tell Lilly Mae it was time to clean out the closet, but then a tiredness would come over her and she'd need her "afternoon coffee". Then Lilly Mae would say, "Next time, Miss Bernice, we'll do it next time."

Sometimes, late at night after she'd been drinking, Grandma got on what Mom called her "high-horse". Then she'd take out those dolls and place them on chairs. She'd carry on something fierce, talking and yelling at those dolls. Grandma's crying would wake up Mom and me. She'd be talking to her father, Old Man Henry. She'd say, "Papa I had dreams. My dream was to leave this town, to get on that big train to somewhere, but Papa, you were always saying, 'You're just going to get married and have kids'." Then she'd shout, "Having kids is a thankless job." And she'd throw her cup and saucer, bam! When I opened my door, Mom would be standing at the top of the stairs and she'd tell me to get back in my room, but I'd crack the door open so I could listen. Grandma would go on about how she snuck off on the train to Houston when she was fifteen. She'd say, "I wandered in Houston for days. I didn't have any money. I had to come back." She'd scream, "Papa, please don't hit me. I just wanted to see things. Please stop. And stop saying I'm stupid. Papa, I'm sorry. It wasn't my fault what happened to you. I can't ever tell anyone about the secret." Then she'd say, "My sweet girls here know things nobody else knows."

Grandma had told me never to touch the dolls, but when I talked to Eunice in the mirror, she told me I could have them. Every time I stood in front of the closet door, I felt excitement and I had to move a lot to keep myself from opening the door. I'd even wake up in the night thinking about those dolls. They were lonely in those boxes, so when Grandma went to the store, I just lifted the lids on the boxes to sneak a quick look. But when I lifted them, I heard their voices begging me to take them out. How could I ignore them? Finally, I couldn't stand it anymore. I thought that if Grandma can do whatever she wants, so can I.

One day, I took them out and ran my fingers over their delicate faces and I felt a pulsing in them. First, I held them close, but they were so happy to be out that they wanted to walk across the couch. Their high-pitched voices said, "We know your father, Jeffrey. Take us to him."

"I didn't know you knew him," I said. I walked them over to the corner of the room and they said, "We're at your father's house now."

I said, "I don't see it."

They said, "But we see it." When they found him inside, they formed a circle around him talking all at once.

The doll with long blond hair told him, "Don't you want Tessa to see your pretty house? You have to bring her here. You have to hug Tessa and be good to her."

Then they all said, "You have to visit Tessa. So, what if your mother doesn't want you to see her? You're a cowboy and you shouldn't be afraid. You have to visit Tessa before she gets too old."

Some of their arms and legs fell off and they told me it was because they were pulling on him to bring him to me. Other dolls in the closet kept telling me to bring them out so they could go after him. I let them out, and with their sweet voices they told him to come to me. Some even cried.

I didn't hear Grandma come home until she swooped down on me. Queen Victoria jumped out of her arm, growled, and grabbed one of the dolls by its human hair and shook it until its head came off. She ran around holding the head while Grandma screamed at her. Then Grandma turned and screamed at me. I told her that Great-grandmother Eunice said that she wanted me to have them. That made Grandma Bernice even angrier, and she told me to stop that crazy talk. She got the switch from the closet and switched my legs.

Before Lilly Mae left that evening, she snuck up to my room and put some lotion on the welts on my legs. Lilly Mae said, "Why do you do those things that makes her mad? She got the temper. It's like she has some of the fire from hell inside of her just waitin' to come out."

"Why can only she take them out of the boxes? I need to talk to them too," I said.

"Those dolls mean somethin' that goes way back. Maybe she tell you someday and maybe not."

CHAPTER SEVEN

Even though I used the word 'pussy' at school mostly to shock the kids, I didn't know what that word and other bad words really meant.

One evening, when I came down the back staircase into the kitchen, I heard Grandma on the black phone in the entry hall. I peeked around the corner and saw her sitting on a wooden stool at a small table. She had her head pushed forward looking like a turtle, which meant she was talking about something important. She clutched the receiver so hard her knuckles were whiter than usual. Her face was scrunched up and her lips were taut.

"Mrs. Thelma at night, they come up through the holes that lead from the bowels of the earth and hide in places, you know, Satan's minions." Grandma's double chin jiggled as she spoke. "Remember, the pastor just spoke about them yesterday. I'm talking about the lust demons. They come in all sizes. They attack ladies in their beds at night." She paused a moment. "Mrs. Thelma, please try to keep up with my conversation."

I felt a creepy fear take hold of me. In the kitchen, I opened the pantry door to see if there were any demons in that darkness. If they were going to shrink down and hide in a can, which one would they hide in? Maybe

Spam …. Yes, they would hide in a Spam can. I picked up a Spam can and shook it to see if any demons would come out. What was Grandma talking about? They couldn't be this small. Maybe they broke open the can when they came out at night?

Again, I peeked around the corner into the hallway. "They turn ladies into foaming sex reptiles. They make them do nasty things." Grandma spat out a little saliva as she talked. I thought maybe I should get a knife in case Grandma turned into a foaming sex reptile herself.

Her nylons were bunched up around her ankles and she sat with her legs apart. Wiping sweat from her forehead, she said, "You won't believe what a woman from our church told me," Grandma paused while Mrs. Thelma was talking and then said, "Yes, I always get all the news first. She told me that some women put that nasty stinking thing in their mouths. Their husbands make them do it. This is what the world is coming to."

Mom came in silently through the back door to the kitchen and she stood behind me, with her arms crossed. She looked beautiful wearing her full print skirt and red leather belt. She listened to Grandma talking, "Mrs. Thelma, we have to know what the sin is to fight it. It's mostly the young women putting it in their mouths. Just think how stupid they must look and they can't talk." Grandma pretended to talk making gurgling sounds. I could feel Mom tensing up behind me. "Mrs. Thelma, how would I know how long they keep it in their mouths?" Grandma asked.

Mom rushed to Grandma. "Stop that crazy talk. Tessa is listening." Mom tried to take the receiver from her, but she scratched Mom's hand.

"Mrs. Thelma, I have to get off the phone because my reptile daughter is here," Grandma said and slammed down the receiver.

Mom followed Grandma into the living room. "Your religion is going to drive you insane and you'll end up in a mental institution," she shouted.

"Before you use my glassware and silverware you wash your mouth out," Grandma said.

I thought that plumbers are men and they spend a lot of time under the sink. I looked under the sink to see if they might have left a nasty thing there.

Even with wine in her teacup and sitting in her flowered chair, other fears would take a hold of her. The tall leaded glass windows in the front had to be locked at night no matter how hot it was. To me, the windows were the living eyes of the house and needed to be open so they could see the other houses across the street. Grandma had installed large locks on the windows that were ugly looking. The locks were supposed to keep out burglars, murderers, and especially rapists.

But that was only part of it. There was one big fear that connected all her fears, and there was no way to avoid it in conversations. And that was her fear of colored people.

I didn't fully understand the secret stories from Yoakum's past. I only heard snatches of dredged up memories. Awful things, gritty things like the dust and stones in long, dry creek beds.

Grandma's talking about colored people didn't make sense to me because I loved Lilly Mae. She comforted me and rubbed lotion on my legs after Grandma used the switch. Often, she bathed me and brushed my hair. All over town, colored people could be seen working, an army of hands cooking, cleaning, gardening, and building. But even then, I knew they were ignored.

When Grandma talked about the colored people, I knew it didn't bother her how they were treated. But Grandma's attitude really upset Mom, and she said Grandma was hateful.

One evening when I came into the kitchen, Grandma, her cheeks flushed, was pointing her fleshy finger at Mom. Mom was backed up against the counter and looked trapped. "Mark my word, they're going to rise up," Grandma said.

"I hate it when you talk like that." Mom's face twisted with disgust.

Sometimes in the daytime, colored men came to the back door and asked if there was any work they could do. Grandma couldn't afford to pay for yard work, so she turned them away. But when Grandma wasn't looking, Mom called them back and gave them a plate of leftover chicken and grits. If they came when Mom wasn't there, I'd make peanut butter and jelly sandwiches, put them in a bag, and hand it to them.

One afternoon when I'd just gotten home from school, I was with Lilly Mae in the kitchen and I could tell by the sound of Grandma's voice coming from the living room that she was giving Mom one of her talks. "I saw you giving away food again. Every colored in town will stop here. We can't afford to feed the whole town."

Lilly Mae silently cut up carrots for dinner. I hated for her to hear Grandma talking that way. Then I took out some cookies from the Aunt Jemima cookie jar and replaced its head, making sure the smiling face lined up with the body.

"I recognize some of them from town and I'm going to feed them if I want to," Mom said.

"What do you mean you recognize them? You wouldn't dare to go to that side of town."

Lilly Mae stopped the cutting and raised her eyes in an exasperated expression.

"Mother, stop the craziness. I'm suffocating with these windows closed. I hate it here," Mom stepped toward the windows.

"Don't touch those windows."

I peeked around the corner into the living room.

"Who's going to break in? We know most the people in town," Mom said.

"Some colored with cockroach fingers is going to grab my silver. I can see them." Grandma pointed to her eyes and pressed her lips together.

"Mother, would you keep your voice down. Lilly Mae's right in the kitchen," Mom whispered.

I hunched over because I was ashamed that Lilly Mae had heard what Grandma said. I stepped back into the kitchen. Lilly Mae's jaw looked tense and she shook her head. "My, my," she said.

"She's not talking about you," I said and I blushed.

"Child, she talks that way about all negroes. We be all the same to her and we're only good for being maids."

I felt pain in my heart. I put my arms around Lilly Mae and said, "Don't listen to her. You're good and I love you." Tears were in my eyes.

I heard Mom in the living room. "You hardly go out, but you made sure those biddies at church spread it all around that you have a shotgun and two pistols in the house."

"My daddy was a bastard. His cock ran around like a chicken with its head cut off, poking everything he could find," Grandma said.

"Mama, stop that language. Tessa has already gotten in trouble at school for saying the wrong things."

"Don't tell me what I can say in my own house. Like I was saying, even with my pudgy fingers my daddy taught me to shoot," Grandma said.

"But you don't need a pistol in the bathroom."

"The bathroom is where a person is the most vulnerable."

"Remember it's 1952. Why do you believe this stuff?"

Later, I snuck into the bathroom and searched under the sink to find the gun. It was stored in one of Grandma's old purses, wrapped in a lacy handkerchief. It was hard black metal. I only touched it for a second before Mom came to the door. "Put that back and don't ever touch it again. Go to your room."

I smiled and thought, you won't always be able to boss me.

Mom said, "What are you smiling about?"

"Nothing. But I know a secret." I went to my room.

"You better not be causing trouble," Mom called after me.

I knew something Grandma didn't know. Late at night after Grandma drank a lot of wine, Larry the ranch hand made visits to Mom in her bedroom. Mom didn't know that their noises woke me up. A couple of times, I cracked my door and saw Larry at Mom's door kissing her and then walking down the hall carrying his boots with his belt buckle open and his pants unzipped. I thought that Larry must have turned into a foaming sex reptile, which was making all the noise. Now he was having trouble turning back and that's why his pants were unzipped.

CHAPTER EIGHT

Finally, it was arranged and Mom was driving me to see my friend Cathy. She always wore her curly brown hair pulled back into a braided ponytail with a pink bow. She had a turned-up nose that made people say she was cute. But I didn't care because I was pretty, too.

Cathy was my only friend, but I hadn't been allowed to play with her for a long time because of the time at school when I said the word … 'pussy'. For years at school I couldn't talk much. Sometimes the kids called me "Cat Got Your Tongue" or "Dummy the Silent Mummy". After hearing Grandma say pussy, I told Cathy the word because I knew if she said it the other girls would copy her. She told the other girls it was a magic word and the girls ran around the playground shouting pussy. One of the girls even called the teacher pussy. Some of the girls used the word at home and all hell broke out. When I said my grandma had said it, nobody believed me. Later that day, the switch made red welts on my legs. But after that, the kids saw me as someone who wasn't afraid to break the rules and didn't call me names anymore.

After a month, Cathy's mother forgot she disliked me. Cathy and I had been friends since our first day of school and we were still in the same class. When I was finally allowed to have Cathy at my house again, I planned something special. In my room I opened the window, but pulled the curtains closed over it. I had covered my little table with one of Grandma's oversized tablecloths. I put candles and Oreo cookies on the table and filled the teacups with soda. I put on a pair of Grandma's white gloves and I gave Cathy a pair. The gloves were too big and the leather fingers stuck out over our fingers.

"I'm so glad you were allowed to come back. I want you as my friend. I want to tell you something I don't tell anyone." I said.

"I can keep a secret."

"I see and talk to the spirits of my great-grandmother and her sister," I said.

"My mother says spirits don't exist." Cathy twisted her braid around her finger.

"I'll show you."

I set up a small mirror and lit the candles placing them in front of the mirror. I spread out some playing cards to help create the mood.

"Does your mom let you have candles?" Cathy asked. She smoothed out her pink ruffled skirt. She wore a bracelet with little hearts on it.

"Of course. She believes in what I do." I put my arms up and started waving them. "Listen. *Hazerfach katterack witterrack latterrack quichemole ticketole.*"

"What are you saying?" Cathy asked.

"It's magic spirit language." I waved my hands above the candles and stared into the mirror. "Great-grandmother Eunice come to me. Let Cathy see you. Please do this for me."

I waited and nothing happened. Luckily, I had prepared plan two. I tied a scarf around Cathy's eyes and made sure she couldn't see anything.

"Sometimes, you have to feel spirits instead of seeing them." Then I went into the closet and wrapped a white sheet around my shoulders and put on my Wicked Witch mask that I'd put red paint on. I had my pet rabbit from the yard hidden in the closet. "Don't you dare open your eyes," I said as I came out of the closet. I put my rabbit under the tablecloth near her feet and said in a deep voice, "A spirit is here. Try to feel it." With my foot, I pushed the rabbit closer to her.

Cathy moved her hands excitedly. "I feel something on my feet. It's soft. It's moving. Is a spirit real small?"

"Yes, yes, it's coming to you. They start small. Don't move and it will get bigger."

I stood behind her. I held two old cut-off turkey claws from when Lilly Mae had plucked a turkey. "The spirit has gotten bigger." I rubbed a turkey claw on each of her shoulders.

"Ouch, why does a spirit feel prickly?" she asked.

"Boo, I'm going to get you," I said in her ear. She screamed and pulled off the mask and scarf. I put the turkey claws in front of her face and she screamed. Then she saw my witch mask and screamed again.

I took off the mask and I couldn't stop laughing. "It's a game."

"Stop. I don't like your games," Cathy said.

I heard a sound. "Be quiet. I really hear something."

We both heard a scraping against the house outside the window. The curtains blew into the room. "See, the spirits are really here. Listen," I said. Then there was more scraping against the outside of the house.

Cathy looked at the curtains billowing into the room and she got under the bed. "Stop it. Make it stop!" The noise got louder.

Then Mom opened the door. "What's going on in here? You're not allowed to play with lit candles."

She noticed Cathy under that bed. "Cathy, what's wrong?"

"Make her stop! She says she can get spirits to talk to her," Cathy said. She broke down crying.

"Cathy, get out from under the bed," Mom said.

"You're a scaredy-cat." I couldn't stop laughing.

"Don't make fun of me." Cathy got out from under the bed. "You think you're so smart." Her bow had come off from her ponytail and some hairs were clinging to her face like wispy fingers. There was dust from under the bed on her shirt.

"Cathy, calm down. Tessa didn't mean any harm. She was practicing for Halloween with the mask. It's just a couple of months away," Mom said.

"It makes her feel good to scare me," Cathy answered. "I want to go home."

"Lilly Mae will walk you home," Mom said.

After taking Cathy downstairs, Mom came back. Her shoulders and neck were tense. "Don't you want to have friends?"

"Yes. But I don't have any. The kids think I'm strange." I wanted to cry, but not in front of Mom.

"If you want to have friends, you can't treat them like that. What are you doing with those dead turkey claws? Throw those away." She grabbed the waste basket and threw the claws in them.

I couldn't let her know that Eunice didn't come to me, so I said, "Great-grandmother Eunice was really here. She's the one who cares about me."

Mom in her tight slacks with her red painted toes peeping out from her new red shoes stood over me. "Stop talking like that. I care about you. You will stop this," Mom yelled, and her hands became fists and her face looked tight.

"I'll talk to her if I want to. Grandma is mean and you're always off someplace or with the Pastor ... the smasher. Nobody else cares about me," I yelled back, and my body shook as I cried.

"I love you more than you know. But please stop defying me. I'm the one in charge. You're going to bed without dinner tonight."

I hated to see Mom so upset. But things just rushed out of me like soda bubbles. This was the first time Mom sent me to bed without dinner before. It was always Grandma before.

CHAPTER NINE

Every Sunday, Grandma laid her clothes, including her girdle, on the bed and stared at them. She could only face the world by wearing her white Sears and Roebuck girdle and she would groan as she pulled it on. Even with it on, her stomach stuck out like a fleshy pumpkin. Only when she was trussed up could she go to church knowing that she was safe, that nothing impure could squeeze its way into her.

For as long as I could remember, I'd had to sit in church with Grandma and Queen Victoria sitting by her side and waiting for someone to get close enough so she could bite them. It always rankled Grandma that Mom wouldn't go. But she felt it was her duty to stand outside Mom's locked door and shout to try to get her to go to church. One Sunday, wearing only her bra and girdle with the garter straps hanging down, Grandma stood outside Mom's locked door trying to open it.

"Get up. You're showing contempt for God by staying in bed on Sundays. If it wasn't for me, Tessa would be a heathen. You're nothing without something to believe in. Please don't turn away from Jesus," she yelled. Grandma's cheeks were moist.

I grabbed onto one of her garter straps. "Grandma's crying," I said.

"That's not going to make me go. I wish you would stop cramming that stuff down Tessa," Mom said.

"While you're both under my roof, she's going with me. I have to do something to counteract your wandering …. You know those little things way down inside of us." Then she shook her head from side to side like she didn't want to speak but the words came out, "Those genes … those puss … puss … pussy genes." Then she looked up to heaven. "Jesus, forgive me. I know it's Sunday."

"What are pussy genes?" I asked, begging to know.

"Be quiet, Tessa," Grandma said.

"Pretty please, tell me. And if Mom has them they can't be that bad."

"She's making things up," Mom said.

Grandma grabbed my arm, hurting me while her garter straps swung from side to side. "Go downstairs."

Mom opened the bedroom door. She looked beautiful in her lacy nightgown. "Leave Tessa alone."

Grandma grabbed me and pulled me toward the stairway. "She's going to believe in Jesus. If you don't like it, you can get out."

Mom looked tired. "I'm sorry I can't do anything, Tessa. I'm religious in my own way," she said to me.

"Just shut up," Grandma said.

Grandma dressed me up for church in my one good dress of pink organdy with ruffles down the front. She tied the organdy sash in a large bow in the back. I put on white socks and my white patent leather shoes. Then she brushed and braided my hair. When she was fixing my hair, it was one of the few times I felt as if she liked me.

She told me to wait for her in the living room and not to wrinkle my dress. As I sat on the gold brocade couch in the living room waiting, I felt like one of Grandma's dolls trapped in the closet. I was becoming two people. I saw a part of myself, the fun part, sneak out and go sit on my bed drawing in my coloring book while waiting for the other me to come back. When I got home, the fun part was supposed to get back inside of me, but I was worried it might not still be there when I got home.

When Grandma was finally ready, having put on her perfume, old lady shoes, and her white kid gloves, she paraded into the room as if people were applauding her. Even wearing her Sears and Roebuck girdle, she still looked chubby. Her short hair had been curled with bobby pins and the curls stuck out from beneath her bucket-shaped hat covered with artificial roses. She looked like she was wearing a flowerpot. She had a whole collection of flowering hats set on mannequin heads covering the dresser in her bedroom.

The only way I had been able to stand the waiting was by bouncing my legs, putting my hands in my armpits, and doing my Chicken Dance. As soon as Grandma saw me, she became annoyed. "You have to get those legs under control. Boys will get the wrong idea when they see you bouncing your legs. You have to sit with your legs pressed together. Jesus wants ladylike legs."

At Church, I had to sit next to her with the adults in the front pew because I needed the force of the sermon. If I moved too much during the sermon, she pinched me hard.

CHAPTER TEN

Pastor Jesse Michael arrived driving down the main street in his sky-blue Cadillac convertible. He was a new young preacher and everybody was talking about him. Mrs. Thelma and the other old women kept repeating the same things because nobody knew much about him.

Pastor Jessie Michael came to replace Pastor Rigby, who in his old age kept falling asleep and drooling during the services. Eventually Pastor Rigby keeled over with his face falling onto the Bible, his tongue sticking out, stone dead. It was seen as a bad omen. The congregation became so dangerously small that its members were walking on eggs, afraid they would be pulled into sin.

Mom must have run into Pastor Jessie Michael in town, because all of a sudden, she was overcome by an interest in going to church.

The next Sunday, Mom got out of bed and started getting dressed. I watched her pull on her girdle. When Mom put on her girdle, it wasn't for the same reason as Grandma. It was because it allowed her to wear a tight skirt. She looked at herself in the mirror and smiled. Then she put on a short skirt, showing off her long legs in stockings and red high-heeled shoes. Her white blouse was tucked into a wide red belt and she finished off her outfit with a red, wide-brimmed hat over her long red hair.

Grandma called me into the living room to wait with her. When Mom came into the room, she glided as if she was floating on air.

"You're not going to church like that? Nobody else wears skirts that short and so much makeup," Grandma said.

"I'm really going to give this town something to talk about." Mom danced around moving her hips.

"Jesus, you even want to flaunt yourself in front of God. I thought you had changed, but you just want to embarrass me out of spite," Grandma said.

Mom held up the keys to the Buick. "Either I go like this or we don't go."

When we arrived at church, the old women, chalky white because they never let the sun touch their skin. They were lined up in the pews like porcelain figurines. Their gazes stuck on Mom, as if they could suck up some of her beauty. Huddled together, they whispered as she walked past them. Mom sat in the front pew, crossing her stockinged legs and tossing her hair back over her shoulders. She turned and smiled at each and every one of them, as if they were friends.

From a door at the back of the podium, Pastor Jessie Michael emerged. The old women sighed and their faces lit up. Pastor Jessie Michael confidently went to the podium, his black cowboy boots squeaked across the scuffed wooden floor. He paused and looked the members of the congregation in the eyes, and some of the women inhaled, as if they hadn't taken a deep breath in years. His face was clean-shaven, with high cheekbones, and radiant skin. I couldn't help but notice his sideburns and his dark hair parted and combed back in a wave above his forehead. He had a thick gold cross around his neck.

He spoke in a velvety voice, sounding honest to the core. He started preaching slowly, but then his voice got louder, and the words seemed to have a life of their own building up inside of him. His words came out like spinning fire. His hair fell across his sweaty forehead as he looked directly at each member of the congregation. The old women were so overcome that no one moved, as if they were nailed to their seats. The way they stared at him said they could eat any fire that he might throw at them.

When he stopped, he took out a handkerchief and wiped the sweat off of his face. I couldn't remember what he said, but I couldn't take my eyes off of the intense shine in his eyes.

Right after the service, Pastor Jessie Michael came out from behind the podium. In the front row, Grandma rushed up to him with Queen Victoria. She held the dog's mouth to keep her from biting him. The old and young women rushed to him, thrusting their smiling faces at him. Still clinging to his words, as if they were being transported to an unearthly beautiful place, they formed a semi-circle of breasts around him. The old women, their skin like crumpled fabric, smiled glowingly at him and the young women smiled lipstick smiles.

A couple of women stepped aside as Mom pushed me in front of the other women. She didn't want to waste any time getting the preacher's attention. She got her breasts in real close and he noticed. I didn't want to be like those silly women, so I looked down and at his black western boots, expensive looking. Then I saw the crease, neatly pressed into his black slacks. I wondered why he wasn't wearing jeans like most of the men in town, especially the ones that Mom was interested in. His leather belt had a gold buckle with his initials on it, and his starched white shirt was tucked into his pants. His shirtsleeves were rolled up, and dark chest hair stuck out at his neck above the golden cross. He was even more handsome than my father Jeffrey.

Within a couple of weeks, Pastor Jesse Michael was coming once a week to our house in the evenings for private Bible study with Mom and Grandma. Grandma felt it was a special honor to have the Pastor teach them privately. She was even bossier now that she was on the fast track to heaven. Around the house, she sang to herself, *I'm a soldier in the army of the Lord,* over and over until Mom screamed for her to stop.

Grandma now had Lilly Mae come more often and watched all her cleaning. "I don't want the Pastor to see any tarnish or dust. You know what they say about cleanliness."

And Lilly Mae whispered under her breath, "There's other things closer to godliness."

One evening when Pastor Jessie Michael came to the house, the dinner table was set with the holiday silver dishes filled with pot roast, string beans, baked sweet potatoes, and corn bread that Lilly Mae had made. In the kitchen, I knew Grandma was bossing Lilly Mae something fierce.

I sat across from the Pastor, who sat next to Mom.

"You make me feel so welcome in your lovely home," Pastor Jessie Michael said.

"We don't have many guests, and Mother has kept the house the same as it was when I was growing up." Mom had on red lipstick and Pastor Jessie Michaels' eyes kept going to her lips.

Some strands of the Pastor's dark shiny hair fell across his forehead, and he brushed them back. His large hands were smooth, with neatly filed fingernails, not like the calloused hands of the cowboys here. He didn't smell like horse and dust the way my father, Jeffrey, did. I wondered if he liked children? I thought: I'd like to ride next to him in his blue convertible and the people in town would notice me.

He put his large hand on Mom's arm resting on the table and slowly slid it down to her hand. She pulled away but he leaned in close to her. "Don't pull away," the Pastor said.

"Your hand is so warm. It's like you have a special touch. What is it?" Mom asked.

"I've had an energy in my hands since I was a child. It's a power from the Holy Ghost."

This interested me because if I squinted my eyes, I thought I was seeing a light around his head. "What's the Holy Ghost Power?" I asked. "I want to see it."

Mom looked at me sharply. "Be quiet Tessa, and stop that thing you're doing with your eyes."

The Pastor put his hand on top of Mom's again and she didn't pull away. "Your hand actually feels hot. So, you had this before you went into the ministry?" she asked.

He kept holding on to her hand looking into her eyes. Mom blushed and looked away.

"Stay with me. I can feel a sadness in you. I want to help," the Pastor said.

Mom looked him in the eyes. "You're intense. It's like you're reaching right inside of me and grabbing onto me. Maybe I don't like that." Mom took her hand away. "What made you realize you had something different?" she asked.

"I don't tell many people this, but when I was eleven, I fell off a ladder in the barn and hit my head. After that I saw things differently. I could see energies, and I would put my hands on sick farm animals and make them better. Shouldn't I wait and also let Bernice hear this?"

"No. Let her stay in the kitchen," Mom said.

He interested me because I hadn't heard anyone talk like that. I said, "I believe what you're saying. And I see the spirits of my great-grandmother and her sister, but I'm not supposed to talk about it because people will think I'm crazy."

"Tessa Louise, obey me and be quiet," Mom snapped. She turned back to Pastor Jessie Michael.

"Let her talk. She's just a child. With my father, I wasn't allowed to say anything I felt," he said kindly.

"I know myself what it's like to feel different, especially in this town," Mom said.

"When my mother got really sick and my father found me laying my hands on her, he said that I was pretending I had some power that I didn't have. He whipped me really good. When I decided to become a minister, I knew no one would question what I was doing," the Pastor said.

"All we have here is a plain old bare bones Methodist Church. People here pride themselves in being boring. They think it keeps them strong and pure," Mom said.

"I think the people here are ready for a change," the Pastor said.

"Since you started preaching, a lot of people are coming to church, even some Baptists. My mother hates Baptists," Mom said.

"People need the experience of the gifts of the Holy Ghost," he said.

I thought: Why doesn't Mom tell him she doesn't believe in any Holy Ghosts? Oh, but she won't do that because she likes him.

"I think this is the best time to bring them the gift of the *Laying on of Hands*," he said. Then he quoted, *"Blessed be our Lord Jesus Christ who comforts us in all our affliction, so that we may be able to comfort those who are in any affliction. II Corinthians 1: Verse 3-4."*

Mom stared into his eyes not really listening to what he was saying. "Oh, Corinthians. Sounds familiar. Whatever you say. I haven't gotten the taste yet for the Bible that other people have."

But Mom must have had needed a lot of energy, or had a lot of affliction that needed comforting, because it wasn't long before Pastor Jessie Michael was making late night visits to her bedroom.

CHAPTER ELEVEN

From then on, every Sunday in church, Grandma Bernice was always wearing one of her flowering hats and holding Queen Victoria. She made sure Mom and I were parked in the front row pew. No one else dared to sit there. With Queen Victoria sitting next to Grandma, trying to see out from under the fur hanging over her eyes, Grandma stared intently at the Pastor like one of her glassy-eyed dolls. She nodded her head even though she didn't understand what he was talking about.

Soon the Pastor made regular visits to our house. I knew not to mention I'd seen him late at night tiptoeing down our hallway with his boots in his hand. But I could bring that up with Mom if she didn't let me have all the cookies that I wanted.

I remember one Sunday morning when he gestured with his large hands and spoke forcefully, "Raise your voice to the Lord and He will hear." I didn't care what he was saying, but I couldn't take my eyes off of the look on his face.

On one side of me sat Mom smiling at the Pastor, her legs crossed and her skirt hiked up. She seemed more radiant than ever and I thought she was getting a lot of that extra Holy Ghost from those late nights with the Pastor. She shouldn't be keeping it all to herself. I was beginning to like the Pastor more and more, and I could see him reading to me at night just like a father and then the kids at school wouldn't say I was the divorced kid anymore. But so far Mom was getting all the attention.

As he walked back and forth across the front of the church, he had a large gold ring with a green stone on his right hand, which he turned while speaking. Wearing a white dress cowboy shirt with a little chest hair sticking out at the neck, he brushed his black hair from his forehead and stopped behind the pulpit. He paused a moment, then said, "Today, we welcome you to receive the gift of the Holy Ghost in a special service where we shall participate in the early church's practice of the *Laying on of Hands.*" His cowboy boots made the floor creak as he walked back and forth in front of the congregation. "This is one of the most fundamental doctrines of the Christian faith." He rubbed his hands together. They were large with neatly trimmed nails. His beefy palms with deep lines were quite red and any minute I thought flames might come out of them.

He glanced up to heaven, as if receiving a message and then looked back at the people. "Even though this may be new to you, there is a definite impartation to be received through the *Laying on of Hands.* Don't listen to any little doubting voice inside you."

The silence in the church was heavy. It was as if the still air was listening to him. I dared to look back to where Mrs. Thelma and her daughter Betty Lynn stared intently at the Pastor. Betty Lynn, wearing her Sunday best, had her bleached blond hair piled especially high that day; her antenna to heaven. She glanced over at Mom like she wanted to burn a hole into her with her eyes. She looked at other people and then at Mom, trying to get other people to also stare at her. I stuck my tongue out at her. Then Grandma's fleshy fingers pinched me to make me look straight ahead.

Pastor Jessie Michael held up the Bible, *"And Joshua, the son of Nun, was full of the spirit of wisdom for Moses has laid his hands upon him. Deuteronomy: Verse 34.9"*. The Pastor put the Bible down and held up his hands and continued, "This shows what hands can do, but remember

I'm only an instrument. I pray for God's awesome power to bring about healing of the mind and body. Praise the Lord." Even though it was cold in the chapel, the Pastor took out his handkerchief and wiped the sweat off of his forehead.

He pronounced his words clearly and slowly and his words shot like arrows into the congregation. He breathed deeply, and I felt that something was building inside him. I couldn't believe my eyes, but he seemed to be growing bigger right in front of me. His chest stuck out and even though he wasn't fat, his belly was expanding and pressing against his gold belt buckle. He looked at the congregation and his gaze had them melted into their pews. I felt afraid and I prayed that he wouldn't look at me.

As his voice got louder, his dark eyes became blacker and more piercing. Then I realized with each inhale he was actually breathing in the Holy Ghost. But nobody could hold that much Holy Ghost. He was puffing up more and more. He was going to explode out over us. I knew the Lord can just bust in on people, so I felt afraid any minute the Lord was going to hit us right then and there with fire or water to show he was the boss. I wasn't sure if it would be fire or water but then I thought that it had to be water because the Lord wouldn't want to burn the church down. This church was going to be flooded. I scrunched down and tried to make myself as small as possible. I prayed, "Please Jesus don't hit me with the exploding water. Let it rush over my head and hit Betty Lynn or Mrs. Thelma." I didn't realize I'd spoken out loud until I saw the adults looking at me as if the snake from the garden was coiled inside me.

The Pastor stopped and gave me a strange look. I thought: Please don't look at me like that. I need you to like me. Grandma immediately pinched me hard to be quiet. I turned my head to give Grandma a dirty look, but when I looked at her, I became afraid. She looked different than I'd ever seen her. But she wasn't aware that her new flower hat leaned to one side, and she had placed her gloved right hand over her heart. Her eyes were bulging, her mouth was slightly open, and she was inhaling heavily. He was making her puff up with the Holy Ghost also. I wanted to tell her she had to be careful because at her age her skin couldn't handle too much expanding.

Pastor Jessie Michael went on. "If you wish, you are invited to come forward to the prayer station here at the alter rail and kneel and receive the *Laying on of Hands.*"

Grandma rushed to the rail and knelt with difficulty. The Pastor faced her and told her to put her hands over her heart. Then he put both of his hands on the shoulders of her linen dress and prayed. "Touch us tender God with the holiness of your spirit. Take all the affliction from this vessel."

Grandma trembled and she couldn't stand up by herself, and when the Pastor took both of her hands in his to help her up, she moaned and went limp. He had to go around the railing and grab her under the arm to lift her up.

Back in the pew, Queen Victoria gnawed on the armrest making teeth marks in the wood. Grandma wobbled back to the pew. When she sat down, she pinched her and Queen Victoria yelped, so Grandma grabbed her mouth and held it closed.

If Grandma could do it, so could I. I pushed ahead of the other people and rushed and kneeled before the Pastor. Then I poked his stomach with my finger to see if he might still explode from being puffed up with the Holy Ghost. He took my finger away and said, "Do you understand this process?" He looked me right in the eyes.

"Of course. I already see spirits, so give me the Holy Ghost," I whispered. "I'm praying for a father and I hope you can get my prayers answered."

I closed my eyes and he rested his hands on my shoulders and they felt warm and wonderful. A tingling went down my body, into my stomach and then down my legs. He smelled of after-shave. My palms became sweaty and I wanted so much to reach out my arms for him to hug me.

When I sat back next to Mom, she said, "You don't push ahead of the adults. Let them go first."

"I'm getting rid of my many afflictions," I said.

"Hush," Grandma said.

We watched as Mrs. Thelma and Betty Lynn went to the railing. I prayed Betty Lynn's hair would catch on fire.

I looked at Mom and she didn't seem to be taking this seriously. She smiled and ran her fingers through her hair. She looked beautiful in her short skirt as she crossed and uncrossed her legs trying to get comfortable on the wooden pew.

In the weeks that followed, Grandma had more healings, and her belief in Pastor Jessie Michael's abilities took over more and more, like guests moving in and refusing to leave. For the first time in years, she was intensely focused on something. In the afternoons, when she sat in her chair in the living room drinking her "daytime coffee," she would break into spontaneous singing. One afternoon she sang, *"Jesus walked this lonesome valley; he had to walk it by himself."* Since she couldn't remember the song's words, she added her own words and then she became angry. She changed so much from moment to moment. Then she yelled, "Jesus, I had to walk my asphalt road with my daddy always on my back. Jesus, why didn't you do so something about him?" Then she started singing again, *"But now I'm a soldier in the army of the Lord. Out there in the front where everybody sees me ... and I've got my pistols for the evil doers...."* Sitting in her chair, she moved her arms like she was marching.

I went into the kitchen where Lilly Mae was eating one cookie after another. Queen Victoria came in and crouched between the refrigerator and a cabinet. Lilly Mae slammed some pots and pans onto the stove to let Grandma know she didn't approve of Grandma's singing. Then Lilly Mae went into the living room.

"Miss Bernice, it's not right what you do to the Jesus songs. You're makin' them ugly."

"Lilly Mae, you don't understand. I'm having something I think it's called a ... cath ... cath ... artic. Anyway, it's new. Virginia told me about it ... it's like you got a spout in your mouth and things are pouring out ... you can't help it ... so you can't blame me ... Things are just shooting out."

"I am blaming you. Miss Bernice, I don't want to be a part of no cath ... cath ... whatever you call it. I don't want no blasphemin'," Lilly Mae said.

"Then go back in the kitchen and don't listen," Grandma said.

Lilly Mae stomped back into the kitchen and threw more pots around, and then she started singing her own song to drown out Grandma. *"Nobody knows the trouble I see, nobody knows but Jesus. Glory Hallelujah. Sometimes I'm up, sometimes I'm down. Oh yes Lord, sometimes I'm almost to the ground."*

Just then, Mom came home from work, looking tired. I followed her into the living room. "Lilly Mae's throwing things again. What have you done now?" Mom asked.

"I have a wonderful voice," Grandma said slurring her words. She had a shine in her eyes. "The Pastor has touched me with his beautiful hands and I feel them on me all the time now. It's like there's another separate little person inside of me making me do all kinds of things. I'm reborn. Isn't it a miracle that I want to sing and dance?" Grandma stood up and tried to dance around in her old lady shoes, but she almost fell and grabbed the chair.

"This is how to dance." I did my Eagle Dance.

Mom had left the room and she came back with her guitar, like other times when she would sing instead of yelling. She sang, *"Hey big cowboy, drive me to the edge of town. Give me a stud and I'll fuck him all night long and sing a song."* Mom strummed loudly and Grandma fell into her brocade armchair.

I sang, *"Yes, pussy day, pussy night, pussy shining bright. Give me a pussy and I'll take flight."*

"Shut up." Grandma spoke as if to wither me like a fig on the tree. Then she stood up and pointed her finger with her garnet ring at Mom and sang, *"Mine eyes have seen the beauty of that wonderful man. He's coming with that flaming swift sword and stamping...."* She paused a second. *"Stamping out the whores, so you're finished, kaput ... dead .... Oh, happy day."*

Mom circled around her and sang, *"Mama you've forgotten how good the moaning is, the heat, the sweat that makes you forget."* Mom made a moaning sound in Grandma's face, and Grandma picked up her cup and saucer and threw it. The glass broke across the floor.

I ran into the kitchen to wait with Lilly Mae for their singing to stop.

CHAPTER TWELVE

With all the singing and rushing to get things ready for the Pastor's visits, Grandma was preoccupied and was forgetting to tell me to keep my legs closed for Jesus. A couple of times just to test her, I sat across from her and let my skirt ride up, but she kept singing to herself. So, after that I did my dances, moved my legs, and showed my panties as much as I wanted to.

Still a lot of things were confusing me, and when I was alone in my room at night the shadows outside seemed alive, as if something was blowing through the house even though the windows were closed. I thought this was because Pastor Jessie Michael was now coming twice a week to Mom's room at night, stirring up all that extra Holy Ghost Power. One night, Mom and the Pastor made a bunch of noise in her room, which awakened me with a pins-and-needles feeling. My clock read 5:00 A.M.

The wind outside tore at the trees, and it sounded like it was calling my name. I felt pulled to contact Great-grandmother Eunice and her sister Gertie, so I put on my pink robe and turned on the flashlight, which I always kept by my bed, for when I needed to walk around at night.

I went into the living room, put the flashlight on the floor and stood on a chair. I stared into the mirror waiting for them. But instead I heard the old wooden stairs creaking, so I got off the chair, turned off the flashlight and quickly went to the stairs. Holding my flashlight like a gun, I turned it on, and I caught him. Pastor Jessie Michael was sneaking down the stairs. He jumped because of the light in his face and then he realized it was just me. He had his boots in hand as he tiptoed down the stairs, and he acted as if he always walked around holding his boots.

"I've seen cowboys on our stairway before, but never a pastor. Grandma would get upset if she knew you were here. But I like you and I won't tell."

"Bless your heart."

"When do I get to ride in your Cadillac convertible down Main Street?" I asked.

"I don't know. But I'm thirsty. Do you have anything to drink?"

"Lilly Mae made her special ginger iced tea. It's in the refrigerator. Follow me." I shined the flashlight showing the way into the kitchen.

In the kitchen, he set his boots on the floor, where they stood like silent strangers watching us. He whispered, "Don't turn on the light." I shined the flashlight on the cabinets, and he took out a glass and poured himself tea from the refrigerator. He drank the whole glass and poured some more.

I sat down at the wooden table, and then I shone the light onto his body. "Your gold belt buckle is unbuckled."

He looked at his belt. "I'm sorry." He closed his belt. "Tessa, you're a smart one."

I shined the light next to him. "I know. But do you like children?"

"Yes."

"Are we getting to know each other?" I ran my hand through my tangled hair trying to straighten it.

"Sure."

"You can have some cookies. We could talk awhile. I'm interesting for my age," I said.

"That's very kind of you, but I best be leaving now."

After he closed the front door, I heard some noise and went into the living room. I put the flashlight on the floor and got up on the chair and stared into the gold mirror. I heard moaning but it wasn't coming from the mirror. Then I realized that the dolls in their boxes in the closet knew it was me, and they started whining for me to take them out, but I hissed at them to be quiet.

I stood on the chair at just the right angle so I could see Eunice's picture reflected in the mirror. Her large dark eyes stared back at me and the mirror seemed to glow and her lips moved, but I couldn't understand what she was saying.

"What good are you to me if I can't understand you?" I asked. I heard the rustle of their dresses and I felt their gentle hands brush me. "I feel you and I'm glad you're here," I said. "But when I can see you in the mirror, it's easier for me to hear you." Then Great-grandmother's face moved into the mirror and her sister Gertie's face pushed in next to hers.

"Can you hear us now?" Eunice asked.

"Yes. I have something important to tell both of you. I've found someone who can be my new father. He's the Pastor Jessie Michael." I listened but all I heard was mumbling, "You have to talk louder," I said.

Eunice's voice came through. "We never went in much for pastors. They think highly of themselves."

"Let me tell her about what I did with my beaus. I had a whole bunch waiting for me to lift my skirt. That will get her mind off of the lying pastors," Great-aunt Gertie said. She adjusted the pink cameo around her neck.

Eunice shoved Gertie's face out of the mirror. "Shut your dirty mouth."

"Please listen to me. The Pastor is handsome and Mom really likes him. He's bringing us the Holy Ghost Power," I said.

"Oh, so that's his story. Those holy rollers can get a hold on you," Eunice said.

"Don't pastors pray for dead people to help them?" I asked.

"We've seen those prayers, white birds with people's names on them going up to the sky. But the sky is so big they don't get that far and they float back looking like crumpled napkins and they pile up on the ground in this place," Eunice said.

"I stomp them," Gertie said.

I was getting tired from standing on the chair. "Tell me that he's going to be my father."

"We know more than you and you need to listen to us," they both said.

"If you're so smart, why are you stuck wherever you are?" I got down from the chair and stomped my feet and did my Chicken Dance. "I need him to come to my school so the kids can see that I have a father," I shouted at their images in the mirror. I'd never yelled at them before and that upset them, and they started to fade.

"Please don't go. I didn't mean to shout. I need you to understand," I said.

"We just don't want you to be hurt," they whispered and faded back into the silver mirror. Then I lost my concentration because the dolls in the boxes started begging again in high-pitched voices to be taken out so they could watch the sun come up. I told them to shut up or I'd pinch them and they immediately became silent. I felt bad for saying that.

The next thing I heard was Lilly Mae's voice. "Miss Tessa wake up."

I opened my eyes, and I was lying on the living room floor with the morning light trying to shine through the draped windows. Lilly Mae stood with her hands on her hips. "Child, what you doin' down there. You can't be sleeping on the floor. That will upset Miss Bernice and you know how she be," she said.

"I guess I fell asleep by accident." I stood up but was dizzy and Lilly Mae grabbed me.

"Come on I'll fix you breakfast. Miss Bernice tires herself out with her singing and she be sleepin' late."

One of my favorite things was sitting at the wooden kitchen table while Lilly Mae made me eggs and bacon. Lilly Mae stood in front of the stove. She had on her white apron tied into a bow in the back. The smell of bacon and toast filled the room.

There was a knock at the back door. I opened it and a colored man was standing there. He asked if we had any work for him. Lilly Mae said, "We don't have no work here."

I said, "Wait a minute. I'll make you something." I made him a tuna fish with Miracle whip sandwich. I wrapped it and gave it to him. He was very grateful. It made me feel good.

Lilly Mae said, "You best not let your grandma see you doin' that." She continued her cooking.

I had something I'd wanted to ask her for awhile. "Lilly Mae, I don't understand the Holy Ghost Power. Our house must be full of it by now. Can you tell me about it?"

"Don't you go to Sunday school where they teach kids your age?"

"No, Grandma makes me sit up front with the grownups because I need the power of the sermon to control the pussy genes. Grandma says they're down inside of me from when I was born just waiting to make me do bad things like my mom does," I said.

Lilly Mae turned and looked at me. "Tessa, your grandma shouldn' be sayin' things like that. You're good and have to learn not to believe everything she says." Lilly Mae stepped closer to me. "Somethin' else is bothering you."

"At school, I feel different. Did you ever feel that way?"

"Everyone feels like they are a shoe that don't fit at times. Ignore those feelings. Tessa, you're smart and those kids at school have no business acting like they're better than you."

"Lilly Mae, did you know your father?"

"When I was ten and my sister was eighteen, 'bout that time he left and went up north. Franny didn't get over being mad at him. After my mama died, I thought about goin' and lookin' for him, but that costs money," she said. She dished up the eggs and bacon on a plate and set it in front of me. Then she dished herself up a plate and sat with me.

"Was your sister like you?"

"Franny had a wild streak. She wanted to be somethin' she weren't. She thought she could dress like and act like a white woman. She got mixed up with the wrong man. She had to move away also."

"Did you know where she went?"

"At first, she had someone write me letters that I couldn't read. But the years started piling up jest like big mountains between us. Her new life jest took her over," she said.

"Franny, now I remember where I've seen that name. That's the name on the back of the faded picture with Old Man Henry. You said she was his fancy woman. Why didn't you tell me she was your sister?"

Tears came to Lilly Mae's eyes and she turned away from me. "Yes, she was my beautiful sister."

CHAPTER THIRTEEN

Every night, I asked Jesus to have the Pastor Jessie Michael take me to the Genuine Circle B Barbeque where my father would see me with him. But even though the Pastor had been making his visits to Mom at night for a couple of months, he hadn't mentioned taking Mom or me out in his sky-blue Cadillac. I kept trying to catch him on the stairs at night, so I could tell him I hadn't told Grandma about seeing him here, and I wanted to know when he was going to take me for a ride in his convertible.

There was a floor furnace with a damper door in my room that also had a door that opened into Mom's room. One night when the Pastor was in Mom's room, I whispered to Jesus that the Holy Ghost was making me pull down the metal door handle so I could hear what was going on in Mom's room.

At first, I didn't hear anything but then the Pastor said, "When you're in that front row on Sunday, I do my best preaching."

"If anybody were going to make me believe, it would be you," Mom said.

Then the Pastor said, "Your skin is so smooth and beautiful."

I felt an antsy feeling and I had to see what was going on. I crept on tippy toes to outside Mom's door. It was an aged, wooden door with long cracks like all the other doors in the house. I peeked through the old-fashioned keyhole and shuddered. I saw Mom's and the Pastor's mouths and noses. They were kissing ... big kisses ... pressure kisses. I saw the upper part of their bodies, and then I saw the Pastor's hands, and he was laying them on Mom's breasts. Then his big-knuckled hands took her flower print blouse off, and they moved slowly over her bra. The Holy Ghost Power had to be all over the place. I saw Mom's mouth was open and she sighed. She was definitely being affected by that power. I pushed my nose harder against the door and tried to see more, and I almost choked when the Pastor unhooked Mom's bra and took it off. There were red strap marks on her shoulders, and Mom moved her breasts a little, but his hands grabbed her naked breasts, holding and rubbing them. Rub a dub Mom and the Pastor in a tub.

I wanted to yell, but I put my hand over my mouth because I wasn't supposed to be watching. I backed away carefully from the door. Now I knew why men were so interested in Mom. They wanted to rub her breasts. What a stupid thing and why would a pastor want to do that also? The Pastor stayed with Mom a long time and I couldn't get to sleep. I kept thinking, what if he wants to take my mom away with him? Then he wouldn't be a father to me and I can't be left alone.

A couple of days later, when the Pastor came again to our house for dinner, he wore a fancy western jacket and a starched white shirt. Grandma Bernice, in a blue linen dress that came down below her knees, immediately put her face close to him and started talking. She had changed a lot in the last few months. Now, she smiled and wore lipstick like Mom.

Grandma took to wearing high heels, even though she couldn't walk very well in them. Her shoes were red like Mom's, but larger because she had bunions. She wobbled when she went into the kitchen to have Lilly Mae bring out more fried chicken, mashed potatoes, and cornbread for the Pastor.

At the table, Grandma was so busy telling jokes and laughing at them that she didn't notice my hands became eagle wings and I swooped down and scooped food into my beak mouth.

When Pastor Jessie Michael wasn't looking, I stared at him to see if he was going to take Mom away. Finishing his third helping, Pastor Jessie Michael moved his plate away. "First, I want to thank you sister Bernice for bringing so many new members into the church."

Grandma took another drink of her "evening coffee" from her flowered teacup and leaned toward the Pastor. "You're welcome. Now, when did you find out your power was from the Holy Ghost?" she asked with a slurred voice. It made me mad when she was like that.

He pushed his shiny hair back off of his forehead and relaxed back in his chair. "I knew as a kid, when I was able to heal a snake."

"How on earth did you heal a snake and why?" Grandma asked.

"Snakes are born evil and I wanted to give them a chance to turn from Satan and accept Jesus."

"That's wonderful. I never thought of that," Grandma said.

"I'd find a rattle snake in the underbrush and I'd grab it and lift it up … I had to be quick. Wham. It would twist and try to bite … But I'd hold it behind the head and pray over it to accept Jesus. At first it would look at me with pure hatred. But I'd stroke it and keep praying. When it relaxed and closed its mouth, I knew I was done. Many times, I did this and never got bitten. I didn't dare tell my father about it. When he wasn't home, I went into the hen house to try to heal a chicken. When our best layer wouldn't lay eggs or eat, I put my hands on her and prayed. The next day she had produced an egg and kept going until she died a few days later. Healing a chicken was hard because no matter what you do, they just stare at you. But I got results. I don't usually tell people this, but I stared hearing voices from the trees and rocks like Moses in the desert but in the woods of Louisiana."

"I never would have imagined something like … like that in Louisiana. We here in Texas tend to think Louisiana people not quite up to par … maybe a little low-class … you know the French marrying their cousins who may be their sisters. But I don't mean you," Grandma said.

I sat up straight and stared at him. "My great-grandmother and her sister talk to me so I've got my own ghost power from my relatives and I'm just as special."

"Tessa, it's not the same. Those are fantasies. Now be quiet." Mom wiped her mouth leaving red lipstick on the napkin.

"I want to learn to heal a chicken," I said.

"Tessa stop interrupting. Let the Pastor finish what he was saying," Mom said.

"Well, when I started studying the Bible, I found out what I was doing was sanctioned in the Bible," the Pastor said.

"I'm so glad you're sanctioned … or did you mean sanitary… I don't know … I'm sorry, I'm a little confused," Grandma said as she took another drink from her teacup.

Grandma had drunk a lot of her "coffee"; her cheeks were flushed, and she was in the mood for talking. "Everyone is talking about your wonderful hands. It's like I can feel them on me all the time … little hands here and little hands there." She pointed to places on her body and giggled.

"I haven't heard it put quite like that but that's a nice thing to say," he said.

Grandma's talking made Mom nervous and she angrily mashed her peas and mixed them with her mashed potatoes. She took big bites and washed them down with mint-iced tea. "Mother, you're monopolizing the conversation." Mom slammed her knife against the plate, cutting up her fried chicken into little pieces.

Grandma looked at Mom with that look in her eyes which she had right before she switched me. She didn't know that her lipstick had run into the cracks above her lips, like they were thin red ribbons. But she must have realized that she had a mean look on her face because she quickly smiled and looked over at the Pastor. Still, lipstick didn't look as good on her as it did on Mom.

The Pastor adjusted his gold watch and pulled down his cuffs. His large hands with neatly trimmed nails rested on the tablecloth like silent guests. Lilly Mae came out from the kitchen with the silver coffee pitcher and filled his cup. His hand gently closed around the flowered teacup as he sipped the coffee.

Mom kept hitting her knife against the plate to cut her chicken and didn't see Grandma's expression change. All of a sudden, Grandma's face twisted and tears came to her eyes. "There's something I want to tell you, but I don't know how." She blotted her eyes with the napkin, smearing her mascara.

"You can tell me anything. That's what I'm here for," the Pastor said.

"It's something in me from a long time ago. I don't know if I can speak of it. The memories are like knives."

Mom chewed a piece of chicken and stared at Grandma as if she wanted to chew her. Now Grandma's tears made streaks through the rouge on her cheeks.

"You can unburden yourself," the Pastor said.

"No, no, I can't. I shouldn't have said anything." Grandma couldn't hold back her feelings and rushed into the living room, wobbling on her high heels.

"She gets like this when she's drinking," Mom said.

"Mom says Grandma gets on her high-horse and wants all the attention," I said.

"I'll talk to her," the Pastor said. He went into the living room, and I followed behind while Mom stayed at the table and stacked the dishes. She liked to help out Lilly Mae.

In the living room, Grandma had plopped face down on the couch and was crying into one of her burgundy pillows. Her shoes were on the floor, her skirt was hiked up, and her girdle with the clips holding up her stockings was exposed. With her face pressed into the pillow she said, "It was my papa … the way he treated me … what he did … awful things."

Grandma's crying bothered me, so I went to the mantelpiece and stared at the picture of Eunice in her blue dress. "Great-grandmother come. Show the Pastor I'm special also." Neither the Pastor nor Grandma paid any attention to me. "Great-grandmother Eunice don't make a fool of me. Come now," I said loudly but nothing happened.

Grandma lifted her head and stopped crying. "Shut up, Tessa, or you'll get a switching." Then she dropped her head back in the pillow and continued crying.

The Pastor knelt beside Grandma and put one hand on her hand and the other on her shoulder. His hands looked red and seemed to become larger. "You can tell me anything. But first let's pray." He closed his eyes, "Jesus, let the Holy Ghost come into sister Bernice and heal her of her affliction." With his red hands still on her, he opened his eyes.

Grandma slowly turned over, but her dress was still hiked up and her legs spread apart. She was not very ladylike and now she was breathing heavily and the top button of her dress was undone, letting her white slip show. She grabbed the Pastor's hand and pulled it to her. She put it against her stomach and held it as if her hands were claws that wouldn't let go. "Just touch me and everything will go away. I've never felt like this in my whole life." Grandma's legs began to shake. "Oh, Jesus, I'm feeling your power now." Her legs shook some more.

Then I felt a gentle touch on my cheek, and I saw Eunice and Gertie over to the side watching everything with disapproving looks. "My spirit relatives are here. Look at them. You can't ignore me now," I shouted.

"Don't pay any attention to her. She's playing one of her games," Grandma said to the Pastor. Now, her legs were lifting up from the couch and falling back down.

"I have the power too," I said.

"Sister Bernice, calm down and sit up. I don't do the healing. Jesus does it. So, pray with me," he said.

Grandma held his hand tightly and tried to force it up to her breast, but the Pastor moved it back to her belly. "I have to have your hands. Please," Grandma said and she started crying and kicking her legs. I'd never thought of this before, but I realized she wanted the breast rubbing that Mom gets from the Pastor … Rub a dub, Grandma and Pastor in a tub. Somehow, I didn't like that picture in my mind.

Now my spirit relatives were standing next to me. "Great-grandmother, look what Grandma is doing. Make her stop. Make him help me." I yelled and jumped up and down, but they just stood there talking to themselves. "Dumb pussy Eunice listen to me," I said.

Eunice said, "Watch your mouth. You don't tell us what to do."

I said, "Pastor, they're right here. You know how to call the Holy Ghost. You should be able to see them. They're talking." But only I could see and hear them. "Damn you, spirits," I said. I went over and stood by the couch. "Pastor you have to listen to me. I'm a kid so help me." Then I did a handstand to get his attention but that didn't work either.

Mom came into the room. "Jessie Michael, what are you doing? Take your hands off my mother. Can't you see she's hysterical? Don't rile her up anymore. She talks to everyone in town."

"That won't hurt anything," the Pastor said.

"No, no, don't stop. Save me Jesus. Pastor, I need your hands," Grandma yelled. She held tightly to one of the Pastor's hands so he couldn't take it off of her stomach. Then she gave Mom a killing look. "You can't stand to see me get help, can you?"

I started crying, and I rushed to the Pastor and grabbed his hands, trying to pull them off of Grandma. "Forget Grandma. You've got to help me. I need you to care about me and take me places." He removed his hands from Grandma and she clawed at him.

Mom took me by the shoulders and shook me hard. "Tessa, this is craziness. Stop it right now. Go to your room."

The look on Mom's face could scare a mean dog away, so I slowly backed away toward the stairs. Mom yelled at Grandma and Grandma yelled back. Pastor Jessie Michael said, "It's best I leave now." He winked at Mom and I knew he would come back later.

CHAPTER FOURTEEN

I felt comfortable and warm. I had no sense of time. Then I heard an excited voice, "I have to tell her."

Then another voice said, "She's too young."

I recognized the voices of Great-grandmother Eunice and Great-aunt Gertie. I saw Eunice sitting on the brocade couch in the living room and Gertie sitting across from her in an armchair. They were wearing long dresses and white kid gloves. "I can't keep this inside. I have to tell a living person," Gertie said.

"I'll hurt you if you tell. This is my secret and my business."

"But I helped you hide it. And now I'm stuck here with you," Gertie said.

"Maybe you're stuck here because you lifted you skirt faster than anyone else," Eunice said.

"I had better love spasms than a lot of men. Men loved it that I made noise. You want to hear how I sounded?" Gertie parted her lips and started to moan.

"Shut up, you nasty thing. This is hell listening to you," Eunice said.

I was standing right in front of them, but they didn't notice me.

Then I heard, "Tessa, Tessa Louise." I was startled awake by my mother's grating voice and I realized I'd been dreaming.

"I'm busy talking to someone important. Don't bother me," I said loudly.

"Don't yell at me. Tessa Louise, get up right now. You're too young to be sleeping late," she said. I felt groggy.

When Grandma Bernice finally got up, she was still mad at Mom. "You can't stand to see me get anything. Don't interfere with my Christian healings. This is still my house."

Mom whispered to me, "This house is a hornet's nest. We're going into town."

We drove down Grand Avenue, the main street, and the sky was filled with clouds that made the buildings seem small. The stores were shaded from the sharp sun by their metal or wood awnings covering the sidewalk. We parked in front of Gus's Shoe store, where so many shoes were stacked in the window that I didn't think there were enough people in town to buy them all. The handsome shoe salesman stood in the door, watching Mom get out of the car. He ran his hand over his slick hair. Mom had a special order to pick up, so she gave me money for a root beer float next door at Mrs. Thelma's Five and Dime. The brick building with a sagging metal awning had the windows filled with kitchen, bathroom items, toys, and all sorts of other things.

When I went into the Five and Dime, Mrs. Thelma and Betty Lynn were in the back next to the caged parakeets and the artificial waterfall. The two women were cutting boxes open and stacking pots and pans on a shelf. I snuck up on them and sat down on the wooden floor on the other side, next to boxes filled with Old Dutch cleanser and Brillo pads.

Then I heard Betty Lynn say, "Virginia." Then nothing more. She had a way of not finishing sentences, and some people said behind her back that she was a birdbrain.

"Virginia? Don't just leave a word hanging in the air. What about her?" Mrs. Thelma said.

"I can't believe she showed up in church showing her legs almost up to her crack."

"With Virginia, she didn't fall far from the tree," Mrs. Thelma said. They were like two chickens pecking at the dirt.

"What do you mean?"

"Don't tell me you've forgotten what I told you. If you can't remember things, people will think you're dumb," Mrs. Thelma said.

"You can't expect me to remember all the things people say. It clutters my mind."

"Just remember what I say. Virginia's got that private kind of itch just like her Granddaddy Old Man Henry. He made a lot of money tanning leather and shipping it up north and he had women all over the place," Mrs. Thelma said.

My pink ruffled skirt was hiked up and the wooden floor felt dusty and cool against my bare legs. Mrs. Thelma and Betty Lynn moved down the aisle as they put the pots and pans on the shelf. I scooted closer to them so I could hear better.

"Old Henry had a hankering for young pretty colored women. They worked in a house out south of town in the colored neighborhood," Mrs. Thelma said.

"And just because people say things that doesn't mean they are true," Betty Lynn said.

"I was old enough to remember what people said. And the men talked about it plenty."

"So, men talked about this house with a young girl?" Betty Lynn said.

"The women also talked about it," Mrs. Thelma said.

"That means your mother never stopped talking about it. Her big stone face going blah, blah, blah…." Betty Lynn said.

"Stop saying things about your grandma."

I felt like sneezing, but I held my nose to keep from making noise.

"Old Man Henry took to this one colored whore, Franny, and he had two children by her. There was a kind of no-man's land with boarded up houses between the poor white neighborhood and the Negro neighborhood. Old Man Henry built her a house, a big fancy house. He put it close to the poor white neighborhood and some people wanted to pull it down," Mrs. Thelma said.

"And this was when Bernice was little?"

"That's right. I was in the same class with her at elementary school," Mrs. Thelma's voice sounded sad as she spoke. She continued, "He drove around with the colored whore in his fancy car. He even dressed her better than a lot of white women. This infuriated people, but he had a whole lot of people working at his warehouses and they were afraid to say anything because they didn't want to lose their jobs. Bernice and I were still friends. That's when they were in the big house on High Street. Sometimes there would be such arguments at her house that the neighbors called the sheriff. People said Old Man Henry had a sex disease in his brain. One day he parked his car right in front of the church, with the colored woman in his car. People went outside and the men told him to leave. I felt so sorry for Bernice. She went to him and kept calling, 'Daddy, daddy,' but he ignored her. Finally, he left and I wasn't allowed to play with her after that. At school, kids taunted her for having colored relatives. One of the whore's bastards used to walk up to Bernice in town and said he was her brother until the sheriff gave him a real bad whipping. One day the coloreds just up and moved away and people said Old Man Henry set them up someplace."

I wondered what a sex disease in the brain was. Do I have a sex disease in my brain also?

"What happened to all his money?" Betty Lynn asked. I heard the dull clank of her stacking dishes on the shelf.

"Besides the colored whores, he spent his money on gambling while Eunice spent his money on bringing spiritualists to hold séances at her house. People said she trying to escape into the spirit world to get away from the sorrow Henry caused her. It was soon after that Henry lost a lot of money and they moved to the smaller house Bernice lives in now. One day Henry was just gone and he never came back," Mrs. Thelma said.

"What did everyone think?" Betty Lynn asked.

"There had been rumors of a "ghastly secret" that Eunice might have shot him. But she was well respected and people didn't like Old Man Henry much."

I had been scooting closer to hear them better and then I sneezed from the dust. Betty Lynn shot around the corner and grabbed my arm and pulled me to my feet. "You nasty stinking girl. You're sneaking around listening to adult conversation?" She gripped my arm harder. Her pink nails dug into my skin.

"I came to get a root beer float, but you were busy."

She put her face right close to my face, her nails still digging into my arm, "How long have you been here? Did you get an earful about your family?"

The old skin around her blue eyes reminded me of alligator skin. Like her mother, she had lost most of her eyelashes and her bird eyes seemed to poke at me. It was all I could do to keep from sticking my finger in her eye. "I don't understand adult conversation," I said.

Just then Mom came into the store carrying packages and saw Betty Lynn's python grip on my arm. "Let go of her!" Mom yelled.

"You better teach your daughter not to eavesdrop. She's going to be a dirty little hussy just like you," Betty Lynn said.

Mom came towards Betty Lynn with her hand raised. "You need to have your face slapped."

Betty Lynn backed away. "You better not try."

"Tessa, let's get out of here," Mom said.

On the way home, I turned to Mom. "They said my Great-grandfather liked colored whores. Do we know any whores? And she said things about our family."

"Let's not talk about it. This town is cutting into me. They're not any better than we are," Mom said.

CHAPTER FIFTEEN

Recently, I had become worried about Mom because she was so nervous those days. She wasn't sleeping and every time the phone rang, she rushed to get it. And when Pastor Jessie Michael didn't come for a week, Mom kept calling the church and leaving messages for him.

Finally, the Saturday night came when the Pastor was going to come, and the silver pitchers and platters were so shined up that I could see my face in them. The glow of the sunset came through the dining room windows, reflecting golden light off the glass doors of the mahogany cabinets.

Steam clung to the windows from the cooking, and Mom said, "Mother if you don't open the windows, I'll tell the Pastor that you constantly worry about burglars." Grandma didn't want the Pastor to think her faith wasn't strong, so she took some deep breaths and opened one of the tall leaded windows.

Mom started drinking wine before dinner, which was unusual, but Grandma had been having her "daytime coffee" all afternoon and didn't even notice Mom's drinking.

The doorbell rang and Mom let the Pastor in and they came into the dining room. The dinner of pot roast and potatoes was on the table, and the Pastor, Mom, and I sat down. But Grandma stood at the head of the table and raised her arms and sang, *"I'm going to get on that glory train. Pastor Jessie Michael is taking me on that glory train to Jesus."* She moved her hips like she was trying to dance.

"I'll show you how to dance." I stood up and started doing my Eagle Dance, but one look from Mom made me stop. Her face had a pinched look and her jaw was tight.

"Please sit down, Mother. Let's have peaceful dinner," Mom said.

"Yes. This food smells delicious. I'll say grace. Thank you, oh Lord for providing this bounty of food," the Pastor said. Then he piled a large helping of roast beef on his plate.

All through dinner, I kept looking from Mom to the Pastor because Mom stared into the Pastor's eyes, as if her eyes were trying to say something. The whole time I had a butterflies-in-the-stomach feeling.

Later that night, when Pastor Jessie Michael came sneaking upstairs to see Mom in her room, as soon as the door closed, I snuck into the hallway to peep through the keyhole. All I could see was Mom in her flower print blouse and tight red slacks moving around the room.

"You left me a lot of messages," the Pastor said.

"Why on earth didn't you call me?"

"I was out of town." Then the Pastor took off his belt with the gold cross on the buckle, tossing it on the bed. Then he pulled off his cowboy boots and took off his western shirt, dropping it on the bed. Then he unzipped his jeans and stepped out of them. His gold cross on a chain rested on the dark hair on his chest. I felt twinges of fear throughout my body. "Jesus, I don't care if I'm not supposed to watch them," I whispered.

"I'm here now and you look beautiful. Come here." The Pastor extended his strong arms and tried to embrace Mom, but she pushed him away.

"You sure take your pants off quickly. Wait a minute; we have a real problem." Her voice sounded urgent and I heard her red high heel shoes clop against the creaky old wooden floor.

Then I heard her crying and I got a glimpse of her contorted face. I felt her sobs as if they were in the pit of my stomach, and I started to cry silently.

"What is it? Tell me?" the Pastor asked.

"I'm pregnant."

"Oh, no. That can't be. We were careful. I'm sorry," the Pastor said in a voice so low I could barely hear him.

"You've got to say something other than you're sorry."

"What do you want me to say?" he asked. He picked up his jeans from the floor and tossed them on Mom's pink bedspread.

"You've said many times that you love me." Mom sounded tense as she pushed her red hair back over her shoulders.

The Pastor tried to put his arm around her, but she pushed him away. "Of course, I love you. You're a wonderful woman."

"We have to get married." Mom twisted her charm bracelet around on her wrist. "I've got it. We can go away and come back married. People will think it was a whirlwind romance."

"Hold on. Keep your voice down. You're going a mile a minute." The Pastor's voice was still low. His black hair fell across his forehead. He put his large hands on Mom's shoulders and tried to get her to sit on the bed. She stayed standing.

"You must know someone in another town who can marry us." The heels of her shoes made more noise as she walked heavily around the room.

"Stop, just stop." The Pastor shouted. He picked up his jeans and searched in the pockets for his handkerchief. He pulled it out and wiped his forehead.

"I have to be married before I get too far along." Mom's voice trembled, and she kept unbuttoning and then buttoning the top button on her blouse.

"Listen to me. I can't marry you," the Pastor said. Then he plopped back onto the bed, making it groan.

"You're just saying that because it's a shock. I'll even believe in your religion." Mom crossed her arms and stood in front of him. "Say something." But the Pastor was silent and she got close to him and yelled, "Tell me why not!"

The Pastor looked down. "Because I'm already married. We're separated. I came here for a fresh start, but she won't give me a divorce."

Mom crossed her arms and shook as she cried, "You act like you have a direct line to God. You're a bastard just like the rest of them."

Now, the Pastor got down on his knees and put his hands together. *"Watch and pray that you may not enter into temptation. The spirit is willing but the flesh is weak. That's from Matthew 26: Verse 41."* He looked up at Mom with a sad expression on his face.

"You're crazy. It's too late for that fucking quote."

On his knees in his underwear, he looked up. "I never wanted to hurt you. Even men of God make mistakes." Tears came to his eyes and he extended his hands.

Mom pushed his hands away. Her eyes were bulging, and I thought that she would turn into one of those demons from the Bible. "Don't cry. Even men of God want to fuck. How many women have you used that line on?" she said, spitting her words.

"I'm sincere. Please pray with me. It will make you feel better." He grasped the golden cross around his neck.

"Stop this bullshit. I need you to marry me. What am I really supposed to do?" Mom yelled.

The Pastor stood up, but looked at the floor. "You could go away for awhile and if you can't take care of the baby, you could put it up for adoption."

"This will be your child also. You want me to make things easy for you," Mom said.

The Pastor moved closer to her. "We can't always know what God wants. I still love you." He tried to put his arm around her.

"Get away from me. And why don't you just go fuck your Bible." She grabbed a glass vase and threw it at him. She missed. The vase smashed against the wall.

I was worried something might happen to Mom, so I banged on the door. "Leave my mom alone!" I yelled.

Then there was a loud crack at the other end of the hallway and I screamed. Grandma had fired one of her pistols. "Tessa, get back in your room," Grandma said. She walked into the hallway dressed in a pink terry cloth bathrobe and matching fuzzy slippers. and holding the gun with both hands. She moved toward the door. "Who's there?" she yelled. I stepped back into my doorway, but I could see everything. Now Grandma was pointing the gun right at Mom's door. "Come out, you thieving burglar. I'm ready for you. I've got the Lord on my side."

There was no sound from Mom's room and Grandma put her ear to the old door and listened. "You better leave my daughter alone. Get out here now. I shoot for Jesus!" Grandma yelled again.

From the other side of the door Mom said, "Mother, put the gun down. There's no burglar." Mom opened the door and stepped into the hallway barefoot. "Are you crazy? Take that gun and go back into your room."

"This is my house," Grandma said.

"Please go back into your room," Mom stood hunched over.

"I knew it. You've been sneaking men up here. Tell him to come out. I want to see him before I shoot him," Grandma said.

"You're not going to shoot anybody," Mom said.

The Pastor came out into the hallway in his underwear. "Bernice, I can explain everything."

"You!" Grandma screamed. Then she looked at his underwear, and the gun went off and the bullet lodged in the floor.

He jumped back, but put his arms in front of his chest. "Bernice, please don't."

"Mother, give me that gun." Mom's face was red and twisted.

The Pastor's legs had a lot of black hairs sticking out. I blurted out, "Why did God put so many ugly hairs on the Pastor's legs?" Nobody paid attention to me.

Grandma lowered the gun and Grandma and Mom turned their demon eyes on me. "Tessa, get back in your room or you'll get a switching like you've never had before," Grandma said. I went back to my room, but stayed in the doorway.

Pastor Jessie Michael stepped toward Grandma and he put out his hand. "Bernice, give me the gun."

"Don't touch my gun." Grandma pointed it at him again.

"Grandma, stop. He's supposed to take me to the Genuine Circle B Bar-B-Que," I said. I looked at the Pastor. "I kept your secret. You have to take me there?" I yelled. I stomped my feet, but they ignored me.

He stepped to the side away from the gun. "Virginia was upset so I came by to counsel her and pray with her," he said in a soothing voice.

Grandma lowered the gun. "You pray with your pants off?" Then she shouted, "You've got something sticking out and it's not holy."

"Mother, you're imagining things. My God, you don't see anything," Mom said.

"Your cock is not for Jesus," Grandma said.

Pastor Jessie Michael went into the bedroom and came back with his shirt on but unbuttoned. He held his jeans and boots in front of himself as if they would protect him. "Bernice, please calm down," he said.

"Mother, give me that gun or I'll call the police." Grandma gripped the gun, but held it at her side. "I'm a grown woman and he's a grown man," Mom said.

"Death to fornicators in my house." Grandma raised the gun again, pointing it at the Pastor.

"I swear I will call the police," Mom said.

Holding his clothes in one hand, the Pastor stepped forward and tried to reach out with the other hand to touch Grandma's shoulder. "I can make you feel better. Pray with me. We all make mistakes. It's the flesh. It's weak. I'm going to pray to be delivered from lust." He bowed his head, but kept his eyes on the gun.

"Lust? You said you loved me," Mom said.

Grandma puffed up even more. She stuck her head out in her characteristic turtle stance. "You don't love her? It was lust. I expect this of Virginia, but not you. You really had me believing in you. I had real faith. I was being uplifted." Her body shaking, Grandma lowered the gun.

"It can be like that again. Remember how my hands felt. Bernice, please forgive me." The Pastor moved forward and reached out touching her shoulder.

Grandma jerked away. "No, you've taken it all away. You just want to stick that dirty thing in whoever you can find" Grandma said.

"What dirty thing?" I said, but they ignored me.

Grandma's hand shook as she held the gun and stepped forward and pointed the gun at his stomach. "You think I won't do it, but I will."

"I am calling the police. You crazy bitch. I want to see you in jail," Mom yelled. She rushed toward the stairs.

"No, don't. We don't want the police." The Pastor stepped back and out of the way of the gun. "Some things have happened before," he said.

Grandma still had her eyes blazing, but she lowered the gun. "You've killed Jesus for me. You've ruined my life. Now get out of my house."

The Pastor picked up his jeans and boots and started for the stairs, but he paused a moment and looked back. "There's a new kind of mental therapy. Maybe all of you should get some help. It's something to think about."

The Pastor started down the stairs. I ran after him and called out, "Don't leave me. I want the ride you promised me in your Cadillac." I rushed down the stairs and grabbed his arm to stop him from leaving.

"Tessa, get away from him," Grandma said.

After he left, I came back upstairs. Grandma had turned on Mom with a look on her face that made me shrivel inside. She stuck the gun in her robe pocket and came toward Mom with her raised hand. "How could you do this to me?"

Mom blocked Grandma from slapping her. "Mother, that's not the only problem," and then she broke down sobbing. As if all the air went out of her, she crumpled onto the floor. "Help me." She put her hand over her stomach.

"Help her," I said. I grabbed Grandma's arm, but she slapped my hand away.

"You're only crying because you didn't get his cock tonight." Then Grandma laughed and poked Mom's ribs with her pink fuzzy slipper as if she were a dead animal.

Mom looked up and said, "Stop it. You have to listen. Help me. I'm pregnant. Mama, what am I going to do?" She shook as she drew her knees up, wrapping her arms around them. She rocked from side to side.

Grandma moaned and grabbed her stomach as if punched. "No, not that. You really do want to humiliate me. You're lucky I don't shoot you and say it was an accident." Grandma patted the gun in her robe pocket. "Nobody would blame me."

"Don't you dare hurt Mom!" I yelled. I yanked on Grandma's robe. She pushed me away hard.

Grandma looked from me to Mom. "You're my daughter and I'm supposed to love you. Lord knows I've tried. I loved you when you were little. But I don't know what happened. I just don't know." Then tears came to her eyes. She went into her bedroom and I heard glass objects breaking.

There was a loud pounding on the front door. Mom slowly got up from the floor and went to the door. I followed her. Two policemen were there. The one named Wilbur said, "The neighbors heard gun shots."

"My mother was just cleaning her gun. It was an accident," Mom said.

They wouldn't have believed her, but Mom was friends with one of the cops. He stood in the doorway looking at her in her robe. He said, "We'll let it go this time. Just don't let it happen again." Mom forced herself to smile at him.

Grandma didn't come out of her room for days and wouldn't eat the food Lilly Mae put outside her door. When she heard Mom in the hallway, she'd open her door and yell, "Damn you. You've made everything dirty and I now I can't sing."

Later, I found Mom's favorite dresses ripped apart on the floor in the hallway.

CHAPTER SIXTEEN

Pastor Jessie Michael didn't come to our house again, but Mom called him many times each day. He never answered and she slammed down the phone.

After a week, when I went into the kitchen, Lilly Mae was cutting up bananas and putting them into a batter for bread. The greased tin was on the sink. She looked at me. "People all over town are talking 'bout your mama. She goes to the Pastor's church several times a day and stands there yellin'. He doesn't open the door. Then at night she throws rocks at his windows. She even went to his Bible study group and started shouting that he wasn't a man of God or a healer. The police were called to get her out. She won't listen to me. Your grandmother won't speak to me or talk on the phone. Tessa, you needs to try to get her to stop what she's doin'."

Just then Mom came into the kitchen. She looked like she hadn't slept in days. Her hair hadn't been combed. I went to her and put my arms around her. "Mom, please don't go to that church anymore. You're too upset. Stay with me."

Mom looked disapprovingly at Lilly Mae. "Why did you tell her?"

"I think it's an emergency," Lilly Mae said.

"This is my business. I'm going to expose him. He's not going to get away with his lies," Mom said.

Finally, a few days later, Grandma came into the kitchen. She walked slowly as if her legs had been injured and just stared at Lilly Mae and me.

Lilly Mae told Grandma that for days some of the churchwomen had been calling to speak to her. When Grandma finally agreed to talk on the phone, Mrs. Thelma told her that Mom was making scenes at the church and outside the Pastor's house. When Mom came home, Grandma was in the kitchen and started screaming all over again, "Don't you realize the whole town will turn against us?" Grandma just sat at the kitchen table. Her eyes took on a harsh blackened look and I knew that look meant anger gathering in her. Her double chins jiggled, and she waved her white arms.

Mom stood there in her flower print dress with the puffy sleeves. She'd worn it for days and it needed to be washed. "Mama, if you don't get a hold of yourself, you're going to bring on a heart attack or stroke."

Grandma screamed and her face looked stretched tight, her mouth an ugly crack. She pointed her pudgy finger at Mom. "You want me to have a heart attack, so you can get the house. But that isn't going to happen. I can't have you here when your belly gets big. I want you out of my house."

"Please, you know I don't make enough money to support myself and Tessa and another …."

"You should have thought of that before."

"I have nowhere to go, and what about Tessa?" Mom asked.

"Let Tessa stay with me and be raised a Christian."

Mom had her own storm in her. She clenched her jaw and her face and neck went stiff. She looked really ugly. "I thought Jesus was killed off for you. And you were giving him up."

The air felt so thick that it was difficult to breathe. I thought: Any minute the anger like lightening was going to strike and explode us into pieces. Queen Victoria hid under the table, but she didn't take her eyes off Grandma.

"Damn you. Get out now," Grandma said.

Mom glared at Grandma. She slammed her hand on the table making the silverware jump. "You'll never get Tessa, you crazy bitch. I'll show you I can get along without you."

That night, I saw Mom pull an old suitcase out of the hall closet and in the morning, she was gone.

CHAPTER SEVENTEEN

As soon as I realized Mom was gone, I felt as if a big hole had opened right across my stomach. Each night I woke up and wiped the tears off my cheeks. Mom had left me a letter. When I read it, she said she loved me and would be back. Somehow, I didn't believe it. I stayed in my room a lot. I wanted to ask Grandma about Mom, but she was talking to her dolls much of the time. When she did come out of her room, she had such a mean look on her face that I was afraid to ask her about Mom because I knew she'd spit words like venom.

At night, I went into Mom's room and slept in her bed with my head on her pillow where I could smell her. I also took out the picture of my dad holding me when I was a baby. I kept thinking, why didn't he come to see me? I slept with the picture under my pillow.

One night, after Mom had been gone for about ten days, I went to sleep in Mom's room and the wind was making the tree branches' bony hands scrape against the windows. The rasping felt as if it was scraping across the hole Mom left in the middle of my body. And I could see the open mouths of little animals, their teeth exposed, being blown by the wind right toward me. I covered my face with the pillow.

Later, when I looked at the clock, it read 5:00 A.M. and the wind had stopped. I thought I heard something and I put on my robe and slippers and went downstairs. From the bottom of the stairs, I saw lights and heard voices in the living room. There were candles on the mantelpiece and also on a table with a lace tablecloth. There were a group of ladies in dresses with long skirts standing in the middle of the room. Their sleeves were puffed out at the shoulders and had lace at their wrists. So many lights were shimmering around their heads, it was hard to see them. I smelled roses.

Eunice and Gertie were in the middle of the group and everyone was listening to them. I pushed my way past the ladies to stand in front of them. "Eunice." Eunice didn't notice me at first. "Eunice. Why are all these women here?"

Eunice realized I was there. "Oh, Tessa. Very good. You came into our time for a moment. You're seeing the room the way it was when we had séances."

"My mother has left me," I said.

"In your time things are so different … I'm sorry that happened," Eunice said. She kneeled and looked into my face. "Don't worry. You are loved."

"Help me. You have to take me with you. I want to be with you." I was shaking.

"Even if we could do that we wouldn't because it would be wrong," Eunice said.

"Your mother loves you," Gertie said.

"No, she doesn't. Please do something. I hate it here. I'll find a way to be with you." They went back to listening to the other women, who were all talking at once. I felt alone.

I felt unsteady and the next thing I knew someone was shaking me. Lilly Mae stood over me, her hands on her hips. "Leave me alone. I don't want to wake up," I said.

"You fell asleep on the floor again. Tessa, I heard you talkin' to those spirits. You can't go on like this not eating. And you have to stop talkin' to those spirits. Child, it's dangerous. They're goin' to take you over and you won't be able to get rid of them. Come into the kitchen and I'm goin' to fix this once and for all."

In the kitchen I sat at the table, while Lilly Mae took a raw egg in the shell and rubbed it all over my head and body, mumbling in a language I couldn't understand. "Now watch," she said. Then she broke it into a cup and pointed to the egg. "See these dark spots. These are the spirits that has been drawn out." Then she smiled and looked proud of herself. I knew that Eunice and Gertie were still in the house, but I didn't tell Lilly Mae.

When I was with Lilly Mae, I didn't feel so alone. I was able to eat some of the eggs and pancakes she made. I said, "Grandma says Mom has the devil in her."

Lilly Mae stood up, and put her arm around me and hugged me against her apron. I hadn't been hugged in a long time and her large breasts felt comforting to me. She smelled of cinnamon from the buns she was making. "Child, don't you dare think that 'bout your Mama. She's good. Your grandma says things when she's got her anger up. She'll git over it. Blood is thicker than water."

"I don't understand why Grandma keeps saying Mom is going to get a big belly."

"Now you sit down and listens to me. That's somethin' you never talk 'bout. That's adults business. Promise me you'll never talk 'bout it," Lilly Mae said. She poured syrup on her pancakes and it dripped down the sides with the butter.

"I promise."

Then the phone in the entry hall started ringing. Lilly Mae answered the phone and called up to Grandma in her room. We were surprised Grandma decided to come down to take the call. Grandma had to hold the receiver out from her ear because Mrs. Thelma talked so loudly that even I could hear her. Mrs. Thelma told Grandma that the Pastor had up and left town and nobody knew where he had gone. Grandma's eyes became moist, but she forced her voice to sound cheerful. "I knew all along he wasn't all that he said he was. He didn't have me fooled one bit. I'm a good judge of character."

When Grandma got off the phone, Lilly Mae said to her, "You've been all worked up for weeks now. You need to rest."

Grandma put some of her "daytime coffee" in a teacup and went back up to her bedroom.

CHAPTER EIGHTEEN

The next evening when the phone rang, Lilly Mae called me to the phone. It was Mom. I jumped up and down. She said she was coming back for me, but she said she'd be coming with a man I'd often seen behind the counter at the grocery store, the butcher. When I'd seen him at the store, he was always trying to get Mom's attention. His eyes would move from her eyes down to her breasts and back like ping-pong balls bouncing up and down.

The next day, Mom brought him into our kitchen. Grandma had stepped out for a few minutes to go shopping. Mom looked uncomfortable and stood there stiffly with Boleslaw. I looked at him closely. He was a burly man with a round red face, bright blue eyes, and a thick brown moustache above his full lips. Mom said, "I want you to meet Boleslaw Grabowski. We went to the Justice of the Peace and are now husband and wife. Tessa, he's going to be your stepfather."

Boleslaw reached out to shake my hand, but I pulled away. "You're a nice little girl and now you're going to come and live with me," he said in his Polish accent. Before I could stop him, he put his wet lips and scratchy moustache on my forehead for a kiss.

I pulled away and wiped my forehead. "I don't want a stepfather."

I ran to my room and Mom followed me. She sat next to me on my bed. "Tessa, listen to me. Your grandma says I can't live here anymore. I know this is difficult, but he is a nice man and I've married him. We are going to be a family. When you get to know him, you'll see he isn't so bad."

"I liked the Pastor. I don't know if I'll like him," I said.

"Don't mention that liar again. Boleslaw's house is on an acre and there's a garden. It's like a farm. The garden is big and there're chickens. You will have a large backyard to play in. You won't have Grandma bossing you around. You'll see. It will be better than here," Mom said.

"I like chickens, but I'm afraid to move. I've never even seen the place. Do we have to move there because you have a baby in your stomach?"

Mom's face became like stone. "Tessa, listen to me. Never mention that to anyone. Give me your word you'll never mention it to anyone. You know when you give your word, you can't break it. You word must be as good as gold." Tears came to her eyes.

"I won't tell anyone, but the Pastor was handsome and Boleslaw is ugly and red-faced. What if I don't like it there?" I said.

"Promise me you'll make an effort to like it. It's a new start for both of us."

"Okay."

We went downstairs and when Grandma came home, she put down her groceries and stood staring silently at Mom and Boleslaw. Mom started to introduce him, but Grandma was quick to speak, "I know who he is. I've never been friends with anyone who works in meat."

"We got married. I told you I could get by on my own," Mom said.

"Well, what a hasty wedding." Grandma looked Boleslaw up and down, her eyes resting on his protruding stomach and red hands. She stepped closer to him and pushed her head forward to make sure she was heard. "I don't know why you'd want to marry her, but you're one of those Euro-pee-ans, aren't you?"

"I've lived here since my family moved here when I was fourteen. Yoakum is my home," Boleslaw said.

"But you and your people came from New York. You're one of those Yankee Polacks, aren't you?" Grandma said.

"I'm from Chicago," Boleslaw said.

"Six of one and half a dozen of the other. If you wanted to marry her, you must not be very bright."

Mom shifted on one foot then the other. "Stop it. How can you be so rude to a guest in your house? He's a good man," Mom said.

"And I'm a happy one. I've had my eyes on your daughter for a long time. She accepts me the way I am. I'm going to be a good husband to her," Boleslaw said.

Grandma's face twisted, and she looked as if her eyes could burn into him. "Well, you better keep your eyes on her."

"Stop it," Mom said.

"How soon will you get your things out?" Grandma asked. "I can rent your rooms to nice people. People who pay."

CHAPTER NINETEEN

While we were packing, I felt nervous and kept thinking what's it going to be like living with a butcher? I pictured dead bodies of cows and pigs stored around the place. But Mom said it would be nice, so I tried to ignore my fears. In the afternoon, Boleslaw loaded our things into a trailer hitched behind his green Chevy station wagon. We drove toward his house on the edge of town. The closer we got, the more run-down the houses were. They were on plots of land with scattered oak trees. Some had gardens, but many had overgrown grasses, weeds, and broken fences under the trees. Boleslaw's house was a two-story wood frame house with a sagging porch and peeling paint on an acre of land. As we pulled up, I could see a large garden and some chicken coops in the back.

When I entered his house, the smell of cabbage hit me. It hung in every room, a pungent smell claiming territory. This had to be what a Polish house was like.

Boleslaw led Mom and me into the kitchen where a big woman sat at a white metal table with its flaps opened out. At first, I thought she was the maid, until I realized she and Boleslaw looked alike. "This is my matka, that's Polish for Mother. Her name is Beata Grabowski." He smiled.

She was big and red-faced and run-down like the house. She wore a red scarf, and when she smiled, you could see she was missing an upper tooth. Her tongue played peek-a-boo, pushing in and out through the hole as she talked. She had some dark hairs growing on her upper lip, and she wore a butcher's apron with something smeared on the front.

One of her large greasy hands turned a handle on a grinder. Her other hand held what looked like a long thin white balloon. Spicy smelling meat was being pushed out of the machine into the long balloon. She looked at Mom. "Hello, welcome to my home and it is my home," she said in her Polish accent. Then she continued turning the handle until the long white thing was stuffed full, and then she tied it off into sections with string. It looked like a long, fatty, whitish hot dog, and she curled it like a snake on a plate.

"Come closer little one and let me get a look at you," Beata said.

Mom nudged me toward her. Beata smiled and her tongue flicked in and out of the hole in her teeth. She took a hold of my wrist. "She doesn't have much meat on her bones." She looked me up and down and I knew it was really to see if I was good enough to eat.

"This is Tessa, my daughter. She's a good girl," Mom said.

"My, my, she's a pretty one," Beata said.

"I want to go home," I said.

Mom stood behind me to keep me from stepping away from Beata. "This is going to be your home now. Remember what you promised," Mom said quickly. Mom even nudged me closer to Beata, but everything was grating on me, the meat, the cabbage smell, and Beata's grin with the missing tooth. I tried to smile to show Mom I was making an effort. I looked out the kitchen window, but I couldn't see anything. Then Beata put her big moist hand on my shoulder and leaned close to me. She wetted her lips and laughed. Even though it was a nice laugh, I knew it was a trick. Any minute her red scarf was going to come off and her wolf's ears were going to pop up. She would rip off her mask and reveal her real wolf's face and teeth.

I leaned forward, easing away from her touch, and I moved my arms and legs doing my jerky Chicken Dance to make her think I was crazy.

Beata sat back and stared at me. "Stand still," she said. Beata pointed to a chair next to her. "Come sit next to me. I'll show you how to make Polish sausage."

"I'm not going to eat that," I said.

Beata scrunched up her nose as though I smelled bad. I thought: Good, maybe she'll stay away from me. I looked at Mom and she looked sad. I'd have to act like I liked it here. I forced my mouth into a smile.

Mom pinched me. "You've never had Polish sausage, so you don't know if you like it or not."

"If you say so. O.K. I'll try it." I kept smiling even though my lips were tired. I thought: I'll have to keep my eyes closed when I eat it.

Boleslaw went to his mother, bending his large body over her and kissed her forehead. With her greasy hands, she pulled his face to her and kissed him on the lips. She tried to hold his face close to hers and he pulled away, but he kept his arm across her shoulder. "My matka, she's always in the kitchen cooking for me."

Beata patted Boleslaw's arm as her eyes stared intensely into Mom's eyes, "I've got a big gentle son. He's never hurt anyone," she said. Then she looked back at Boleslaw. "I never thought I'd see the day you'd be married. I'm glad. But you only called me after you were married. You knew I had my heart set on a big wedding in the Catholic Church," she said.

I stiffened when I heard the word *Catholic*. Grandma didn't like Catholics because they were Pope worshippers.

Boleslaw stood up straight. "All of our relatives in Texas are dead, and the ones in Chicago are too far away. Virginia and I got married the way we wanted to."

Beata looked at Mom again as if her eyes could bore holes into her. "This is his first marriage. He hasn't had a lot of experience with women," she said.

"Virginia is all the experience I want," Boleslaw said. Boleslaw put his arm around Mom's waist and slid his hand down her rear, resting it there.

Beata didn't see what Boleslaw was doing because she was leaning in so close to me. "This is your house now. It's not fancy but I want you to feel at home."

"No, I want Lilly Mae. I'm at home with her," I said. I felt as if fingernails were clawing me. I started swinging my arms side to side and making a moaning sound.

Mom gripped my shoulders hurting me. "Stop that now or I'll swat you. Sit down and behave."

I pinched myself to hold back my anger. "Great-grandmother Eunice come to me now. I need you. Help me." I looked around, but she wasn't there.

"Who's she talking to? Does she do that a lot?" asked Beata.

"I talk to the spirits of my great-grandmother and her sister all the time," I said.

"Hush, Tessa. It's just a fantasy of hers." Mom pointed to the chair beside Beata. "I told you to sit down."

I sat on the edge of the chair as far away from Beata as I could get, almost falling off the other side. But she could still reach me and touch my arm with her greasy hand.

Mom and I were not the same anymore. My mother was being pulled away and Boleslaw's big stomach was coming between us like a wall of flesh. I stared at his bulging belly. Then I looked him right in the eyes. "Do you have a baby in your belly?" I asked.

When I saw the panicked look on Mom's face, I wished I hadn't said that. Her mouth tensed into an ugly shape. "Tessa, hush your rude mouth."

Boleslaw laughed. The ends of his moustache turned up and he patted his belly. "I like good food and I'm not ashamed of it. Matka can't stop cooking for me."

I had to think of a way to remember his name. I thought that the name Boleslaw reminded me of cold slaw, so in my mind I'd call him The Big Slaw. Now his last name Grabowski reminded me of the word grabber and he liked to grab. He kept putting his large hands around Mom's waist and pulling her up against his body … fat man and Mom like two bugs in a rug. So, in my mind I decided to call him The Big Slaw Grabber.

"She's my little woman now. I've waited a long time for her," he said.

When I'd seen him in the meat department, he was always wearing his white butcher's hat, but without it I could see the shiny bald spot on the top of his head. I couldn't stop imagining him eating, putting big juicy bites of meat into his mouth, and then some of the juices oozing out of his large red lips onto his chin.

Beata stared at me. "Child, why are you crying?" Beata licked her lips.

"I don't know," I said.

Mom came around to my chair, grabbed my arm, and pulled me up. "She's tired from the moving." Then she turned to me, "Tessa, I'll show you to your room while Boleslaw is bringing in our things."

"Her room will be the third door on the right. Nobody has been in there for awhile. It may have to be cleaned." Boleslaw put his arm around Mom and pulled her toward him. "Be sure and warm our bed up for me."

As Mom and I walked up the creaky staircase. I said, "Mom I've tried to like it here. Now, I need to go home."

"Try a little harder. We've only been here an hour," Mom said.

Mom took me into my room where the wooden floor squeaked, and faded wallpaper was peeling off the walls. The bed was saggy and there was a musty smell. "It stinks in here," I said. My tears were falling on the backs of my hands. "Take me home."

"Don't you want to stay with me. You're my baby. I need you here with me. Sometimes we have to accept things the way they are. You'll get used to it," Mom said.

Mom hugged me and it felt good for a moment. She said, "This is a brand-new place. It is good for you to get away from talking to those imaginary spirits all the time. You will become normal if it's the last thing I do."

"This place isn't new. It's old and rotten," I suddenly yelled.

Mom held my arm tightly hurting me. "Don't yell at me. I don't know what I'm going to do with you. You don't know how to make people like you. Sometimes I think you don't want anyone to like you. You'll stay here until I tell you that you can come down for dinner."

I noticed the poster in a frame on the torn flower wallpaper. It was a poster of a lady with a see-through tee-shirt showing her big breasts sitting on the hood of a shiny new car. She was smiling as if she stuck her pink breasts out every day for the camera. I moved close to look at it. Then Mom noticed the picture. "Is that a whore? Does Boleslaw know them?" I asked.

"He should have taken this down." Mom grabbed the picture off the wall and took it with her, closing the door behind her. I looked around the room. There was a dresser with wooden drawers that got stuck when I tried to pull them out. Also, there was a white dressing vanity with an old cracked mirror above it. I sat down on the bench and opened the drawer in the middle, and it smelled of old wood and perfume from an old bottle left inside it. As I looked in the mirror, the crack in the mirror divided my face into two parts. I took out the yellowed picture of Eunice and Gertie that I brought from home and put it in the corner of the mirror. I stared at the picture, calling for them to come to me, but I didn't see their faces flash, nor did I hear their voices. I felt empty inside and the best part of me was left back at home.

At dinnertime, when I did get to go into the dining room, on one wall was a red and white Polish flag with what looked like a two-headed chicken sewn on it. On the wall opposite the flag was an old sword in its sheath, and above it an old helmet with a point on the top. The table wasn't set pretty like Grandma's because there wasn't any tablecloth, just some red and white plastic place mats with "Lone Star Beer" printed on them. The green plates were also plastic, and so were the glasses. Around the table were red plastic chairs with the word "Coke" across their backs. I liked the chairs and Boleslaw said something about how he got them from the market.

As Mom, Boleslaw, and I sat at the table, Beata brought in plates of food, one of sausage and cabbage, one of potatoes, and one of steaks piled high on a platter. She set them on the table and she smiled proudly. She sat down and held the crucifix she wore around her neck in her hands as she put them together in prayer. "Let's say grace … I want to give thanks …" she said.

Boleslaw grunted, "Enough, Matka, I'm hungry." He grabbed the potatoes and started piling them onto his plate.

"Can't you show respect for the Lord?" Beata asked.

"Matka, don't irritate me." He looked at Mom. "I think religion should stay in the churches," he said.

Beata kept her eyes closed and said the grace to herself, saying, "Amen," loudly at the end.

Boleslaw with his piled plate high, and ate just the way I pictured he would, stuffing his mouth and chewing with his mouth full and laughing at things that weren't funny. When he laughed, his hard belly didn't jiggle like Beata's. He got some pieces of food stuck in his moustache, which he wiped off, leaving his moustache shiny.

Beata and Boleslaw washed down their food with beer. The white foam clung to Boleslaw's moustache. Beata would swig the beer and then she'd belch, a large rumble making her stomach bounce, and then she'd laugh.

At home, Grandma would say that sound was so unladylike that good people wouldn't invite you back if you made it at their table.

Watching them wasn't very appetizing, but then I looked at the steak Mom had put on my plate. Boleslaw had brought it from the market and I could hear Lilly Mae's voice in my head, "Child you has to learn to take the good with the bad." We hardly ever had steaks at home and the T-Bone smelled delicious. I couldn't resist it, but I kept my face as close to the food as possible so as not to watch Boleslaw and Matka chewing.

"Would you sit up straight and get your face out of the food. That's not the correct way to eat," Mom said.

Mom looked at Boleslaw. "I put clean sheets on the bed. The ones with the roses on them."

"Those are my best sheets," Beata said.

"We have to have clean sheets. Sometimes men aren't aware of those things," Mom said.

Boleslaw stuffed a big piece of bloody meat in his mouth and chewed with his mouth open looking at Mom. He licked his moist lips and smiled. "Then we'll be snug as two bugs in a rug." Mom looked away from him and Boleslaw said to his mother, "If my wife wants nice sheets, she gets sheets. And she can go and buy more." Boleslaw looked at Mom and pointed to his mother with a piece of meat on his fork. "Matka does the cooking and the cleaning. It's been that way since my father died. She's old-fashioned. She'll show you what you can do to help."

"Don't you have a maid come in once in awhile?" Mom asked. She sat up straight and pushed her long red hair back over her shoulders.

Boleslaw pointed at Mom with meat on his fork. "Now that is something I wouldn't waste money on. But now I have a wife to help her, to take some of the burden off of her."

"Really," Mom said.

I was sent to bed while the adults stayed downstairs. I peeked into the room Mom was going to share with The Big Slaw Grabber. There were two more pictures on the walls of ladies with see-through tee-shirts and wearing shorts. One was smiling from a motorcycle and the other from the back of a horse. Boleslaw seemed to like breasts more than the Pastor.

There was a shag rug on the floor. I walked back and forth over it. It felt soft under my bare feet. On his dresser, he had a large plastic "Lone Star Beer" can and a metal replica of a Chevy.

Besides the ladies, the only other picture on the walls was of a big black bull and his eyes stared at me wherever I went in the room. He looked sad and I felt guilty for enjoying the steak I'd just eaten.

CHAPTER TWENTY

The next morning after The Big Slaw Grabber went to work, I walked into the bedroom to see Mom, and the pictures of the ladies had been taken off of the walls. The faded wallpaper was lighter where the pictures had been. The walls were nude and Mom was nude under the covers.

Before I got a chance to talk to Mom, Beata was calling from downstairs. Her voice was harsh. "Virginia …Virginia, would you come down here. In my house, nobody stays in bed all day."

Mom put on her clothes and we went downstairs to the kitchen. Even though the sun was coming in through the old curtains, it didn't cheer up the house. It highlighted dust particles floating in the air and dust on the windowsills. Through the kitchen I could see the back-porch door was open, leaving the screen door visible. The screen was torn in several places at the top, and a piece flapped in the breeze like a ghostly hand waving.

I noticed that stacked on the counters, in their corners, were white turnips with their stems and leaves attached. Also, they were on the floor by the refrigerator. "Look at those," Mom said and shrugged her shoulders. She went to the stove, and started looking though the cabinets, noisily moving some pans. Beata came in from outside like a guard dog. "What are you doing? I have the pans just the way I want them."

"Why do you have turnips on the counters?" Mom asked.

"Never you mind those. They keep away the evil spirits," Beata said.

"O.K. Where's your kettle for boiling water? I want to make coffee."

"We're out of coffee. If you want coffee, you have to go to the store. Everything has been so sudden. When Boleslaw told me you were coming, I didn't have time for shopping. We only have bread and eggs." Beata pulled out a cast iron skillet. "Here, use this and there's the toaster." Beata went back out through the screen door letting it slam. The ghostly hand frantically waved at me.

When we were almost finished eating the scrambled eggs, Beata came back in standing with her hand on her hip. "Be sure and wash the dishes. I don't want any dishes left for me. After you're finished, you can come out back. There's a lot of work around here. I'll show you how to feed the chickens and clean the coops and then there's the tending to the vegetables."

Mom let out a sigh and kept her face looking straight ahead, her back to Beata. "I guess you grow a lot of turnips. And just to let you know, I don't clean chicken coops," she said.

Beata retied her red scarf tight under her chin, and she looked irritated as she talked to Mom's back. "Everyone works around here. Tessa, come with me and I'll show you how to get the eggs." As it turned out, I liked going into the chicken coop and collecting the eggs while the chickens stared at me with their round eyes.

∽

A couple of days later, at dinnertime the afternoon sun had made the kitchen hot and sticky and Mom, fanning herself with a newspaper, had opened the back door. Mom was wearing an apron, slacks, and her red peep-toed pumps. She started to make fried chicken, sweet potatoes, and peas for dinner. I was shelling the peas into a bowl and I'd eat some every once in awhile. Just like at home, Mom was a little clumsy when cooking and some flour had spilled on the floor and was getting on her red shoes.

Beata rushed in from the back and came up behind Mom like a delivery truck edging up to the loading dock. She was standing so close behind Mom that Mom couldn't move. I could smell the chicken coop smell on Beata.

"What's this flour all over my floor?" Beata asked.

"I'm making fried chicken and sweet potatoes for Bo's dinner."

Beata's tongue was quick to slip in and out through the hole in her teeth. "No, no, no," she said in her Polish accent with some saliva shooting out of her mouth.

Mom extricated herself from being pinned between Beata and the counter. "What do you mean, no?"

"My Boleslaw can't eat that. He has to have his good Polish food to keep his strength up," Beata said.

"You've lived in Texas a long time. Everybody likes fried chicken." Mom wiped her hands on the front of her apron that said, "Mom and Apple Pie."

I wasn't going to let her scare me or Mom either. "I only eat fried chicken," I said. Neither one looked at me.

"No frying chicken in my kitchen spattering grease all over the place," Beata said.

"Bo said this would be my house too," Mom stood with her legs apart, so even Beata's large body wouldn't be able to get her to move.

"He meant the other parts of the house, not my kitchen." Beata opened the refrigerator, which made the statue of the Virgin with the red heart on top wobble a little. She peered inside. "I'll have to show you how to make his food. Tonight, I show you how to make Golabki." She closed the refrigerator and the Virgin wobbled again. From a drawer, Beata took out an old white butcher apron and put it on.

"What's that?" Mom asked.

"It's stuffed cabbage with turkey. Or maybe I show you how to make Chlopski Posilek. It's bacon and cabbage," Beata said.

"I want fried chicken," I said.

"Neither Tessa nor I like cabbage," Mom said. Her red hair was hanging down in front of her blouse. She crossed her arms and stood with her feet apart.

I made a gagging sound and Beata's eyes stabbed at me.

"Hush up, Tessa," Mom said.

"It's not my fault you don't like cabbage. This is a cabbage eating house." Beata washed her large red knuckled hands at the sink.

"What do you make without cabbage?" Mom asked. Mom pushed her sweaty hair back over her shoulder.

"Pork Knuckles and beer." Beata got some wrapped meat and two cans of beer out of the refrigerator. She opened one can, took a long drink.

"Then show me how to make the cabbage stuffed with turkey," Mom said.

"Cabbage, Slabbage. Yuck. Yuck," I said.

"Tessa, be quiet," Mom said. She took a step in one direction then another. She didn't know where to go or what to do.

As I watched Mom and Beata in the kitchen, they reminded me of two chickens trying to scratch and peck at the same ground. Mom tried to follow Beata's instructions, but every time Mom picked up a pan, Beata said that it wasn't the right one. By the time Mom was cutting the cabbage, she was angry and chopped at the cabbage viciously until Beata yelled, "No, no, no, you're ruining my cabbage."

Beata kept telling Mom that she wasn't using the right knives or spoons and she made Mom so nervous that Mom cut her finger.

"You're so clumsy," Beata said.

"You're so bossy." And then Mom left the kitchen. I followed Mom, but I looked back at Beata and said, "Yuck. Give the cabbage to a Polish duck." Then I stuck out my tongue. Mom didn't see Beata raise her hand in the air as if to hit me.

That night at dinner when Beata was in the kitchen clucking over her Polish food, Mom said to Bo, "Your mother won't let me cook normal food like fried chicken and peas. I'm not a cabbage eater."

"I can't eat that stuff either. I'll die," I said. I stuck my tongue out and put my head on the table like I was dead.

"She's so critical of me," Mom said.

"Cooking is all she knows. It's her life," Boleslaw said.

"She's the commandant of the pots and pans," and Mom gave a Hitler salute, "Heil, heil."

"That's not nice. She's never had another woman here. Just give her time. She's the best mother a son could have," Boleslaw said.

Mom turned the ring on her finger, her knuckles becoming white. She had sweat circles under her arms and she looked sad.

CHAPTER TWENTY-ONE

In the backyard, an enclosed area of chicken wire with a wire gate was nailed to upright log poles. On one side of the enclosure was a small house of old cracked wood. The wood planks came to a point on the roof. It had a front door, also of planks, and next to it, a window with dirty glass. There was straw on the ground around the little house, and inside, the straw covered the wood floor. Inside, on one wall there were long wooden boxes. The boxes, painted blue, were divided into smaller square boxes. These were the nests for the hens, and there was a ramp going up to a walkway, which the hens used to get into their nests. The nests were filled with straw, pieces sticking out every which way, like wild hair. Even though straw was covering the floor, white and brown chicken poop was splattered everywhere. It stank.

Since that first morning when Beata showed me how to collect the eggs in a wicker basket, I collected them every morning. Beata was always giving me instructions, and I had to make sure I stood back far enough so I wouldn't get hit with the saliva bullets that sprayed from her mouth.

There weren't that many children out here on the edge of town, and even though the chicken coop was smelly, the chickens became my friends. When she left me alone with them, I talked to them. I had names for each of the chickens: Big Mouth, Big Feet, and Fancy Feathers. They were big white chickens with long necks and red combs from their beaks across the top of their heads. My favorite was Big Mouth, who had a larger than normal yellow beak, which she kept open a lot, as if everything she saw surprised her. There were also the two I called Fat Lady and Noisy Bird, who squawked a lot. They were a reddish-brown color, with their eyes a red orange. There was one funny looking chicken that was small, skinny, and dark colored, with feathers sprouting around its face like a flower. Beata told me it was a Polish chicken, so I called it Polack. I'd go into the chicken coop and do my Chicken Dance with my hands tucked in my armpits. When I danced for them, they stopped whatever they were doing, cocked their heads, and opened their beaks as if they wanted to say something. Their round lidless eyes followed my movements. When I'd leave the chicken coop, but while still inside the wire fence, the big brown rooster with a red comb would rush out of the box in the corner and try to peck me. He made me laugh and I loved those chickens.

After being there two weeks, I still didn't like Beata, but I wasn't scared of her anymore. She seemed afraid and crossed herself all the time to make sure bad things wouldn't happen.

When I came home from my new school, I helped her pull weeds out of the garden. She had rows of cabbages, carrots, squashes, onions, and beans. I imagined the cabbages were the heads of midgets growing in the ground and that a midget army was going to come out of the ground and chase Beata away. She didn't seem to mind that I talked to the plants. Beata would sing songs in Polish from when she was a girl on a farm, and she was glad I was helping her because Mom refused to work in the garden or in the chicken coop.

Several times I'd overheard Beata saying to The Big Slaw Grabber, "You married a lazy woman. She stays in bed all the time. Why do I have to put up with this?"

"She's not a farm girl nor a servant," Boleslaw said.

"She thinks she's better than us."

"Hush, Matka. I love her and I need her," Boleslaw said.

In our third week, on Saturday morning after breakfast when Mom had gone back to bed, Beata told me to come with her to the chicken coop. She was holding a burlap bag and a large butcher knife. She went into the chicken coop and brought out Big Mouth. She had her in the crook of her arm and Big Mouth looked up at her calmly. Then she grabbed Big Mouth by her legs, holding her upside down while she flapped her wings wildly, and her beak was wide open. Beata announced, "I'm going to show you how to fix a chicken for dinner."

Those words hit me with terror. "You don't eat these chickens, do you?" I asked.

Beata smiled. "Oh, yes." She licked her lips.

I wanted to run, but I couldn't move. Big Mouth tried to get away. "I was plucking chickens before I was your age." Then Beata grabbed Big Mouth's body in one hand tightly. "You hold it like this in one hand and with the other hand you twist the neck off real quick."

She twisted Big Mouth's head all the way off and dropped it bleeding on the ground. The poor chicken's head lay there jerking. Her beak was open, while her eye stared up. Then she let Big Mouth's body fall onto the ground and it ran around the coop with no head. Her body didn't know where it was going and ran into the fence. I opened my mouth and a shriek came up from my gut. She might as well be killing me. I screamed and finally the body stopped running and fell over on its side, a pile of breathing feathers. Blood from her severed neck leaked out onto a puddle on the ground. I stared at Beata. I opened my mouth, but I couldn't speak.

Beata laughed. "Don't tell me you've never seen anyone wring a chicken's neck before? That's what God gave them to us for. We have to kill them before we can eat them. Look, I'll show you how to pluck the feathers and dress it for cooking."

I ran out of the coop screaming and I heard Beata laughing. I didn't look back, but I knew she had her hand on her hip and her belly was shaking.

I ran into the house and went into the bathroom and threw up. When I knew they were eating Big Mouth, I stayed in my room. Mom didn't come to my room.

The next morning when I wouldn't get ready for school, Mom came in my room and tried to explain that things have to die for people to live. "You've always eaten chicken. Remember you said that you had to have chicken or you'll die."

I cried harder. "I didn't know. Why didn't you tell me?"

"I thought you knew," Mom said.

"She murdered Big Mouth. I hate her." My body shook.

Mom looked like she didn't know what to do. She shook me. "I can't talk to you when you're like this. Get control of yourself. A normal child accepts things the way they are."

"I hate that word, normal." I pounded my fists on the bed.

Mom looked scared and tried to hug me, but I pushed her away. "Please stop crying. I don't know what to do with you."

I couldn't stop my tears. "I want to go home … even Grandma is better than this."

Mom's anger came quickly, making her face as hard as stone. "I'm her flesh and blood and she turned me out. We're not going back there." Then Mom put her hand on her throat, holding it to keep herself from crying.

That night when Beata was in her bed down the hall snoring, I snuck down to the chicken coop, opened the door, went in, and shooed out the chickens. I sprinkled some feed in the open field next door and got the chickens to go over there. I told each one that they had to run away and never come back.

The next morning Beata went out back and found the chicken coop door open. Mom and I were in the kitchen when Beata came in out of breath. She was furious, and saliva was shooting out from the hole in her upper teeth as she spoke fast in Polish. Her scarf was tight around her bulging double chins, and her hands looked like claws. I started to laugh, but Mom pinched me. I thought: Beata would explode and all the chewed-up chicken she'd been eating would spray all over us. Mom told her to speak in English and she told us how somebody, maybe some colored, had gotten into the chicken coop and taken a chicken. A wave of joy went through me because I realized one got away. And I thought:

Jesus if you save the chickens, I'll love you and I'll pray to you every day even though it's boring. When I went out there later, I found out it was Big Feet that had escaped.

The next night when I went down into the backyard, I froze in my tracks. In front of the chicken coop was Beata sleeping on a chair with a shotgun in her lap. I tiptoed back inside.

Later that night when in bed, I heard Beata fire the shotgun and it woke us all up. I overheard her telling Boleslaw that she scared someone off. During the next few weeks whenever Beata took the knife and burlap bag into the backyard, I'd start screaming and crying.

That made Mom mad, but I couldn't help it. I'd never be the way she wanted me to be. I kept having nightmares about headless chickens. Even in the mornings when I first woke up, if I went into the living room, I'd see a headless chicken sitting on the couch gurgling. Or if I went into the dining room, I'd see one sitting on the dining room table flapping bloody wings. I even saw one in the bathroom sitting on the toilet and wearing a hat with flowers like Grandma's over its headless body. If I woke up at night, I'd see them in my room inching toward me, wings flapping, and I'd scream and Mom would come into my room. I couldn't tell her what I was seeing because that would upset her even more. She'd say, "Please stop crying. Please sleep. There's nothing I can do." Some days I'd refuse to go to school.

A few weeks after the first chicken kill, one morning early, I snuck down to the kitchen and heard Beata talking to The Big Slaw Grabber. Mom was now sleeping late every morning and not making Boleslaw breakfast. This time Beata wasn't complaining about my mother being lazy, she was complaining about me. "How do you say it? Tessa's swallowed one of those screws. It's in her head," Beata said in her accent.

"No. You say she has a screw loose in the head," Boleslaw said.

"It doesn't matter how you say it. She cries too much and the look in her eyes gives me the chills. Now, I have two princesses to take care of."

"You don't have to take care of them," Boleslaw said.

"Why can't Tessa stay with her grandma sometimes, so I can have some peace with my sweet son?"

When I peeked around the corner, I saw Beata lean over Boleslaw and kiss him on the mouth. Yuck. Yuck. Later I told Mom I saw them kissing again because I knew that bothered her, and I even added a few things, like Beata sticking her tongue in Boleslaw's mouth, because I wanted Mom to take me away from here.

CHAPTER TWENTY-TWO

After about three months, I wasn't seeing the dead chickens anymore, but something else was twisting and turning inside of me. I was worried about my mom. Every day I looked at her closely and her belly was getting bigger. It looked like she had half of a volleyball sticking out of her stomach. So, Grandma had been right about Mom having a baby inside of her.

Mom stayed in her room sprawled across the bed a lot. She didn't say anything about it, but I knew the ball in her belly was why she looked pale. She didn't get up and put on makeup every day like she used to. She didn't brush her hair and just kept it back in a ponytail, and the new roots were brown against her red hair. I must have noticed Mom's belly before Boleslaw because I hadn't heard Boleslaw talk about it. Maybe he was concerned about his own belly, which he did pat at times, and therefore didn't notice hers. But a couple of days later Mom and Boleslaw were in their bedroom talking for a long time.

The very next morning I heard Boleslaw in the hallway, whistling to himself. He said something about little feet in the house. He went into the bathroom for his shower and was singing, *"The patter of little feet is so sweet to hear and can be so dear."* Then I saw Beata, wearing her scarf and hunched over like a big bear, come out of her room and stop outside the bathroom putting her ear to the door.

I wanted to irritate Beata, so I took a deep breath and ran into the hallway and did my Chicken Dance around her. "Beata, I've brought the spirits of my great-grandmother Eunice and my great-aunt Gertie here into your house. I see them and talk to them."

Beata crossed herself. "Don't you bring your evil spirits in here."

"They protect me and they don't like you." I danced closer to her and she took a swing at me. "You missed me, old lady."

"Get away from me," she said. She crossed herself and held onto the crucifix around her neck as she went downstairs.

Then I snuck into her room and I saw the statues of Christ, the Virgin, and a whole bunch of other saints on her dresser, a miniature world. I took a statue of a suffering saint from the back that I thought she wouldn't notice was missing. I was a Protestant, so the statue didn't mean anything to me.

On the way back to my room, I passed Boleslaw in the bathroom. Why couldn't Mom just have a big egg inside of her that would become a chicken? I'd like to live with a big chicken. I could take it to school with me. I prayed, "Jesus, if you let Mom have a big chicken inside of her, I'll mean it when I pray to you."

Holding the statue, I went back in my room. I took out pictures of saints that I found in magazines in corners of the house. In the pictures, children knelt in front of the statues. The saints had red tears on their cheeks and the captions said they were crying real tears of blood. I thought: Beata doesn't like spirits, but she believes in statues.

After Beata had gone into tess garden, I went into the kitchen and collected a bunch of things: red food coloring, flour, glue, raspberry syrup, and body lotion from the bathroom. Sitting at the vanity table in my room, I tried mixing different combinations to make fake blood. With my watercolor paintbrush, I put each concoction on the cheeks of the statue to make it look as if were crying real tears of blood. Finally, I got it right.

The next morning at breakfast, Beata kept staring at Mom's belly. She squinted because she couldn't see that well, and, as usual she couldn't find her glasses. Actually, I had hidden them. Beata just kept staring at Mom's belly, and I tried not to look at her because that wolf was back inside of her, twisting her face. With the wolf inside of Beata, it was hard for her to talk, and she sputtered and slammed plates down on the table.

∾

That evening before dinner, while Mom was throwing up in her room, I heard Beata talking to Boleslaw in the kitchen. "Wake up. You're such a fool. She's too far along to have gotten pregnant after you married her. That's why she was in such a hurry to grab you."

"It's none of your business. We were together before we were married." Boleslaw sounded angry.

"So, you were fornicating a couple of weeks before you got married. It still doesn't add up."

"Shut your mouth, Matka. You should be happy you're going to be a grandma. I want a son," Boleslaw said.

There was that word again, 'for-ni-cating'. Sounded like a good word to remember.

The next morning before school, I went to Mom in her room and sat next to her. "Mom, so it's true about you getting a big belly and somehow a baby."

Mom put her arm around me. "Tessa, you have to be a big girl now. I'm going to have a baby in a couple of months. You'll have a brother or a sister."

"No. You've told me many times men don't want fat women. Please just stop eating and make it go away."

"It won't go away. There's a baby inside of me. A woman gets pregnant and after nine months gives birth," Mom said.

"Please. I want it to be just you and me like it used to be." I wiped the moisture from my face.

"Tessa, things change. Nothing stays the same. This is part of nature. We have to accept what life brings to us. You'll like having a brother or sister," Mom said.

"I don't like nature or life just bringing any old thing." Mom put her arm around me, but it didn't make me feel better.

Since Mom's clothes were tight, she was now wearing Boleslaw's shirts and his big jeans. Since they both had big bellies, I called them the jellybean pork bellies.

❧

Mom and I hadn't gone into town for months, but one day she drove me in Boleslaw's green Chevy wagon. As we drove down the main street, women I recognized were on the sidewalks and they stopped. Their heads swiveled on their necks to stare at us. I stuck out my tongue.

When we went into Mrs. Thelma's Five and Dime, Mrs. Thelma stopped in her tracks and pushed her head forward as if she was a long-necked bird. Her lash-less eyes stared so hard I thought that she's going to emit some kind of x-rays. Mrs. Thelma positioned herself behind the cash register, a giant crow on guard. I smelled her dime-store lilac perfume wafting through the store.

Mom grabbed some things and pulled me away from the candy and went to the counter. Mrs. Thelma pounced, "It must be nice to be married again. I bet your husband is bringing home a lot of good meat … meat for dinner."

Mom didn't look at her. "Boleslaw is a good husband. Why didn't you ever get married again? Couldn't you find a husband? Anyway, how much is this?"

Mrs. Thelma didn't answer tend pressed her lips together like she didn't know what to say. "Just a minute. Let me ring it up." She punched the keys on the cash register. "That's ten dollars and fifty-nine cents." Then she forced a smile, accentuating all the cracks around her mouth where her lipstick had run into them. "When is the blessed event? Be sure and tell us. Everyone wants to know."

Mom looked at her as if she could stab her. "You're a disgusting vulture that eats other people's lives because you're empty inside."

Mrs. Thelma leaned her skinny body over the counter. "How dare you talk to me like that. Now you're stuck with those foreigners." She patted her belly and continued, "Maybe you're not so special now. Are you having a lot of romantic nights with Bo … Bolly … what's he called … Bellyslaw? I never could say his Pollack name."

"Shut up, you old coot. It's better than being with people like you. And all the cold cream in the world won't help your wrinkled bag face," Mom said and grabbed her packages and pulled me out of the store.

"Go on, get mad. I guess I got your goat." Mrs. Thelma laughed, a cackle aimed at burning us.

We got in the car and Mom drove down the street where Mrs. Thelma couldn't see us and parked. She pounded her hands against the steering wheel and cried. "I hate it here … these mean small-town people. I've got to get out of here." She kept crying and I cried with her.

"I don't want you to be sad." And I tried to hug her, but her belly and the steering wheel were in the way.

Mom wiped her tears. "Tessa, don't cry. You can't be like this. You have to be in control or people will think you're weak and they'll hurt you any chance they get."

CHAPTER TWENTY-THREE

As the ball in Mom's stomach inflated, things were deflating between Mom and Boleslaw. Every afternoon, evening and weekend, Mom sat on the back-porch singing and playing the guitar, which was propped against her stomach. She was composing a song, but never seemed to finish it. She said, "I have to polish up my music because I'm going to sing in public."

One evening when I was with Beata in the kitchen, on the porch Mom was working on her song, which was called, "Donkeys Jumping." Mom sang loudly, *"Men come and go, like donkeys jumping thinking they can fly. They hurt me to the bone, when I should have had a home."*

Beata grumbled in Polish, sounding like a meat grinder. Her face turned so red I thought she might catch on fire. She slammed her pots and pans around.

Mom continued singing, *"Hooved creatures fly away so I can live another day. Leave my Texas heart alone, so I can find a home."*

Wham! Beata slammed the cast iron skillet down on the stove and she was about to slam another pan down, but she froze in mid-air holding the pan and cocked her head to better hear the song.

Mom must have heard her because she sang louder, *"Being stuck with a donkey, doesn't let you do the honky-tonk. Boy, do I need that hot … honky-tonk day and honky-tonk night."*

Beata's eyes widened and she turned to me. "What's that crazy thing she's singing about, donkeys trying to fly? Is she calling me a donkey?" Beata clenched her fists. I moved out of her way.

Even though I enjoyed seeing Beata upset, I didn't feel like fighting. "It's a country-western song like the ones on the radio. When Mom took me to a rodeo, there were cowboys on horses singing with their guitars."

Beata stepped toward me, her eyes wide. "And I suppose cowboys sing about donkeys to the cows."

"They sing about everything. They make up the words," I said.

Mom kept singing, *"Gimme me some good ole' honk-tonk in the hot Texas night in the back of a pickup, so I can soar past any creatures to my dream sky. And so I can laugh before I die."*

Beata repeated the words, "Honk … honky … tonk … tonkee." She turned to me, "What's this … this honky-tonky thing and why is it done in the back of a pickup?

"I think it means fun. Mom likes to dance and have fun," I said.

"Really." Beata's mouth turned into an angry crack. "She's not fooling me. Is that another one of those words like, how do you say, to Get the Fuck?"

Immediately I felt excited. I said, "I don't know what that means, and you're not supposed to say that to me because I'm a kid."

"You always pretend you don't know things. Is it this?" Beata made a motion with one hand, the finger and thumb together in a circle, and with the other hand she moved her index finger in and out of the circle like she was stuffing something. "Is that what she means by the honky-tonky?" Beata asked.

"I'm a kid. Don't ask me." I knew that was bad, so I did it right back to her.

"Don't do that to me. Just be quiet," Beata turned and looked through the window over the sink where Mom was singing on the porch and yelled, "Virginia, shut that racket up so I can make dinner in peace."

I enjoyed making Beata mad. Since Mom kept on singing, I thought I'd sing my own song to bother her. I said, "Hey Beata." When she turned to me, I sang, *"The world is full of donkeys pooping all over the place. Smelly and big they're like old ladies and pigs. And that makes me want to do a jig."* I marched my legs up and down while moving my arms. Then I drummed on the metal kitchen table with my palms. This infuriated Beata and she came after me with a wooden spoon. As I ran out of the room, I said, "The spirits of my dead relatives are coming after you. Just wait and see."

I looked back and saw Beata take a turnip off of the counter and put it in the pocket of her apron. "Leave me alone, you devil child. Satan is coming to take you away."

That evening when Boleslaw got home, Beata rushed to get him alone in the kitchen. I was watching from around a corner, and first thing Beata did was to kiss him several times making a smacking sound.

"Virginia's singing crazy songs about donkeys trying to fly. She thinks we're donkeys," Beata said.

Boleslaw put his hand on her shoulder trying to calm her. "She's not saying that. It's just a song. Cowboys sing about silly things."

"She's singing about a honky-tonky thing. That's something dirty. She's really singing about to Get the Fuck."

"Matka, keep your voice down," Boleslaw said.

"This is my house. She did this American honky-tonky thing before you were married, and I know that baby isn't yours," Beata said.

Boleslaw slammed his hand down on the metal table and I jumped. "She's my wife. Stop criticizing her. Women do things when they are pregnant."

Beata stood up and put her mouth right in Boleslaw's face. "This isn't from pregnancy. All I'm wanted for is the cooking and cleaning. Your princess can finish the dinner and wash the dishes. I'm going to bed."

"Matka, don't be like that," Boleslaw said softly.

Later that night, I heard Mom and Boleslaw arguing in their bedroom. I heard Mom say, "I have to have my music. I don't feel well from the pregnancy."

"At night when I lie next to you, I feel alone. I need to know that you still love me. I love you. You're everything to me. Come and hug your Bo," Boleslaw said.

"Bo, you're good. You deserve to be loved," Mom said.

"I hope soon you will feel well enough to be a wife again."

I couldn't hear anymore. I just wished there was something I could do to get Mom to leave this place.

CHAPTER TWENTY-FOUR

When I told Mom how Beata talked to Boleslaw about her, she'd only say, "Things will be better after the baby is born. He wants the baby."

The ball in her stomach was all she could think about. She ran her hand over it quite often, but she was irritated a lot and I wanted to laugh with her, sing with her, and have her take me places again.

For as long as I could remember, Grandma had said that besides keeping my legs together for Jesus, I had to be a good girl. Recently, it occurred to me that I didn't feel like a good girl anymore. I hated Beata morning, noon, and night. I could even see a black energy around me in the mirror. I hoped Beata wasn't right about me having the devil in me.

At my new school, I hadn't made any friends. The kids had known each other for years and I was the outsider. And ever since I had moved here, I hadn't been able to see or hear Eunice or Gertie. I had placed a picture of them in the corner of the cracked mirror over the vanity and stared at it many times, but they wouldn't come to me.

One day, I came home from school and went to my room. I looked at myself in the vanity mirror where the crack made my face look split into two sides. My hair had not been brushed and a voice from the silver mirror said, "I see you, but there's only emptiness here. I can't do anything for you."

I lay on the bed and put my head on the rough pillowcase and cried. After awhile, I felt feathery touches on my face and shoulders and I smelled roses. I opened my eyes and sat up. There they were, staring at the cracked walls and peeling wallpaper. They wore their white dresses, gloves, and summer hats. Gertie held her parasol and her little white shoes stuck out from her long dress. I wiped the tears from my face.

"Tessa, don't cry. We've been trying to reach you. There's a fog between you and us," Eunice said. Then she looked around my bedroom. "It's this house. It's blocking us out. Why in God's name are you living in this awful place?"

"This is Boleslaw's house. That's Mom's new husband. I hate it here. You have to help me get Mom to take me away from here."

"We're also stuck in a lonely place with boring old people. We haven't been able to find a way out," Eunice said.

Gertie said, "Eunice don't start complaining. We're supposed to cheer her up. Tessa, your mother is to be admired because she knows how to get men. In my day, first I said things to get my beaus excited, then they would climb over the fence and up the tree and look in my bedroom window. I'd be lying on my bed and … I would lift my skirt. They knew father would kill them if they came into the house. But they did things to themselves that were so exciting."

"My God, stop talking like that, "Eunice said.

"I want to hear what they did," I said.

"She has to learn about things. A person has to do what they want, so they won't regret it," Gertie said. Then she smoothed out her white dress and ran her hand over her curly hair to smooth it.

"I need you to help me. I feel like I'm dying here," I said.

They nodded their heads. "We'll do our best to help. But we have trouble staying here very long. We're being pulled away," Eunice said.

"I need you," I said.

They looked around as if they didn't know where they were. They went to the wall and started to move through it. They turned around with their faces protruding from the wallpaper.

For a moment, they seemed to be frozen, their eyes staring straight ahead like two statues. They blinked and turned their eyes toward each other.

"You should see how dumb you look with your face sticking out of the wall," Gertie said.

"We could get stuck in a place like this. Follow me," Eunice said.

"You have to take me with you," I said.

They moved gracefully toward the bedroom door. I stood up and tried to follow them, but everything was fuzzy and I felt like I was floating. I touched my arms and they felt like cotton. Nothing felt solid. Then I fell back and landed on the bed and I laid on top of the sagging mattress. They were gone and even though the room was cold, I was sweating.

CHAPTER TWENTY-FIVE

The next day was Friday, and I knew Mom would go shopping in town. So, very early that morning, I went into the kitchen and stood on a chair in front of the refrigerator. With my paintbrush, I put a mixture of red food coloring, flour, glue, and lotion on the statue of the Virgin, just the way I practiced on the statue I'd taken from Beata's room. Then I poured my mixture around the base, making a puddle.

When Mom got up, I said, "I vomited this morning."

"You'll have to stay home from school. I'm going into town, but it's not a good for you to be alone with Beata," she said.

"I'll stay in my room out of the way of the old hunched-back buffalo." I could tell Mom didn't want to argue, so she left for town by herself.

Beata was down in the kitchen baking, as she did on Fridays. I had to hurry, so in my bedroom I took out my special box where I had precious things. I took out my white gloves and put them on. I also had my Wizard of Oz wand and an old rattlesnake skin that I grabbed from a neighborhood boy who tried to scare me. I took out the wand and the rattlesnake skin. Sitting in front of the vanity mirror, I waved the wand and said my magic words, *"Hazzerfact katterack witterack latteract."* I shook the rattlesnake skin as I marched around the room. "I have the power and I can do what I want."

I stood in front of the mirror, with the picture of Eunice and Gertie tucked in the corner and I stared at it and waited. "You said you would help me. If you care about me, come now." But nothing happened, and I had that empty feeling just like when my father didn't come for me.

I stared in the silver mirror and its emptiness stared back. The silence bounced off the faded wallpaper. I became angry. "Where are you … you dumb pussy bitches? If you don't help me, you can go to Get the Fuck."

Still, they didn't come and I was about to abandon my plan, but then I realized I'd told Beata I talked to spirits and she didn't know if I was really seeing Eunice or not. She was afraid of having spirits in the house, and that's why she put turnips on the countertops.

I went downstairs and stood outside the kitchen, gathering myself together for what I had to do. All I had to do was think about how much I wanted to leave here, and tears came to my eyes.

I said under my breath, "No smelly woman with missing teeth is going to frighten me."

Then, as though there was a power inside of me, I screamed and ran into the kitchen. I shook my rattlesnake skin and I yelled, "Great-grandmother Eunice is here, and her sister Gertie is too." I pointed across the kitchen table as if I was seeing my relatives, standing there between the table and the wall. "See, they come when I want," I yelled. I looked at Beata, and she was wearing her red scarf, black dress, and heavy shoes. I forced myself to sob harder because my crying bothered her.

Beata hit her metal spoon against the side of the pot. She looked at me, her mouth open. "What in God's name are you crying about now?"

I kept crying. Then I looked at the space where I was imagining I saw my relatives, and I abruptly started laughing and paused as if listening to them. I said as if talking to them, "Oh, you've come to keep me from being lonely. That's so nice of you to say that. I love you both."

Red-faced, Beata turned and looked at me and then to the place I was pointing to. "They're right there." I continued talking to my imaginary vision. "You're all dressed up today. You look so pretty in your hats and white gloves." I looked over my shoulder at Beata and said, "They always dress up wearing beautiful dresses with lace. Not like you." Then I looked around the room and back to my vision. "This house isn't much, but I have to live here now. I know you're used to much better. Would you like some tea and biscuits?"

Beata wiped her wrinkled hands on her butcher's apron. She walked around the place of my imaginary vision, but did not step into it. She looked at the space from top to bottom. She even bent down as if looking where their feet would be and squinted. "Why are you saying my house isn't much? And there's no one there, you rude, crazy girl."

"Oh, yes there is. There's my great-grandmother Eunice and her sister Gertie. Their spirits come to me when I call them. I want them to feel welcome, so I'm going to make them tea."

I went to the cabinet and started getting down cups and saucers, but Beata grabbed my arms. She shook me. "You stop that right now. You show respect for the dead. This isn't a game."

I pulled away from her. I pointed again to the space I had been staring at. "You can't stop me. I talk to them all the time. And you better let me make them feel welcome by giving them some tea or they might do something bad, like come after you at night …." I tried to sound as menacing as possible and I shook my rattlesnake skin again.

"Put that down and stop your games. You really have the devil in you." Beata crossed herself.

"You can cross yourself all you want, but that won't make them go away. They say you're mean down in your soul and you have to quit bossing me," I said.

Beata's face flushed. "You don't know what's in my soul."

I felt a warm breeze in the room and my body tingled with excitement. Maybe they had finally come. I looked around the room and listened for them to speak, but I heard nothing. "Damn it," I said.

"Don't you swear in my home. Your mother puts up with all your nonsense. She's too easy on you. You'll respect my wishes in my house."

I heard small gusts of wind kicking up outside. It was just the wind, but I had to make her believe it was really them. "See, the room is getting warmer and there's something moving inside the house. I know you feel it." I pulled my shirt away from my chest as though it was hot and I grabbed my snakeskin and pointed it at her and shook it.

Beata stepped back, and looked around the kitchen as though she felt something. Her eyes widened, but then she shook her head. She went to the closet in the hallway and brought back one of Boleslaw's big leather belts and slapped it against her hand. I didn't move.

Why didn't they come? How could they leave me alone with her? I thought.

All of a sudden, just when I needed it, I got lucky, the hot Texas wind that always blew the dirt, the sagebrush, and the plants was here. A lonely whining licked the corners of the house. The curtains over the sink billowed out. Then the cabinet doors slammed shut and then with the next gust, they opened as if they had their own life. I got close to Beata and stared straight into her eyes. "See, they're really here right now and they're rapping on the cabinets. I know you can feel them. So, you better beware."

The back-porch door was open with only the screen door closed. The torn piece of screen flapped wildly as the screen door opened and slammed closed. Beata closed the back-porch door, but it blew open again and she jumped.

I grabbed some of the turnips from the kitchen countertop and threw them on the ground. "These won't protect you. Great-grandmother Eunice won't let you hurt me. She has a power."

Beata froze and listened and looked around the kitchen. She trembled a little, but she didn't want me to know she was afraid. I stared intensely to keep up the act that it was Eunice who was making the cabinets blow open and then close again. Beata moved slowly and looked at the cabinets as though she was seeing something. Just then the house creaked and groaned. The wind surrounded the house. The moaning of the wind could be mistaken for a voice. Beata looked at me, her wrinkled face had a twisted look. "I told you. She's saying she doesn't like you. Listen," I said.

Beata crossed herself. "Blessed Virgin."

She kept looking around the kitchen as though she was hearing something. She crossed herself again and went to the refrigerator where her statue of the Virgin was on top but pushed back where it was hard to see it. "Who moved this?" She got a chair and stood on it to pull the statue forward. She reached for the statue, and that's when she saw the red drops that looked like blood on the statue's cheeks and heart. It looked like a pool of blood was around its base. Beata got down from the chair and slowly backed away. She breathed in gasps. "Get out of my sight and take your evil spirits with you!" she yelled.

I paused outside the kitchen door and saw her open the refrigerator and take out a new bunch of turnips and put them on the kitchen table as she glanced around the room, afraid.

That evening she didn't come down to dinner, and I heard her yelling at Bolelsaw from inside her bedroom that she wasn't coming out of her room until the devil child was out of her house.

I'd won, so I did my Eagle Dance. There was a lot of talking that night in the kitchen between The Big Slaw Grabber and Mom.

The next morning was Saturday and I remember that early in the morning Mom was on the phone downstairs. After she hung up, she came into my room and kept her voice low so as not to wake Boleslaw. She reminded me of a fat duck waddling because when she walked, her stomach swayed side to side. When she sat on my bed, I wondered, how could she stand to be so big? Her face was sad and worried. "Tessa, I've told you not to talk to those imaginary spirits and especially not to tell people you see them."

"They're a part of me. I can't live without them," I said.

"You've upset Beata really bad."

"She's a chicken murderer. Anyway, you're the wife, so why aren't you in charge?" I asked.

"This is her house too. Some people think that ghosts are evil and against their religion."

"Why don't you take me away from here?" I asked.

Mom wiped the tears from her cheeks. "You're going to get your wish. You're going back to your grandma."

I jumped up and down and did my Marching Dance around the room. "We'll be going home together."

Mom shook her head. "I'm staying here. The doctor says I need to rest. I can't be around your grandma. I'll visit you on the weekends."

"No, please don't leave me again. I need you." Tears filled my eyes. I kept saying, "No, please don't leave me."

"You aren't paying attention at this school. You'll be going back to your old school where I think you'll do better."

I went back into my room and stood in front of the picture of Eunice and Gertie. "I kept calling for you, but you two dummies didn't come." I took the old perfume bottle from the drawer and threw it against the mirror, making a spider web of cracks.

CHAPTER TWENTY-SIX

That afternoon Mom drove me home in Boleslaw's Chevy wagon. She was silent much of the way, but when we pulled up to Grandma's house, she turned to me. "Tessa, this is the way it has to be. You have to control yourself and act normal." Lilly Mae came out to get my suitcase. I wanted to hug Mom, but instead I asked, "When will I see you?"

"On the weekends. You'll be all right now, so go inside."

Once inside, I stopped in the entry hall to take off my jacket. To me, the house was an old friend and alive. The walls were breathing and the floor, a living skin, gave off little moans and laughed, as if tickled, when I stepped on it.

As Lilly Mae went upstairs with my jacket and suitcase, the creaking of the old wooden stairs turned into a female voice, "Finally, you're home, our darling girl."

I glanced into the dining room where the silver pitchers and the silver plate serving dishes were shined up. Then I went into the living room. The mahogany end tables and bookcase were in the same places as when I left.

By the tall leaded windows, the green brocade couch was placed with plumped-up pillows. From it, I heard a female voice, "Tessa, dear come and sink into me. I want to hold you and you can relax. We all love you." Other people didn't know that furniture had voices in them just waiting to speak, but I did because I was special.

I went to the picture of Great-grandmother's where she was wearing her blue dress with the high collar and little buttons up the front. I knew if I stared at her face long enough, I would hear her and Gertie also.

As soon as I smelled their perfume and felt some movement in the room, I said, "Hey, you stupid pussy ladies, you wouldn't help me so just stay in your lonely place and talk to yourselves. I had to do everything by myself."

Before I could hear them answer, I heard Grandma's loud voice, "Tessa. Stop staring at that picture. Your mother says you're still talking to those spirits and that is going to stop right now."

"I've just come home. Please don't be mad at me," I said.

"I'm trying not to be angry. But I know what's best for you and you have to stop this behavior."

Now, all I could think about was doing something bad. I looked at Grandma and she looked different. She was wearing a burgundy linen dress with a wide white collar belted at her chubby waist. She never used to wear jewelry, but today she had on a string of pearls.

Grandma put her fleshy palms on my shoulders. "Your mother wants you to see one of those new mental doctors and she wants me to pay for it. She says you have problems. A nine-year-old doesn't have problems and I told her not in my house. But you better straighten up. Talking to spirits will lead you down an evil path. It isn't what Jesus wants."

"I love my great-grandmother Eunice. How can you say that? And you're right, there's nothing wrong with me."

She sat on her gold brocade chair and pulled the string on the Victorian lamp on the round table next to her chair. With increased light, she could better stare at me. "I know what's right in the Lord's eyes. My mother, Eunice, thought she was above the Lord. She used to carry on something fierce at night in her bedroom. She was doing some ungodly things, maybe fornication with her so-called spirits."

I felt excited. "What is fornication with spirits?" I asked.

"It's evil to think about it. Just listen. She didn't stop my father from treating me the way he did. He cheated on her and she ran herself crazy thinking she had some power. I'm going to save you from that. Your salvation is in Jesus Christ. You haven't been to church and that's going to change."

I could already feel the hard pews on my backside and smell the old ladies' perfume and hair spray. "But Pastor Jessie Michael left."

"Don't ever mention that scum-sucking false prophet again."

"But Mom said you gave up the Bible thumping," I said.

"How dare she call it that!"

Her feet in her black old lady shoes were firmly on the ground with her stockings wrinkled around her ankles. Her head was forward in her turtle stance. Her lips were pressed together, and there was a flush in her usually pasty face. She seemed to be puffing herself up like a chicken, ready to give me the full force of something.

"Well, I'm back with Jesus and I've found a new church. Very new … And in fact, I'm a leader of this new church. Do you know what that means?" I shook my head no. She continued, "People listen to me now. I'm getting back some of the respect I lost due to your mother dragging our name through the mud. Now people realize I have abilities. I'm the preacher in this new church. Well, the lay preacher, but that's as good as any preacher. I bet you didn't think I could be a preacher?" Grandma picked up her flowered teacup from the end table next to her chair. She took a sip of her "daytime coffee."

I tried to keep my face blank. "I've always thought you would be a good preacher," I said.

She set the teacup back on its saucer. "You were right." Then she turned toward me and stood up straight. As she spoke, she exhaled deeply as if she could breathe her religion into me. But her religion smelled like wine. I didn't what to breathe in her air, so I held my breath.

"You listen to me. The sins of the mother fall on the daughter. You're going to have to work hard to overcome the Whoredom influences from your mother and that dirty scum-sucking Jessie Michael. I want to be loving, but any more of that evil conjuring or talking to spirits or demons and you'll feel the full force of that switch." She spoke with such a fury. She clenched her teeth and her body shook.

I couldn't hold my breath anymore and inhaled. I smelled the wine on her breath. This was what it was going to be like all alone with her.

"Stop looking at me like that," she said. I looked down at the ground.

As it got closer to dinnertime, Grandma told Lilly Mae to make me dinner. Grandma stayed seated in her gold brocade chair having what she called her "evening coffee". She refused to eat even though she used to always be hungry.

Lilly Mae, wearing a flowered print dress, was in the kitchen cooking. She wiped the sweat from her forehead as she cut up some potatoes. For dinner, she served me pork chops, lima beans, mashed potatoes and gravy.

"Lilly Mae, I missed you and your cooking so much. Why isn't Grandma eating?" I asked.

"She's all tuckered out cause of this new church business. She's a preachin' there too. I never heard of a woman preacher 'fore. These white folks git so worked up praisin' the Lord. Sometimes she can't get out of bed the next morning. I think she keeps herself busy cause she misses your Mama, but wonts admit it."

"She looks different," I said.

"She say the Holy Ghost come right out a heaven and got inside her makin' her do the speakin'."

I felt a tingly feeling in my stomach. "So, she's talking to Eunice like I do. Why did she tell me never to do that again?"

Lilly Mae's eyes got wide. "No, it's not the dead spirits … not relatives. It's the kind of speakin' the Lord likes. It's called the speakin' in tongues … the tongues of fire … Go look in the backyard."

I went out on the back-porch and opened the backdoor. The backyard had been transformed. On the left side of the yard was the big oak tree and nailed up on it was a wooden cross. I heard a sad female voice from the tree saying, "Get this cross off of me. The nails hurt."

"I wish I could help you," I said.

Under the big oak tree, a large raised wooden platform had been built. A big canvas held up on poles covered the platform. To one side there were stacks of folding chairs and lanterns with bulbs were strung on cords around the yard.

I went back into the kitchen. "What's all that for?"

Lilly Mae shrugged her shoulders. "Now she has special meetin's here after church."

After dinner, I felt lonely and I went into the living room and stood in front of Grandma. Sitting in her brocade chair, her palms were closed into a claw shape resting on the arms of the chair. Queen Victoria was at her feet and licking the air in front of Grandma. Grandma's eyes were half-closed and turned up toward her gray eyebrows. At first, I thought she was sick. She opened her mouth wide and sounds started coming out of her, *"Aracosh coudacouda boya arakash coura leelakesh moura boyamata kato harakato fatamata seeta nabara."* Her breath was a long exhale at the end of *"seeta naabaraaa."*

"Grandma," I said but she didn't respond. "Grandma," I said loudly.

She opened her eyes and aimed her sounds like bullets at me, *"Sarabediki dora harakesh doraaah."* The *kesh doraah* was held a long time as she stared at me. Then she continued, *"Doe doebadara napepi badara pepi nalouche arakesh doralouchi louche napepe beedora."* Then she drew out the sounds as she said, *"Naaaaapepe beeeedorrrrraaaa aa aa aa."* Her eyes got bigger and her voice louder like she was bringing forth some of that Manna stuff or the fire that the Bible was always talking about.

"You're scaring me. What are you doing?" I asked. I felt stiff and I couldn't move.

Queen Victoria curled at her feet and whined, but Grandma poked her with her foot to make her be quiet.

Grandma opened her eyes and stared at me. I was really scared now. "Don't interrupt when the Holy Ghost is upon me."

"I've just come home. Don't you want to talk to me?" I asked.

Grandma looked right at me and her face was flushed. She stood up and said, *"1 Corinthians 14: Verse 2: For one who speaks in a tongue speaks not to men but to God."*

"I never heard you do Bible quoting before."

"I've got a few Bible quotes under my belt now," she said. She raised her arms and turned her eyes to heaven and said, "*Acts 2; Verse 17: And in the last days it shall be, God declares, that I will pour out my spirit upon all flesh, and your sons and your daughters shall prophesy.*"

She looked at me and put her hand over her heart and came toward me one step. I took a step backwards.

"Do you know what that means?" Grandma asked.

"What?" I took another step backwards.

"It means women can prophesy and preach," Grandma said.

"I never knew that."

"The Holy Ghost has come into me and given me the gift of tongues. They're all inside of me, little tongues that have never spoken before. They're waiting to come out, to speak, to be brought forth, to be given life. It's wonderful to let new things come out. It's my duty to let them out," Grandma said.

I imagined a bunch of tongues wiggling inside of her belly waiting for their chance to speak. I felt nauseous and held my stomach.

"I also have the gift of prophesy. This house lives by the Bible. Don't you forget that." Her eyes were bulging. The way she looked at me made me tremble. I took a couple more steps backward. "Don't back away from me. Come pray with me," she said.

The wine had made her wobbly and she stepped backwards and plopped into her chair. She pulled her skirt down and reached her white hands towards me and for a moment she looked like a loving Grandma. "Tessa, come here. I just want what's good for you. I know it's hard that your mother sent you away. I'm sorry if I sound harsh, but I have to keep you away from the dirty sin … that's like a snake just waiting to wiggle into everyone." She twisted her round body trying to imitate a snake.

I didn't want to hear about anymore sin. "I just started back at my old school. I have to do my homework now." I ran upstairs and shut myself in my room. I was shivering, and I was worried about her saying that she had the power of the Lord and that she had the tongues inside of her wanting to speak. Anyway, I didn't need any Holy Ghost Power because I could see spirits and talk to them all by myself. If Mom found out about Grandma's new religion, she might not want to come here. So, I decided not to tell her that Grandma was Bible thumping more than ever.

CHAPTER TWENTY-SEVEN

The next day was Sunday and when Grandma and I came home from church, she took off her flowered hat and gloves and set them down. We went into the kitchen where Lilly Mae was cooking up a feast. Grandma told me to help Lilly Mae while she went upstairs to get ready for the prayer meeting.

I turned to Lilly Mae. "We just got back from church. What's she talking about?"

Lilly Mae wore a red and white apron that had picture of a smiling Betty Crocker printed on the front. Lilly Mae leaned over the black-eyed peas in a big pot. "There's another church meeting startin' this afternoon. I got to set out lots of food for 'em. I think that some of 'em come jest for the eatin' and to see your grandma's preachin'. I never knew women could preach."

"She said the Bible says that they can," I said.

"The way she carry on makes me afraid the sky goin' to open up sooner than it's supposed to. And the whole Judgin' Day will come right down into your backyard." She got a pitcher out of the refrigerator and poured herself some iced tea.

"Lilly Mae, you're good. Nothing bad will happen to you," I said.

"I jest wish your Mama would come back."

I went out back with Lilly Mae as she took a large platter of food into the yard. People were arriving, and some were nicely dressed, but some were dressed in a way my grandma would say was low-class, with the women wearing tattered flower print dresses and the men wearing jeans that had holes in them. I recognized some and others I didn't.

The women had taken charge of the food tables set against the side of the house. Men were setting up the folding chairs and the people in the back were waiting to take their seats. Under the canvas covering, at the front was a raised platform like a stage with a rough pine pulpit on it. The first row of chairs on the ground were set back from the platform, leaving a space covered with a carpet in front of the seats. I found a chair not far from the front.

All of a sudden, it became very quiet and everyone turned as Grandma came out the back-screen door and glided down the stairs. She wore white gloves and a white linen dress that came down below her knees. She had on one of her bucket-shaped hats with pink artificial roses sticking out like antennae. Queen Victoria with a bow on her head was cradled on her right arm.

Grandma had always said that makeup made Mom look like a hussy. But today her face was powdered, her cheeks were rouged, and she had on lipstick. As she moved past me, I smelled perfume.

An usher held her hand and guided her up onto the stage platform where the new minister, Mr. Gabriel Goodbank, waited for her. She put Queen Victoria in a little bed on one side of the stage. Then the minister took her gloved hand, and she stared into his eyes smiling, as if she was melting into him. He helped her step behind the pulpit. He was fat, dressed in a suit, with the bottom buttons unbuttoned, exposing his white shirt. I saw some skin peeking out from where the shirt stretched over his stomach. He had full pink lips and eyebrows sprouting every which way like grass. His hair was brushed straight back, and when he smiled, he had big horse teeth.

The pastor raised his hand for everyone to be quiet. "I want to welcome the new people. You've all come to the right place. The Holy Ghost sanctions whatever happens here today. But you've already heard me this morning and I know you've come to see our truly gloriously re-born Sister Bernice. She will guide us in receiving the gifts of the Holy Ghost. Whatever happens, don't hold it back."

From behind the pulpit, Grandma looked at the audience and then back to the Pastor. "We all have Pastor Goodbank to thank for his guidance." Then she raised her eyes to heaven and everyone followed her gaze. After a few moments, she looked at the audience. "Some of you may truly believe and others may be questioning why you have come here. Let me remind you why it's so important that you're here today."

She opened her Bible and read, *"Acts 2: Verse 19-21."* Her voice was slow and forceful. She stood up straight and raised her arms to heaven and in a deep voice quoted, *"And I will show wonders in the heaven above."* Then she outstretched her arms level with the ground and said, *"And signs on the earth beneath."* She moved her arms around like she was going to make the earth rise up and clenched her fists and spoke slowly, *"And signs on the earth beneath, blood, and fire, and vapor of smoke."* She looked heavenward as though she was seeing something, and members of the audience also looked up. Then she pointed to the setting sun. *"The sun shall be turned to darkness and the moon into blood."* Then she pointed to where she thought the moon was, but it hadn't come up, so she waved her pointed finger around. *"Before the day of the Lord comes, the great and manifest day."* She slowly pointed to the audience, her voice growing louder. *"And it shall be whoever calls on the name of the Lord shall be saved."* She stabbed her finger as she pointed at the audience, "How many of you are going to call on the name of the Lord?" The audience answered, "All of us. Hallelujah." As if her eyes would scorch them, she stared at the audience and closed her Bible.

My new grandma was so powerful. Everyone was watching her, but what she was doing didn't seem quite real and I also felt embarrassed. Then Grandma walked back and forth across the platform in front of the audience. "Speaking in tongues is the evidence of being baptized in the Holy Ghost. Let the tongues of fire come up from your belly. Let them warm you. They will be your truth. Let them make you lie down in green pastures. Give the tongues life so you will know the wonders of the Lord and speak the language of the angels."

Then with her eyes turned up, she started speaking fast with a strength I'd never heard before. *"Shaba bakar ayabras shata bakar yayaka brasshata shatabaha ayaya frata shatabakar yama nena yar."* Then she started singing the sounds. *"Naya frata shaker yarafrata shaker pakaar neyara kaya jarapakar fra shatapakar yaya maya pakaar."* She didn't sing well, but nobody else seemed to notice and her voice kept getting louder. I wondered if the Lord couldn't hear unless people shouted. Queen Victoria howled from her bed as if she was trying to speak in tongues also. Grandma kicked her bed.

The Pastor said, "The Holy Ghost is upon you. Feel free to join in." He moved his fat arms and moved his big shoulders forward and backward awkwardly. I think that meant he was overcome. Compared to him, Grandma looked pretty good. He said slowly as if he couldn't think of what to say, *"Watcha gotcha fatcha her ee boom bada boom ser ee boom ba da matcha gotcha tata toom ye hoomie zoom dada boom dekoo boomie dede maataa … aah."* He extended that last sound and exhaled heavily as if he was breathing out the Holy Ghost. Then he marched his feet in place as if he was going to do a little dance and didn't know how. The Holy Ghost sure made him look funny. I was proud my grandma was a better speaker in tongues than him.

People in the audience became wide-eyed and surprised and moaned as the Holy Ghost descended upon them. With their mouths wide open, the audience members joined in with their own speaking, softly at first and then their voices became fervent. They stood up, their arms in the air, and some cried out like the Lord was piercing them. Some rushed to the space in front of the platform and were so overcome they collapsed on the carpet with tears running down their cheeks. It was amazing how the Holy Ghost made the people roll around on the ground while they continued their speaking. Each had their own sounds and the sounds became louder and became all jumbled up. It sounded like. *"Lula moolasha tatakata Moooooo."* One person kept saying, *"Toota dede toota dede toota sese yaya dedeeeee,"* over and over as if he couldn't think of anything else to say. Some others were saying, *"Oh oh oooh,"* and then, *"Ah ah aaaah."* I wondered if the invisible Lord was touching them.

The women ushers went up to the ladies rolling on the ground and when their skirts hiked up, they pulled them down so their underwear, and girdles wouldn't be shown to the Lord or to the men watching from the back. There were some men in jeans and cowboy boots standing up against the garage wall and they were staring at what was happening, but they didn't look like they were overcome with the Holy Ghost. They just stared with their hands in their pockets and stood on one foot and then the other.

Grandma was getting more worked up as she continued speaking in tongues. She had sweat rings under the arms of her linen dress. But she was my grandma and I couldn't take my eyes off her. I felt a rushing as if a wind was inside of me pushing me. I stood up. Then all of a sudden, I saw red cut-off tongues floating around her head. My body trembled as I saw them fall from above her head to down around her feet on the platform. They were flopping on the ground like dead fish and then bursting into flames and sizzling. It was frightening. But she didn't see them. She stepped on a couple of tongues and they screamed. A pins and needles feeling swooshed through me. I had to stop her from stepping on more tongues. I shrieked loudly to get people's attention, "Holy tongues are falling. Grandma, I see cut-off tongues falling. The Holy Ghost is making its tongues fall around your feet. And the tongues are catching on fire." I was glad that people were now looking at me. If Grandma could speak in tongues, then I could see things just as important. I screamed again and waited until more people looked at me. "Stop Grandma from stepping on any more of God's holy tongues," I shouted. "Grandma listen to me, the holy tongues are falling. Stop squashing God's tongues. Watch where you step. Stop hurting the tongues!" I yelled. Then I saw Grandma look at me.

Her face was red and her eyes became large, as if they were the angry eyes of God.

Out of the corner of my eye, I saw a boy coming toward me. I thought I recognized him from my old school I had just begun attending again. His thick black hair was combed to one side and he had a round face with black-rimmed glasses. He was chubby and had his shirt tucked in his short pants with a brown leather belt buckled over his stomach.

I yelled again, "Stop hurting the tongues."

A bunch of women sitting close to me glared at me, and one got up and came toward me. Dotty, a big-breasted woman who knew me, grabbed my arm, hurting me. I smelled her sweat and felt her breasts on my face, as she lifted me off of my feet by my arm. "Little lady, you don't see anything, and you shut your dirty mouth, or your grandma will whup you real good."

But I was seeing this all on my own. There wasn't any Holy Ghost coming inside of me. I was shaking, and I couldn't stop seeing the tongues falling and catching on fire every time I looked at the platform.

I pulled free from Dotty. "Get away from me. You can't stop me." I rushed closer to the front. What I was seeing was just as real and as important as whatever Grandma's tongues were saying. The boy followed me and stood next to me, his arms folded in front of him.

I felt confused. On the one hand, it seemed Grandma really meant her preaching, but then also her preaching reminded me of her high-horse sessions when she was drinking and yelled at her dolls.

Maybe Lilly Mae was right that this calling on the Lord was going to open up the heavens right here in the backyard and bring the Judging Day. I wished Mom were here. Now I couldn't ignore the boy because he bent over and got close to my ear. "I'm Carl. You're Tessa and you used to be in my class," he said. Then he straightened up and pushed his black-rimmed glasses back up his nose.

I pushed my hair back over my shoulder. "That's right. This is my grandma's house. I've been away but I'm coming back to school next week."

"I heard you yelling that you see tongues falling around Sister Bernice's feet," he said.

"Yeah, but nobody pays attention because I'm a kid."

His face lit up and he made a motion with his hand like an airplane crashing. "Can you show me how to see bloody tongues crashing and catching on fire?" he asked.

"Maybe. Have you been coming here long?"

"Since it started. Maw makes me come here. She says it's to keep the devil out of me. Paw says he can't talk to Maw anymore cause she's always speaking in tongues. I can't talk to her either. Paw says he's tired of Maw's Holy Roller shit. That makes Maw mad and then she yells in tongues. One time, I yelled in tongues back at her, but I got whupped," he said.

I looked around to see if anyone heard him say shit.

"I don't see my dad," I said.

"Are your parents dee-vorced?"

I nodded my head and tried to smooth out the wrinkles in my pink dress.

He shrugged his shoulders. "Maw don't believe in dee-vorce."

"Do you want to come to my room?" I stood up. I pushed back my curly brown hair.

"Yeah, I guess so."

I wrapped some cookies from the dessert table in a napkin and went up the backstairs. He followed me.

CHAPTER TWENTY-EIGHT

When Carl and I entered into my room, he walked around and jumped up and down on the floor. "Nice wood floor. I wish my room was big like this. I have to share a room with my snotty little brother and I'm supposed to be a Christian and love him. Yuck," he said.

We could hear shouts of "Save me, Jesus" from the meeting in the backyard.

He stared at me. "Can you show me how to see bloody tongues falling on the ground?"

I motioned for him to sit on a wooden chair at my child's table. "I would if I could, but things like that just happen to me during all the excitement."

"You're kind of strange. My paw says women are not normal. Maybe it starts when they're your age," he said. He pushed his glasses back up his nose and stared at me as if to figure out why I was strange.

"Don't stare at me," I said. I put the napkin with the cookies on the table. Since I'd never been allowed to play with boys, I didn't know what to do. I went to my dresser and opened the top drawer and started to take out my teacups.

"What are ya doing?" he asked.

"I'm getting my teacups and we can pretend we're having tea and talk about things."

"That's sissy stuff." Then he took two cookies and pushed them with the palm of his hand into his mouth. He chewed with his mouth open. That made his round face look even rounder. "Let's take the blankets from your bed and make a tent." His blue-striped cotton shirt was a little too small and his belly stuck out above his short pants. He tried to tuck his shirt back under his belt.

"OK," I said.

"But I'm in charge of the tent making." Carl wiped the sweat off of his forehead. Then he roughly pulled the blankets and sheets off of my bed, ripping one of the sheets. He pushed the table closer to the bed and with some twine and scissors I helped him tie the two ends of the blanket to the bedposts. Then he draped the other end of the blanket over the table, dropping it down to the floor. He put some books on the table to hold the blanket in place. Now there was a covered space between the table and the bed. Then he draped a sheet across the back and front. At the front of the tent he folded the sheet back and used another book to hold it in place making something like a flap of a teepee.

"Do you have any kid's guns to play cowboys and Indians?" he asked.

"No." I took off my white patent leather shoes and pushed my curly brown hair over my shoulders. My bow on the right side was still in place.

"Well, we'll play anyway. You're the Indian and I'm the cowboy," he said. His belt was tight around his stomach, so he took it off and threw it across the floor.

"I want to be the cowboy."

"Girls aren't cowboys," he said.

"But I know how to sing cowboy songs."

"We're going to fight, not sing. You're the squaw, so get into the teepee. I'm the cowboy and I'm gunna to come into yah camp and kill you, the injun squaw. Go on, get in."

I took my pillow into the make-believe tent under the blanket and sat on it. But so far this didn't seem like much fun.

He went over by my desk. "I'm on my horse and I see tracks down by the river. It's the injuns. They've been stealing my cattle. I'm following their tracks," he said in a deep voice.

"Who are you talking to?"

"Uh, I guess my horse," he said. Carl neighed like a horse so I'd believe he had a horse.

"What am I supposed to do?"

"Do what squaws do. Make moccasins. Now, I'm circling your tent. I know there're injuns in this here tent. I have my knife." He crawled into the tent and waved my magic Wizard of Oz wand with the star on top in front of my face. He looked excited and he opened his eyes wide. "What do you say before I kill you?"

"Don't kill me."

"Lie down," he said.

I took off my white belt and carefully lay down because I was wearing my pink organdy dress, which was my Sunday best. Grandma always dressed me like one of her dolls. He got on top of me straddling me and crushing my dress. I touched his round belly with my finger, but he pushed it away. I'd never had a boy this close to me. I smelled him, and his chubby legs felt warm around me. He held up my magic wand and moved his hand up and down pretending to stab me.

"That's my magic wand. Don't break it." I was sweating.

"It's my knife. See, I'm killing you. It's fun. Stab. Stab. Kill. Kill." His glasses slipped down again and with his other hand he pushed his glasses back up. His glasses were becoming foggy from the moisture on his face.

The weight of his body was squashing me. "You're heavy. Get off of me." I put my hands on his fat stomach and pushed on him. I'd never touched a boy's skin before. He felt softer than I had expected.

"I have to finish killing you. Remember this was my idea. Stab. Stab. You have to pretend you're dying," he said.

I didn't want the sweat on his forehead to drip on me. "Get off of me now. I don't like this game."

He rolled off of me, sat down, and pushed his black hair away from his moist forehead. "That's because you're a girl and a chicken. You're no fun."

"Don't say that. Don't you want me to like you?" I asked.

"Yeah, I guess so."

Even though he was bossy, I looked in his brown eyes and I felt as if feathers were tickling me. I laughed. When Mom had Pastor Jessie Michael in her room, whatever they did they did it naked. There was some secret about being naked. I moved closer to Carl and smiled.

"What are you laughing about?" he asked.

"Nothing. But I have an idea. We're two cowboys on a cattle drive and this is our camp."

"I told you girls aren't cowboys."

"Pretend. You can be anything when you pretend," I said.

I put my leg up against one of his legs. Since he was wearing short pants, my calf and part of my thigh was right against his leg. I didn't expect touching him to feel warm and good. He didn't know it, but it seemed like his skin was saying it wanted to be touched.

"Cowboys don't sit so close together," he said. Then he scooted his leg away.

"So, pretend we're camped by a river. After riding all day we're tired and dirty. There's a beautiful cool river right in front of us. Do you see it?" I asked.

"No."

"Try to see it." I was getting sweat rings under the arms of my organdy dress.

"Now, I see a bunch of snakes on some rocks."

"It's so hot let's take off our clothes and get in the river," I said.

"Why would I want to do that?"

"Because I've never seen a boy naked and I want to see you naked," I said.

"So, you want to see my thing. Paw says it's called a pecker. Paw says women are pussies and that makes you a girl pussy."

"Have you seen a girl's privates?" I asked.

"I peeked through widow Crandall's window when she was dressing but I couldn't see much, and she was all wrinkles."

"My mom used to have Pastor Jessie Michael in her room next door. I peeked through the keyhole and I could only see a little bit of their kissing but mostly I heard them making noise. Kind of like this." Then I breathed and moaned a little, imitating their noises.

"You sound silly. But jeez, your mom really had a pastor in her bed? And you tried to look?"

"Yes, and one night, Grandma caught them and said they were 'forni… cating'," I said.

"That's in the Bible and Maw says forni… ni…ca…cat is bad. Even worse than bad."

"It's pronounced fornication. I know because I'm smart."

"When Paw's mad, he goes around the house yelling Maw's tight-assed. And Maw says he's a forni…ni…cating devil."

"At the other house where I stayed, the old woman there would say, to Get the Fuck. But I'm not sure what that is," I said.

As I scooted closer to him, I pressed my hand down on his thigh. "Ouch! You're pressing too hard on my leg."

"I'm sorry." I took my hand away. His glasses slid down his nose and he pushed them up.

"If you take off your pants so I can see your thing, then I'll pull down my panties and you can see my privates," I said.

"Why should I?" He rubbed his palm around on his stomach that was sticking out.

"Because maybe you won't get another chance to see a girl naked, and besides, I'm pretty," I said.

"I know what's going on. I seen animals do it."

"Well, I haven't. Come on, unzip your pants." I rested my hand lightly on his thigh again.

"Watch where you're putting your hand." He moved my hand away. I kept staring at him, but he wouldn't look me in the eye. We heard the voices from downstairs shouting, "Hallelujah, hallelujah, Jesus is here. Just reach out."

"I think you're scared. But I'm a girl, so how could I scare you?" I asked.

"No, I'm not. But boy o boy!" He put his mouth up to my ear. "O.K. If I do this you won't tell anyone, will you?" he whispered.

"I promise," I said. He half-stood up and half-crouched in the tent and unzipped his short pants. He stumbled as he tried to get them off his chubby thighs. He grabbed the bedpost to keep from falling. I also stood up and lifted my skirt so he could see my panties. "See it's easy. I have pink panties."

"You said you would take them off or are you chicken?" he asked.

"Both at the same time."

He pulled down his underpants and I pulled down my pink panties. I couldn't take my eyes off of what was between his legs. This was exciting. I felt a tingling in my chest. I was doing something Grandma said was bad and it felt good.

But when I looked at his face, he didn't seem excited. He just stared at me. He had one hand at his neck and rested his chin on it, as if he didn't know what to say. How could that be? I wanted him to look excited.

"I can't see much. You're flat. Lay down and put your legs apart," he said.

There wasn't much room, but I lay down on my pillow and propped myself up on my elbows. Then I spread my legs but only a little. I hadn't planned this. I kept staring at his pecker. How did boys walk around with that thing dangling? Compared to him, I felt I didn't have much. He was right that I was flat. I couldn't think of anything to say.

He sat down and moved close to me, then his finger made a beeline to poke me between my legs. I closed my legs quickly before he touched me.

I sat up. "Hey, don't touch me."

"Jeez, there's nothing wrong with my finger. I told you I seen animals do it and the boy animals poke at girl animals. Anyway, there's not much to see," he said. He crossed his arms in front of his stomach.

"Don't say that. Your pecker reminds me of a Vienna sausage. You know, like the ones in the can." I got this picture in my mind of the boys at school walking around with Vienna sausages between their legs and I started to laugh.

He stood up, his head pressing against the blanket at the top of the tent. "Are you making fun of me?" he asked.

"No, I wouldn't do that. It's bigger than a Vienna sausage. I'm just trying to say what it reminds me of."

"You talk too much. All girls do…blah, blah."

I got down on my knees and looked closely at his pecker. Boys have something special, even if it's stupid. I reached out with my index finger to touch it. But he pushed my hand away.

"I didn't say you could do that," he said. He pulled his shirt down, but his pecker was still out as if to tell the whole world, "I'm here and I won't go away."

Then we heard Carl's mom calling from the bottom of the stairs. "Carl, come down here right this minute."

Carl rushed to get his pants on and pulled the blanket down on us. We struggled under the blanket, bumping into each other, trying to get our clothes on.

"I know you're up to no good. I better not have to come up there." Carl's mother's voice sounded threatening.

Carl yelled back, "I'm reading."

"Since when do you read? Carl Rogers get your butt down here."

Carl pulled up his pants and rushed to the door. He stopped and turned back. "Yuh better not tell anyone about this." His belt was still unbuckled.

I went to bed that night feeling different. Mom does what she wants to do so I can do what I want.

On my first day back at my old school, when I was out on the playground, I looked at the boys and I couldn't stop imagining they had Vienna sausages dangling in their pants. I counted the boys and there were a lot of sausages on that playground. I wondered if the heat affected their sausage peckers.

When I went up to Carl on the playground, he wouldn't even look at me. I hadn't expected that.

By my second day, several boys from Carl's class came up to me on the playground and bumped into me. "Pull your pants down. I want to see your pussy crack … And your face looks like a pussy," they said. They laughed so hard they doubled over and they patted each other on the back.

I blushed, and I got a knot in my throat. All the excitement of doing something I was not supposed to do went away. For the next few weeks I felt trembling in my stomach. I did not look at any boy who looked at me because he might have a cruel smile on his face.

Cathy had forgiven me for how I treated her the last time we saw each other. She must have overheard them because she came up to me. "Boys are mean. Ignore them and they'll leave you alone."

"Have you seen a boy naked?" I asked.

"I have a brother and I saw him doing something in the bathroom." Then she got close to my ear and whispered, "Did you pull your pants down for Carl?"

"Of course not. He's ugly."

I told myself if I ever wanted to do something like that again that I'd find a boy who couldn't talk because of some disease.

CHAPTER TWENTY-NINE

For the next couple of months, I went to school and hoped the boys would stop making fun of me. I attended Grandma's church meetings where the tongues always knew when it came time to speak through Grandma. I wondered what they did on other days. Where were they while waiting for the next person to speak through? Did they wait on benches, like in a bus station with the door opening to the sky filled with clouds? Were they in line holding numbers to be called when someone was ready to be spoken through? Was there any pushing to get to the front of the line?

On Saturdays, while Mom was parked out front waiting to pick me up, Grandma would peek out from behind the living room curtains at her. Mom's stomach was so big now that it was difficult for her to get in and out of Boleslaw's Chevy wagon.

One Saturday when we arrived at Randy's Hog on the Spit Barbeque, Mom parked between two pickups with rifles in their gun racks. Tears started running down her cheeks making streaks on her red cotton blouse. From her red leather purse, she took out a handkerchief and wiped her tears and looked around to see if anyone was watching her.

I scooted as close to her as I could get. "Mama, what's wrong?"

"I'm sorry I had to send you back to your grandma's," she said. Seeing her sad made me cry also. She wiped my tears with her handkerchief. "Let's not cry. I didn't know Beata would be the way she was."

Two men walked by wearing cowboy hats, and one leaned in the window. One tipped his cowboy hat at Mom. Without saying anything, Mom rolled her window up, to make them go away.

"I miss you. I need to see you more than once a week. Please come home," I said. Mom hugged me against her big stomach.

"I know it's hard, but my mother doesn't want me there. Has she said anything about me?"

"No, she doesn't mention you. She's too busy."

She sat up straight and looked at me. "What on earth is she doing now?"

"She's fixing up the house. She even cleaned up the whole backyard." I didn't dare mention Grandma's speaking in tongues because then Mom wouldn't want to come back home at all.

"I'm your mother and I love you no matter what and I won't forget you," she said.

"Grandma prays everyday you'll get back to Jesus."

Mom's neck got stiff and she gripped the steering wheel. "She can stick those prayers where the sun doesn't shine and maybe they'll sprout into turnip greens sticking out of her ass."

I laughed. "I do hear her praying in the bathroom. 'Jesus, Jesus. Oh, Jesus', she says again and again."

"She's lost her mind over religion. Don't ever let that happen to you," she said.

Then Mom put her hand over her stomach and bent over the wheel and moaned. I took her hand. "Mama, I don't want you to be sick."

She squeezed my hand. "Don't worry. I just felt a pain, but it's gone."

She put her arm around me. "Tessa, I may not always understand you but I love you. There's something fine in you. You're going to grow up to be a wonderful woman." She smiled. "Do you want to hear my new song

I'm working on?" I nodded and then she sang, *"A Texas woman has to stand her ground, even if she's in the lost and found. Especially when you're hurt, and you're treated like dirt. Sing from your heart, let them know that you are smart. The world is full of dumb asses, make them take off their glasses. Shout your song to the sky, before you say goodbye. Nothing is what it seems."*

It felt so good to hear her sing. She rolled the car window down because both of us were sweating. Then she slapped her palms on the steering wheel. "I just have to be a good singer."

"Mama, I think you're a good singer," I said.

Tears came to the edge of her eyes, but she brushed them away. She put her arm around me. "I'm sorry, honey. This is your day. I'm not going to cry."

CHAPTER THIRTY

I'd been back with Grandma about two months when early one Monday morning, as the darkness outside was clinging to the trees, Grandma called to me. I didn't open my eyes because this was the time when the night spirits, the ghosts of children, were outside and they walked around on their little feet.

"Tessa wake up," Grandma said. I still didn't move. "Tessa, don't play possum. Wake up."

I opened one eye, hoping the child spirits would think I was still asleep. In the early morning, they didn't want people disturbing them. "Stop Grandma. It's still dark outside. You're disturbing everybody."

Grandma came over and shook me gently. "You have a new baby sister. Wake up."

I got out of bed and Grandma got my clothes out of the closet. "Hurry up, get dressed. We're going to the hospital."

"They're outside. We can't go out there while it's still dark. They need their private time. It's the only way they can be happy," I shouted.

"Don't raise your voice, and what crazy thing are you talking about? You better not be conversing with those evil spirits again. That makes me so angry I could spit," Grandma said. Her face turned red and her double chins wiggled. Then Grandma quickly turned and left the room.

When Grandma came back, she was wearing one of her bucket hats with lavender roses piled on top, and a blue linen dress. She had on her lace-up old lady shoes and carried a leather purse full of things she might need in an emergency, like her gun, which she took with her when going out in the dark. As we left, she stopped in the hallway and looked in the mirror and rubbed off the extra lipstick where it had run over the sides of her lips.

When we got into Grandma's 1948 maroon Buick, she put the gun in the glove compartment.

"You told me never to mention Mom because she's a fornicator," I said.

"Tessa, don't say that word. Children don't say that word. People will think you're low-class." Grandma pressed her lips together. "She's my daughter and Christians are supposed to turn the other cheek even if you want to bite the person." She spoke in her preaching voice like she did when she was in front of an audience.

"Are you going to bite Mom?" I asked.

"No, no. I'm just trying to explain the turn the other cheek expression. I don't fully understand it myself. I had a vivid dream that seemed so real. I was holding the baby. Maybe Jesus wants me to try to get along with her."

As we drove, the leaves on the dark trees moved as if a breeze was blowing them, but I knew we had disturbed the night spirit children. Since the edge of the sky was turning into orange light, the night children would have to sink back into the earth in a few minutes. It must be horrible for them to be stuck in the earth all day.

We pulled into the empty parking lot of the hospital. "Aren't we too early?" I asked.

"Nope, I don't want to run into that butcher with the meat cleaver hands."

"His name is Boleslaw," I said.

We went into the old brick hospital with faded white walls, and walked down to Mom's room. Mom was propped up on pillows on a mattress that was covered with a white knit blanket. The old white metal frame bed had a headboard and footboard of metal rods. The paint on the frame was chipped away in places, showing the dark metal underneath. In the corner was a furnace with pipes reaching across the painted brick walls as if they were living tentacles.

"Mom," I said. I leaned across the white blanket to hug her, but I couldn't reach her.

She turned her head toward me and took my hand. She seemed half-asleep and her face was white, and her eyelids looked heavy. "Tessa dear, I'm glad you've come." Then she noticed Grandma in her room. "It was nice of you to bring her."

Grandma's hat had an artificial rose hanging down. She pulled it out and threw it away. She stepped closer to Mom. "I thought we could try again. It's the Christian thing. Since you're laid up, maybe you won't be up to your old ways so soon." Grandma's purse was heavy, so she set it down. Then she ran her hand down the front of her skirt.

Mom tried to sit up straighter, but it caused her pain. "What's that supposed to mean?"

"Let's try to have a nice conversation."

"I've just had surgery. Don't come in here and criticize me." Mom ran her hand through her tangled hair.

"You take everything the wrong way. Anyway, where's Mr. Meaty Man? Is he happy to be the proud father?"

"He was here all night. He's a good man. I need to rest so why don't you take Tessa to see her new sister, Gertrude," Mom said.

Before I realized what, I was doing, I blurted out, "I can't wait to tell Aunt Gertie about the baby being named after her."

Grandma grabbed my arm. "How dare you defy me and still do that evil con ... consort ... You know what I mean." She squeezed my arm hard.

"Let go of her. Really, Mother, she's not consorting. It's her imagination," Mom said.

"She has to stop it. Anyway, I came to pray over the baby. I want one of the first things she learns to be Jesus' name," Grandma said.

Mom sat up straighter and raised her voice. "Mother, no you don't. Leave my baby alone. I knew it was too good to be true that you wanted to patch things up." She put her hand over her stomach and winced in pain.

"You're hurting Mama." I jumped up and down.

"Relax, it's just a little prayer of thanks. You can't be against that." Grandma took my hand and pulled me toward the door.

"I don't want a sister. I want it to be just Mom and me. Like it's always been," I said.

"You're going to love your sister." Mom gave me an angry look.

Grandma led me down the hall to the nursery. Grandma addressed the nurse in the hall, "I want to see the Grab … Grabo baby … You know, the butcher's baby."

"Wait here at the window," the nurse said. She went inside the door and brought the baby up to the window. Her face was red and wrinkled and wasn't as cute as a puppy. I'd been praying for a puppy, but Jesus was ignoring me.

The nurse pulled the white blanket back from the baby's head and a mop of thick black hair jumped out and stood straight up. She had thick black eyebrows and there was even black fuzz on her forehead. It was as if the hair was saying, "Look at me. I'm here. I'm strong and won't be kept down."

Grandma let out a gasp and let her jaw drop as she exhaled loudly. The nurse smiled at us. I guess she thought we should be happy. Grandma didn't want the nurse to think anything was wrong, so she forced a smile. Her cheeks had quite a bit of rouge and I hadn't gotten used her wearing makeup since she'd become a preacher.

"Look at her nose and all that black hair. What can be done with that? It's obvious whom she looks like. I wonder if the butcher has noticed? We'll have to cut that hair off. Can a baby's head be shaved?" Grandma asked. I shrugged.

The baby looked exactly like Pastor Jessie Michael. Then the baby opened her mouth and moved her lips. She was actually saying something.

I heard her say, *"In the beginning God created the heavens and the earth. The earth was without form and was void."* I yelled, "No, Gertrude, stop that Bible talking right now. You can't do that. I won't let you. You're the second daughter." I put my hands over my ears. It had to be my mind causing me to hear her voice. I hit my head with my fist. She couldn't really be speaking because that would mean she was smart. I said loudly, "She can talk all she wants but I'm smarter than she will ever be." The nurse heard me through the glass and got a pinched look on her, face but then forced herself to smile again. I wished Jessie Michael would come back and take his baby.

"Hush your mouth. Don't yell in public. Look, the nurse thinks there's something wrong with you," Grandma said.

"Is Mama going to take her home to Boleslaw's house?"

"Of course. She's your sister now," Grandma replied.

"No. Please no. There's not much room there."

"You're not there, so there's room," Grandma said.

The baby moved her tiny red hand and opened her tiny mouth and she was cute in a toothless sort of way. I was afraid Mom would think she's really cute. The nurse started to take the baby away. But Grandma tapped the window with her white finger. The nurse forced another smile for us. Grandma took my hand. "Bow your head." She started praying, "Thank you, Jesus for this new life you have entrusted to us. But, Jesus, I have just one thing to ask. Could you keep people from noticing who she looks like? Jesus, give the whole town a little forgetfulness for your devoted servant? Thank you, Jesus. Amen."

I stood up straight. "I don't forget anything."

CHAPTER THIRTY-ONE

For quite awhile, Mom couldn't drive because of the surgery. So, when I hadn't seen her for over a month, I felt as if I was sinking into a big hole. Finally, Mom called and said she had talked Boleslaw into letting me spend Saturday afternoon at his house, but that I had to stay out of Beata's way. Grandma had Lilly Mae drive me over there. Grandma said to me, "I have a reputation to keep up and I can't be seen talking to Boleslaw's peasant mother."

When I got there, Mom was dressed in a pink terrycloth robe over a red flannel nightgown. She was in the kitchen sticking a long scrubber on a wire handle into baby bottles washing them. They had a sour milk smell. Her face was pale, and her long red hair was combed back into a ponytail. Her brown roots were showing. She moved with difficulty and she wiped the sweat off of her forehead.

The bunches of turnips were still stacked on the countertops. The kitchen smelled of turnips and cabbage, and in front of the turnips were statues of Jesus. Each Jesus had a raised red heart in the center of his chest. Beata had put them there to keep out the evil spirits she thought I was bringing into the house. I liked the hearts, and when no one was looking, I'd try to cut them off of the statues.

I rushed and put my arms around Mom, but she pushed me away. "Honey, you can't squeeze my stomach so hard. I have an incision," she said. She took some Betty Crocker fudge brownies out of the cookie jar and put them on the table. She opened the refrigerator to get milk. The statue of the Virgin was in its place on top of the refrigerator watching us. It still had the artificial tears I had painted on it. It wobbled, as if dancing, when Mom closed the door. Maybe Beata believed they were real tears.

Mom put the brownies and milk on the table and I sat down. She eased herself carefully onto a chair and pulled her robe tightly around her, holding her arm across her stomach.

"So, Gertrude the beach ball just came out of you. Plop! What's it like to have a baby come out of you?"

"It's painful, but when it's over and you hold the baby, it's wonderful. She's a beautiful baby," Mom answered through dry and chapped lips.

"Why is she here with you while I'm at Grandma's? Is she that beautiful?"

She moved her chair closer to me and took both my hands in hers. "Tessa, nobody will ever take your place. You're my precious daughter and don't forget that."

"If I'm so precious, you should keep me with you," I said.

Mom looked down. "I'm doing the best I can."

After the brownies, Mom and I went out onto the back-porch. We sat down and I handed her the guitar and we started singing. In the garden, humped-back Beata hunched over the plants, as if she were a buffalo and furiously pawed up the carrots. Her large hands tightly grabbed them by the stalks and tossed them on a pile. She seemed angry at them and then I heard the carrots screaming, "You're killing us. Leave us in the ground!" I kept hearing the carrots whimpering as they lay in piles slowly dying in the sun. The breeze blew Beata's red scarf as she ignored us.

After awhile, we heard Boleslaw's heavy footsteps coming down the gravel driveway on the side of the house and into the backyard. Beata rushed to hug and kiss him on the mouth and he pushed her away. Mom watched with a grimace. He would want to kiss her after kissing Beata. I felt sorry for Mom.

We went into the kitchen and heard Boleslaw come up the back staircase, his big work boots sounding heavy on the old stairs. He carried grocery bags with beer bottles clinking inside, and as he came into the kitchen, Mom smiled at him. He wore a beige work shirt and slacks. He still smelled of meat. His brown hair was combed to one side and he kissed Mom on the lips.

Mom looked over at me. "Tessa, go upstairs and play until I call you for dinner."

I went into the hallway, but instead of going upstairs, I tiptoed into the dining room. I snuck behind the swinging door to the kitchen and ever so carefully moved the door so I could see through the crack. I saw Boleslaw plop himself down at the table and open a big bottle of "Lone Star Beer." He took a long drink and wiped the foam off his thick moustache and smoothed it out with his thumb and forefinger. He focused his blue eyes on Mom, but didn't speak.

I couldn't see Mom, but I heard her. "How was your day?" she asked.

Boleslaw put the beer bottle to his mouth again, taking a long swig. He looked at Mom with a hard face. "That mother of yours looks down on me."

"What difference does that make? You don't see her," Mom replied.

Boleslaw raised his bushy eyebrows, wrinkling his big forehead in an angry look. "Oh, yes I do. She came into the store today wearing white gloves and a huge flowering hat like a crown. She came toward me and tilted her head back but couldn't get her nose as high in the air as she wanted because it's so short. I laughed a belly laugh. She puffed up and said to me, 'Why are you laughing? You look better with your blowhole shut and covered with that briar bush moustache'. She had me pull out a bunch of steaks and weigh them like she was rich enough to buy them. After all that trouble, she only bought ground chuck." Boleslaw's face turned red and with his clenched fist he hit the table. Wham! The bottles in the bag clinked. I jumped. "It was all I could do to keep from rubbing a steak in her face," Boleslaw said. Then he slammed the table again.

"Bo, stop it. I've never heard you talk like this," Mom said.

"She called me Mr. Meaty Man."

Now I could see the side of Mom's face as she stood next to Boleslaw. "I can't keep her from shopping." She put her hand on Boleslaw's shoulder, but he pushed it away.

His neck tightened. "She looks down on me because I'm Polish. She has no right. It hurts me." Boleslaw put his hand on his heart.

"You have to ignore the hate in this town," Mom said soothingly.

He looked at Mom with his clear blue eyes. "Don't you know what everybody is saying about her?"

"What do you mean?" Mom took the steaks out of the bag and put them in the refrigerator.

Boleslaw took another long drink of beer. "People say she has a church in her backyard. That she's a preacher now. They say she has words coming directly from the Holy Ghost. They call it some kind of 'speaking'. She may have a bunch of people fooled, but not old Boleslaw. She doesn't have anything holy coming from her. She's rotten inside," he said.

"My mother preaching. I don't believe it."

"Ask Tessa. Bernice is up in front of people shooting off her big mouth. It's disgusting. Women aren't supposed to be preachers." he said.

Mom stood up straight. "Who are you to say what a woman can do?" Her voice was angry.

Boleslaw didn't seem to hear. "When will you be able to help Beata with the cooking and cleaning? I don't want her to think you're mad at her."

"I'm still recovering from surgery. Why should I help her when she talks behind my back?" Mom asked.

Boleslaw's face was still red, but he sat up straighter. "I see how you look at my Beata. She's from a farm and she eats sloppy and she burps because she likes the beer. But she loves me from the bottom of her heart."

"She's trying to turn you against me," Mom said.

"No, it's not her, Virginia. I don't feel like I'm your husband anymore."

Mom looked confused. "Don't say that. Women get depressed after a baby and I'm still recovering from the caesarean. I need some time," Mom pleaded. She stood up, moved behind him and put her arms around his shoulders and her face against his cheek. "I know you want to feel loved."

Boleslaw put his large hands on Mom's arms. "Come sit down." Boleslaw pulled the white metal chair in front of him. "It's time to talk serious." Mom sat down facing him, her hand holding her stomach, and he leaned in close to her, his face like stone, his blue eyes wide and watery. "I always thought if I just have Virginia, my life would be perfect. I so much wanted a son ... my son. But you know that baby doesn't look anything like me ... all that black hair. How do you think Boleslaw feels?"

"That's from my side of the family which is black Irish. She's a sweet baby," Mom said.

"I'm a good husband and I deserve to be respected in my house."

"I know you're a good husband." Mom took a Kleenex out of her robe pocket and wiped her nose. Her hand was shaking.

"Listen. It's hard for Boleslaw to say this. People think Boleslaw is dumb Pollack, but Boleslaw is not dumb. I was willing to accept the baby if I thought you really loved me."

"But I do love you," Mom said. She took both of Boleslaw's big hands in hers.

Tears started rolling down Boleslaw's cheeks and off of his moustache. I'd never seen a man cry and I felt afraid. His head was bent over, and he reminded me of a boy. Then he looked straight in Mom's eyes. "We have to talk honest. I know you try, but you don't really love me."

He rubbed his palms over his eyes, cheeks, and moustache, as if they were a washrag, wiping the tears away. His eyes looked red and his shoulders were forward. I felt a knot in my throat.

Looking through the crack between the door and the wall, I could see Mom's eyes were moist. "Don't cry. I never wanted to hurt you. You're a good man," she said. Some tears fell onto the front of her robe. She kept holding onto Boleslaw's hands and he held hers. "I'm sorry," she said. Then both of them cried.

"I know you're recovering from surgery and I'm not going to pressure you, but we have to talk … to decide things. It's no good this way," Boleslaw said.

He's right. It's no good, I thought. I accidentally moved the door making noise.

Mom looked toward the door. Holding her stomach, she came behind the door and grabbed my arm and pushed me down the hallway. "I've told you before not to listen to adult conversations." She pulled me to the foot of the stairs and squeezed my arm. I knew better than to resist her. She still had tears in her eyes. She swatted me on the butt, but then put her hand over her stomach and bent over, as she had hurt herself. Everything stopped for me. I held my breath and stared at her because she had hardly ever spanked me. My shoulders shook from the sobbing. "You're becoming like Grandma."

"Go up to up to your room and stay there until I come and get you," she said.

I started up the stairs. "All you care about is that dumb baby."

Mom's jaw stiffened. "Don't you ever talk like that again or you'll get a real whippin'."

I knew she meant business. Upstairs, I slammed the door to my room and then I kicked the door, making a dent in the old wood.

I felt parts of my heart were being pulled out just the way Beata yanked up the carrots. I put my hand over my heart because I saw dead clumps of red flesh falling onto the floor and whimpering. I lay on the bed and cried until I was completely tired out.

CHAPTER THIRTY-TWO

Two weeks passed without Mom inviting me back to Boleslaw's house. So, what if I listened to adult conversations? Kids do things like that all the time, but that doesn't mean their mothers stop seeing them. I'd go into Mom's room and call out, "Mama I need to talk to you. Please don't leave me." Lilly Mae couldn't get me to stop me pulling out strands of my hair. I liked the pain. Another two weeks went by and I was alone in my room every night.

Then early Saturday morning as I looked out of the living room window, I couldn't believe my eyes. Mom drove up in Boleslaw's green Chevy station wagon. The baby was in the passenger seat and the back was stuffed with suitcases and boxes. Lilly Mae got to the car before I did. From the porch I heard her say, "Miss Virginia, I'm so glad you're back. Tessa misses you somethin' awful."

Through the car window, Mom handed Lilly Mae a package wrapped in brown butcher paper. "Put these steaks in the refrigerator."

"Sur' Miss Virginia." Lilly Mae passed me as she went inside.

The only thing I liked about Boleslaw's house were the steaks. When I asked Grandma for steaks, she said, "Hamburger is just as good as steak and people who follow the Lord are grateful for hamburger." I told myself to remember when I said my prayers that night to ask Jesus why he was so stingy with Grandma getting steaks.

I went down the front steps. Mom had gotten out of the car, but I didn't try to hug her. I was thinking about how she had swatted me the last time I saw her. I just stood there in my wrinkled dress and matted hair. She put her arm around me and pulled me close. Now, my mom was back and I felt better. But Gertrude started crying. Mom backed away. "I have to get the baby inside." She opened the back of the station wagon, and Lilly Mae came and took out the folded crib and lifted it into the house.

Mom took Gertrude out of the canvas car seat and she made a fussing sound. "It's all right, sweetheart," Mom cooed.

I followed Mom up the stairs. Now, it was always going to be the baby this and the baby that. I stomped up the stairs.

I heard a voice from inside the stairs say, "Please don't take it out on us. You know we love you."

Lilly Mae set up the crib in Mom's bedroom. Mom gently put Gertrude inside. Gertrude had on a white sweater, white knit hat, with her black hair spikes sticking out. Her little red fingers were closed in fists. I looked at Gertrude's mouth and her lips started moving like in the hospital. I heard her say, *"And God said; 'Let there be light'; and there was light. And God saw the light was good."*

I put my hands over my ears and I jumped up and down. I went to the crib and yelled, "Don't start that again. You think you're so smart, but you're not. Shut up. Baby's got a big mouth."

Gertrude's face scrunched up and she started crying. Mom grabbed me by the shoulders and turned me around. "You don't yell at the baby and stop that mean talk."

"She's like Grandma," I said.

"She is not."

I put my arms around Mom's waist and held tight. "I've been waiting so long for you to come back."

"I'm not going to hug you when you act that way." Mom loosened my arms and pushed me away. She picked up Gertrude, putting her over her shoulder. "Why don't you go and amuse yourself?" Mom turned her back to me and Gertrude looked at me and smiled.

I moved around in front of her. "But Mom, I need to talk to you, to tell you things."

"I know but later, Tessa. I'm tired and I have to get the boxes up here and soon I'll have to feed the baby." She put Gertrude back in the crib and patted her back.

I heard Grandma's new shoes clacking down the hall and she came into the room. She held a small photograph. She had on a new rose-colored linen dress, with a wide white collar. Her new shoes didn't look comfortable and had only small heels, like little beaks. The bunions on her feet pushed out the leather of the shoes. She held her head high and had on red lipstick and bright rouge on her cheeks. It wasn't Sunday, so I didn't know why she was dressed up. "Before you get comfortable, we have to get some things straight," Grandma said. Her lips turned down. She looked as if she smelled something bad.

"I noticed you were wearing makeup at the hospital. When did you start wearing lipstick?" Mom asked.

Grandma stood up straight and took a deep breath, which made her bosom stick out. "Because of my position. I'm a preacher now and my appearance is important."

Mom pushed her red hair over her shoulders and paused. Then she said, "Boleslaw told me that people are talking about you all over town."

Grandma had a shine in her eyes, the way she looked when she was preaching on the platform. "Well, I'm glad. People sit up and take notice of me now. I have the gifts. I'm doing the Lord's work." Grandma went to Gertrude in the crib and held up the photograph, looking from it to Gertrude. Grandma smiled. "Now that I see her up close, I can see she looks like me when I was a baby. It's a sign."

"I just said the same thing," I said.

Grandma fluffed her hair and stepped toward Mom. She had the look on her face I called her angry God face. "Now you listen to me. I won't have you bringing your Whoredom in here," Grandma spoke loudly as if an audience were listening to her.

Mom looked down at the suitcase she was unpacking. "Mother, can't we talk about this later?"

Grandma stepped close to Mom and said, "You're not going to be spreading your legs for every red-faced butcher, cowboy, or shoe salesman that comes along."

Mom stepped back as if she didn't want Grandma to breathe on her and turned away. Her face had a pinched look.

"I need to know if spreading your legs is something like to Get the Fuck?" I asked.

They both turned angry eyes on me. Mom's face became pale and stiff. Grandma took a deep breath and puffed herself up. "It's your fault Tessa has a nasty mouth on her." Grandma grabbed my arm. "If you ever say that again, I'll wash your mouth out with soap." Grandma shoved me away hard and turned to Mom. "You better get her under control. But she's not going to get me off of the subject, which is your Whoredom. I better not have to use that word in relation to you in my house again. I hope things are crystal clear," Grandma said.

"Whore … dom, I can use that word. It's like King … dom? It's in the Bible so I can say it. Whore … dom, Whore … dom" I said.

"Children don't say that," Grandma said.

"Tell me why? Whore … dom," I said.

"I don't have time for this. Do you want me to get that switch?" Grandma said to me.

Mom stood up straight and looked her right in the eyes. "Stop it. With all your religion, you should realize you're still my mother and the Lord wants you to take care of your own."

"You better be at the meeting I'm leading tomorrow afternoon," Grandma said close to Mom's face.

"I'm tired. I need to rest," Mom insisted.

"I suppose a second divorce is more tiring than the first. Tomorrow afternoon and no sulking. Put on a happy face. I want everybody to see the new you," Grandma said. Mom forced an ugly smile. Grandma clacked away in her small beak-heeled shoes.

I tried to hug Mom again, but she pushed me away again. She said, "I have to feed the baby now."

I did my Marching Dance and as I went toward the door, I sang, *"Oh baby, baby, yuck, yuck. Maybe she can go to Get the Fuck."* Mom rushed toward me, but I got away.

CHAPTER THIRTY-THREE

The next day was Sunday. In the afternoon, a lot of people started filing into the backyard. Mom stood in the back holding the baby and nodding at those she knew. Mrs. Thelma and her daughter Betty Lynn rushed up to Mom and stared at the baby. Before Mom could stop her, Mrs. Thelma pulled back the baby's hat and ran her hand over Gertrude's hair. "Now, I wonder where she got all that black hair?" When they walked away, Mom had one of those looks that could kill.

Mom sat in one of the folding chairs in the last row by the garage wall, holding Gertrude. That was where the four cowboys were standing against the wall. They were handsome, tanned, and standing all in a row. They pushed their cowboy hats back, and leaned against the wall, talking amongst themselves.

Pastor Gabriel Goodbank, with a red flushed face, wore his blue suit jacket stretched over his fat torso, with little clumps of flesh visible between the buttons of the white shirt. His horse teeth were yellow when he smiled. He put out his arm and escorted Grandma up the stairs and onto the center of the platform. Grandma's eyes became big, and she blushed as she stared into the Pastor's eyes. The pastor sat in a chair on the side of the platform and Grandma said, "We are so lucky to have him." I saw the red fiery tongues gather above Grandma's head, waiting for their chance to speak through her. Then Grandma took over the meeting and walked back and forth across the platform with her gloved hands raised to the sky. The tongues above her head wiggled and her lips moved letting them speak, "*Kaya mose koo ya base kooya mander wooya shoom laka yayaaash*" … and everything blurred together as she spoke faster.

Mom stared at Grandma and then at the people as they started to cry and get down on the ground in front of the platform. They rolled around as the Holy Ghost came into them. Mom's face looked like stone. She wasn't smiling and her face wasn't becoming shiny. She just slumped down in her chair. I said to myself, "So, Grandma isn't able to get the Holy Ghost to come into Mom or those cowboys in the back." I was happy Grandma wasn't as powerful as she thought.

Then Mom turned and looked at the cowboy right behind her. He pushed back his hat and put out his hand to her. Holding Gertrude with one arm, she took his hand and he put his other tanned hand over hers. She sat up straight and smiled in a way I hadn't seen in a long time. From under his hat, his golden-brown hair covered his ears, and his sideburns ran down his cheeks. His curly chest hair poked out of the top of his dark blue denim shirt. The outline of his muscles could be seen through his shirtsleeves and his leather belt had a large gold buckle.

He leaned forward, smiled, and stared into Mom's eyes. She kept looking at him and now her face was getting all shiny the way the Holy Ghost people's faces became shiny. Mom adjusted the towel under Gertrude's head so she wouldn't spit up on Mom's flower print dress. Then she took his hand again and he leaned in close to hear what she was whispering. Mom looked around to see if anyone was watching her, but they were all too busy moaning for the Lord. Holding Gertrude, Mom got up and went up the backstairs into the house.

Then I noticed the cowboy walking down the driveway. I felt afraid. I thought: Grandma wasn't going to like this. I waited until Grandma was facing the other way, then I snuck up the backstairs and went inside. The kitchen was empty, so I looked into the living room. Mom had put Gertrude on a blanket on the floor, and as I looked into the hallway, Mom was opening the front door. The cowboy came inside, his big brown boots squeaking on the floor. He took off his hat and kissed her on the cheek. Mom looked as beautiful as she was before Gertrude was born.

Mom took his hand and led him into the living room. I stood just out of sight next to the door, but where I could see into the living room.

The cowboy paused, looking at Gertrude. "She's pretty," he said. Mom had him sit on the couch. He put his hat on the coffee table and Mom sat next to him. I thought: No that's too close. Crossing her long legs, Mom let her skirt hike up. I heard the couch whispering to me in a feminine voice, "Trouble, trouble, on the double, make them stop." He put one arm around her shoulder and took her hand with his other hand. I felt a pang in my stomach. I wondered exactly when does the Whoredom start.

He kept looking into her eyes. "I'm Johnny Hartman, but people call me Buck. I'm from Boerne up north." He had a deep voice. He leaned back making himself comfortable.

"I've never been there."

"It's a little town just north of San Antonio."

"So why did you come to Yoakum?" Mom asked.

"My rodeo buddy Tommy and I are training some horses here and then we're going down to the rodeo in Sinton and then on down to the one in Corpus Christi."

"So, you're a rodeo cowboy," Mom said.

"Yes, ma'am, but I also have a little spread outside of Boerne. It's some of the best ranch country anywhere."

"What events are you in?" Mom asked.

"Bare-back bronc riding, bull riding, team roping and tie-down roping … just about everything."

"I'm going to be a country-western singer. I write my own songs."

"I like an ambitious woman. Where have you played?"

"Only in the diner where I worked."

"As far as I'm concerned, country music is the only real music," Buck said.

I relaxed. They're talking so maybe the Whoredom wasn't going to start after all. Mom didn't know that sometimes women from the meeting entered the kitchen and when no one was watching they snooped around the house. They wanted to see if Grandma kept things cleaned up enough for the Lord. Once I found an old woman looking in Grandma's doll closet. I snuck up behind the old woman and said, "Lady, the Holy Ghost isn't in the closet."

Since I couldn't let Grandma find out about Mom and the cowboy, I went and locked the kitchen door from the inside.

I poured lemonade into two glasses. I had to do something to keep Mom from being sent away again. I put the glasses on a tray and went into the living room and stood there. Buck was trying to kiss Mom, but she had her hand on his chest keeping him away. They didn't notice me. I cleared my throat and Mom looked at me. Buck kept his arm around her.

"Tessa, why aren't you outside?" Mom asked.

"I'm so tired of those meetings. I thought you might want some lemonade." I put the glasses on the table in front of them.

"That's sweet of you, but you better not be sneaking around," she said.

"I locked the kitchen door so no one can come in. Sometimes women from the meeting come in to use the upstairs bathroom and then they walk down the front stairs like they own the place."

"Even with a portable toilet outside?" Mom asked.

"That's just for the men. Grandma says she doesn't want the women to share the outside toilet with the dirty men. She says the men pee on the floor."

"They will have to use the bathroom by the laundry room. They won't know that's the one Lilly Mae uses." She turned to Buck. "This is my daughter Tessa."

Buck smiled. He had smile lines on his tanned face. Up close, I saw he had green eyes. He reached out his hand for me to shake. "Buck Hartman."

"He's a rodeo cowboy," Mom said.

I took his hand and it felt warm, strong, and rough. "What a lovely girl. I bet she's smart too," he said.

"Yes, I am smart and I remember things." I pulled on my hair.

"Don't brag about yourself and stop pulling on your hair. If you don't want to go to the meeting, then go upstairs," Mom said.

I picked up a Bible from an end table and held it up. "Don't you remember what Grandma said … you know from the Bible … that nasty woman?"

Mom said to me, "Tessa, put that Bible down. And don't talk about it." Mom looked at Buck. "My mother has lost her mind over religion. I'm stuck here in this crazy place."

Buck took one of Mom's hands and turned it over. "Do you know you have pretty hands?"

"Thank you. I'm at a bit of a low point."

Buck squeezed her hand and held onto it. "Why?"

"I just got divorced and I had to move back here," Mom said.

"Was he the father of your children?"

"He was Gertrude's father."

I wanted to stamp my feet and say she was lying but I didn't dare open my mouth.

"What about Tessa?" Buck asked.

"This was my second divorce. I'm not good at relationships."

"I don't believe that. Maybe you don't want to be tied down," Buck said.

Mom looked at Buck. "Most women want to succeed at marriage. But tell me about you. You don't look like the type to take all this preaching seriously."

Buck still had his arm around Mom and he pulled her closer. "I got over that years ago."

"So, what got you over religion?" Mom asked.

"My father was the bad draw of my life. He was a rancher, but imagined himself a preacher. Any religion I might have had got whipped out of me," he said.

"Then what brought you to our genuine Holy Ghost revelation here in our backyard?"

"Everybody is talking about your mother. My friends wanted a look-see and we heard the food is really good," he answered.

I heard the feminine voice from the couch again, "He's not leaving. Hurry. You have to try harder."

I jumped up and down on one foot then the other. "Mom, please remember that woman in the Bible," I yelled.

"Tessa, don't yell and stop jumping around."

Buck looked me in the eyes and then back at Mom. His green eyes were so intense. "The preachers grab you right from the start. They stick pitchforks into your guts and turn you into a puppet," he said.

I was afraid. "You know how mad Grandma gets if you go against her." I did my Marching Dance trying to make Mom understand.

"Go upstairs right now," Mom said. I turned to leave and as I looked back, Mom had her head on Buck's shoulder. I walked into the front entry hall.

As I went upstairs, I yelled, "Jesus, please you have to stop the Whoredom now. I'll pray more if you do."

I heard Mom say, "I worry about what my mother's influence is doing to her."

I went into Mom's bedroom and took her makeup bag and then I went into my bedroom. In the middle of my room, I heard Grandma's voice from the meeting outside. "Raise your voice to the Lord, praise Jesus," she said.

The congregation's voices were deafening. I put my hands over my ears, but I couldn't shut them out. I went to the window and I stretched my arms out and pushed my matted hair back over my shoulder. I yelled, "Jesus, open up a hole and throw all these scaly abominations, especially Mrs. Thelma, Betty Lynn, and that nasty Carl into the fiery pit! And don't forget Carl's friends with their Vienna sausages also throw them into the fire. I see them burning. See, Grandma I can preach just like you. You're not so special, so shut up!"

I grabbed a pitcher of water and threw the water out the window, getting a couple of women wet. They looked up at me with their demon faces. I ducked out of sight and laughed.

I sat down and propped the mirror on my child's table and looked into it. For a moment I saw Grandma's face. That scared me. "No, Grandma, you can't be in me. I'm just like Mom. I look like her and I talk like her."

I brushed my curly hair trying to get the mattes out, but they wouldn't come out, so I brushed out the top layer over the tangled part. I put Mom's mascara on my eyelashes. But I wasn't good at it. I smeared black around my eyes. I did the lipstick well, even if it was over the edges of my lips. Looking in the mirror, I put a hand on each shoulder and hugged myself.

"Buck, so you're a rodeo cowboy. You're wonderful. Buck hold my hand." I put my hand out pretending he was holding it and walked around the room. "My father is a jerk. The Pastor ignored me and I didn't like Boleslaw, but now you're here. You're a real gentleman, and now that we're together maybe the Whoredom isn't such a bad thing after all."

CHAPTER THIRTY-FOUR

I'd been marking off the days on my calendar until my tenth birthday, so I knew that Buck had been sneaking into Mom's bedroom for three Sundays after that first one. The Saturday finally came that was my birthday. Mom told me to get dressed up because she was taking me to Randy's Hog on the Spit Barbeque for a birthday lunch.

Mom put on a new red dress, held tight at the waist with a white leather belt. The dress hugged her from the waist down. Because of the baby, she said that she had to pour herself into her girdle, and after awhile she'd be saying her girdle was killing her. She wore new red high heel shoes. Her wavy red hair hung down her back like a cape.

I put on my pink-checkered dress with a stiff petticoat that made my skirt fluff out. Standing up straight, I walked down the stairs behind Mom. My curly brown hair was down my back. I was beautiful, and people were going to look at me the way they looked at her. Outside, we got into Boleslaw's green Chevy station wagon.

When Grandma had asked Mom when she was taking back his car, Mom had said that Boleslaw had given it to her.

"There's a reason people think Polacks aren't very bright," Grandma said.

That Saturday when we were in the car and ready to leave, Grandma rushed out onto the front porch. She was wearing her green linen dress with her large bosom resting just above her waist. She wore one of her bucket hats and white gloves to protect her skin. She waved excitedly and called out, "Virginia, wait for me." Mom kept her head turned away, looking back down the driveway as we backed out.

"Grandma wants to come with us," I said.

"I don't want any arguments. We'll bring her some cake."

We drove away, leaving Grandma on the porch. Her shoulders slumped over, and she went back inside.

On the edge of town, the smell from smoke clouds billowing out of the back of Randy's Hog on the Spit Barbeque wafted across the asphalt highway. The dirt parking lot was filled with Ford and Chevy pickups with gun racks and American flag stickers. Mom parked between a pickup and a Cadillac. She looked in the rearview mirror, her large eyes sparkling. She put on more red lipstick and unbuttoned a couple of her buttons. She told me to pull down my skirt over my white petticoat. I wore my white patent leather shoes and held my white purse Mom had bought at the Five and Dime. We got out and Mom took out a couple of presents from the backseat and carried them inside.

Randy, with his gray hair and fat belly, was at the cash register greeting people, and he gave Mom a big smile. "Virginia, it's good to see you. I've saved the corner booth just like you wanted." He led us to a big round booth with a red plastic seat. In the center of the table was a cowboy boot vase filled with daisies. Large red and white checkered cloth napkins were next to the forks.

On the wall was an old wooden wagon that had been sliced in half, old saddles, western ropes and whips. I could see a layer of dust on them. Lower down on the walls above the booths were pictures of Old West cowboys and famous outlaws. I recognized a grumpy looking Billy the Kid. There were even pictures of women holding guns and whips. "I need a whip," I said.

As I slid into the round booth, the edge was cool against the back of my knees. Mom slid in next to me. I picked up a plastic menu with pictures of the food.

"This is a big booth," I said.

"Buck is coming also. I want you to have a chance to spend some time with him."

"Oh." I thought that Mom must have seen I was disappointed because it wasn't just Mom and me.

"When you get to know him, you'll like him," Mom said.

"I don't know."

"But, Tessa dear, please don't talk about those spirits you see."

"They're your relatives too. You should be glad I talk to them. Do you want them to be lonely?" I asked.

"I don't want him to think there's anything wrong with you. I mean there's nothing wrong with you. I just don't want him to think you're uh … different. Thank God you haven't been seeing those headless chickens you saw at Boleslaw's. That was terrible. Don't bring anything up like that, and don't start that crazy yelling."

I didn't like her bossing me. I just kicked my feet against the back of the booth and waved my arms. Mom grabbed my arms to make me sit still while she watched the door for Buck. Vicky, the waitress, came to our table. Her hair was piled up in a beehive with a pencil stuck behind her ear. She chewed gum, set down our water glasses, and said, "Virginia, it's been ages. I heard you got married again and had a baby."

"I was married."

"With you everything changes so quickly. You're like one of those, whatchamacallits? That's you. Nothing changes for me." She laughed showing her crooked teeth. She took her pencil from behind her ear. "Are you ready to order?"

"No, we're waiting for someone."

When Buck came through the front door, he was wearing a cowboy hat and black western shirt with embroidery across the front. His brown boots strode across the wooden floor. He was tall and strong and had a big smile. "Will you get a load of him," Vicky said. As he walked toward our booth, Vicky said, "Oh, I didn't know he was with you." And her eyes strayed from his green eyes down to his gold belt buckle. Other women in the restaurant turned and stared, their eyes moving up and down him, as if their eyes could touch him. At that moment, I was proud he was with my mom.

He moved my presents to the other side of the booth and slid in next to Mom. He put his arm around her and kissed her cheek. Vicky came with silverware for Buck. "We'll need another place setting," he said. He turned to Mom. "I hope you don't mind. I asked a buddy of mine to join us. He just got into town and he's staying with me out on Tommy's ranch."

"Oh," Mom said.

Another cowboy came in and walked toward our table. He had a scruffy beard and he wasn't as handsome as Buck. "Sit down. I want you to meet Virginia," Buck said. The other cowboy took off his hat and reached out his big hand for Mom to shake. "I'm Vern."

He slid into the booth on my side, putting his hat next to my presents. There was a sweat ring around his hat. I moved my presents away from it.

"This is my daughter, Tessa. It's her tenth birthday," Mom said.

His smile was warm and made me feel good, even though his front teeth stuck out and rested on his lower lip. "Well, little lady, we gotta celebrate."

Vicky came back and Mom ordered barbeque brisket sandwiches. Buck and Vern ordered baby back ribs, cold slaw, French fries, and a pitcher of beer.

Buck noticed the jukebox in the corner. "How about some music?" He went to the jukebox. It had bright yellow and green curved neon tubes around the front. Bubbles were moving through the tubes.

Buck selected a song and it started. *"I'm in luck. I got a beautiful woman who likes to cook ... Day and night she treats me right."*

Back at the table Buck put his arm around Mom and drew her close to him. "So, what do you think of my lady?" he asked Vern.

"I didn't know Yoakum had such pretty women," Vern said.

When our sandwiches were brought, I licked the sides of mine before the sauce dripped all over. It tasted like heaven. I wondered if Jesus served barbeque brisket sandwiches there. If he was going to call it heaven, he should provide them. Thinking about angels flying around eating dripping sandwiches made me laugh. But then angels probably had little angel servants to do their dirty laundry. I laughed from deep in my belly and kept it going because it felt so good.

Mom looked at me. "Tessa, remember what I told you." I wanted her to stop telling me what to do, so I laughed harder. "Stop that," she said.

But I had gotten Buck and Vern's attention. Seeing I could get some attention away from Mom, I kept laughing and Mom put her hand firmly on my leg, but I had trouble stopping the laughter.

"Mom doesn't want you to know that I see and hear things other people don't. I talk to spirits and I'm not supposed to tell you. It's a secret," I said. A couple of little laughs were bubbling up, but Mom's expression made me kill them. I burped instead.

"Is that so?" Buck said.

Mom looked at him. "She just wants attention."

"We're all a little different," Buck said. He took a long drink of beer and turned his attention back to Mom. "Vern's decided to go with Bear and me down to the rodeo in Sinton and then we'll go on down to the one in Corpus Christi. Early next year we'll be doing the big one in San Antonio."

Then Buck looked at Vern and said, "Recently, I've been drawing some real hogs. At San Antonio, I gotta draw better bulls and horses. I want another chance at Sidewinder. He'll be there."

"He's a real spinner. When has anyone done eight seconds on that bull? Jessie Martin got hung up on him. They said he busted his hand in twenty-four places. Nobody knows if he's going to come back," Vern said.

"I'll be the one to do the eight seconds," Buck said.

Mom looked at Buck. "Have you had any serious injuries?"

"It depends upon what you call serious. My cutting horse Storm busted his leg and had to be put down. That was one of my worst moments,"

Buck answered. He poured himself more beer. "But now I have my black stallion, Panther."

"Storm meant more to him than any woman, and he buried him next to his bedroom on his ranch," Vern said.

"Really, more than any woman?" Mom asked.

I wondered, is it possible to see the spirit of a horse? Anyway, stop talking about the horse and look at me. I propped my elbow on the table and stared wide-eyed at Buck. His green eyes made me feel something I hadn't felt before.

He couldn't avoid my stare. "Does Tessa ride?"

"She hasn't had anyone to teach her," Mom answered.

"I want to ride," I said. But he didn't hear me because his attention was back on Mom. She had that honey on her tongue that attracts the men. She pushed her red hair back over her shoulders.

Halfway through the meal, I saw Jeffery, my father, walk in. I couldn't believe my eyes, and it was as if needles shot through me. He wore on an expensive brown suede jacket. On his pinky finger was a diamond ring and he had on a gold belt buckle. Mom was so busy looking into Buck's eyes she didn't notice him. My father noticed us and sat at a table across the room and stared. He was alone. Why was he just staring? Why didn't he come over?

I told Vern I had to get out. He picked up the presents and his hat and let me slide out. "Be careful with my presents," I said.

Then Mom noticed Jeffrey as I started walking over to his table. "Tessa come back here."

"No," I said.

I was nervous, and I could feel the butterflies wiggling in my stomach. I took a deep breath and exhaled, and the butterflies flew out of my mouth and landed on the crisscrossed rafters on the ceiling. They made little moaning sounds.

I slid into his booth close to him, but not too close. He looked at me and I looked at his left eye that was slightly crossed in toward his nose and then I stared at his good right eye. I wondered how many people had made fun of him for having a crossed eye. But he was rich, so maybe people didn't make fun of him. He smiled, and his tanned face creased into lines around his eyes. He put his arm around my shoulder. "Hi, sweetheart. How's my girl?"

"Daddy, I haven't seen you in so long."

"I've been out of town working." He took his arm away from my shoulder.

"Daddy, at home I have a picture of you holding me when I was a baby."

"You do? That was years ago, sweetheart," he said. He looked sad as he looked down.

"I keep it so I won't forget you."

"I'm sorry, but things change. Adults can be busy." He looked over at Mom, Buck, and Vern and he lit a cigarette. "Who are those guys?" he asked.

"Mom's friends."

"They look all snuggled up like peas in a pod," he said.

"Why don't you come and see me?" Tears were at the edges of my eyes. I wiped the bottom of my eyelids to keep the moisture from falling. I wanted Mom to look at him and smile the way she looked at Buck, but she didn't look over.

"Last I heard your mother was married to Boleslaw the butcher. I couldn't call you there," he said.

"She sent me back to Grandma's awhile back and now she's back with Grandma too."

"Looks like she popped out that baby everyone was talking about," he said.

"Yes, Gertrude, Miss Noisy Face. She's not as smart as I am."

He kept looking back and forth from me to Mom and Buck. Buck looked over at him and then put his arm around Mom's shoulder. My father's neck tightened. "How long has she been cozying up to him?" he asked.

"Not very long. She wants me to spend some time with him. She says I'll like him."

"Is that so? She sure lines them up," he said.

"Daddy, do you know what day it is?"

"Should I?" He turned the gold ring around on his pinky finger. Then he took out a cigarette and lit it with his gold lighter.

"It's my tenth birthday."

"You don't say? Well sweetheart, you're almost grown up." He took out a twenty-dollar bill and handed it to me. "I'm sorry for forgetting. Here, get yourself something. I bet there's something over at the five and dime that you'd like." He kissed me on the forehead and then he looked back at Mom.

"Quit looking at her. She's not important. I'm right here. When I called your house, your mother said you weren't there. Why didn't you call me back at Grandma's?"

"Like I said, I've been out of town."

"But I want to see you. Don't you want to see me? How can I love you if you don't see me?"

He looked sad. "Things happen between a husband and wife, adult things. People hurt each other and it's hard to get over. I know it's difficult to understand. I'll call you next week, I promise."

He'd said that before. "I wish that was true. I'm your daughter. Would you see me if I was a boy?"

He put out his cigarette in the ashtray shaped like a bull's head. "That's not it. Now you better go back to your mama," he said.

"You can't tell me what to do. Grandma says your mother doesn't want you to see me. She says you're a mama's boy, that you do whatever your mother wants." I wished I hadn't said that because his neck and mouth tightened.

He slammed his hand down on the table. I jumped. "Your grandma has always talked shit. That's her specialty."

I felt the "divorce crack" pain in my heart and I tried to talk, but I couldn't find any words.

He wiped the tears off my cheeks with his fingers. "Tessa I'm sorry. It's not your fault. I know this can be hard. Maybe, I'm not so good for you after all."

It felt so good that he had touched me. "Don't say that." I pulled on my hair.

He took my hand away from my hair. "Now you go back to your mama," he said. He looked down as he turned the gold ring on his finger.

I stood up, turned away from him, and put my hand over my heart to keep any clumps from falling out. The butterflies still up on the rafters started moaning again.

Vern let me slide in over by Mom. He put my unopened presents next to me, but I didn't care about them now. Mom put her arm around my shoulder.

My father got up to leave. I'd failed again to make him care about me. He pushed his brown hair back and put his hat on. His jaw was set like steel as he walked out. His boots sounded heavy on the floor. I wanted to call out to him, but I didn't.

Then Buck looked over at the jukebox in the corner where there was also a guitar case. "Let's get this party started." He motioned to Vicky, the waitress, and told her to have Randy come over.

When Randy came to the table, Buck asked, "Do you have a guitar in that case? I'd like my girl here to sing us a little song."

"I can't. I'm not ready," Mom said.

"The only way to get ready is by doing it," Buck said. "Can you get that guitar out Randy?"

"Sure thing."

"Come on, beautiful," Buck said.

Mom looked around the room noticing there weren't many people in the restaurant. She went over by the jukebox and Randy handed her the guitar and he set up a microphone. At the tables were some old couples, the wives had bleached blond hair. Also, a couple of families had squirming kids. Mom saw that the people weren't watching her. Even though Mom's cheeks turned red, she sang, *"Men come and go like donkeys jumping, thinking they can fly. In the Texas dirt, men have big eyes and lying smiles. They hurt me to the bone, when I should have had a home. Hooved creatures stuck in the mud, chewing their cud. Rise up and fly away, don't say goodbye. Just leave my heart alone, so I can find a home."*

Buck and Vern smiled, and I felt so proud. I tried not to think about my father. I knew the song and I joined in singing from the table.

Mom stood by the jukebox, played the guitar, and danced. A couple of old men turned their heads, looking at her. I stood on the booth and danced at the table. I said, "I want people to look at me." I sang my own song loudly, *"Donkeys and birds have really big turds. Throw those turds around and you won't need any hot wonky … tonky …."* The old men stared at me and I gave them my prettiest smile.

Mom finished singing, *"Just leave my heart alone, so I can find a home."* The two old men watched her. Their wives, without even looking up, wiped the barbeque sauce from their lips and nudged their men to make them to stop looking at Mom.

Mom came back and sat down and said, "'Donkeys Jumping', I know that wasn't very good." She had a couple of wet spots from tears on her blouse.

Buck put his arm around her shoulder. "Don't worry, you're doing fine."

The waitress, Vicky, brought my chocolate birthday cake with lit candles to the table. I kicked my legs against the back of the booth while Mom, Buck, and Vern sang me Happy Birthday. I ate as much cake as I could before Mom said we had to get back. In the parking lot, Mom put my unopened presents in the car. She had said I'd open them at home. Buck kissed Mom, holding her close. Then kicking up dust, Buck and Vern drove off in Buck's pickup.

In the car, Mom loosened her white belt and with the rest of my birthday cake in a box on my lap, we drove home. Mom started singing her new unfinished song, "Kiss This Town Goodbye." Then she turned to me. "What do you think of Buck?"

"He was talking to Vern a lot." Through the opening in the box I was sticking my finger in the icing and licking it.

"Yes, but do you like him?"

"Yeah, I guess so. He's better than The Big Slaw Grabber." I moved my fingers grabbing at the air like he grabbed at her. "But why weren't you nice to my father?"

"I know this is hard for you, but things aren't going to change between us. It's not your fault."

"I know it's not my fault. It's your fault. If you'd been nicer to him, he wouldn't have ignored me. You're nice to everybody else," I said.

"Tessa, I wish I could make you understand, but I can't talk about this anymore."

"Well, I'm going to talk about it if I want to."

CHAPTER THIRTY-FIVE

The next day, Sunday, was the same as usual, with Buck sneaking up to Mom's room during Grandma's meeting. I looked through the keyhole and I saw them kissing, but I couldn't hear anything because of the shouting of "Save me Jesus" from the backyard. When I saw him put his arms around Mom, it occurred to me that the Whoredom and to Get the Fuck might be the same thing. I knew the Whoredom could get a woman dragged right into hell. I was glad Mom didn't seem to be afraid of it.

Later that night, when Grandma had fallen asleep in her chair, Buck was gone and Mom had gone to bed early. I was alone in my room. The wind blew outside, a twisted angry whine and I heard a light tapping on the roof. I hoped it was the spirit children calling to me. Since that night when we went to the hospital, Eunice hadn't been able to get them to come again. I looked out my window and I saw that the first drops of rain were making the noise. It started raining harder. The rasping noise of the wind blew through the trees and branches like witches' hands scratching at the windows. Water falling from the tips of the leaves made the trees seem to weep and their tears became puddles. It rained harder and water fingers stabbed at the earth. I stretched out my arms like the outstretched branches of the large oak tree outside my window. The wind began violently blowing and the trees poured even more tears. The trees looked like large, battered people stranded in the darkness. But their voices came to me, "We know that you're really a beautiful princess. Someday, your father and everybody else will recognize you for the royalty that you truly are." I moved my arms violently pretending I was a tree being blown around and suddenly tears came to my eyes. I thought: Will people ever see the real me? I got into bed and covered my face with the blankets.

It rained cats and dogs for six nights and five days. The only thing people could talk about was how the river was flooding the homes and businesses, and nobody could remember anything like it. Trees crashed onto things, but I knew it was because they got tired of standing alone with no one paying attention to them. I went outside in the rain and I told the trees around my house that I loved them and asked them not to fall on Grandma's house.

People telephoned the house and Grandma spent a lot of time on the phone. Sitting at the table in the entry hall, holding the black telephone receiver, she told whoever called, "God is flooding Yoakum because Yoakum is wallowing in the Whoredom. The people wallow in it at night in the bars. They're wallowing in it in their houses, on their farms, in the boarded-up buildings in the old western part of town. That's where the young ones start their dirty Whoredom careers. The men go to colored town to indulge their fleshy fornication."

That day when I looked around the corner, I saw Grandma was excited and breathing heavily. Her legs were apart and her blue linen skirt was hiked up. Her nylon stockings came only above her knees, held tightly by garters. The white flesh of her thighs was bunched out above the garters. "I see it in the darkness, the flesh is rubbing, the protrusions are rubbing … the bulges like filthy snakes are thrusting … thrusting. Oh … These visions are invading my mind and I can't make them go away," she said loudly. Grandma put a hand across her bosom and let out a moan. She paused, listening to the person on the phone. "Of course, I'm all right. The

Lord is punishing us the way he punished Noah. The Reverend Goodbank and I have the mission of trying to save these people. Isn't he wonderful? I can't stop thinking about him." She kept her hand on one of her breasts. She was sweating and then she moaned some more. Then she paused again and said, "The nastiness makes me want to scream, but we are so lucky to have the Reverend Goodbank." Then her legs moved farther apart and she yelled, "Save me, Jesus … please." I heard a loud voice coming through the phone and Grandma calmed down a bit. "I've told you that Jesus wants the Reverend Goodbank and me to show everyone what the sin really is. Remember you need us," she spoke loudly. When she put the phone back in the receiver, her face was flushed. When she noticed she had a hand on her breast, she removed it. Her chest heaved up and down.

I rushed into the hallway. "Grandma, are you all right?" I said.

She fixed her glassy eyes on me. "I'm fine. It's the sin that's penetrating, pushing into everything."

"Can I do anything to help you with the sin? I could clean my room."

"You? No, you're like your mother." Her legs were spread and her skirt was still above her knees.

"Grandma, you told me ladies keep their skirts down and imagine their legs to be glued together."

She noticed her skirt hiked up and pulled it down. "Tessa, quit sneaking around and go find something to do."

I went into my room and prayed, "Jesus, please don't punish Mom because she likes the Whoredom. Please don't flood our house, because Grandma will say it's Mom's fault and send her away again."

CHAPTER THIRTY-SIX

I woke up early Saturday morning. Everything was quiet and the sunlight coming through the blinds made light squares on my blankets. I went out onto the back-porch and looked around the backyard where everything was shiny and wet. The canvas covering Grandma's wooden preaching platform was completely ripped apart with pieces hanging from its frame. Puddles were in the yard and on the platform. A branch from the old oak tree had fallen on the upright pine pulpit, splitting it. A couple of other large branches had fallen through the floor of the platform. Jagged edges of wood were sticking up. Where the tree branches were torn away, a wound was left with beads of sap. I listened, and I heard a faint female voice coming from the tree softly moaning as if in pain. "Help me," the voice said.

The yard had always been higher on the oak tree side and mud had flowed up against the side of the garage. The folding chairs leaning up against the garage were stuck in a sea of mud.

I got my rain boots from the back-porch and put them on. I imagined I was going forth like Noah to explore this new land after the flood. I climbed up onto the ripped-up platform and carefully walked around where the branches hadn't fallen. Was God angry with Grandma? Was God angry with everybody? I went around the other side of the platform by the back fence and looked at the backside of the oak tree and I saw something round and yellowish white with two partially exposed holes sticking out of the mud. That had never been in our backyard before and I felt a chill. But it beckoned to me. I went inside and got some bath mats and towels from the laundry. Going back outside, I trudged through the mud, my rain boots making a sucking sound.

Standing next to it, I could see it was only partially exposed, but I knew what it was. I'd seen cow's skulls and I'd seen pictures of human skulls and it was a human skull. My whole body shook and, even though my hand was shaking, I put down a bath mat and sat next to the skull. With a towel, I began wiping away the mud. As I exposed more of the skull, it seemed to be staring at me from the holes where the eyes should have been. I scooped away the mud from the jaw and, using the towel, wiped it until the yellow teeth were exposed. Then I stuck both hands down in the mud where I thought I'd find the chest bones. I took away gobs of mud and reached back into the mud and then I felt a bone. My hand shook but I closed it around a curved hard bone, maybe a rib. While digging away the mud from the ribs, some rotted fabric came off into my hands. When I had the ribs partially dug out, I stuck my hands in the mud and I touched long bones that I thought were an arm. I moved to where the hand should have been and I continued digging away the mud and cloth. I felt little pieces of bone like pebbles, and I pulled up one finger-shaped piece. Reaching back into the mud, I gently touched more small bones. I didn't want to mess them all up because I thought the skeleton wouldn't like that. Now that a large part of the skeleton was partially sticking out of the mud, my stomach twisted and even though I felt afraid, I took a deep breath. I had found it, so it was mine. I didn't care that I was getting mud all over my dress.

After moving my bath mat to the other side, I started digging where I thought I'd find the other arm. I uncovered two yellow cracked long bones and they lay there as if saying, "Secrets don't stay buried forever." I ran my finger in the mud along one of the bones. It felt cold. Then I touched something in the mud by the ribs. I pulled it out. It was a chain with an old gold watch attached. Carefully wiping it, I opened it. The engraving was barely visible. Henry ... Henry O ... Henry O'Connell. I said out loud, "This is Old Man Henry's watch. So, this had to be my great-grandfather's skeleton. What was he doing out here?" My body tingled, and my breath came in short bursts. The skeleton must have been glad it was finally found.

Then I remembered overhearing Mrs. Thelma talking to Betty Lynn in the Five and Dime. She had called it a "ghastly secret." She said that two women in the neighborhood had heard a gunshot at this house a few days before Old Man Henry supposedly left town. Mrs. Thelma had said there had always been talk that Eunice might have taken things into her own hands, but she was well respected. A lot of people didn't like Old Man Henry, so nobody cared if he had left town.

I looked at the skeleton and spoke, "You must be lonely." I laid my hand across its forehead.

Then I seemed to hear a deep man's voice, but I couldn't tell where it was coming from. "Who's there?" the voice asked. My body shook and I jerked my arm back. I looked around to see where the voice was coming from and I saw a dark shape by the tree. Maybe this skeleton wasn't mine after all. I forced myself to touch the forehead again. Then I heard a forceful voice, "Who ah ... ah ... are you?" The voice came from the dark shape and it definitely was a man's voice.

"I'm Tessa. Who are you?" I wiped my hands down the front of my dress.

"I'm Henry. It's like I'm in a fa ... ah ... fog. Where am I? Why can't I ... ma ... maa ... move?"

"I've been digging in the mud and you're stuck out here in my backyard," I said. I looked around, but all I could see was the dark shape and the voice sounded as if it was talking through water. The wind blew and it felt as if little knives were sticking into me.

"You're not making sense, but you tell that bitch of a wife, Eu … Eu … Eunice, that she can't lock me out of my house," he spoke in a slurred voice. The dark shape was turning into a man.

His mention of Eunice's gave me chills. "Do you know Eunice?"

"Of course, I know Eunice, that foaming hyena ma … ma … mouth. I can't wait to get my hands on her. Sh … sh … she better let me in." I could now make out a man's bulging eyes in the shape.

"I think these are your bones, and you're too muddy to bring inside." I pushed my hair back, not caring I was getting mud in it.

"Why can't I see or feel anything? Nothing seems so … saa … solid. What is this pla … pla … place?" Henry's strong voice pushed itself into my head, and now I could clearly see the dark shape of a man standing by the oak tree. He had a neat gray beard, and wore cowboy boots, a western suit jacket, and a fancy vest underneath. He turned his head to the side as if trying to see something.

"Eunice is my great-grandmother. I love her, and no old skeleton man is going to scare me." I tried to sound forceful.

"That's nonsense. Sss … ssta … Stop that lying. Where's my good-for-nothing daughter, Bernice? Get her out here," Old Man Henry said.

"She's my grandma and my mother is Virginia, her daughter."

"Bernice, pregnant and a mother? She's not married. I'll whip her good for thaa … that."

"You're mean and you're dead and I don't have to listen to you. You stop that talk now or I'll throw the mud back over your skeleton and leave you out here." I stood up. "But the watch is mine."

"Wait, don't leave me. It's dark. I'm lonely. I can't get my bearings." His voice sounded as if he was on the verge of tears.

"I think you're my great-grandfather Henry. You're in what Eunice calls the spirit world. You're a spirit and you're in a place where you go when you die." I tried to make my voice sound like I knew what I was talking about.

"I've got to stop drinking. Could you call a doctor?" Standing by the oak tree, he turned his head from one side to the other, still trying to see something. "Help! I can't see. I must be temporarily blind. Somebody help me!" he yelled.

"Nobody can hear you. You're dead. Really dead."

"No … I don't believe you. Where are we? Tell me exactly what you see," he insisted.

"I'm in the backyard over by the big oak tree. I'm sitting next to your skeleton. We had a lot of rain and flooding and it came up from the mud. I found your gold watch and all your muddy bones."

"A skeleton, oh my god. I think I'm starting to re … re … remember." He put his face close to the oak tree. "Yes, that's the oak tree. I can barely see it." Henry broke down crying. He said, "I don't know what's happening to me. I've never cried before. Crying is a weakness."

I felt his pain. "Don't cry, Great-granddaddy." I cried also and wiped my face with my muddy hands.

"Now, it's coming back. She did this." His body shook and his face contorted. "Does anybody know I that I died?"

"I heard Mrs. Thelma say how nobody ever knew what happened to you. People said you ran off with one of your colored whores. What is a whore? No one will tell me."

"How old are you?" he asked.

"Ten-years-old."

"And you say you're my great-granddaughter. Well, if I'm in that spirit world Eunice always talked about, why can't I see her? That nasty old fart."

"Stop it. I don't have to listen to you. Goodbye." I stood up, but my boots were stuck in the mud and I fell back down.

"No, don't go. Please. I'm not used to anybody telling me what to do. Wait, I'm starting to see something. It's blurry. That's the back of my house but the paint is peeling off."

I felt a presence, as if it were a wind, brush past me. I saw a shadowy outline in an old-fashioned dress. Then the figure became clear. It was Eunice. "Tessa, you woke the bastard up," Eunice said in an angry voice.

The wind brushed the oak tree, there was a crack, and a branch fell on the wooden crucifix. By the tree, I could now see two figures. Eunice had on her long dress with the small buttons up the front. She was standing next to Old Man Henry in his western suit and cowboy boots. Eunice's wavy brown hair was down her back and she pointed her white-gloved finger at him. "Henry, go back to your hellish rathole."

"Now I remember. How could you murder me and with my own gun? I would never have dumped you like trash in the backyard?" Henry yelled.

"All you ever did was give money to your colored whores. I put up with it while you kept it quiet, but you had to build that one a house and drive around town with her."

"A man of my position deserved a decent bah … bu … burial," Henry said.

"Do you realize the shame I had to live with? You with your whore-sniffing penis," Eunice, yelled at him. The wind blew harder and more branches fell onto the preaching platform.

"Eunice, you loved me once." Tears rolled down Henry's cheeks. "Eunice, did you put me in this dark place?" He crossed his arms to try to maintain some control.

Eunice put her face close to his. "You put yourself there because you never believed in anything. Go back into your darkness."

I felt angry winds blowing around me. My stomach was twisting. "Stop it both of you. I have enough arguing between Grandma and my mother!" I yelled.

Behind me, I heard the back-screen door open and slam closed. I heard someone walking on the platform behind me. "Childs, you know your mama and grandma don't want you talkin' to yourself," Lilly Mae said as she put her hand on my shoulder. Then she noticed the skeleton. "Oh, my God. Lordy, oh Lordy, look what's washed up from the rains."

"He's my great-grandfather Old Man Henry. I found his watch." I showed her his watch, but I wouldn't let her touch it.

"I've been thinkin' all these years he was out here," Lilly Mae said. I started wiping the bones again. "Stop doin' that," Lilly Mae insisted.

"I have to clean him up. He even talks to me."

"Stop that crazy talkin'. I told you to stop messing wit them spirits. Now look what you've done. Go inside," Lilly Mae said. She put a towel over his skull.

"Don't cover his face. He doesn't like the dark," I said.

"Tessa, go inside now." As I went inside, Lilly Mae covered the skeleton with some towels.

I stood behind the door and watched as Lilly Mae told Grandma that her father's bones had floated up in the backyard. Grandma yelled. "I don't want this to affect my preaching. It's the sins of the father coming back on me. Jesus, please do something; it's not my fault. It's not fair." Grandma broke down sobbing.

"Years ago, I overhear your mama saying somethin' 'bout this. I think you knew 'bout it."

I saw Lilly Mae following Grandma as she rushed out onto the back-porch and started grabbing gardening tools from the shelf and throwing them on the floor. "No, I didn't know. I mean I'd forgotten," Grandma said.

"You're not supposed to forget somethin' like that." Lilly Mae picked up the tools from the floor.

"My mother wouldn't let me speak of it. As the years went by, I thought I'd dreamt it. Lilly Mae, help me bury him deeper. No one has to know," Grandma pleaded. She picked up a small shovel and looked at it and then she threw it down. She yelled, "Help me get a bigger shovel from the garage!"

"I can't do that. You has to call the police."

"But this will get all over town. I can't bear to have people saying bad things about me. It hurts," Grandma moaned.

In the entry hall, Lilly Mae picked up the phone. I took it from her. I said, "I'll make the call."

Two policemen from town came and dug out all the bones, and they stood there looking at them as though the bones might say something, but the bones remained silent. I couldn't hear or see Old Man Henry with all the people there. One policeman brought Mom out and she stared at the bones too. Her face was white and she bit her lip.

Then a man came who they said was a special kind of doctor and they loaded the skeleton piece by piece onto a stretcher. The hand bones were put in little piles and they covered the bones with a sheet. When they lifted the stretcher, some of the finger bones slid off onto the ground. I yelled, "Hey, you be careful. That's my great-grandfather." Then one policeman picked up the bones and put them back under the sheet and they loaded everything into the ambulance.

Soon after the police left, the phone rang. From behind the kitchen door, I listened to Grandma talking to Mrs. Thelma. "You know I was a teenager when he disappeared. I pushed it of my mind, but it's coming back now. It was my mother who shot her whoring husband. I'm blameless."

I peeked around the door and Grandma wiped the tears and the rouge from her round cheeks as she clutched the black telephone receiver. She continued, "My mother should have considered what this would do to me to have him float up in the backyard. Just as my star is rising, now this happens." Tears fell onto her linen dress making a wet spot on her bosom. "What do you mean you want to know what he looked like?"

As Grandma listened, her lips trembled, and she leaned her head and wrinkled neck forward like a turtle. Then she said, "No, you can't see him. The police took him away. We're not allowed to bury people in the backyard. I have to go." Grandma's hand was shaking, and she pounded the receiver on the telephone table making dents in it. Then she kicked the table, knocking it over, hurting her foot.

CHAPTER THIRTY-SEVEN

Before I moved to Boleslaw's, I hadn't played any more tricks on Cathy and we had become friends again. I missed her while I was away. Back at my old school the next Monday, I was on the playground with Cathy. Lilly Mae had braided my hair and put a pink bow on each braid. Cathy had her curly brown hair pulled back into a ponytail. People said that Cathy's turned-up nose made her look cute. I didn't care what they said because I was pretty, too.

Since I'd been away, she had become friends with Molly. Molly had short curly black hair and was putting herself between Cathy and me. Just when I was happy to be back with Cathy, Molly came over, put her face close to Cathy and they laughed and whispered back and forth. It felt like bees stinging me in the heart.

At least when the three of us were together, Carl's friends, the ones he'd told that he'd seen my pussy, didn't come up to me and say they wanted to see it too. And they weren't bullying me so much now because I brought a metal box with batteries and wires to school. I told them it was a science project with invisible waves that could shrink their Vienna sausages into little worms. When I pointed it at them, they moved away from me.

We three were sitting on the bench by the swings next to a chain-link fence. Cathy tossed her thick ponytail over her shoulders.

"My mom said the police came to your house. So why did they come?" she asked.

Cathy was holding Molly's hand and they were leaning close to each other and smiling as if they had a secret. I felt left out. Cathy was my only friend and I had to get her back.

I leaned in close to them. "The police were at my house for hours. They asked me questions. It was a matter of life and death," I said.

That got Cathy's attention and she let go of Molly's hand. Both of them became silent. "Well, go on, tell us," Cathy said.

I told them, "After the storm, I found a skull sticking out of the ground in the backyard. It was a human skull. I put my fingers in the holes where the eyes would have been, and I scooped out the mud." Their eyes got wide. "It was the skeleton of my great-grandfather Old Man Henry." I tossed my braids over my shoulders. I said, "I put my hand on his forehead and he spoke to me." They inched away from me, but I moved in right next to them. Cathy stood up. Molly looked as if she would cry.

"Tessa, stop. You're always trying to make me believe that you see or hear things that aren't there, like spirits. You want me to think you have special powers. I don't believe you." Cathy sat back down and stuck her chin out. Her turned-up nose made her look as if she could take on anything. She whispered something in Molly's ear.

Even though their whispering hurt, I leaned forward. "Please believe me. I don't have anyone else I can talk to."

Cathy faced me. Her face was cold. "My mom says talking to spirits is Looney Tunes." Cathy and Molly faced each other and played pat-a-cake saying Looney Tunes over and over.

Other kids on the playground turned and looked at me. I wanted to scream, but didn't dare. Then a dark emptiness descended on me. I was all alone. The bell rang ending recess and the two of them arm in arm walked in front of me back to class.

CHAPTER THIRTY-EIGHT

The next week in the afternoon, I sat in the back of the class by the window. My curly hair was in a ponytail and I was wearing my pink dress with the white lace collar. The golden sunlight fell across my desk revealing specs of dust in its light. I figured that the dust was probably there all the time, but couldn't be seen unless the light hit it just right. On the wall at the bottom of the window, a small brown spider inched its way along. I heard the spider's squeaky voice say, "Look at the teacher. Don't think about squashing me like those other kids."

At the front of the class, old eagle-eyed Miss Stanley stood next to the blackboard. Her back was straight, and her gray hair was wrapped in such a tight bun that it looked like it grew out of the back of her head. She was the leader of this room of freshly washed fourth graders.

Miss Stanley cleared her throat often, as if something was permanently stuck in her craw. She unfolded four well-worn pictures and tacked them on the wall next to the blackboard. One was a picture of an old stone building with two columns on each side of the thick wooden door. Above the door, the roof formed a curious round semi-circle shape at the top.

The other pictures were of old-fashioned men, two in military uniforms, one with a single star on his collar and the other with a high fancy gold collar and some gold strings hanging on his shoulders. The third one had sideburns and a long straight nose. He wore a black suit, and his arms were folded in front of him, making him look strict.

Then squeaking the chalk on the blackboard, she wrote *Alamo & Siege.* She pointed with the pointer, which also doubled as a rod for knuckle whacking, to the word *Siege.* "A siege is where an army surrounds a place and won't let anyone in or out until everyone inside surrenders. At the Alamo, who surrounded the Texans?" she asked. A few girls raised their hands. I knew the answer, but I didn't raise my hand. Miss Stanley pointed to Cathy in the front. "The Mexicans," she answered. She smiled as if she'd just gotten the biggest piece of cake.

"It was the Mexican army led by President General Antonio Lopez de Santa Ana," Miss Stanley added. She stuck the pointer on the nose of the military man with the high gold collar. Then she turned to the class with her arms crossed, holding the pointer as she searched the room for any infractions of her rules. The room was silent.

The sun was still streaming through the window onto my desk. For a second, I thought I saw a shadow flicker through the sunlight. I looked toward the window, but I saw nothing. Then I felt a presence next to me and I smelled cigar smoke. I looked around to see where the cigar might be. Then something brushed over my shoulder and I jumped.

"Tessa, I have to talk to you." It was Old Man Henry. His voice was in my ears, my head, and all around me. I froze, and I looked around to see if anyone else had heard him, but no one had.

The spider had stopped farther along the wall. Its faint voice whispered, "I can't help you."

At the front, Miss Stanley pointed to the picture of the man with the sideburns in the black suit and said, "James Bowie." Then she pointed to the man with the single star on his collar and continued, "And Lieutenant Colonel William Barrett Travis were co-commanders of the 250 men at the Alamo."

"Tessa, you have to listen to me." Old Man Henry's voice was so strong it blocked out everything else. His presence felt heavy and sucked up the air around me. I looked toward the window. He was in his brown western suit jacket, with a black vest and wearing a cowboy hat. How could he be here? My stomach hurt and I felt cold all over.

"Tessa, I need your help." Now his presence pressed against me as I tried to breathe. I pinched my arm to make him go away, but he didn't.

"You can't be here," I whispered.

"Don't ignore me," Old Man Henry said forcefully right in my ear. It felt as if he was touching my shoulder. I kept pinching myself, and then I pulled on my hair until it hurt, while I kept looking straight ahead at the teacher. "Go away, Great-granddaddy, and take that cigar smell with you."

I looked around the room and Miss Stanley was talking in her grating voice about a letter Commander Travis had written. She wrote on the blackboard *Victory or Death.*

Old Man Henry pressed against me harder. I glanced at him then quickly looked back to the front of the room. I bit my lip and bounced my legs.

"You can't ignore me," he said.

"I'm in school and you can't butt in," I whispered.

"I can't find Eunice. You have to bring her to me," he insisted. I felt confused, and dizzy, and for a moment I thought I was back in the yard with the skeleton. I smelled the mud and I pulled harder on my hair.

"You're not my boss. I can't bring her to you." I didn't realize my voice was becoming louder. The kids around me were looking at me and smiling. Two seats away from me, Carl stuck his tongue out. Miss Stanley at the blackboard was saying, "The Battle of the Alamo was a turning point in the Texas Revolution. All the Texans were slaughtered, but to this day their spirits live on with us."

I bit my lip and pulled out some strands of my hair to keep from screaming. I saw Carl imitate me pulling on my hair and he crossed his eyes.

"You have to help me," Old Man Henry said.

"I'm sorry that you were murdered but you have to go away."

The kids around me whispered, "Tessa's talking to herself."

"I'm lonely. I've never felt like this." Old Man Henry started crying.

"Please, don't cry. I'm learning about the Alamo." My voice was loud and sounded as if it weren't a part of me.

I looked to the front of the classroom and Miss Stanley had stopped talking. All of a sudden, Old Man Henry stood at the blackboard. "You can learn about the Alamo some other time!" he shouted. He did a little dance making fun of Miss Stanley.

"Stop! I want to learn. Don't make fun of Miss Stanley. Now, get away from that blackboard," I shouted back before I realized what I was doing.

I looked at the class and everyone's eyes; brown eyes, blue eyes, and green eyes were staring at me. The room was full of open silent mouths. Cathy put her finger across her mouth to signal me to be quiet. Miss Stanley, holding her pointer, had on her knuckle whacking face as she moved deliberately down the aisle toward me. "Tessa, we're glad you want to learn about the Alamo. We also want to learn about the Alamo. Who were you talking to?"

My cheeks felt hot. "Nobody." I tried to hold back my tears.

She whacked her pointer against my desk and I jumped. Carl and his friends giggled. "Don't lie to me. You were talking to yourself. Come here." She walked back to her desk and scratched forcefully on a piece of paper. I wiped tears from my red cheeks as I went to the front of the room. She handed me the note. As if it were on fire, I took it between my index finger and thumb.

"Take this to the principal's office," she commanded.

I left the room and everyone's eyes burned holes into my back. In the hallway, my stomach twisted becasue Miss Stanley's notes had the power to get a kid swatted. Boys were swatted on their rears with a paddle, while girls had to put out their palms to be hit with a rod or ruler. For some reason, girls' rears were more delicate and couldn't be hit. The principal looked mean as he read the note. "I supposed this is that new mental thing." He sent me to the nurse's office.

Nurse Channing, a large-bosomed, heavy-set woman, was behind her desk reading a movie magazine. She quickly stuffed it in the drawer overflowing with other movie magazines. She read the note and had me sit next to her while she took my temperature. Then she stuck a big popsicle stick in my mouth and looked down my throat. She took it out and stared into my eyes. "You can tell me if there's something unusual happening at your home. Who is that person Miss Stanley heard you talking to?" I looked at her with angry eyes, but didn't answer. "I know all about a little girl's fantasies," Nurse Channing said.

I didn't answer.

"You have to tell me. We don't allow students to imagine things that aren't there. We take pride in the fact that our students here are very normal," she said.

I looked straight ahead.

"Look at me. I'm tired of stubborn uncooperative students. Little lady, you're going to sit in that chair until you tell me."

I stared at her and she stared at me and then I shrugged. "He's my great-granddaddy, Old Man Henry. I dug up his skeleton in the backyard. Now, he talks to me whenever he feels like it. I didn't know he would follow me to school."

"I heard about that being found. And all these years later. Shocking … Is he here now?" she asked.

"No, he doesn't like nosey old nurses. He fancies colored whores. He was rich and he had a lot of them, pretty ones. He's going to tell me about them," I said.

Nurse Channing's eyes got wide. "Where are you getting this awful talk? A nice little girl doesn't talk like that."

"I don't care." Then I couldn't hold back my anger. "I'm not one of those dumb normal students. I know about boys' Vienna sausage peckers. Carl taught me the word pecker. He said that's what they're called. Why don't you get mad at him? I know about to Get the Fuck, and Pussy. Now, I want to know about whores. You have a pussy, so how do I know you're not a whore?" I saw Nurse Channing's mouth open, a big hole with a fat pink tongue. "Nurse Channing," I said, "if you keep your mouth open too long, the flies will get in."

"You can't talk this way in school. Your grandma, a good Christian, would be very upset. I'm sending you home," she said. She started scratching on some paper.

I saw a movie magazine under her desk and bent over and grabbed it. "You're fatter than this woman on the cover," I said.

Nurse Channing grabbed it from me and stuffed it into her already full drawer. Then I thought about Grandma and a panic came over me and I started crying. "I'm sorry. Please, please don't tell my grandma. You don't know how she gets. I won't do it again. I'll be normal." Tears came to my eyes, but I held them back and pulled out some more strands of my hair.

"Give this note to your mother," she said.

CHAPTER THIRTY-NINE

As soon as I saw Grandma driving up in the maroon Buick, I knew Mom hadn't been home when the school called. Grandma had a look on her face that cut through me. She was wearing one of her bucket-shaped hats with the roses. She thought it was low-class to go out in public bareheaded. As soon as we got home, she grabbed the note from my pocket and read it. She started puffing up in front of me, her own personal thunderstorm. Her face became red and her eyes got large. She looked as if she was going to bite me. "Go to your room," she snapped.

I went and hid in the closet. I called out, "Great-grandmother Eunice, this would be the time to help me."

Grandma came into my room and slammed the door behind her, "Tessa, come out of that closet."

When I came out, Grandma had a switch in each hand, like an outlaw with two whips. These switches had nubs from where she tore off the smaller branches. I ran to my bed and she came after me, switching my bare legs and buttocks with her right hand, and when that hand got tired, she hit me with her left. She'd punished me before, but never like this. I screamed and cried. "I warned you to stop that evil ghost talking. It's from the devil!" she yelled.

"It's not my fault. He came to me. He made me talk to him!" I screamed back at her.

Grandma screamed, "My father was a mean dirty evil man. My only brothers and sisters were from his colored whore. The shame I had to live with. I'm glad my mother murdered him." She whacked me with the switch in her right hand.

I screamed, but I also felt anger and it didn't matter what I said. "He was your father. He doesn't remember what he did and he's lonely."

"He always said 'spare the rod spoil the child'." Since you like him so much, I'll give you a taste of what it was like with him. Don't you ever mention him again in my house." She whacked my buttocks harder.

I kept crying, but my anger made me talk through my tears, "You think God talks to you." I imitated her speaking in tongues, *"Woolatoola massamoola coolacoola, moo moo …* See I can do it too. You sound like a dumb cow for the Lord."

"I'll whup that smart aleck out of you." She whacked the backs of my thighs.

I felt welts rising on my legs. I had to do something. Somehow, I was able to turn and get on my knees, and before she could hit me again, I lunged and sunk my teeth into her arm. It was only for a second then she snatched her arm away. "Damn you," she said.

"You always told me not to swear. Is this your real Jesus? Is this your Holy Ghost? They're mean like you and I hate them. I'm special and you can't take it from me. Mom says you're crazy."

"I'll put the fear of the Lord in you yet." She started with another round of blows. I grabbed one of the switches and it broke. She kept going at me with the other one. "See, you can't fight back."

Mom had come home and must have heard my screams because she ran into my room. She had on a wide-brimmed hat and a flower print dress. She threw off her hat and yanked the switch from Grandma. "Stop it, you crazy witch. You've lost your mind," she yelled in her face.

Anger flared in Grandma. "I'm not going to let her turn into a whore like you." She tried to grab the switch from Mom, but Mom broke it into pieces.

"You're always spouting your pompous shit. And some dumb asses believe you," Mom said.

Grandma looked confused. "Pom … pom … us. What are you saying?"

"Pompous shit… Look it up," Mom said.

"Pompous," I said. "Go on, look it up. You're not as smart as you think you are." My eyes were swelling up from the crying.

"If you ever touch Tessa again, I'll take a bull whip to you," Mom yelled.

Grandma started for the door, but stopped. "Read the letter from Tessa's school. You're raising one of those psycho … psycho … otic … daughters." Grandma slammed the door behind her.

Mom took me in her arms. She hugged and kissed me. She ran her hands over the welts on my legs and got the Mercurochrome. She put it over the broken skin. Then she rubbed Jergens lotion with its sweet smell all over my legs. "I'm so sorry Tessa. I should have been able to take you away from her, but I didn't have the money. Then I got pregnant. I'm not doing things right." Mom started to cry. "I promise I won't … I can't let this happen again." She hugged me until I stopped shaking and then she said, "I have to make a phone call. Stay right here."

CHAPTER FORTY

Early the next morning, Mom woke me. I followed her into her bedroom, where there were a bunch of boxes, some of which smelled of fruit. She must have gone early to the grocery store to get them. "Tessa, we have to pack. We're going to a new life." She started tossing her clothes and Gertrude's clothes, baby blankets, and diapers into a box without folding them. Her eyes were all shiny; she was full of energy and moving around in a hurry. "Hand me, the night cream, and the jewelry box from the nightstand."

"Are we going far?"

"Not that far. We're going to Buck's ranch a little north of San Antonio. He says it's beautiful there. There're horses and a river." She was talking fast and her cheeks were flushed. "There're horses and a river."

"You already said that."

I handed her the cream and jewelry box and she quickly put them in a box and started dropping clothes on top of them. "We'll be happy there." She started laughing. I had never seen her laugh so much. It reminded me of when I had started laughing and couldn't stop, so I lay on the bed and laughed with her.

I raised my head. "Are you going to marry him?" I asked. I continued laughing.

She abruptly stopped laughing. "I don't know. Don't tell anyone we're not married."

While her back was to me, I went to the box with the baby clothes and blankets and took out Gertrude's things and piled them on the chair.

Mom took her underwear from the drawers and dropped it in a box. I picked up some red underpants and held them up to me. "I need some like these."

"Put those down and listen to me." She continued tossing clothes in the boxes. "This isn't going to be like at Boleslaw's. In the new place, there'll be no more talking to Great-grandmother or Great-Aunt."

I looked at Mom's reflection in the mirror above the dresser and there were tears in her eyes. She turned to me. "Tessa come here." I walked over to her and she embraced me. "Tessa, promise me you'll get control of yourself. There's a whole world out there. You don't need those fantasies," she pleaded as she ran her hand over my hair. "Promise me." I nodded. Then she saw Gertrude's things on the chair. "What are you doing?" she asked.

"Gertrude has to stay here so Grandma can keep her from becoming a whore. We don't need another whore in the family."

"Tessa, stop that nasty talk," she said. "She's your sister and she's going with us. Go take your clothes out of the closet and put them on the bed." I went to my room.

CHAPTER FORTY-ONE

That night, I thought about leaving Great-grandmother and Great-aunt Gertie. I opened my curtains and let the moonlight fall on the silver face of the mirror on my dresser. I put a brown aged picture of a young Eunice by the mirror and stared at it and after awhile I felt a breeze and smelled roses. They were coming. They brushed past me and stood in the center of the room, grand in their long dresses with the moonlight behind them.

Eunice's voice insisted, "Tessa, you can't let Old Man Henry near you. You have to be strong enough to resist him."

"I have to tell you something important." I took the rubber bands off of my braids. "Tomorrow, Mom and I are moving a little north of San Antonio." I ran my hand through my hair loosening it.

"We've never been there," Eunice said.

Then I heard Eunice and Gertie gasp. "No, what are you saying? You can't leave us. We won't glimpse your shining world anymore. We'll wander inside of our past," Gertie said. She wiped her cheeks with her gloved hands.

"I'm going to take the big picture of Eunice and the mirror, so I'll be able to contact both of you."

Eunice and Gertie moved around the room. "Yoakum is all we know. I went to the edge of town once. I wanted to leave but I panicked," Eunice said. She clutched the skirt of her dress.

"Everything is so different from when we were alive. You're going to leave us in your past," Gertie said.

"No, no. I still need you," I said.

"Tessa, it took a long time for us to believe you were real ... that something so good could come into our dreary world. It was some quirk of nature that let you contact us. Now it's like we're dying all over again," Eunice said.

"Don't say that," I said.

"Tessa, you're growing up. Soon, you will come to believe we never existed," Eunice said.

"No matter what anybody says, I know you're real." I got out my diary and I spoke to them while I wrote: "Two ladies ... I will keep you in my heart. You are the women who went before me. You're in my breath, and my blood, and I will write about you. Don't worry, you won't be forgotten." I looked down at the few words on the page that were wet from my tears.

"That's beautiful. You're going to do more and be more than us." Eunice spoke with such love in her voice. I looked up and they were by the door smiling at me. I rushed toward them, but they went into the hallway and disappeared, leaving the smell of roses behind. I heard their soft voices echoing all around me. "We love you."

The next morning, I snuck downstairs and took down the picture of Great-grandmother Eunice from the mantel and the mirror with gold bows and hid them in a box and packed it in the station wagon.

Lilly Mae helped Mom load up the car. Every inch was full with boxes, suitcases, Gertrude's playpen, and bassinet. She took up a lot of room. I wanted to sit in the front seat as Mom's co-pilot, but Mom put Gertrude there in her metal frame car seat. Her plump cheeks moved as she sucked her pacifier.

Alongside the car, Lilly Mae, Mom, and I stood together without speaking. Lilly Mae had a hand on her chest and Mom hugged her. "We'll miss you."

"Miss Virginia, I wish you the best in your new place," Lilly Mae said.

Leaving Lilly Mae put an ache inside of me. I held onto her. "You be good to your Mama and no more of that talkin' to those spirits." She gently ran her hand over my curly hair.

Then Grandma came out onto the porch holding Queen Victoria who was barking. Her face was stiff as wood. The silence between her and Mom was as heavy as the air before a rain. But then she started crying. She came toward us and stood in front of the car. "I know I made mistakes, but you are my family. Please don't leave me."

"You should have thought of that before," Mom said. "Get in the car, Tessa."

I got in the backseat behind Gertrude, squeezed in next to some boxes. I'd brought a pillow to sit on because my rear and legs were still sore. We waved to Lilly Mae as we pulled out of the driveway. I looked at the house and told myself to remember every detail, to freeze it like a picture in my mind. Even with the good and bad of it, this was a part of me I was leaving behind.

The sun shone through the windshield as if to say, "Hello traveler." It warmed the car even though there was a chill outside.

"Does it take very long to get north of San Antonio?" I asked.

"It's a couple of hours or so to the city and then less than an hour to his ranch, but we're going to take our time. We're going to see things. We're finally free of that vulture. I'm working on a new song and here's what I have so far." She smiled and sang, "*The cowboy in the heart is giving us a new start. Let old Mom stand at the door, she can't say no, no more. Stones that were thrown now become birds on the wing, that let your soul sing. So, kiss this town goodbye, and spit right in its eye, nobody can say no, no more.*"

"I have a song too." And I sang, "*The earth is opening and Grandma is going down. With dirt in her mouth, she'll come out with a pig's nose and twenty toes."* I started laughing. "Pig's nose." I pushed my nose up with my finger and continued laughing.

Mom stopped smiling. "Tessa, don't let yourself give into meanness."

CHAPTER FORTY-TWO

We drove down Lott Street, and passed Mrs. Thelma's Five and Dime. We turned north on Grand Avenue and drove until it became Highway 111. On the outskirts of town, we passed Randy's Hog on the Spit Barbeque, a cloud of smoke rising from it. I would miss that smell and I told myself to freeze that in my mind because it was a part of me also.

As we passed the city limits, I looked back at the big yellow sign that read, "Welcome to Yoakum, the Leather Capital of the World." I thought: It was the only home I've known. I wondered if I'd ever come back.

Then we passed the turn that went down to the river where the blue bonnets bloomed in the spring. It was a cool October, but everything still looked burnt from the summer's sun. Farther down the highway, we passed the turnoff to the ranch where we got the turkeys each Thanksgiving. We weren't that far out of Yoakum, but we were the only car on the road.

But soon, everything looked different; we had gone farther than I'd ever been. Inside Mom, Gertrude, and I were silent as dust swirled in the wind and blew the lonely sagebrush. I looked across the vast expanse of land and strained to see what was on the horizon. Is this what they talk about when they talk about infinity? Then I felt as if I was expanding, a freedom I'd never felt before. The cotton-colored clouds stretched across the sky, tucked in along the straight horizon, a bit of heaven hugging the earth.

As I looked out the window, it felt as if my heart reached across at the endless flat land, the scruffy trees, the underbrush, the dirt, and the dust. We passed little dirt roads off the highway going into the distance, man-made veins on the living earth. Along the highway, the old fence posts were cut-off bare logs sticking up, wooden fingers pointing to the sky. Tightly wrapped barbed wire cut into the fence posts and the cattle in the fields stared silently into space. I got on my knees and I stuck my head out the window. My hair blew against the side of the station wagon. The wind put its sharp mouth against my ears and whispered, "You were born here. This land is in your flesh and bone … Its song is your song … Let it sing to you … Deep in the heart … Deep in the heart forever."

The land, as if an ancient being rising up, was just waiting to whisper its stories to me of ages past. Across the horizon, for a moment I saw them in the sunlight. The shadowy apparitions of horses and cowboys, merged into one creature moving in their own time, the true people of this land. I was pulled into the forever time. I heard the sounds of the cattle lowing and the cowboys shouting. Even the smells came to me; the horse sweat, the cowboy sweat, the cattle stink, the leather, and the smoky campfires.

With the wind still whipping my hair, we passed a cow's skull on a fence post, an unwritten warning from the mighty land. We kept driving down the dark gray highway, and we passed old wooden crosses on mounds set back a little from the highway. The land had swallowed the dead and their dry bones whispered in the earth, waiting for someone to listen. They had stories to tell. They were calling to me, but we were going so fast down the highway that I couldn't hear them. I was interrupted.

"Tessa, get your head back inside the car. Do you want to get yourself killed?" Mom yelled.

"I'm listening to the wind. Be quiet," I yelled back at her.

"Sit your butt down on the seat," Mom said. Then I was just a girl again in the car with her mother and sister.

I sat back down on the pillow, but I kept my ear close to the open window in case there were more whispers. Then I took out my diary and wrote what I had heard.

My thoughts were interrupted again because Gertrude started crying and waving her pink fists in the air. We were now driving on Highway 183 and we passed a sign saying, "Gonzales, the Lexington of Texas."

We continued on the same highway until we turned west onto Highway 10 going toward San Antonio. We drove into San Antonio and I'd never seen a place so large with so many buildings. This had to be the center of the world. People must get dizzy going up in such tall buildings.

"Buck's not at his ranch right now. He's away at the rodeo in Corpus Christi. He wants us to see some of San Antonio. He's going to treat us to one night in the historic Menger Hotel. First, we'll check in, have lunch, and then see the Alamo," Mom said.

We turned onto Alamo Plaza and pulled up in front of The Menger Hotel.

Standing in front of the hotel were doormen wearing neat green uniforms and white gloves. Along the curb were old-fashioned light posts with two lanterns atop each one. The three-story building had large green awnings above the windows. Balconies were across the top two floors. Each one had a green wrought iron fence around it.

We stopped in front of the hotel and Mom got out and the doorman followed her to the back of the station wagon. When she opened the back, the doorman caught the boxes as they fell out and he helped stuff them back inside. Mom put Gertrude in her stroller and put the diaper bag over her shoulder. With the doorman carrying the luggage, we entered the hotel lobby.

The lobby soared up three stories and I'd never seen anything so high. There were white wooden columns rising up to the third floor. At each floor, there were brass lights coming out of each column like tree branches. We walked across a floor of white, gray, and blue squares.

"It's almost one hundred years old. This is Victorian architecture and the furniture and paintings are antiques," Mom looked at the floor. "This is marble. It's expensive."

I started jumping up and down on the floor, my shoes making noise.

"Tessa, stop that," Mom said.

Mom went to the desk to check in. There was a polished wooden table in the middle of the lobby. Its legs were curved and it had gold trim around the edges. I pushed it a little to see if it was wobbly on its legs.

After we got the room keys, we took the old elevator with the folding metal door upstairs to the third floor. In the room, Mom powdered her face and refreshed her lipstick. She took her hair out of the ponytail and brushed it out. She took off her slacks, put on a girdle and hose, and slipped into a skirt, while I braided my hair and put on my red bows, two on each braid.

We went into the dining room for lunch. There were more white columns and large semi-circle windows. We sat at a table covered with a white tablecloth with the initials MH in gold. On the tables were silver pitchers with moisture veins running down their sides. The glasses even had real silver trim. The waiter who came to our table mentioned that Ulysses S. Grant, Teddy Roosevelt, and Babe Ruth had stayed at the Menger. During lunch, I knocked over a water glass and it broke. The waiter didn't even get mad that I had broken it. He wiped it up and brought another one.

CHAPTER FORTY-THREE

After lunch, Mom pushed Gertrude in her stroller, and we walked across the side street to the Alamo. The south walkway had stone walls with round tree trunks across the top, creating a roof. I felt pins and needles first in my feet, then up my legs and into my stomach. We came out onto the plaza facing the Alamo mission. The Alamo was right in the middle of the city and looked small compared to the tall buildings surrounding it. The sunlight reflected off the irregular beige stones on the front. It was as if the building was saying, "I don't care how many tall modern buildings you build. I'll always be here." The Alamo was in the forever time and it knew it.

All five of the different sized rough wooden windows had bars on them, a prison look. The largest window was above the door, and the two windows on each side of the door were like the silent eyes of the building, witnesses to what had taken place there.

As soon as we got in line by the chain fence, a handsome cowboy in a denim shirt came up to Mom. He took off his hat and pushed his way up next to Mom. Up close, I could see that his cowboy hat and boots were worn and cheap, not like Buck's or my father's. "I'm Walter," he said in a deep voice, as if he didn't know he looked poor.

"I'm Virginia." She smiled, showing her straight teeth that weren't like my teeth that stuck out in the front. Right away I knew this was another case of Mom having the honey that attracts the bees. She tossed her long red hair over her shoulders. Her blouse was tight. Walter's eyes slid down to her breasts, like he had won a prize and wanted to claim it.

I thought: Mom please hunch over. When men look at your breasts, it never turns out well.

"This is Tessa," she said.

I turned my face so Mom couldn't see me and put on an angry expression which I turned to him. That startled him.

"Tessa, say hello," Mom said.

Now I scrunched up my nose as if he smelled bad and I pushed myself in between them, stepping on his foot. "Are you, all right?" he asked me.

"I'm always like this," I said.

He looked at Mom. "Would you like me to show you around? I've been here many times."

"I'm meeting my boyfriend tomorrow, but I guess that would be O.K."

Mom pushed Gertrude, and they walked ahead of me. While standing in line, he had Mom stop to look at something. There was a long straight line made of metal embedded in the stone walkway and a bronze plaque explaining it. Before I could read the plaque, Walter said, "This is where Lieutenant Colonel Travis drew a line in the sand and told anybody who was with him to step across it."

We went inside the mission and the first thing I saw hanging from the ceiling were the six flags that had flown over Texas. There were murals on the walls showing the Mexican times and also murals showing the American immigrants that came later. Around each wall were glass cases with bronze plaques telling the history of the Alamo. There were display cases with clothing, muskets, tools, letters, and shaving kits.

We got in line to look at the plaques. Walter stood up straight. I could see that he was trying to impress Mom by telling her the events that had happened. "The Battle of the Alamo was from February 23 to March 6,

1836. Several months prior the Texans had driven all the Mexican troops out of Texas. President General Antonio Lopez de Santa Anna was furious and classified foreigners fighting in Texas as pirates."

I thought, so, big deal he has the story memorized. But stop sneaking peeks at Mom's breasts.

Walter walked with confidence to the case that held yellowed letters. "Here's the letter Santa Anna wrote to President Andrew Jackson, informing him of Santa Ana's decision banning the taking of prisoners." Mom moved alongside of him and he put his arm around her shoulder.

I pushed in between them. "I can read the plaque right here. I don't need you to tell me."

"Tessa, hush. Don't' be so rude." I could tell Mom liked his deep voice, but I noticed his jeans were tight and I wondered how he rode a horse.

Then we got to the case with the letters from Lieutenant Colonel William Travis. Holding his cowboy hat, he put his arm around Mom's shoulder, pulling her close. "At first there were approximately one hundred men at the Alamo. James Bowie arrived with thirty men and then on February 3 Colonel Travis arrived with another thirty men. Later Davy Crockett came with some volunteers." Walter pointed to the case.

"Blah, blah, blah. If I lived here I'd have it memorized too," I said. Before Mom could get mad at me, I walked ahead to the other side of the room. On the wall was a sign with the battle cry, *"Remember the Alamo."* Underneath, there was a table where under glass the whole battle was recreated in miniature, the Alamo inside and out with the soldiers, cannons, and all the fighting. It was amazing. The miniatures of Colonel Travis and Davy Crockett were shown fighting, and James Bowie was in his hospital bed.

I looked up to the painting above it, with Davy Crockett swinging the butt of his musket at the Mexicans surrounding him. That's when I started hearing it. I heard the cannons and muskets firing and the men shouting, screaming, and yelling in pain. I smelled the gunpowder. I couldn't move. Then I heard the shouts. "Remember the Alamo."

I couldn't stop myself and I slapped my open palms down on the glass case. I yelled, "I can feel it." And I shouted, "Remember the Alamo!" I ran along the front of the case and into the middle of the room and back to the case. I brought my palms down on the glass again. I said, "I smell the gunpowder." I shouted, "Remember the Alamo!" People stopped and stared. There were a couple of other kids by the case and their mothers pulled them away. I yelled, "Remember the Alamo … Remember the Alamo!" I was breathing heavily. Mom and Walter got to me at the same time as the security guard in a blue uniform. "Ma'am, this is sacred ground and proper respect has to be shown. I'm going to have to ask you all to leave."

Mom grabbed my arm hard and pulled me toward the door. "Tessa, how many times have I told you that you can't yell in public and run around like a crazy person?"

"But it's like I'm really there. I hear it and I see it." I started crying.

We stepped into the sunlight and Walter squinted and put his cowboy hat on. Mom grabbed my shoulders and started shaking me. "Can't you see how much you're upsetting me? I'm taking you to a new life. I'm doing all this for you." Mom was on the verge of tears.

"You're hurting me."

Mom kept shaking me. "You get me so upset."

"Stop, now you're acting like Grandma," I said.

She let go and hunched over as if crumpling. "I know things affect you more than other people. Where we're going there's no room for acting like this."

"I can't help it. It just happens. I really feel what happened to those men. It's like it's inside of me. I can't make what I feel and see go away," I said. My shoulders shook.

"Don't say that and please stop crying, Tessa." Mom had such a painful look on her face. I knew I was hurting her, and I told myself that I had to be the way she wanted me to be … to be normal.

Walter stood there looking at us. "Is there anything I can do?"

Mom looked at Walter. "No, this is the first time she's been out of Yoakum."

He raised his eyebrows. "Does she have one of those new-fangled, what do you call it … mental problems? I haven't seen one of those before."

"She's excitable and sensitive," Mom said.

"But she seems more than just excitable," he said.

My anger came back and I said, "Don't butt in."

Mom grabbed my arm, pulling me with her. As we walked on the stone walkway, Gertrude started fussing. "I've got to change her. Tessa, come with me."

Walter sat on a stone bench. "I'll wait here." He pushed his cowboy hat back.

I followed Mom as she pushed Gertrude's stroller into the lady's bathroom. She stood me in a corner. "I don't understand everything you're seeing or feeling. Please, you have to try to control yourself. I'm so sorry I left you with your grandmother. She's mean and has been a terrible influence. But we're going to a wonderful place. Now, about these ideas of the dead talking to you."

"I don't talk to them. They talk to me," I corrected.

"Many folks don't understand such a thing. It would be a big favor to me if you could pretend they weren't always chatting to you," Mom said.

"But I'd be lonely."

"Not anymore. Everything is going to be different now," Mom said.

Gertrude started fussing again and when Mom got busy with Gertrude, I snuck back outside and sat on the bench next to Walter. I looked him right in the eyes. "You're not a real cowboy, are you?" I asked.

"I work in a western clothing store. It's honest work."

"I knew you weren't real right from the start. I'll tell you a secret," I said.

"What?"

"It's all right for my grandma to say this, so I'm going to say it. Mom likes the Whoredom. Grandma calls it the dirty Whoredom."

"Who taught you to talk like that?" He sat up straight and looked around to see if anyone heard me.

"My grandma says it when she's preaching. But it's important to say what's on your mind. You like my mom and I see the way you look at her," I said.

He leaned toward me. "If you were mine, I'd wash your mouth out with soap." He had a mean look on his face.

"Do you want to know a secret?" He looked surprised, but he was interested. "Somehow, Mom got my sister Gertrude from the Pastor Jessie Michael. I saw him touching her breasts. Then she had to marry Boleslaw, so people in town wouldn't know. She's had two divorces. It's as easy as pie for her to get married. Lots of men want to marry her."

"You shouldn't go around airing your family's dirty laundry," he said.

"I don't know about that but there's a reason I'm saying this." I put my face real close to his, looked him in the eyes, and said slowly, "Mom's engaged to Buck, a real cowboy who owns a ranch up north. We're going there tomorrow. I don't know exactly what this means except that it's bad and Grandma says all men want it. I have to tell you that you're not going to Get the Fuck with my Mom."

He jumped up and was angry, but he looked like he didn't know what to say. "You're a right nasty little girl. You need someone to take you over his knee. There has to be something wrong with a mother raising a daughter like you. All you run into these days is damn cockeyed people."

"You need to put your hands on a cow and squeeze it instead," I said. He quickly walked away. I was so glad that I put my hands in my armpits doing my Chicken Dance while jumping up and down on one foot then the other.

Mom pushed Gertrude out of the bathroom. "Now, why are you jumping?"

"I'm happy."

"Stop that jumping. Where did he go?"

"I don't know. But he wasn't a real cowboy," I said.

"It's better that he left," Mom said.

Mom pushed Gertrude as we headed back to the Menger Hotel. That night, back in the hotel room, I wrote in my notebook about the Alamo, its stones, its windows, and how it was in the forever time. I also put down that I had made the fake cowboy go away.

CHAPTER FORTY-FOUR

The next morning, we drove northwest now on Highway 10, which had two lanes on each side and a wide dirt strip down the middle. On the outskirts of San Antonio, we passed new houses right next to each other, one after the other. They didn't look like the ones in Yoakum and they gave me a lonely feeling. They were one-story rectangles with over-hanging roofs that came to a point over the front door and the garage. The box-shaped garages stuck right out in front and the houses were all the same, except that the front door might be in a different place and the windows different. I felt afraid that we were going to a place crowded with these houses.

"Mom, why do these houses all look the same?"

"They're called tract houses. They lay a bunch of foundations one after the other and then erect the walls on them. They make more money that way."

Those new houses seemed to say to me, "We bring an emptiness and coldness on the land. We'll expand one box at a time. We bring the straight lines of cement and asphalt. We divide the land, we make it small, and you can't do anything about it."

Then I saw a smiling box house jump out of the roof of the house at the end of the block. It planted itself alongside the one it had come from. Then another one jumped out of that one and so on going on up onto the hills, growing out of control across the land. They were laughing and saying, "We will take over everything." They didn't have any of the forever time in them. I couldn't stop seeing them and put my hands over my eyes.

We kept driving northwest on Highway 10 until we were completely out of San Antonio. There were a few diners along the highway and some old farmhouses set back on small bits of fenced property. We stopped for gas at a Humble Gas Station. It had a sign saying Est. 1932 and a large red and white Coca-Cola sign stuck on the sagging roof. There were two skinny long-necked gas pumps with the hoses dangling down like dead snakes. An attendant came out wearing a cap that said Humble Gas and he filled us up and checked everything under the hood and smiled at Mom.

As we drove farther northwest on Highway 10, there were fewer diners and gas stations. The land took over, but there wasn't a flat horizon like outside Yoakum. There were rolling hills on each side where the horizon would have been. We turned off on Boerne Stage Road and went about a half mile and turned onto Ranch Road. The sun reflected off the green hood of the Chevy station wagon.

Gertrude started crying and Mom stroked her head. On each side of the road, standing or lying in the shadows of the large oak trees, were the cattle. The smell of dirt and cattle stink filled the air. The cattle stared across their pasture and their mouths moved slowly as they chewed; they were going to suck out all the juice from each bite because they had all the time in the world. The cows were saying they owned this land and the people were nothing without them, the land was nothing without them. They were in the forever time.

We came to a sign made of wrought iron over a gate that read Buck Hartman's Horseshoe Ranch. Mom got out of the car and pushed open the gate. We bumped over the metal pipes that were across the road.

"That's a cattle crossing. They can't walk over the pipes," Mom said.

Mom got out and closed the gate by looping a chain over the upright fence post. She got back in the car, but didn't move. Then she looked at me and said, "I've never done anything like moving in with a man I haven't known very long. I hope I haven't made a mistake."

"It's pretty here," I said.

She drove down the road where there was a wooden fence on each side of the road. Between each upright post there were logs crossing in an 'X' shape in the middle. On each side of the fences, oak trees were scattered, stand-alone strangers spreading their branches. On the left side, where the pasture backed up against the rolling hills, the trees stood in clusters, large and small families of trees. The leaves moved as if the trees were speaking to each other. But they had trouble making words, so in the breeze they made brushing and breathing sounds.

As we drove farther down the road, in a fenced pasture were horses, some head to tail and some head to head, sharing secrets. They were all colors; light browns, dark browns, white ones, and a couple that had huge brown and white spots. Mom said, "Those are called Paints." They flicked their tails and turned their shiny brown eyes toward me and I felt a twinge on my thighs. I loved them immediately.

When we got closer to the ranch house, in a separate pasture was a large muscular brown stallion with a long black mane, and black socks on his legs. He trotted along the fence following us, his neck arched, and his nostrils flared. I thought I heard him say, "The cows are nice but slow. I'm the power and I'm in charge of this place."

Mom said he was a bay. We stopped in front of the ranch house. It was on a small rise overlooking the pastures. Mom held Gertrude as we walked up the plank steps. The house was a long rectangular building with a rock chimney. The roof jutted out from the house, creating a wide porch. An assortment of old chairs and wooden crates were spread across the front of the porch. On the tops of the crates were ashtrays and beer and whiskey bottles. I smelled beer. The walls of the house had round gray rocks up to the bottom of the windows. Mom looked out at the pastures and said, "I told you it was beautiful here." Everything about the ranch said the forever time.

On a beam above the door, horseshoes were nailed into the wood. Mom knocked, but there was no answer. I asked, "What if Buck really doesn't want us to come here?"

"He invited us to come," Mom said.

Mom peeked into the windows as I walked to the other end of the porch, the wooden planks creaking under my feet. An old hand-made child's wagon was against the wall and hanging above it were old branding irons. Mom rang the brass bell and still nobody came.

Mom carried Gertrude over her shoulder, and we followed the path to the back of the house where there was a screened in porch and a rock pit for fires. We went up a few steps to the back, and it wasn't a yard but land going as far back as we could see. To the right was a large red barn with a sloping roof. On one side was an old black car, a tractor, and a stack of alfalfa bales. The sweet alfalfa smell was carried all the way to the house. On the other side of the barn, wooden gates were on the front of each horse stall. Two white corrals stood in front of that side of the barn. Looking over to the left of the property were two red bunk houses with porches.

We followed the dirt path back. Gertrude hadn't fussed or cried since we arrived. She bobbed her head as if trying to see everything. She liked it here, and I had to admit she was cute. She was my sister and I could love her. Too bad Mom was always kissing her so there was no room for me. Gertrude must have known what I was thinking because she looked me in the eyes and I heard her voice in my mind, "If you would stop thinking I'm in your way like you're the queen bee, maybe I could love you too."

On the porch of the first guesthouse, Mom rang the metal bell.

"I'm coming. Hold yur horses," said a gruff voice from the back. Then suddenly the front door opened and a slender, tough old man stood before us. From his tanned face to his short gray beard down to his bowed legs, everything about him said, "I was born a cowboy and I'll die a cowboy and don't dare give me any trouble." He was wearing an old denim shirt and jeans. "You must be Virginia, and these are yur little ones." He smiled, and the crow's feet bunched up around his clear blue eyes. He had a face that made me feel as if I'd always known him. He stuck out his large rough hand to Mom. "I'm Jeremiah and I'll get you settled in. Buck wants you to feel right at home."

Out of the other guesthouse came a colored man about Jeremiah's age and a boy about my own. They were dressed in denim overalls. Both of them took off their straw hats as they approached us. "This is Virginia, and Tessa, and baby Gertrude," Jeremiah said to them.

Then Jeremiah turned to the two coloreds, "And this here is Willie and his son, Josey."

Willie and Josey nodded their heads, "Pleased to meet ya Miss Virginia and Miss Tessa," Willie said.

"They keep this place running," Jeremiah said.

I looked Josey in the eyes and thought that he might actually become a friend. Grandma had always told me not to stare into the eyes of strange colored men or boys. She always got nervous if when alone, she ran into colored men at a gas station or parking lot. For years, she'd been saying that they were going to break into our house. I was breaking one of Grandma's iron-clad rules and it felt so good. Since I'd never talked to a colored boy, I looked closely at Josey. He looked strong. His large brown eyes were framed with long eyelashes and he had high cheekbones and smooth skin. His full lips had an edge around them that made them look as if they were sculpted.

"Josey, how old are you?"

"I'm eleven, Miss Tessa."

"I'm ten, but I'm grown up," I said.

"Yes, Miss Tessa. I'm learning to take care of the horses round here." He smiled, showing his white teeth and a happiness. I could tell that he didn't have any of the meanness in him.

Jeremiah took us into the house through the back-porch while Willie and Josey went to get our luggage and boxes out of the car. From the porch, we went into the kitchen.

We stopped in the kitchen. "This was Buck's father's house. It used to be a two-bedroom, but Buck made the kitchen and living room larger and added what he calls the Master Bedroom," Jeremiah said.

"Did you know Buck's father?" Mom asked.

"Yessup. I worked for him for many years … a man of few words. How do you like this kitchen? Buck made it real fancy."

Over the stove hung some shiny copper pots. On the other wall there were two sinks side by side. I'd never seen a kitchen that had two sinks. The cabinets were all new honey-colored wood and the countertops were brown tile. It was open from the kitchen into the dining room because there was no wall. Also, the kitchen and the large living room were separated by only a counter with leather stools.

Jeremiah said, "Buck said he wanted to be modern and he got the ideas for this from looking at some pictures in ladies' magazines. Imagine that … from ladies' magazines. I threw out them ladies' magazines as soon as he wasn't looking."

The thing that truly drew my attention was the dark wood beamed ceiling with knots in it above all the rooms. When the wood sensed my presence, I heard its voice, "We remember being alive, but now we're stuck up here."

I went to the wall where there was a large photograph of Buck riding a bull. Also, a shelf was filled with gold trophies.

While we were standing in the living room, Willie and Josey brought in some suitcases, set them down, and stood there. "I need you to bring in the crib and changing table," Mom said.

A burnt wood smell was coming from the stone fireplace. The chimney's round gray stones went up to the ceiling. The other smell was from the brown leather sofas and armchairs that looked like they were from Buck's father's time. I guess he ran out of money to get new furniture.

Cattle skin rugs were on the floor and a cow's skull on one wall, while another wall had old guns and pistols in a case.

"It's a little dusty. Buck's gone a lot, so it builds up. He'll be glad to have a woman around," Jeremiah said. Mom didn't say anything.

A gray layer of dust was on the chairs and the end tables. I felt excited, so I got up on one of the sofas and jumped up and down even though my feet sank into the leather.

"Tessa, stop. You don't jump on leather."

Willie brought in Gertrude's furniture, and Josey carried some boxes into the dining room. Jeremiah led us down the hallway to the bedrooms and sang to himself. *"Hear that old crow. His cry is so lonely at night. He's too mournful to fly. That big rig truck is moving so slowly."*

Then Mom joined in, *"I'm shouting out my loneliness under the dark blue sky."*

Jeremiah stopped and looked at Mom. "You have a nice voice."

"Bet you wouldn't guess I'm planning on being a singer," Mom said.

"There're not a lot of singing places out here."

All of us went into the bedroom on the right of the hallway, where the bed had a knotty pine headboard and footboard. All of the furniture was also made of knotty pine. Even the window frames were of that wood. I opened a dresser drawer and smelled raw wood.

"This will be Tessa's room," Mom said.

"Buck is proud of how he got everything to match."

I wrote my name with my finger in the dust on top of the dresser.

The other bedroom across the hall had the exact same furniture but there was no desk. Mom held Gertrude over her shoulder, and I said under my breath, "I get the desk and you don't." On the dresser I wrote Gertrude's name in the dust with my finger.

Then Jeremiah took us into the master bedroom, which was much larger than the other two. The desk, the dresser, and the trunk were all fancier than those in the other rooms. There were more pictures of Buck at rodeos on the walls.

The wooden headboard and footboard had posts sticking up, and it had a wool bedspread and pillows with images of horses. "This is really nice," Mom said. She sat on the bed and ran her hand over the spread.

I went to Jeremiah. "I'm not supposed to tell people that Mom and Buck aren't married. In that bed are they going to do things my grandma would say is the Whoredom? Do you know about the Whoredom? Do you have the problem of doing it yourself?" I asked Jeremiah.

"Well, I'll be. She's pretty, but does she always talk like that?" Jeremiah asked Mom.

"Tessa, go in your bedroom and don't come out until I call you."

I went to my new bedroom and wrote in my diary about the square houses jumping one out of the other and growing up the sides of the hills. I named them "The Land of Square Boxes." Then I wrote about how the cattle just chewed and chewed and how the stallion looked me in the eye and talked to me and a thrill went through my body that I had never felt before. The houses, barn, and the land that stretched to the mountains were all in the forever time.

CHAPTER FORTY-FIVE

That night when I was alone in my room, I walked across the creaky wooden floor and looked out my window to the back of the property. There were lights on in both guesthouses, but other than that the darkness stretched for miles. I'd never seen such blackness surrounding everything. It was heavy and somehow alive as if it was breathing. The hills and trees had disappeared because the darkness ate them. That's what darkness does: it eats things. What did the cattle and horses do at night? Do they eat at night or stand there feeling lonely? I wondered if snakes, rats, or an army of potato bugs were out there or in the house. I shuddered because I could almost hear little feet moving across the floors.

It was cold, and I got into bed wearing my flannel nightgown with the dogs on it and a tail in back. As soon as I closed my eyes, the image of the last time I saw my father in the restaurant came to me. He wouldn't know where I'd gone. Even though I'd left Yoakum, my parents' divorce, which created my "divorce crack", was still inside of me making me feel split like an opening filled with my own darkness. The huge darkness outside was pulling on the crack inside making it larger. Why didn't Mom know that something was hurting me? I kept thinking, you're not the same as other kids. You can't get away. I pulled up the covers around me.

I had no idea how long I'd been sleeping, but I was startled awake. There was something cold against my face. Maybe it was just a breeze, and I got out of bed and went to the windows. But they were closed. I ran my finger through the moisture on the inside of the windows. I got back in bed and I saw a shadow move in the room. I thought: Please, there can't be anything in here. I told myself to stop imagining things, but I felt afraid, and my stomach twisted with nausea. Then I smelled cigar smoke, and there was a dark shape next to my bed and I covered my face with the blanket.

"Tessa, wake up." It was Old Man Henry's voice.

I kept the covers over my head. "How did you find me here?"

"I had to because you're the only one who can hear me."

I stuck my head out from the covers. "I was dreaming about you. You were driving in an expensive car with Franny, the colored woman. She was all dressed up fancy, with a hat and gloves?"

"Something from my life came into your dream. I didn't know that could happen," Old Man Henry said.

"Go away. I have to sleep."

Now he had become fully visible and his presence felt heavy as he stood next to me. He was dressed in his western suit, his brown vest, and black cowboy boots.

"You're crowding in on me." I got out of the bed and turned on a small lamp on the dresser. It cast a shadow on the wood plank wall and it fell across the scuffed floor. For a moment, I thought that this was just my imagination. I stepped across the cold floor to get back in bed, and when I turned Old Man Henry was still next to my bed, smelling of cigar smoke. I said, "You will eat me the way the darkness outside eats everything." I got back in bed. "I can't breathe. You're too close."

"Oh. What if I move over here?" I saw him move by the dresser. He stood there wearing his cowboy hat and his hands on his hips as if he was in charge of everything. He puffed on his cigar.

"Listen, you got me in so much trouble at school. Grandma beat me. She says talking to you is evil. And put out that cigar."

"I'm sorry. Bernice has a meanness in her," he said. He opened his hand and the cigar vanished.

"Well, she got it from you. It's in your genes. Go away."

"We're connected. I don't know how I do this, but sometimes it's like I look through your eyes for a second. I get glimpses of your life, even though you're a girl." He started to move closer to me.

"But I'm a smart and beautiful girl." I ran my hand through the tangles in my hair.

"You didn't see me, but I rode part of the way here with you in the car." He pulled down his brown vest with the gold buttons and stood with his legs spread apart.

"Don't say that."

"I saw you writing and talking to yourself. What you were saying was beautiful. It's coming back … I used to feel those things about the land, the sky, the cowboys, and the cattle."

My arms tightened, and I clenched my fists and my breath was short. "You can't have my thoughts and feelings."

"I'll always be part of you, an unbroken chain from me to you. You need me," he said.

"I do not. Go away."

Then he moved toward me, and his large form came into me, overlapping me. I held up my hand to the light and there was an image of a large man's hand with a diamond ring superimposed over my hand. My hand was so small, and his hand covered it like a large glove. Old Man Henry was making me small and I was disappearing. I pulled on my hair to keep from screaming.

"See, I'm a part of you now. It's wonderful," he said.

"Get your spirit body or whatever you are out of my body and go to Get the Fuck," I said. I kicked my legs against the bed and brought my fists down on it. Then I held up my hand and I could see he was still merged with me. "Go away. You're making me crazy," I said. I shook my hand again to get rid of him, but he still moved when I did. I couldn't get him out of me. I got out of bed and put on my robe, but there he was inside of me, a transparent person, moving with me exactly the way I moved. He bent down with me as I put on my shoes.

"Think of your own movements. Don't copy me," I said.

"I just feel better when I'm a part of you," he said.

Tears started rolling down my cheeks. It felt as if nails were in my stomach and my throat tightened. I put my hand over my mouth, so I wouldn't scream and wake Mom. I said out loud, "I have to be normal for Mom. See if you can do this, Old Man." I did my Marching Dance, moving my arms like in a parade. For a moment, I didn't feel him, but when I stopped he was still there. I opened my door and rushed down the hall, through the back-porch and then outside. The cold air hit my face, but I still felt him inside of me, a heavy double.

"I just want to feel alive. Why is that so bad?" he asked.

"I will get rid of you," I said.

I saw a light on in the barn. The dirt was hard under my feet as I ran toward the barn.

"Slow down," he said. My running pushed him out of me. Now he was running behind me, his cowboy boots clomping on the ground.

I turned my head and yelled at him, "You can't make me talk out loud in front of people again. Can't you see what you're doing to me?" My tears fell on the ground.

He kept running close behind me. "I won't bother you. I can make myself smaller."

"Just go away."

The heavy barn door was slightly open, and I squeezed through. There were ropes and chains hanging from hooks that were fastened to the beams across the high ceiling. There was a wheelbarrow, shovels, and buckets. There was a room at one end where equipment was stored. On one side, there were bales of alfalfa. There were three horses in the stalls, a black one, a white one, and a Paint. They put their heads over the doors and whinnied. Their shiny eyes stared at me. I felt calmer. "Good, I think he's gone," I said. But then I felt a horrible pain in my left eye. I pressed my hand over my eye.

"I got back inside of you. I'm in your eye. I like it here. I can see things," Old Man Henry said.

I spoke to the horses, "You're animals, you must know things I don't. Please do something."

The black one pawed the ground and the others just stared and whinnied. "Tell me this isn't real." The white horse closest to me shook his head up and down, like he was saying "Yes" it is real. "Please help me to make him go away."

I jumped up and down and stomped my feet, but the pain got worse. The horses whinnied and pushed against the doors to their stalls.

"Don't jump. You're bumping me around," he said.

"You're hurting me." The pain stabbed my eye. Then I heard someone behind me and I jumped. I turned and there was Josey in overalls, work gloves, and a bucket in his hand. "Who's hurting you?"

"Nobody. I had a bad dream." I blushed with embarrassment.

"Tessa, why aren't you asleep?" Josey asked.

"I thought it was something, but it's gone. Mom says my imagination runs away with me." I still held my eye.

"Why are you holding your eye? Is there somethin' in it?"

"There's nothing in my eye. I hold my eye at times for the fun of it."

"Let me take a look." He put down the bucket and moved closer to me.

I heard Old Man Henry's voice clearly in my head, "Keep him away from me."

"Pull down your lower eyelid like this," Josey said as he pulled down his eyelid.

"No, no, don't let him look at me," Old Man Henry said, but his voice was fading as Josey stared in my eye, his face close to mine. Josey smelled of alfalfa. Then I heard Old Man Henry moaning as he slipped out of me and the pain went away.

"I don't see nothing," Josey said.

"You made him go away." I jumped up and down.

"Tessa, who are you talking about? There's no one else here. And what are you doin' out here in the dark?" Josey asked.

"I always walk round in the dark."

"You're scared of something. You can tell me what's it is."

"What are you doing up so early?"

"There's work to be done. You want to watch me milk Ruby Jean?" Josey asked.

"Yes."

"We only need one milkin' cow cause it's just for us. She be back here."

He set the pail down by Ruby Jean's stall and grabbed a large square of alfalfa from a bale and put it in her trough and the fresh smell filled the air. Josey wet a clean rag at the faucet. He held the bucket as we went into the stall. Straw was spread all over the floor of the stall. Ruby Jean chewed as she looked at me with her thick brown eyelashes. She had a soft, light brown coat with a cream color under her neck and stomach. Josey put a small bench alongside of her and sat down. He ran his hand gently along her side stroking her, comforting her.

He pointed to the pinkish swollen bag between her legs. "This is the udder." I already knew what an udder was, but I hadn't seen one up close. It looked like puffed-up fingers on a rubber glove. "These are the teats." He ran his hand along one of them, and Ruby Jean moved her tail. "See how she moves her tail to one side to make the milkin' easier. First, I have to clean her up." He wiped her swollen udder with the wet rag. Then he put the bucket under her udder and rested his head on her side, smiling. "She be just like a big pillow."

I tensed because I thought that I smelled old Man Henry's cigar again. "Can I hug her?" I asked.

"Sure, but no quick movements," Josey said. I moved closer and put my arms around her and my nervousness went away.

"Watch me," Josey said. He took a teat in each hand, squeezed, and the milk shot into the metal bucket making a ringing sound. The milk filled the pail and little bubbles danced around the inside of the bucket while he hummed a song to himself.

"Josey, where do you go to school?"

He lifted his head from Ruby Jean. "The Negro school is about a mile and a half from here. I walk there."

I stroked Ruby Jean's soft coat. She turned and looked at me with her gentle brown eyes.

"Grandma is always saying things about coloreds. But Lilly Mae, the maid who works for us, takes care of me. She's so good. I'm beginning to see that everything Grandma says is a lie," I said angrily. "I hope you will be my friend?"

"You'll make friends at school. You best be gettin' back to the house. You don't want your mama wondering what ya doin' out here," he said.

I went back into the house, and when Mom got up she made us a breakfast of toast with peanut butter. It was Friday and Mom said I'd start school on Monday. Then Mom loaded Gertrude and me in the station wagon and we drove back toward San Antonio to the Piggly Wiggly for groceries. Because it was named the Piggly Wiggly, I wiggled my hips as I walked down the aisles.

CHAPTER FORTY-SIX

That evening, Mom made dinner and Jeremiah came in and lit the fireplace. The smell of burning wood filled the room. Jeremiah ate with us and he slurped his beans and I slurped with him because it was fun. I was happy because Grandma wasn't telling me how to sit and how to eat.

"This here is real home cooking," he said. He shoveled more beans into his mouth and chewed with his mouth open.

After dinner, Jeremiah, singing to himself, went out to his guesthouse. I helped Mom with the dishes and as soon as I could, I headed for my room.

"Where are you going?" Mom asked.

"To my room."

"Don't you want to sit with me for awhile and keep me company? It's so quiet out here. We can listen to the radio. I haven't always spent enough time with you, but I want to make up for that."

I felt antsy and a pull to try to contact Eunice and Gertie. "Please, I want to go to my room. You can talk to Gertrude. You prefer her to me. She's the normal one."

"Tessa, stop being jealous of your sister. I treat you both the same. And you don't ignore your mother. Stay with me."

"No. I need to do something," and I rushed to my room and closed the door. I carefully unpacked Eunice's picture in the carved gold-gilded frame. I bet Grandma was angry when she found it was missing.

I put it on the dresser and stared at the picture, waiting for Eunice's face to move and change and for Gertie's face to appear and then to feel their feathery fingers touch my cheeks. I squinted my eyes but the light hitting the glass of the flat picture only reflected my face with my two front teeth sticking out and my long hair that was matted. Butterflies came into my stomach and my eyes started to hurt, but nothing moved or changed in the picture.

I raised my voice, "Dumb picture. I thought you were alive and special, but you're not. Bring them to me." I felt so alone in the empty room. I started hitting the mattress with my fists and yelling.

Mom opened the door and had an angry look. Her mouth was twisted in a way that made her look like a cartoon character. "Tessa, what are you yelling about now? If you keep carrying on the way you do, you'll end up in a mental institution," Mom said.

"Grandma said that you were the one who would end up in a mental hospital. Seems like I come from a whole line of crazy women."

"Stop talking back," Mom said. She noticed the picture. "You took that picture."

"I need my relatives."

Mom came in and sat on the bed. "Come here and sit next to me." I sat down and she put her arm around me. "Tessa, I've told you many times you don't need those fantasies. Now you have me. I'm going to be here for you, you'll see."

The next morning in the kitchen, Mom made Gertrude and me Aunt Jemima pancakes with bananas for breakfast. I cut up a pancake into little pieces and fed Gertrude. I liked watching her round cheeks and pink lips move as she chewed.

After breakfast, Mom went into the living room where the boxes she had brought were stacked and giving off a musty cardboard smell. She opened some boxes, pulling out crumpled newspapers. She opened a closet door, but it was full. Then she slammed the boxes around as if she could force them to unpack themselves and that made her tired. "This isn't my house. I don't know where I can put our stuff. I don't feel at home yet. I hope I didn't make a mistake coming here. I need Buck to come back." She held Gertrude as she walked from room to room. Finally, she put Gertrude in her playpen, and I went into my room.

After a half an hour, I heard my mother in the living room strumming her guitar. I came into the hallway to watch her sing her new song. *"When your man's away it's a long day, but he'll be coming home soon. So, dig your roots into the Texas dirt. Stare at the fields and horses all day but you can't run away. You have kids. You have to stay put. No matter how much you want to put the pedal to the metal, you have to settle down. So, put a smile on your face and count your blessings. You have kids. You have to stay put."*

I'd never heard this song before and Mom noticed I was watching her and stopped singing.

"Are you singing about Gertrude and me?" I asked.

"No, it's just a song." She pushed her hair back over her shoulders and wrote in her singing notebook.

"You have to stay put. Are you saying we are in your way? That you want to go someplace?" I asked.

She closed her notebook. "They're just feelings that come up and I put them in a song."

"But they're real so you do feel that way."

"I have two children and I'm alone. Sometimes it's difficult to handle everything myself," she said.

"Now that we're here, you won't be alone. We're going to be with Buck. I thought you loved him."

"He's a wonderful man and he has a good heart. It's so generous of him to let us come here. Of course, I have feelings for him," she said.

"I think he's going to be a father to me and I love him."

"We need to get to know him better. And I wish he'd come home," she said.

"No matter what, I still love him," I said.

"Go find something to do. I have to make it or break it now."

"Look around, nobody is listening to you."

"Don't criticize my dreams," she said.

I just stood there, and I thought: Back in Yoakum, I felt myself to be a smaller version of her, but now she seems different and always thinking about something. Still, I couldn't tell her that Old Man Henry was really scaring me because that would upset her. I didn't want to do that.

"Tessa, why are you just standing there? You have a strange look on your face. Are you off in one of your fantasy worlds again?"

"No."

"I have very little time to practice," Mom said.

"I have to practice for what I'm going to be when I grow up and I'm not going to be like you." I didn't know why I said that. I wish I hadn't.

Mom slapped her hand against the guitar. "You've got to stop this attitude. Now go find something to do."

As I left the room, Gertrude started crying. I thought: When I grow up to be an Indian, I'm not going to worry about the things Mom worries about.

I put on my coat, and even though it was cold, I went out on the property. I walked behind the barn to explore and I was glad I didn't feel Old Man Henry sneaking up on me. I heard the sound of water running and followed a dirt path through some trees, and after walking awhile I came upon a creek. I could find water, which meant I was an Indian.

In the grass by the creek, I saw something. I thought it was a turtle, but when I rushed over to it, it turned out to be just an empty shell. I bent down and ran my finger over the raised pattern and gently turned it over. There were empty holes where the legs and neck would have been. It lay there silently, and nobody knew it had died. The empty holes and the dark shadow inside of the shell reminded me of the darkness that takes over everything at night and how it pulled on me. I felt scared, and I carefully placed the shell back the way it was. It shouldn't be moved. Even if nobody knew or cared about the turtle, it deserved not to be disturbed.

I wondered what happened to animals when they died. Was it different than what happened to humans?

I went down to the edge of the creek where the water ran between the smooth gray rocks that stuck up like round heads in the middle of the creek. The rushing and gurgling sound seemed to enter me. I felt as if I was flowing with the water down the creek. I was part of the water and the water was part of me, free and pure. Then I was back, all alone, standing on the bank. Green moss clung to the rocks closest to the bank, right beneath the water. I slid my hand in the water and along the slippery cold moss.

But out of the corner of my eye, I saw something watching me; a horned toad. I was an Indian so I had to move slowly. I carefully grabbed him. His legs moved in a frenzy. The dark brown horns sticking out of his head were rough when I stroked them. He wiggled as I put him in my pocket.

CHAPTER FORTY-SEVEN

Early Sunday morning, the darkness outside was still walking around on its heavy damp feet. I was half asleep and half awake, and I had been dreaming. The dream came back. I was in that colored neighborhood again. The houses were run-down except for one, separate from the rest. It was a blue and white two-story house with a porch and a balcony, and a white wrought iron railing. Then I was inside the house seeing Franny, Lilly Mae's sister, and she was wearing a white lace dress and the table was set beautifully. There were two colored children about eight and six sitting up straight and silent. She was serving Old Man Henry pot roast and he looked at her and said, "After what's happened, I'll have to arrange for you to go away … maybe San Antonio."

Then I felt the bed beneath me. I stretched my legs under the blankets. I got up and looked out the window. The early morning light was just beginning to creep along the horizon. But the night shadows were not yet being forced back under the pieces of wood and leaves where the insects hide.

The smell of Old Man Henry was in my room. It seemed as if even the air didn't like him. It was stuffy and I had trouble breathing.

"I know you were dreaming about me. You have time to talk to me now," Henry said.

I got out of bed and turned on the lamp on the dresser and quickly got back in bed.

"You're crowding me." He was wearing his cowboy hat, and cowboy boots.

"Do you have to sound so angry?" Old Man Henry asked.

"I like sounding angry. Everyone thinks I'm weird. My life is strange and now I have to deal with you. Get over there by the dresser." He moved over by the dresser. "You drove Eunice and Gertie away from me. I hate you for that."

"Wasn't me. They never wanted to leave that boring town," he said.

"I dreamed about you and Franny, Lilly Mae's sister. Is she the reason why Eunice shot you?"

"Eunice was quick to find fault with others. And unlike her, I never killed anyone." His voice cracked.

"Do you know what's wrong with my mother? She seems so different now."

"Females are a mystery to me. Now let me merge with you. I need to feel alive," he said.

"No, stop." I got up and looked down at my feet. His cowboy boots covered my feet completely, but I could still see my small feet through them. I was really angry. "You're killing me."

Wham, I felt the pain in my left eye. "This is becoming easier. See, I can make myself small in an instant," Old Man Henry said. He was stuck in my eye again, and things were blurred when I looked through that eye.

"This is the worst thing you've done to me. You're making me crazy," I said.

"I'll just watch everything from here. I want to see the morning sun."

I covered my mouth with the palms of my hands and screamed, hoping Mom couldn't hear me. I tied a scarf around my eye like a pirate to keep it covered while I got dressed. "Now you can't see anything … ha, ha, … and I'm going to find Josey."

"No, not him. He's not good. And take that scarf off," Henry said.

I walked to the barn and peeked inside. It looked empty and I went to the trough and splashed water on my eye. Then I went into an empty stall and lay down, burying my face in the sweet-smelling straw. I couldn't tell anyone about Henry. What was I going to do? I pushed my scarf onto the top of my head and looked at the straw. It felt like he was gone.

"No, I'm still here, in your eye watching everything," Old Man Henry said.

I slammed my face in the straw and tears fell on my hands and arms. I spoke softly, "How can you keep doing this?" My shoulders shook.

"Stop crying. It makes me dizzy," he said.

"Stop talking in my head," I yelled at Old Man Henry, and I hit my head with my fist.

Then I looked up and saw Josey. He was wearing denim overalls with straw stuck on them. I hadn't seen him come in. "Tessa, you can tell me who you are talking to."

I was embarrassed, so I pulled the scarf back over my eye and I kept my head down. Josey sat down next to me.

"Get away from him. When he's here I can't stay with you," Old Man Henry said.

I sat up and inched closer to Josey. "I got in a lot of trouble back in Yoakum because of this thing. I can't talk about it."

"I know what's it like having things you can't talk about. Anyway come, I want to show you somethin'," Josey said. He led me into another stall with fresh straw where a golden-brown foal lay on its side with its legs and small hooves tucked against it. It turned its head and its deep eyes stared at me. It had white down its face and on its legs. "Isn't she beautiful?"

Standing next to him, I felt safe and without thinking, I ran my hand down his arm and rested it in his warm hand. He quickly took his hand away.

"Tessa, don't do that. We can't be doing anything like that," he said.

"I only touched your hand."

"People will say it's not natural for us to be touchin'… that it's sinful. You hear. They will say that it's the devil," he said.

"But when I'm with you this awful thing goes away." I pulled on my hair until it hurt.

"Don't pull on your hair. Maybe you'll tell me about it when you're ready," Josey said. "But watch this." Josey picked up a bottle and sat down next to the foal. She grabbed the nipple in her small mouth and started sucking.

"Was she just born?"

"Today, she be five days old. Pa and I rescued her from the slaughterhouse. They was goin' to kill her. She lost her mother and they usually don't live when they lose their mother so young." He stroked her neck as she sucked on the bottle and I carefully sat down next to her.

"Can I touch her?"

"Just a little. She's been through a lot."

I touched her soft nose and felt her gentle breath on my hand. Then I saw the cuts at the top of each front leg in the crease between her leg and her chest. There was some greasy ointment on the cuts.

"She's hurt," I said.

"She strong and I'm going to get her well. She be pure quarter horse and she's mine. I named her Glory 'cause she's got some of that glory they sing about in church," Josey said.

I looked at the blankets on the straw in the corner. "Did you sleep out here last night?"

"I have to sleep here. She has to be fed often. Foals nurse all the time. Also, I don't want her to feel lonely."

"Do you give her milk from Ruby Jean?" I stroked her short mane that stood straight up.

"No, I have to feed her goat's milk from Daisy back over there. Pa borrowed her for me." He pointed to the back.

I went in the stall where Daisy, a black and white goat, was eating alfalfa. She stared at me and kept moving her jaw back and forth as if to say she could chew me. She looked easier to milk than Ruby Jean. She had only two dark teats and each one was bigger than a cows'.

"Show me how to milk her and I'll help," I said. Josey put a pail under Daisy and showed me how to hold the teat. Then I put my hand around it. It was swollen but felt smooth and soft and I squeezed and made the milk come out. I looked over my shoulder and smiled at Josey.

CHAPTER FORTY-EIGHT

The next week from the window, I saw three pickup trucks with horse trailers coming down the road, pulling dust clouds behind them.

"Buck's here." Mom was excited and rushed into the bedroom. I knew she wanted to gussy herself up.

They stopped in front of the house and Buck got out of the first pickup and two other men got out of their trucks. Willie and Josey went to meet them and started taking the horses out of the trailers. First, they took out Buck's black stallion, Panther. As they let him loose in the field, his long mane blew in the wind and the first thing he did was buck. The sun glittered on his coat, and he held his tail up as he ran off. They took out the other horses and put them in the same field and closed the gate.

Buck, holding three trophies, came up the front steps with his two friends. I opened the front door and smiled my prettiest smile. I was so excited that I couldn't stand still. I got my Eagle Dance going.

Mom came out from the back, wearing a pretty dress with a red belt and red high heels. Boy, I had to say the dress looked tight on her hips and everywhere else. She had on red lipstick and her wavy red hair was down her back. Buck put down his trophies and hugged Mom, lifting her off her feet and turning her around.

As soon as he put her down, I went to Buck and I put out my arms. "Tessa, don't bother Buck," Mom said.

So, she wants to get all the hugs, I thought. I smiled at Buck.

"Come here, little lady," Buck said. He put his strong arms around me and lifted me. It felt so good and I couldn't remember when my father, or for that matter any other man, had hugged me.

My skin and my body felt alive. The stubble on his cheek rubbed against my face. He smelled of horse, sweat, and himself. This is what men smell like, I thought.

He put me down and turned to his friends. "This is Virginia." Buck turned to Virginia. "You remember Vern." He was wearing a brown cowboy shirt with white stars.

Vern shook Mom's hand. I quickly put out my hand to him and said, "I remember you from my birthday party." He also shook my hand. He smiled and the crow's feet bunched up around his eyes. His front teeth stuck out like mine and I liked that it didn't seem to bother him.

Vern looked back at Mom. "You're just the right person to give this place a woman's touch."

Buck turned to his other friend. "And this is Bear."

Bear was a large barrel-chested man with a bunch of chest hair sticking out of the top of his unbuttoned denim shirt. The hair seemed to be saying, "I need to be free and breathe." Right before my eyes, I saw it sprout into grass and become a small front lawn. It could be a home for ladybugs and crickets. I moved really close to him and stared at his chest to see if anything was crawling in it.

Since I was right in front of him, Bear couldn't help but notice me staring.

"Tessa, you don't stare at people," Mom's voice grated on me.

"Do you ever get any bugs in all that hair?" I asked.

"Tessa, hush your mouth." Mom smoothed out the front of her dress.

"Sorry, I forgot that I'm not supposed to say what I think."

Bear ran his hand over his chest hair, and strands curled around his fingers like tentacles. "I was born this way. I'm used to it," he said. He took Mom's hand in his gorilla fist and squeezed it hard. Mom pulled away and tried to keep her face blank, so not to show that his grip hurt. Bear smiled, and he was missing a tooth in front. "Buck is lucky to have found a filly as pretty as you."

"I'm planning on being a country-western singer," Mom said.

"I heard you sing that song you wrote, 'Donkeys Jumping'," Vern said. He tucked both his thumbs into his belt.

Mom blushed. "That was the first song I'd ever written. It was silly."

Vern and Bear looked from Mom to Buck as if they knew something I didn't. After a moment Buck said, "They're going to the ranch-hands house and get settled in with Jeremiah."

"I'm making a big pot roast for dinner," Mom said.

"Sure thing," Vern said. "We'll get cleaned up."

As soon as they left, Buck put his arms around Mom and kissed her. Mom's eyes got all shiny and reminded me of the way people looked when the Holy Ghost came into them. For a moment, I thought the Holy Ghost had followed us here, but the way they looked at each other made me realize it was something else. With his arms around her waist, Buck led Mom into that master bedroom. I followed right behind them and Mom closed the door right in my face. It was as if I wasn't there and I hated that feeling. I put my ear to the door, but I could only hear laughter, and then I went around to the patio off of their bedroom, and just as I looked through their window, Mom's hand pulled the curtain closed.

In my room, I swung my hips the way Mom did. Then I wrote in my notebook, I love Buck and I know more important things to say than Mom. Buck, you must notice she's boring.

I opened my door and they were still in the bedroom. I stood by the door and said, "Mom, why is it taking so long for you to do the Whoredom? Grandma says that's what you do." I heard Buck laugh softly.

"Tessa, shut up and get away from that door or you will get punished real good," Mom said.

Then I smelled cigar smoke as Old Man Henry snuck around outside my window, but before he could corner me, I rushed outside to find Josey. When I found him in the barn, he was cleaning saddles and bridles. I felt Old Man Henry slink away.

A pretty colored girl a little younger than me was with Josey. She had a turned-up nose and two braided pigtails. She struggled with rubbing a saddle with a rag, and she smiled at Josey. I could tell she really liked him.

"Tessa, you're always in a hurry. Nothing goes fast around here," Josey said.

"Josey, you're always working," I said.

"I help my pa. He cain't do everything around here."

The girl looked at me. "This is Tillie, my uncle's girl. He came to visit my pa," Josey said.

"Josey is my best cousin," Tillie said.

"I want to help," I said.

Josey took another saddle off of the rack and propped it on a saddle box and gave me a rag and saddle soap. He showed me how to wipe the clean smelling soap onto the leather.

"You wait for it to dry. It turns white and then you use elbow grease to rub it off," Josey said.

"Since Buck got home, he and Mom have been in the bedroom the whole time. I saw the way he kissed her. They're doing what my grandma called the Whoredom. But when we lived with Beata, the mother of Boleslaw the butcher, Mom's second husband...."

Tillies' eyes got wide and she twisted one of her braids.

"Your mom has been married twice?" Josey asked.

"Yes. Men want to marry her all the time. But as I was saying, Beata called those goings on to Get the Fuck. So, I figure they're doing both things, maybe one then the other so they don't get bored," I said.

Josey stared at me. "If I said those words my papa would whup me good."

I said, "I don't have a father. I can talk anyway I want. I like the way people stare at me when I use bad words."

"If you talk like that, other kids will think there's something wrong with you."

"I don't care what they think."

"I don't believe you. And I think you want to have friends," he said.

CHAPTER FORTY-NINE

At dinnertime, Mom was hurrying around in the kitchen, her red high heels thumping against the floor. Her lipstick was called Red Thunder. She brought extra tubes from Yoakum so as not to run out. Her red dress with puffy sleeves and a full skirt was covered with a big white apron that said Betty Crocker on it. I didn't know a woman dressed up when cooking for men. A checkered red and white Betty Crocker cookbook lay open on the counter.

"You took Grandma's cookbook," I said.

"She never used it. Don't go running off."

"I don't like cooking. That's for you and I want to go to the barn," I said.

"No, I need your help."

At Grandma's, Lilly Mae did most of the cooking and Mom didn't look like she was enjoying it. She wiped sweat from her forehead and dropped utensils on the floor. She'd tell me to pick them up and put them in the sink and then she'd grab a big spoon. You'd think we were fighting a war the way she ordered me to put plates, napkins, glasses, and a basket of biscuits on the table.

"Can you believe we've been here for two months now?" Mom said.

"I feel like I've always been here."

"Buck just talks to his buddies all the time. I can't get a word in. I didn't think I'd be so ignored," Mom said.

"I love everything about this place."

While she dished up potatoes onto a platter, she told me to run and get her purse. When I gave it to her, she quickly took out her compact and looked in the mirror to see if the sweat had messed up her makeup. She put on more Red Thunder and rubbed her lips together.

She finished dishing up onto platters the green beans, black-eyed peas, and of course the main course that men want … that men need … that they come to the table for … the beef. The beef that night was pot roast. I hoped for Mom's sake the pot roast was really good for these male meat eaters. Mom tasted a little bit of it and it seemed to pass her test, but she was still nervous. She looked at the table and moved things here and there, trying to get them in the right place.

The smells of the food mixed with the smell of the wood burning in the fireplace. Buck, Vern, Bear, and Jeremiah came in from the back-porch talking and laughing. Mom was pouring gravy into the gravy bowl and the men stood around the table waiting for her.

I went to Buck and took his hand. "Buck, can I sit next to you?"

Mom brought the gravy bowl to the table. "Tessa, you sit there." She pointed to a seat on the other side of the table away from Buck.

"If the little lady wants to sit next to me, she can sit right here. She just wants to feel at home." He pulled out the chair next to him. "Each of my ladies will sit on one side of me."

Mom's face looked tense. But I smiled and sat down.

Buck passed around the platters of pot roast, potatoes, green beans, and black-eyed peas. The men piled the food on their plates. Mom waited silently for Buck to take that first most important bite. After taking a mouthful of pot roast, he nodded his head. "That's real good cooking." Mom relaxed and smiled as if she'd gotten an "A" on a test. She started eating, but glanced at each of the men as they tasted her pot roast.

I didn't take my eyes off of Buck, even if I dropped some food in my lap, I brushed it off onto the floor. When Buck finally looked at me, I put my head down a little and looked up trying to make my eyes big and winked the way I'd seen Betty Boop do in cartoons.

"Tessa, stop making those silly faces at the table," Mom said.

I wasn't able to get Buck's attention, but neither was Mom. He, Vern, Bear, and Jeremiah talked rodeo and then more rodeo.

"Sidewinder is a real ball-breaker. When I saw that crazed killer look in his eyes, I didn't think you could do it," Vern said. He took the ladle and drowned his potatoes in gravy.

"He gets so high and then does that twist around to the left. Then he pounds his legs like jackhammers. He sure earned his twenty-five points from each of the judges," Bear said. He was chewing meat with his mouth open.

"I needed that purse," Buck said.

"I wonder when they'll be putting him out to stud?" Vern said. He filled his mouth with beef and potatoes. Some of the gravy dripped down his chin, which he wiped with the back of his hand.

"Not anytime soon. He's such a big draw," Buck said.

"When I got my hand hung up on White Lightening and was bouncing off of his side," Bear said. He scratched the hair on his chest and I looked to see if any bugs came out. None did. Then he continued, "I thought I'd get trampled for sure." He opened and closed his sore hand.

Vern dished up even more mashed potatoes and gravy. He looked from Buck to Jeremiah. "My back isn't getting any younger. The doctor says I should retire. I'm thinking of just sticking to roping and cutting. My Danny Boy is one of the best cutting horses around," Vern said.

"You love the rush of all that power between your legs. It's hard to give it up," Buck said.

"I don't have a ranch to fall back on," Vern said.

"We've been through so much together," Buck said. He gave Vern a warm look. "You'll always have a place here with me. I've got plenty of room."

Mom sat up straight and looked surprised. She pushed her red hair back over her shoulders, cleared her throat and looked at each of the men. Finally, she had their attention. "Have you heard the song by Kitty Wells, 'It Wasn't God Who Made Honky-Tonk Angels'? She's the first female solo artist to have a Billboard number one."

"I think I heard it on the radio," Vern said.

"Isn't it amazing what a woman can do now?" Mom said.

"Well, I'll be. One filly made it to the top, I wonder if she lives up to her name and is a real pussy...." Jeremiah looked at Mom and saw her disgust. He added, "....cat." He laughed showing his yellow teeth.

"A lot of people seem to say pussy," I said. Mom gave me an angry look.

Mom looked at each of the men again. "I'm working on my country-western singing."

"Of course, we wish you the best," Vern said. He rubbed his nose with the back of his tanned hand.

Mom said, "Maybe I can sing you my new song I wrote."

All the men became silent for a moment and looked at each other. Jeremiah scooped more black-eyed peas and pot roast into his mouth. Mom looked at Buck. "Buck, the song is about you. Listen, this is the last line." Mom sang, *The cowboy in the heart is giving me a new start...So, kiss this town goodbye and spit in its' eye. Nobody can say no no more."* Mom looked at each of the men. She said, "'No. No more.' That's good, isn't it?"

Buck patted Mom's hand. "Honey, let's wait until after dinner."

"I hope you would be interested but if not, I'd think you'd listen out of politeness," Mom said.

"It's not that often we all get together, so we'll listen later," Buck said.

All of a sudden, the air in the room felt heavy. Nothing was said for a few moments until Bear said, "This is one hell of a ranch."

"This is all here because of Buck's father. Buck reminds me of him sometimes," Jeremiah said. He took out his red handkerchief and wiped his forehead.

"God, no. He was one hell of a bullhead. Nobody believed he'd own his own ranch someday. We lived in a trailer for years on this property," Buck said.

Mom looked down at her plate and bit her lip. She was acting ladylike the way Grandma had taught her, taking small bites. But her Red Thunder lipstick had become an uneven smear across her lips. I knew she was quiet because they weren't paying attention to her. Also, she didn't know anything about rodeo. I thought: She should act interested in rodeo. But Mom started singing her song again to herself, *"The cowboy in the heart is giving me a new start."* Buck patted her hand to make her be quiet.

"Buck, I never get tired of hearing about rodeo," I said.

"Tessa, that's my girl," Buck said. But he didn't take his eyes off of his friends.

I plopped a second helping of potatoes on my plate the way they did. They didn't worry about getting fat. The only other men I'd eaten with were Pastor Jessie Michael and Boleslaw. Now, I was rubbing elbows with strong men who did dangerous things. Their deep voices and laughter made me excited. I looked at each of their faces and there seemed to be a light coming from their eyes as if energy from the sun, wind, and even the animals had gone inside of them and was radiating back out now. When they talked about the bulls and the bareback broncs, I imagined myself sitting on a bronc full of muscle and power. I said, "Yee haw." But the men just talked a little louder.

Gertrude started crying in the other room, and Mom went out and brought her into the living room. She gave her a bottle and returned to the table, bringing more biscuits. She sat and looked from Buck to the other men, as they told a story and laughed. She hummed one of her songs and they heard it, but ignored her.

I dropped a biscuit under the table, so I could look under it. There I saw four pairs of strong legs, with their feet in black, brown, and red dusty cowboy boots. They didn't care about how far apart their legs were spread showing the bulges in their jeans. They weren't affected by Grandma's special rule for ladies that said, "Ladies have to sit with their legs pressed tightly together to keep their pussy genes from causing miserable trouble."

"Tessa, what crazy thing are you doing now?" Mom asked. I didn't say anything. "Get your head up from under the table."

CHAPTER FIFTY

The next day I decided to become a cowgirl. When I got home from school, I went to the barn and Buck took me to a stall where there was a gray horse. Its back and face were a light gray, while its chest, stomach, and legs were covered with dark spots. "This is Suzy. She's a dappled gray. She's getting on in years and very gentle. I'll give you your first lesson."

"I want to become a cowgirl, so I can go to rodeos with you." I stood up straight and I wasn't wearing braids. I had let my hair down my back to be grown-up like Mom.

"You can't miss school."

He put the saddle blanket and then the saddle on Suzy's back, fitting it in just the right position by the bone at the back of the horse's neck that he called the withers.

He brought Suzy over by a platform, so I could get up on her. He told me to put my left leg into the stirrup and swing my right leg up and over her back. I tried to swing my leg, but I didn't make it and Buck had to help lift me. I sat in the saddle and twinges of excitement moved from my thighs and belly throughout my body. I was on top of this beautiful animal and she was going to go where I wanted. I ran my hand over her neck and her coat felt like soft velvet. Then I touched her mane that was coarse and black with some gray hairs.

Buck moved Suzy away from the platform and stood alongside of me. He had on his cowboy hat with the sweat ring around it. He put the reins in my hands.

"You can hold the reins in one hand like this or in two hands like this." He demonstrated both ways of holding the reins with his large hands on top of mine. "That's good." His touch made me feel calm.

Then with his hand, he positioned my heel in the stirrup. "You keep your heels down and toes straight ahead. There should be a straight line from your shoulder to your hip to your heel."

He stood sideways and squatted, showing me how to sit with everything in a straight line. "Don't lean forward or backward." Then he put his hand on my thigh. "To hold on, you grip with your thighs," he said.

I looked into his green eyes and thought: Mom, I've got Buck all to myself right now.

"Tessa, you're a really sweet girl. Sometimes I wish I had children."

He led Suzy and me outside and into the corral and closed the gate. There were smells from the alfalfa bales under a tarp, the horses, and the dirt. He stood alongside of us with his hands holding the reins. He said, "You lay one rein across her neck to turn her in the opposite direction. If she doesn't turn, you gently kick with the heel on the side opposite the direction that you want her to go." He demonstrated laying the reins across her neck, with it loose on one side. "Now, you try." I did. Buck stepped back a few steps. "Now, loosen the reins and gently kick her with both heels and she'll walk forward," he said.

I did as he said, and Suzy started, barely lifting one foot and putting it front of the other, the dead horse walk. How could I be a rodeo cowgirl with a horse this slow? Was this the best he thought I could do?

Buck stepped back a little farther. I looked down and I froze. I said, "Buck stay right next to me." The horse was so big. It was so far down to the ground. I didn't want Buck to see my fear, so I forced my mouth into a crooked smile.

"You're getting it. Just grip with your thighs and keep your heels down," Buck said.

I couldn't let him think I was a sissy.

Suzy stopped walking and turned her head towards me. I whispered, "Don't look at me? You're making me look bad in front of Buck."

Buck smiled. "Sometimes she's lazy. Kick her with both heels again and she'll go."

I kicked her again and she snorted and shook her head. She didn't move.

"You have to kick her a little harder," he said.

I did, and she walked forward. I started to get used to gripping with my thighs and moving with her and I was beginning to feel comfortable. I felt a part of this living creature. I sat up straight because I wanted to look pretty for Buck. I turned and smiled at him. I'll show him, I thought, and I kicked Suzy harder and she started trotting, but I forgot to grip. I'd never bounced this hard, my butt hitting the saddle, my legs loose. I was a chicken flopping around. I looked down … it's too far. I grabbed onto the saddle horn with both hands.

Buck moved toward me. "Don't let go of the reins. Pick up the reins. You have to be in control. You have to remember to grip with your thighs and press your feet down, so you won't bounce so much. You can do it."

I couldn't get the reins while I was bouncing, and I looked silly, but Suzy immediately got tired of trotting and started walking before I looked like a complete fool. I took the reins and sat up straight. I was in control again. Buck said that after a few lessons Josey could take me out on rides.

When we went back to the barn, Buck lifted me off of Suzy and swung me around hugging me. He smelled of sweat and horse. "You did good," he said. I felt thrills go through my body.

I thought that was the second time he had hugged me.

CHAPTER FIFTY-ONE

When the day came that Josey was going to take me on a ride, I went into the barn where Josey had saddled Suzy. I got on her and Josey went into a stall with a bridle and brought out Liberty, a brown and white Paint. He jumped up and his belly landed on her bare back and then he swung his leg over.

"Don't you need a saddle?" I asked.

"I've been riding a long time."

Josey sat up straight, his legs hugging her belly, and he led us out of the barn and down a path toward the back of the property. As soon as we got out of the barn and on the dirt path, I looked at an oak tree to my right. I tensed with fear. In the broad daylight, I saw Old Man Henry leaning against the oak tree staring at me. He was wearing his cowboy hat, his gold watch, and was smoking his cigar.

"I've never seen you outside or when I'm with Josey. You're making me crazy," I said.

He said, "Maybe I'm learning things, too. Tessa, talk to me. I won't let you leave me."

I pulled back on Suzy's reins, stopping her abruptly. "Don't you dare follow me, Old Man. Go away," I shouted.

"I'm not bothering you that much."

"Go away!"

Josey was still ahead of me and he stopped Liberty and turned back. Coming up alongside of me, he had a concerned look on his face. "Tessa, you're frightened. Who's this Old Man you're talking to?"

I was having trouble getting my breath and I was shaking. "There's nobody there I tell you." I was trying to convince myself as much as Josey. I tried to smile, but tears were on my cheeks.

"Tessa, you see someone who's not there. You can tell me what it is. I won't make fun of you. I see you get real upset at times. I know what it's like to be different ... to have people look at you in a certain way," Josey said.

"Back home there was a big storm, and in the back yard I found in the mud, the skeleton of my great-grandfather Old Man Henry. From that day on, I have seen him and he talks to me. He can even make himself small and somehow get into my eye." My cheeks became red from embarrassment.

"So, that's why you hold your eye. He's selfish to cause you such pain," Josey said.

"My grandma says I'm one of those psycho crazy children."

"She shouldn't say that. You have to find a way to stop it. I wish I could help." He brought Liberty alongside of me and reached out and held my hand for a moment. That made Old Man Henry back off and walk away over the field.

I relaxed and I looked at Josey. "You helped to make him go away. But I can't seem to stop him because it's in my genes. It's from my relatives. Let's just ride. How far back does the property go?"

He pointed ahead. "Our property goes all the way to the hills. There's a river back there." He pointed to his right where the trees were clustered by the creek. "The creek flows into it."

We were silent, and I was glad because I didn't feel like talking. The only sound was the horses' hooves on the dirt and their snorting. Maybe it was Suzy's age, but she seemed to like to shake her head and snort.

As we walked, Josey looked calm with the sun on his skin and his legs relaxed around Liberty. I looked ahead to the hills where the trees were clustered at the bottom. I looked to my left at the land that stretched flat and went on and on. Out here a person could become the same as a rock or a tree. I imagined in the distance the flat land becoming hills then rock formations, then mighty mountains like spears reaching for the sky. And on the other side where the birds go, the land became desert. I imagined the lava flowing deep in the earth. Down inside there must be hidden voices that went back to the beginning, whispers of creation. I listened, but all I heard besides the horses' hooves were bird sounds and some rustling in the brush.

I felt small, but when I looked at Josey sitting erect on Liberty, he looked as if he was getting larger; the open land made him grow and didn't swallow him. As he held the reins, the muscles in his arms clung to his denim shirt. He looked older than his age.

Josey looked at me and smiled. "Tessa, you have a strange look on your face. You're not saying much."

"Before this, I was always in Yoakum, in our house or in the stores in town. When we drove here, I never realized how big everything is … the city, the highways, and the ranch land."

"Do you like it out here?" Josey asked.

"Yes, but everything is so big that I feel small." Suzy had sweat on her neck and my cheeks were hot from the sun.

"When I'm riding, I think 'bout how I want to be a rodeo cowboy like Buck when I grow up. Bet you didn't know they're some Negro rodeo cowboys," he said.

He pulled Liberty to a stop. I stopped Suzy, and she immediately went to the side of the path and firmly put her head down to grab shoots of grass. Josey looked straight ahead and his face had a serious expression.

"When I'm out here on Liberty, this here is the one place where I'm really free," he said.

Suzy was pulling on my arm and I made her raise her head. "But you have to go back to your papa, the ranch, and everything else in the evening."

"Let's go over under that tree," Josey said. He guided Liberty to a large oak tree and I followed him under the tree. The cool shade fell across us. Josey looked me right in the eyes. "Out here for a little while, I'm the person I want to be and nothing is holdin' me back," he said.

"I understand." I pushed my hair back behind my ears.

"I want to tell you somethin' I never tell anybody."

"What?" I asked.

"The way I see things is that people have their rules 'bout how things are … 'bout how things should be … Look at this Paint horse. She has two colors. Now, horses don't care which color another horse is. Now, some people are always sayin', 'God has given us this and God has given us that. Because we has our God-given rights. Everything will be our way and we are supposed to own everything.' That's the way things are," he said. He looked as if he would cry and I felt I might cry also.

"I understand what you're saying. You're talking about the white people. There are lots of rules for Negroes. I've seen the signs all over the place all my life," I said.

He lifted his arm and motioned across the land as if he owned it. "I forget those signs when I'm out here. This here place is bigger than all those peoples' rules. They can't put their signs over all this. The land will go on forever and will outlast all those people. There's somethin' out here that gets inside you and makes you stronger," Josey said.

"I want to feel that. Take me all the way to the river." I kicked Suzy, but she only moved slowly back onto the path.

CHAPTER FIFTY-TWO

We watched Bear drive away, his large body stuffed into his truck. "Thank God he's leaving. I had to cook for two more just to feed him," Mom said. But Vern had settled in for a long stay and bought a rocking chair to sit with Buck on the front porch in the evenings. They'd play poker and drink beer and I'd sit with them listening to their stories of the old-time cowboys until Mom made me go to bed.

We settled into a routine. I came home from school and Mom was always busy with Gertrude, or cooking, or cleaning. Since moving here, dust had become her enemy. She was always rubbing the wood or leather furniture as if someday it would thank her.

She practiced her guitar whenever she could steal a few minutes for herself. She said everyone was trying to keep her from the one important thing that she was supposed to be doing.

Mom rarely came out to the barn because she said the dust made her sneeze, so she didn't know Josey was taking me on rides every day after school.

Since we moved here, I didn't feel as if I was a smaller version of her anymore. Every time I tried to talk to her she was distracted or else singing country-western songs. I loved the horses and she could take them or leave them. I was beginning to see that I was different from her.

Back in Yoakum, she'd have nervous attacks and rush out of Grandma's house saying she needed to get some air and then she'd drive around for hours. But here it was as if an invisible fence or corral was keeping her inside Buck's house. She'd walk from room to room and even open the front door and look outside, but wouldn't go out. But I liked to think the house was a barn and the bedrooms our stalls and we were gorgeous horses with long manes. I'd go around the house stomping and whinnying. When Mom wasn't looking, I'd bring Suzy halfway onto the back-porch. I'd put pieces of carrots on a plate and put them at the end of the table where she could reach them. I liked for her to eat lunch with me, so I didn't have to eat alone.

Other than driving me back and forth to school every day, Mom didn't have the energy to go into San Antonio, or explore the other ranch roads, or even drive around the neighborhood by my school.

She'd sit silently as we drove around in the car. If I said something it would hang in the air, without an answer. Her silence made me feel like I was sinking.

When we were back in the house, sometimes I'd find her staring out the front windows at the pastures and trees. Once when I asked her what she was staring at, she said, "I didn't know Buck's ranch was so far out. It feels so empty and alone here. All this space swallows my thoughts. I have to have my music."

"I like it here," I said. But she didn't hear me. She filled the house with the sounds of country-western music morning, noon, and night.

When I showed Gertrude how to dance, she bounced up and down in her playpen to the music, but it was hard to get Mom to hear me over the radio. I'd have to speak louder and louder until I could get her to turn the music down.

One afternoon when I came back from riding with Josey, the music was blaring, and Mom was on her knees scrubbing the oven. She wore yellow rubber gloves that were too large for her hands. She was using

Dutch Cleanser and Brillo pads inside the oven. The white O'Keeffe and Merritt had a double oven and one side of it had a window with stuff stuck to it.

Without her noticing, I got a bag of cookies and milk and sat at the table. She was singing along with the radio, *"Well I left my farm down on the old south road. I told my maw I'm going out two-stepping all night and will surely get those honky-tonk blues."* On her knees, she was wiping the oven window in rhythm to the music. The bucket of water next to her was black from the dirt. She stood up and wiped the sweat off her forehead with the backside of the rubber glove. She moved her feet to the music then she turned and noticed me. "Don't sneak up on me. Where have you been? You know I don't like being alone in this house."

"I didn't think you could hear me," I said.

"What did you say?"

"I said turn the music down, so you can hear me."

She turned the music down a little bit. "Does it matter? You never seem to want to talk to me. You're in your fantasy world," she said loudly. She got back on her knees and again started cleaning the inside of the oven.

That thick lonely feeling like the dark night came over me. I said under my breath, "Why can't you just listen to me?"

She continued cleaning the oven and moved her hips to the music. But then she stood up and faced me. She looked tired. "Look at me," she still spoke loudly. "Can't you see I'm tired? There's too much work here. Buck needs to get a maid. He better not be thinking I can do this all the time." She dipped the Brillo pad in water and turning away from me, she shook more Dutch Cleanser into the oven and put her head back inside.

The loneliness covered me like a new skin. "Ask me about my day," I said. I didn't know if she was ignoring me or couldn't hear me, so I decided to turn into a horse. I whinnied and dipped my cookie in the milk and bobbed my head up and down. I chewed with my mouth open, pretending I was a horse eating alfalfa.

Mom with her head in the oven, shouted along with the song on the radio, *"Yeah those honky-tonk blues are floating around everywhere. Well,*

I caught them." She added her own words, "*Too many dishes…too much scrubbing. I got the housecleaning blues. Lordy, I'm not a maid. I'm that honky-tonk lady that will tear this house down,*" she yelled. She stood up and danced to the music.

She faced me and turned the music down just a little more. "Tessa, why don't you ever listen to me?" she spoke loudly over the music.

"I try to Mom."

"But your mind is always off somewhere in your daydream place. And you ignore me."

"Because it's hard to talk to you. And you play that loud music all the time," I said angrily. She just continued scrubbing the oven.

I bobbed my head up and down. I stomped and pawed the floor with one foot then the other. I felt just like a horse.

In a loud voice from inside of the oven she said, "I don't think Buck has ever cleaned this oven. He's dumping this on me." She took her head out again and looked at me. "Tessa, do I look like a household drudge to you?" The yellow gloves had a lot of black stuff on them.

"No, Mom, everyone says you're pretty." But she wasn't looking at me and it didn't matter what I said.

She stood up and went to the sink with the bucket and dumped the dirty water. She filled it with fresh water. "Don't tell Buck any of this while Vern's here."

"Nobody listens to me anyway," I said. I got up and bent over and started moving my rear side to side, as if I had a tail and was swishing it around.

"What are you talking about now?" Taking the fresh water back to the stove, she looked at me. "What are you doing?"

"You're dancing and I'm dancing," I said.

"That's a strange way to dance."

"We don't seem to be able to talk, ever," I said loudly. I pushed my hair back over my shoulders and whinnied and pawed the floor.

Finally, she turned the music down. "Why didn't you tell me you felt that way?"

"I've tried to tell you," I said.

"I don't know what to say. I'm here all the time. I don't ignore you the way you ignore me." She wiped the sweat off of her forehead with her forearm. "I have to talk to Buck when Vern leaves, if he ever leaves."

I moved close to Mom. "I like Vern. His front teeth are like mine and they don't bother him." I opened my mouth showing my front teeth that stuck out.

"Stop worrying about your teeth. They're hardly noticeable." She looked away and started cleaning the top of the stove.

"That's easy for you to say." I went back and sat at the table.

"Are you listening to me? I'm not cut out to be a housewife. I need time alone with Buck. Don't you agree?" Mom rubbed around the burners as if she were mad at them.

"Sure, so you can be all kissy face." She didn't hear me and I started laughing, and then I danced around moving my rear, and with my lips I made some farting sounds. Horses make farting sounds. They can't help it. I laughed some more.

She turned and looked at me and stopped cleaning. Her face became tense and she wiped more sweat off of her forehead. "Tessa, don't you dare laugh at me."

"But I'm happy. All you do is worry," I said.

She took off the yellow clown gloves and got a dust rag out of the broom closet. "Don't criticize me. I've made sacrifices for you. I came here for you. And I never switched you like your grandma. Anyway, I need your help. You can start by dusting in the living room," she said.

I grabbed the rag from her and rushed into the living room to do the job quickly. I wanted to get to the barn where Josey would soon be milking the goat to feed Glory.

In the living room, I looked at the large leather sofas and chairs. I always imagined the sofas had little dwarfs inside making their forms lumpy. I hit my fists on the sofa seats. "Little people inside, wake up. You're not going to sleep while I'm working." I quickly wiped the coffee table and knocked over an ashtray, spilling cigarette ashes on the cattle skin rug.

Mom came into the living room. "Now look what you've done because you don't want to dust."

I felt guilty and picked up the ashtray. "No, I'll help you."

She went back to the broom closet and came back with a dustpan and broom and started sweeping. "I have to do everything myself."

"I said I'll do it." I took the boom and swept up the ashes. I finished wiping the table and the other end tables. I dusted off the sofas and chairs. I took the old newspapers into the kitchen where Mom was cleaning the countertops. "From now on, you're going to help me for an hour when you come home from school."

I jumped up and down. "O.K. I finished the dusting so can I go to the barn now?"

"All you want to do is rush out to the barn. And after dinner, you just want to sit with Buck and Vern on the porch. But you're going to finish your homework first. Girls don't sit with the men all the time. They talk about things you shouldn't be hearing."

"I already know all the bad words. And girls sit with their fathers," I said. I stared at her and I thought she looked down because I had reminded her that my father didn't see me.

CHAPTER FIFTY-THREE

The best part of my day was riding with Josey, and I felt something with him I didn't feel with the girls at school. When I dared to write in my diary that I loved Josey, I blushed. It was forbidden, but who would know?

By then, I'd become a better rider, so I rode Black Betsy, who with one kick would take off like a speeding car.

One day as we were riding toward the river, the sunlight shone on Josey's face and I knew he was feeling that freedom he felt when riding. We kicked the horses and took off in slow cantor, my favorite gait, rocking with the rhythm of the horse. We approached Buck, Vern, Jeremiah, and Willie out in the pasture on the left side of the dirt road. Vern had a post-hole digger that he was raising and slamming into the dirt. They were building a fence around a pasture where I'd heard them say they were going to plant alfalfa in the spring.

We slowed the horses to a walk. Buck and Willie were moving some logs for posts, and as we got closer Buck stopped, took off his red scarf, and wiped the sweat off of his face. Then he smiled and waved to us, and a warm feeling went through my body. This had to be what it felt like to have a father. Willie pushed back his straw hat and his gaze followed Josey on Liberty, his smile creasing the lines around his eyes.

I realized that just as Mom cleaned and made the house orderly inside, the outdoors was the house for these men, and it had to be shaped and ordered to their will. But they weren't gentle cleaners; they wore heavy gloves, sweaty shirts, and old jeans as they prodded and poked, pushed and pulled logs, rocks, and tree stumps. With tight muscles, their faces strained as they pounded the post-hole digger into the dirt.

They never talked about the land the way Josey did. But I could see their determination as they worked. The property was to be divided into planted fields, pastures, and holding pens for cattle and horses. As we passed, I took off in a fast gallop. My legs gripped the saddle and I waited for that moment when I felt it, that feeling that Black Betsy and I had merged into one strong being. Josey galloped up alongside of me, and I told myself to freeze that image of him in my mind. He was in the forever time. As we rode, I looked back at the cowboys and they had become four dark shapes, small against the land. There was only the sound of our horses' hooves on the path.

I saw that the men worked as though something deep inside pushed them, a presence telling them, "You can toil and struggle, but things won't last. See the remnants of houses dotting the land from the people who went before you. All that is left are small burnt logs. Listen to the wind whining across the mountains as if saying, 'Your bones will become the same as the bleached cows' skulls. So, hurry and build while you have the time.'"

At dinnertime, Josey brought me back to the barn. Black Betsy and Liberty were sweating, and Josey would have to walk them to cool them down before putting them in the stalls.

As I watched Josey loosen the cinch of Black Betsy's saddle, I reached out and touched his arm softly. I hadn't tried to touch him in a long time. Even though his hands were rough, the skin on his arm was smooth.

"Tessa, stop it," Josey said.

I took my hand away. "I didn't mean any harm."

He lifted the saddle off of Black Betsy and took it into the tack room. When he came out, he said, "I'm just the same as anybody else."

"I think friends touch each other." I pushed my sweaty hair back over my shoulders.

"I'm jest a ranch hand, not your friend," he said.

Just then the men pulled up in a truck, stopping outside of the barn on the side where the farm equipment was stored. Buck and Vern got out of the front, and Jeremiah got out of the back and unloaded the post-hole digger and other equipment. I went to Buck and he put down a coil of wire and hugged me, lifting me off of the ground.

"You look beautiful on a horse. But isn't it time for you to help your mama in the kitchen?" he asked.

I knew they were going to say things that I wasn't supposed to hear, so I pretended to walk toward the kitchen, but I doubled back around the other side of the barn. They were in the storage area under the overhanging roof, and I crouched out of sight behind a tractor, so I could overhear their conversation. This was how I was learning cowboy language. I didn't know that with cowboys the words "shit" or "oh shit" were so popular. I also heard Jeremiah say, "tight-ass," which I thought had something to do with a person having trouble going to the bathroom.

They were unloading the fence posts from the truck and stopped to take a break. Jeremiah stuck some chewing tobacco in his mouth. Jeremiah said, "You sure got yourself a pretty lady."

"She seemed so glad to be here at first, but now I don't know," Buck said. He sat down on a crate and took off his work gloves.

"A woman could feel isolated out here. No other women to chit-chat with," Vern said.

"She's always playing music and singing. Something may be bothering her, but I don't know," Buck said.

"Trying to figure out what a woman is thinking is out of my league," Vern said.

"I'm a simple guy. I can't come up with fancy language," Buck said.

"I think she loves you. Don't doubt yourself," Vern said.

"As long as she is good in the sack, don't complicate things with too much talking," Jeremiah said.

"I don't feel right talking about her when she's not here. We got to unload the rest of these fence posts," Buck said. Buck put his work gloves back on and went to the back of the truck.

After they finished unloading the truck, Vern got behind the wheel, but the engine wouldn't start. He tried a couple of times and the engine made a clicking sound. "Fuck, it's the starter," he said. The way he spoke was as if a hole had been punched in the air. I realized I'd been saying the expression wrong all this time. I'd learned from Polish Beata the expression to Get the Fuck. Well, cowboys didn't waste words and said just plain old Fuck.

I felt I had to go in and help Mom. In the kitchen, Mom was dancing to the loud country-western music, and when she saw me, she slammed some pots around. But she didn't touch the pretty copper pots over the stove. I figured she was trying to tell me without using words that she was angry because I hadn't come into the house earlier to help her.

She pulled open the silverware drawer, which I knew meant she wanted me to set the table. She pressed her Red Thunder lips firmly together. Even with the music, her silence made the room feel empty.

Since the music was so loud, I could talk out loud without her hearing me just as I did every night. I took out the silverware and as I placed the forks and spoons on the table, I felt a shudder go through them. I could feel their fear. I told them not to be afraid when they were put in the big mouths between the teeth. I reminded them that they went through this every night, but were too skinny to remember it. I reassured them that afterward they would be cleaned, dried with the dishcloth, and put to rest in their drawer. This calmed them because they liked being rubbed all over.

I didn't talk to the knives because they were boys. Their memory was even worse than the forks and I knew they would never listen to me.

Finally, Buck, Vern, and Jeremiah entered through the back-porch slamming the screen door and then the door to the kitchen. Their boots stepped loudly on the floor, as if they were saying they owned the place. The men were joking and laughing, and the first thing Buck always did was turn off the music. Buck hugged me. He smelled of dirt and sweat. Jeremiah smelled of chewing tobacco, even from across the room.

Their sweaty hats, dirty gloves, and jackets were their outdoor male selves. As they took them off, they landed where they were dropped. Mom had worked all day to clean the place, but dirt came in with the men.

The men made the house come alive and the walls took on a shine. The knotted beams across the ceiling weren't like the forks. The beams had good memories. Only I heard them whisper, "We remember being made by men and we love to hear their voices."

Mom sat Gertrude in her highchair while the men warmed their hands by the fire. Then Mom brought platters of food to the table. The men took their seats. I never got tired of watching them dish up piles of food.

After dinner, I followed the men as they headed for the front porch where they would drink beer and play poker. "Young lady, where do you think you're going?" Mom's voice pulled me back like a rope around my neck. "You're going to help me with the dishes right now."

I stomped over to the table whinnying and shaking my head. Instantly, I was a horse again. "Don't make that sound and don't give me that look," she said. I cleared the table and stacked the dishes and silverware on the counter while Mom put away the leftovers in the Hotpoint refrigerator with a big round thing on top. Mom said that Buck needed to get one that went with the remodeled kitchen.

Mom put on her yellow rubber gloves, scraped the dishes, and then filled one side of the double sink with soapy water.

I moved my arms through the air like an eagle. "Can I go out now?" I asked.

"First finish helping me."

"Why don't you sit with them after dinner?"

"I'm not interested in poker, beer, or rodeos."

I wanted to understand what the men had said. "What does 'tight ass' mean? Is it something just a woman has or does a man have it too?" I tried to imagine a man in jeans that tightened his ass to make it look better.

Mom stopped washing the dishes and her face had a twisted look. "You heard that from Buck and his friends. Who were they talking about?"

"I don't know," I said.

"It's a crude expression. So, after you finish here, you're going to your room and do your homework."

I heard the wind blowing outside and I knew little swirls of dust were being kicked up as if wandering spirits were exhaling on the dirt. The darkness was descending and cloaking everything outside. I wasn't afraid of the darkness, but I was afraid of Old Man Henry. He had a way of knowing when I wasn't supposed to leave my room. "Please, don't make me stay alone in my room. Please don't make me." I was on the verge of tears and I pulled on my hair. I couldn't tell her about Old Man Henry because that would really upset her. Many times, she'd told me that what I saw was all in my imagination. But I couldn't make him go away.

"Tessa, now what is wrong with you?" Mom said.

I had to pinch myself to keep my mouth from letting unwanted words come out.

CHAPTER FIFTY-FOUR

As soon as I went to my room, I took out my diary with the daisy print cover from under my mattress and wrote, "Fuck you, Old Man Henry, and don't come tonight." I wrote that many times and it made me feel better.

I opened my door and I heard Mom in Gertrude's bedroom getting her ready for bed and singing to her. I closed my door, lay down on my bed, and fell asleep, but I was awakened by a voice. I froze. Was it Old Man Henry's? I became alert and I heard a man's voice say, "Go on, say what you want to say."

I looked around my room and Old Man Henry wasn't there. Then I heard, "Go on, spit it out. I can tell you're chewing on something." It was Buck's voice coming from the master bedroom. I'd never heard him sound so angry. The floor was cold as I put on my robe and tiptoed into the hallway and put my ear to their door.

"When is Vern going to leave? He's been here for months," Mom said in a low voice. The wood floor creaked as she walked back and forth across it.

"He can stay here as long as he wants. He does a lot of work around here," Buck replied.

"Every night you sit on the front porch with him and Jeremiah for hours."

"He and Jeremiah are my family."

"Don't you want to spend time with me?" I could tell that she was crying.

"Virginia, we have time together."

I held onto the brass doorknob and put my ear against the cold door to hear every word. "I feel ignored and I'm stuck in this house all day." Mom made little choking sounds as she spoke.

"Honey, I'm not much of a talker. I've never been very good at conversation. It's like my tongue is all thumbs," Buck said.

"When are you going to take me to dinner in San Antonio, or to a movie, or dancing?"

"I have a lot of work to get done before the rains come."

"When we met in Yoakum, you were so lively."

"A cowboy always looks good when he's working a rodeo."

"We didn't get to know each other very well before I came here." Mom was definitely crying now. I imagined the tears making streaks on her cheeks.

"I'm a simple man. It takes a certain person for ranch life. I was hoping you'd love it like I do. There's nothing like watching the sun come up across the land with the drops of dew on the ground. Then breathing in the cool air," Buck said.

"I want to feel I'm special to you."

"You know I love you and I appreciate all you do. You don't have to work so hard."

"That's another thing I need to talk to you about."

"Can't we talk about this tomorrow?" Buck asked. The bedsprings of the brass bed moaned loudly so it had to be Buck who had sat down.

"This is exactly what I mean." I heard light footsteps, as Mom walked around the room.

"Come here, my pretty lady. Don't you want me to want you?" Buck asked.

"And when are we going to talk about marriage?"

"Whoa, hold on a minute. I'm not a person to be roped down and it's the man that does the asking when it comes to marriage," Buck said.

"So now you're all formal with rules. We have to talk about this."

"I'm happy with things the way they are," Buck said.

"What about my feelings?"

"In a couple of weeks, I'm going away to some rodeos," Buck said.

"Do you have to? Do you make that much money at it?"

"Sometimes. But that's not why I do it. It's in my blood."

"What am I supposed to do here all alone? Please don't go so soon." Mom's voice sounded sad.

"Why don't you come with me?"

"Tessa can't miss school and it's hard hauling a baby around."

"A lot of kids miss school for a few days for a rodeo. We can have fun. Tessa would like it."

"You're making me feel pressured."

"You're my girl, so I think you should come," Buck said.

"Did you hear what I said?"

"Let's not argue. Come here, pretty lady."

"I don't want to." I heard walking in the room.

"O.K. I get it. You're independent, but I know you want me," Buck said.

"Please stop. I can't give you whatever you want whenever you want it."

My feet were cold and when I moved the floor creaked.

"Tessa, get away from that door, you dirty little sneak!" Mom yelled. I felt a knot in my stomach as I tiptoed away.

CHAPTER FIFTY-FIVE

The next morning when I came into the kitchen, Mom and Buck were kissing. Then Buck held Mom and looked her right in the eyes, and I felt relief. I thought that if they are kissing then Mom's not so unhappy after all. I couldn't bear it if she wanted to leave here.

Mom dished up the eggs, bacon, sausages, pancakes, and biscuits and put them on the table. Then she added the butter and the little crock of honey. Just as Buck and I sat down, Vern and Jeremiah came in, slamming the back-porch door. Mom jumped.

They were laughing, and Jeremiah was rubbing his hands together to warm them. They were eager to start their work for the day. As soon as they sat down, I lathered my biscuit with butter and honey.

Buck looked from Jeremiah to Vern. Buck said, "Jake Russell's mare, Honey Lady, has just come in heat. He needs a quality foal this year to help with his bills, so I'm going to breed her with Panther."

"I was there when Panther was born ... strongest foal you ever saw, black as night and graceful. He has great quarter horse bloodlines," Jeremiah said.

"Jake's done me favors many times and I didn't want to charge a stud fee, but he insisted on paying something," Buck said.

"I'm sure Panther has plenty of sperm to spare. Squirt, squirt.…He's got strong swimmers." Jeremiah moved his hand as if a fish was swimming. "And what's a little extra sperm between friends?"

He looked from Buck to Vern smiling as if he had told a funny joke. Vern smiled, but Mom's face was taut and twisted.

"Virginia, you have to forgive Jeremiah. He hasn't been around women that much," Buck said. Jeremiah stroked his beard, looking embarrassed.

I wasn't sure what they were talking about, but it was as if the word "sperm" hung over the table … a floating word, maybe a slimy fish word. Since it was one of those secret words, I sounded out its spelling in my mind. But it had something to do with boys and I felt my cheeks turn red.

Vern and Jeremiah put on their jackets, gloves, and cowboy hats and went outside. Buck looked at Mom. "Jake's coming this morning. I don't know if you want Tessa out there. We will get a little rowdy."

"She's getting her crude language from listening to your friends. Today, she's going to spend time with Gertrude and me. I need time with my daughter," Mom said as if I wasn't in the room.

"Of course, you do," Buck said, and he went out the back.

Mom turned to me. "You're going to stay inside and first you'll clean your room." She sounded angry.

"Why are you angry? I haven't done anything yet."

I went to my room and after a few minutes, I heard Mom singing to the loud country-western music on the radio. I knew she'd get absorbed in the music and forget she said I had to spend time with her. I waited a little while and then climbed out my window, stepping on the wooden box that I always kept under it.

The four men were gathered on the side of the barn, which had the two corrals side by side, separated by a walkway in between. Without being seen, I snuck around the backside of the barn getting closer to the corrals. The men were standing by the corral that was closest to the front of the barn. Josey was in the walkway between the two corrals. He was next to an old wagon and he had one boot on the bottom fence rail. As I came around the back of the barn and climbed into the wagon, I was careful he didn't see me. The bottom of the wagon was rough cracked wood, so I was careful as I scooted across and stopped behind Josey. His back was to me and I thought that I was in the clear.

Josey stuck his head over the side of the wagon and I jumped. "Tessa, do you think I don't see you? Does your mama know you're out here?"

"My mama lets me do what I want."

"Do you know what's going to happen?"

"Yes, back in Yoakum I've seen it lots of times." I had no idea what he was talking about.

Willie put Panther in the second corral behind the one at the front of the barn. Panther had two ropes attached to his halter and Willie tied him to the fence next to the walkway, not far from us.

"You're going to see the works of pure nature. The preachers can jaw all they want, but there's no sin here," Josey said.

"You're right. Those boring preachers always talking about sin." I made my voice a little deeper to sound like I knew what I was talking about, but Josey wasn't listening to me. He was watching the men.

Even though the men were just standing around talking, I felt the excitement in the air. Vern put his hands in his pockets and leaned back on the heels of his black boots for a moment, and Jeremiah took out some chewing tobacco and put it in his mouth. Buck pulled the sheepskin-lined collar of his denim jacket up around his neck. Then he looked at the gold watch he'd won at a rodeo.

"He should be here soon," Buck said. He took out his work gloves from his pocket and put them on. The others pulled on their work gloves.

Patches of sunlight broke through the large clouds, gently falling on the cowboys. They looked up the road where an old pickup pulling a beat-up horse trailer was approaching the barn, a dust cloud following. The truck stopped by the empty corral and Buck and the others walked over to the trailer and a cowboy got out. He was bowlegged and shorter than the other men, but had a pleasant smiling face. He put one hand on Buck's shoulder and with the other grabbed Buck's gloved hand and shook it.

"Buddy, I'm grateful for this," Jake said to Buck.

"You know Vern and Jeremiah," Buck said. He motioned toward the two men.

Vern and Jeremiah each shook Jake's hand. "It's been awhile, but it's good to see you two again," Jake said.

Jeremiah was smiling at Jake. "As I was telling Buck, what's a little extra sperm between friends? We got plenty," Jeremiah laughed and was proud of his joke.

As they were talking, Panther snorted loudly a couple of times. He pulled against the halter, lifting his head, straining to see the trailer. He flared his nostrils, stuck out his upper lip and inhaled. He took deep breaths, trying to suck up as much of the smell as possible. I sniffed, trying to figure out what was exciting the horse. But all I could smell was dust, horse sweat, and manure. Panther's eyes widened while he kept inhaling and he pawed the ground and kept pulling against the halter, trying to get a better look at the trailer.

I felt drawn to him and I forgot about hiding. I got out of the wagon to get a better view and moved next to Josey by the fence. Buck noticed me, but didn't say anything.

Buck and Jake went to the rear of the horse trailer and unlatched the tailgate, pulled it open, and set it on the ground. "She's a little testy today … you know female hormones," Jake said.

Panther snorted. I looked back at him, and his large eyes with a little of the whites showing had a wildness in them I'd never seen before. Even though I didn't have the words for it, I felt his primal nature and maleness. There was something deep in earth's creatures. Something that was always there. Sensations shot through my body and my stomach. I hadn't really noticed Panther before, but looking at him now, he was grander than anything I'd experienced.

Jake went inside the trailer and started backing Honey Lady, a sturdy quarter horse, down the ramp. She was golden-brown with a lighter colored mane and tail, and I wondered why her tail was wrapped up with a cloth. Jake stroked her neck and gently spoke to her. "That's my girl." He led Honey Lady to the gate on the side of the empty corral and still stroked her neck. Buck opened the gate to let them in and then closed it. Jake walked Honey Lady over toward our side of the fence. She wasn't paying any attention to Panther. She nuzzled the arm of Jake's denim jacket. He stopped and took a cube of sugar out of his pocket, and with his palm flat, let her take it from his hand.

Jeremiah went to Panther and he took the rope from Willie. Then Jeremiah and Vern untied Panther from the fence and each held one of the ropes attached to his halter. They started walking him toward the gate at the front of his corral. He pawed the ground and strained toward Honey Lady. Jeremiah and Vern held him back. "Hold on, Buddy. Just a few more minutes," Jeremiah said. Panther nodded his head up and down, as if he was agreeing with him.

As they walked him through the gate of his corral, Panther flared his nostrils and inhaled again.

The sun glistened on his sweating coat and then he reared, but Jeremiah and Vern pulled him down. Jeremiah leaned toward Panther's ear and said, "Don't worry, Big Boy. You'll get her."

I stood near Josey, but he wasn't paying attention to me. Panther looked toward us and for a moment his eyes fixed on me as if I were a fellow animal, and I felt his power and rawness. He looked as if he were telling me that he could run right over me.

Josey and I moved over to the fence of Honey Lady's corral. As they led Panther to her corral, he pawed the ground, trying to get Honey Lady's attention. But Honey Lady only glanced at him and then went back to rubbing Jake's jacket with her muzzle. He was excited and she wasn't. I didn't know why.

Jake checked to see if Honey Lady was firmly tied to the fence. I looked at Josey. "Honey Lady doesn't seem interested in that pure nature after all," I said.

"She don't have to be. She just has to spread her legs and hold still. He's the male. He does everything. He's the king," Josey said.

This was the first time Josey had said something that bothered me. I thought: What does that mean? Is he saying that the female doesn't matter? I looked back at Vern and Jeremiah holding Panther's ropes and my stomach knotted up. My God what is that? I thought. I couldn't believe the size of the thing hanging down between Panther's legs. I was sure I'd never seen anything that size before. I'd seen something hanging from male horses, when they peed, but nothing like this. This was hard and looked as if it could pierce its way through the earth. This was important. Excitement and tingly sensations ran through my body.

"Most males get gelded, but Panther's a stallion and has all his equipment the way God made him … like I said, it's beautiful pure nature," Josey said.

I felt like I had to say something. I didn't want him to know I hadn't seen this before. "His equipment? You mean his pecker hanging down?"

"Where you'd learn that word?" Josey said.

"At my old school, Carl told me that boys have peckers," I answered.

"You're a nice girl and he shouldn't be talking to you that way. It's called a cock," Josey said.

As Josey said that, I thought: But it's too big. That would scare any girl. I looked at Honey Lady. She was calm and didn't look scared.

Buck took the rope Vern was holding, and he and Jeremiah continued leading Panther along the side of the corral where Honey Lady was tied. The closer Panther got to Honey Lady, the more excited he became. I had to admire that Panther wasn't embarrassed having his cock hanging out for everyone to see, and as he moved, it swayed from side to side, like a big snake moving. Yes, like a python, like the ones I'd seen in pictures.

When they were at the gate, Vern opened it and Buck and Jeremiah led Panther into Honey Lady's corral. As soon as he got inside the corral, he reared again, but the men pulled him down. "Buddy, you behave. You don't get her until we let you," Jeremiah said.

I thought: Aren't they bossy and what is he going to do with that anyway?

It was as if Josey heard my thoughts. "You know he's going to put it inside of her. He'll do her good … fuck, fuck, boom, boom," Josey said.

He smiled at me, his white teeth showing. But then he stopped abruptly. "I'm sorry for usin' that word with you. I shouldn' talk that way around a nice girl. It's just the excitement."

"Fuck. I like to say that word," I said. But I couldn't stop the redness from coming to my cheeks. I didn't want him to see my blushing, so I kept my eyes on Panther. I felt afraid and I didn't believe that could fit in her. I didn't think human females would like that.

"Tessa, you have a strange look on your face. He has to fuck her … I mean innercourse her … in and out … because it's the only way she can get pregnant. It's the nature," Josey said.

I had no idea how Mr. Python would fit in her. I thought: So, this is really what fucking is. Because I'm a girl, nobody would tell me this.

I kept staring at Panther. Then I looked at Buck and Jeremiah holding Panther. I looked at Vern and Willie, now inside Honey Lady's corral, leaning against the fence. They were smiling as if ready to cheer Panther on. Buck and Jeremiah were walking Panther with his cock hanging down; they were standing erect with their chests stuck out. They thrust their boots firmly down on the dirt and strutted with their tight leg muscles. The stallion was their brother. They laughed while controlling Panther with his cock big enough for the whole world to see. Were these cowboys also part of the pure nature Josey talked about?

Now that Panther was in Honey Lady's corral, she turned her head, pulling against the rope, watching him. Jake stroked her head. Panther pranced, sweat like diamonds glistened on his neck, as Buck and Jeremiah held him. "I know it's been a long time for you, Buddy," Jeremiah said. Jeremiah patted Panther's neck and then he unhooked the rope he was holding and moved out of Panther's way. Buck still held onto his rope, but he stepped back, letting Panther have a lot of room.

Panther went to Honey Lady's head, whinnying softly as if he was talking to her. She turned her head, and he gently touched his nostrils to hers, still whinnying softly. They're kissing, I thought. Then he moved his muzzle down along her neck, to her side sniffing her. Honey Lady lowered her rear legs and surprised me by peeing a big stream.

"She's getting ready for you, buddy," Jeremiah said.

Panther moved his muzzle gently along the side of her rear, sniffing, and then on the back of her hind leg, smelling her urine. He lifted his head high, curled his upper lip, and inhaled deeply that thing only he could smell. Then he put his nose back on her leg again to smell some more.

With his big cock swaying, he moved around behind her. Jeremiah grabbed Honey Lady's wrapped tail and pulled it over to one side. Panther got up on his hind legs. He put his front legs over her back, letting them hang down on each side of her stomach. He slipped off of her, but he got up on her again, taking little steps on his hind legs to balance himself. He was graceful, almost as if he was dancing. He was in a hurry and started thrusting his cock at her rear. But he was just thrusting into the air. Then he moved his hind legs closer, and kept thrusting until he partially entered her, and then with a big push, all of his cock sank into her. I had no idea she had a place big enough for that. I wanted to yell "stop" because I thought he was hurting her, but she stood calmly. I thought: How can she stand that? Panther held his head up, his front legs hanging along her stomach, and he thrust inside of her again and again, his whole body taut. Honey Lady didn't seem to mind Panther's weight on her back.

"You go, buddy. Fuck her good," Jeremiah said. Jeremiah put his hand out palm up, and Vern slapped it with his palm. "That's our boy. He can out fuck any stallion," Vern said.

So, this is what it's all about, I thought. I took a deep breath. Why would a female want to be stuck with that thing inside of her? Human females can talk, and so we're different than animals. So, a pussy is for a male to stick his cock inside. And all she has to do is hold still. Maybe I should be more careful when I say the word pussy. Well, that isn't for me. Somebody else can hold still.

Panther, sweat foam on his black neck, had his head hanging alongside of Honey Lady's neck. He was resting and then he lifted his head, backed up, and came down off of her. His cock wasn't as hard as it was before. Buck came up and grabbed Panther's rope close to his halter. Everything was finished. I thought: *So, this is what all those big secrets were about. I'm not so impressed.*

Jeremiah on the other side of Panther patted his neck. "You did good, Buddy."

Josey turned to me. "He done it. She'll get pregnant ... and get a big belly,"

I didn't know what he was talking about, but I blushed and I couldn't look at him. I stepped back against the wagon. These were men I admired and I wanted to be a part of their world, but in that moment, I realized I was different. I didn't want the cowboys to look me in the eyes and think because I was a girl that somehow, I didn't measure up.

At night did Mom just lay there and get poked by him? Is that the way women are supposed to be? I had a butterflies-in-the-stomach feeling. I felt confused. I was alone and shut out of the important things in life. Adults around me were always saying, "Girls can't do this, and girls can't do that." It's so unfair. I wiped tears from my cheeks. I felt a hot anger inside of me. I thought: *They can take all the cocks in the world and stick them someplace else. I hate all that pure nature and it's not going to control me. And I won't hold still for it either.*

I did my Marching Dance as I went back to the house to my mother and Gertrude ... to the cooking and cleaning, and watching my mother take care of Gertrude while waiting for Buck to come inside.

I looked at Mom standing by herself in the kitchen, wearing her lipstick and an apron, and she looked like she could use my help. I helped her make Toll House cookies.

CHAPTER FIFTY-SIX

That night in my room, I looked out the window. The moonlight shone around the edges of the blue-black clouds and I saw the lights on in Jeremiah's and Willie's and Josey's houses.

I thought they were sitting around and congratulating themselves on helping Panther do such a good job of fucking Honey Lady.

In the morning, I got dressed for breakfast and when I walked through the living room, Buck's duffle bag was by the front door. That gave me a pins-and-needles feeling.

Buck was already seated at the table, and Vern and Jeremiah noisily came in through the back and sat down. Mom was dishing up food in the kitchen. Her hair was in a tight ponytail and her lips, without lipstick, looked pale. As she put the food on the table, the men smiled and said, "Morning." She nodded her head, but didn't speak.

Buck was going to leave and I felt an emptiness inside of me. It became like a mouth that demanded to be fed. I started piling up pancakes, bacon, and eggs on my plate. Mom looked at me. "Tessa, what have I told you about eating too much?"

"I don't care if I get fat." I put a fork full of eggs in my mouth.

Jeremiah had put such a mouthful of pancakes in his mouth that he was having trouble closing his jaw. Buck and Vern talked about who they would run into at the rodeos. Cowboys such as Terry Burke, Tommy Tex Rawlings, and Mighty Jim McKinney were mentioned. I could tell by the sound of the men's voices they admired these men. It was as if they all had a little superman inside of them. Because it was Texas, these were spitting tobacco supermen, bowlegged supermen, and foul-mouthed supermen. They all had muscles of steel, and they leapt on horses and bulls with a single bound.

Buck, Vern, and Jeremiah were part of the man's world in a way I hadn't realized before. I imagined them at a rodeo running into each other and shaking hands and patting each other on the back, confirming that their cocks hung down the way Panther's did. The word "cock" was right on the tip of my tongue and I wanted to shout it.

The men were acting as if Mom weren't there. "I bet Jeremiah never heard the story about Tommy Tex after he won roping in San Antonio," Vern said. "The next morning, I went to his room at The Big Boot. His door wasn't locked, and he was still drunk and in bed with two pretty fillies, their legs intertwined like … like a giant drunk octopus. He tried to pull on his pants, but couldn't figure out which leg was his," Vern laughed.

Staring at Vern as if her eyes could burn him, Mom took an apple and cut it into small pieces, slapping the paring knife against the plate.

"Maybe it wasn't so funny. I'm sorry, Virginia. I just forgot myself," Vern said.

I was being ignored because I was a girl and it was making me angry. I looked at Vern. "Did you congratulate Tommy Tex for poking those girls the way you praised Panther when he poked Honey Lady with his pecker … I mean his big hard cock. His cock was so big it could stab its way to the center of the earth." My words hung in the air for a moment before Mom slapped the table.

"Tessa, not another word. I told you not to go out there yesterday," Mom said.

"So, I saw the big secret … the secret of fucking … in and out, poking … and even old ladies know about it. Do they fuck, too? And I'm going to say fucking as much as I want," I said.

"Go to your room right now," Mom said. I saw that Jeremiah and Vern had little smiles on their faces, which vanished when Mom gave them her scorcher look.

Instead of going to my room, I hid behind a big leather chair in the living room. Mom looked at Buck. "If you saw her out there, why didn't you tell her to go inside? She's talking like a gutter cowboy."

"Virginia, I'm sorry for telling that story. We don't all act like that at the rodeos," Vern said.

"Maybe you do, maybe you don't," Mom answered.

Jeremiah and Vern stood. Vern said to Buck, "We best be loading the gear and the horses, so you can leave." Vern put his hands in his pockets and looked at Mom. "Thank you so much for the great meals. You make this place a home." They slammed the screen door as they went out the back.

"I don't want Tessa talking like that. Couldn't you say something to Vern and Jeremiah about their language?" Mom said.

"I can't tell them what they can say. I don't know anything about kid-raising and I thought you, of all people, wouldn't be so old-fashioned," Buck said.

"What do you mean by that?"

"Nothing. It just seems to me Tessa was already kind of sassy when we met. I think she's a fine girl the way she is," Buck said.

I started doing a little dance behind the chair.

"Virginia, let's not argue before I leave," Buck said.

"I just never knew I'd have to compete with other men, horses, bulls, and maybe women for your attention."

"I'll take you out to San Antonio when I get back."

I peeked around the chair. At the door, Buck kissed her and held her close. I ran to Buck holding out my arms, and he let go of Mom and lifted me, hugging me and turning me around.

"I'm your cowgirl and I'll be waiting for you forever," I said.

He put me down and hugged Mom close to him again. "I wish you didn't seem so down in the mouth."

"Two months is a long time," Mom said.

We heard the pickups pulling the horse trailers drive up to the front of the house. Buck picked up his duffle bag and went out the front door. Mom and I watched from the front porch as he and Vern drove away, their trucks kicking up dust and gravel on the road. Mom looked sad and rubbed her forehead, as if she had a headache. I went to my room and cried.

CHAPTER FIFTY-SEVEN

The next morning was Friday, and I was awakened by Mom taking some of my clothes out of the closet and throwing them into a suitcase. Her cheeks were flushed and her red hair was sticking out all over the place like a wild woman.

"We're going to P.T. Flood's Café and Saloon over in Helotes," she said.

"I'm not going. What about school?" I asked.

"You'll miss a couple of days. You're not going to fight me. Hank Williams is singing there this weekend."

After breakfast, she came out of the bedroom dressed in tight jeans with the cuffs turned up, red high-heeled shoes, and a red and white checkered shirt. She put the suitcases in the back of the green Chevy station wagon and Gertrude in the front. I stood by the car with my arms crossed in front of me, wearing a wrinkled pink cotton dress with spots on it. I also had on my pink cowboy boots which were scuffed.

"Why don't you mind me? I told you to put on a clean dress. You'll change when we get there. Get in the car," she said.

I got in the back behind Gertrude and looked at the house and a shiver went through me. Old Man Henry stood on the porch, watching me. "You're not coming with me," I said.

"Tessa, stop it. Gertrude is coming," Mom said.

The tires made noise as we drove down the gravel driveway. We turned onto a two-lane highway and drove past a lot of open ranch land and past a billboard with the paper peeling off of an advertisement for Brill Cream. Mom had to tell me when we arrived at Helotes because it had only one street with a few stores spread out on each side of the two-lane street. They were of weather-beaten wood; a hardware store, a feed store, and a post office.

We came to a large sign on top of a building that said, "World's Best Food and Drink," and underneath it said, "P.T. Flood's Café and Saloon." The building was a wooden, dark green structure with a roof overhanging the porch. Vertical banners on poles were in the front and one said, "World Famous Enchiladas" was next to the one that said, "Hank Williams, Fri, Sat, Sun." A couple of horses were tied to a hitching post at the other end of the building, and cowboys were sitting in wooden chairs on the front porch. Some were napping.

Mom parked the station wagon on the dirt next to a pickup truck. All the cowboys' eyes followed Mom as she got out of the car and went to the other side to get Gertrude. The cowboys still watched Mom, holding Gertrude, as she walked up the front stairs. One cowboy said, "That's a pretty filly." Mom didn't even turn her head toward him as she went inside. I wished I had put on a clean dress before going out.

The place was dark and sawdust covered the floor. Cowboy hats and boots hung from the ceiling, and the whole place smelled of beer and cigarettes. There were wooden tables, some with names carved into them, and an assortment of chairs. The bar was lit up with red and blue neon tubes and in the middle of the bar was a mirror that said, "Pearl Beer." Another mirror said, "Lone Star Beer."

At one end of the room was a stage with shiny guitars propped up on stands. I could tell they were male guitars because they looked so strong. I went toward them and all of a sudden, I heard waves of country-western music coming from them, as if they were playing themselves. The invisible waves skidded off of the tables and I started moving my arms and legs in a dance. I felt wild. Then my mother grabbed my arm and pulled me back to the bar.

Mom sat at the bar holding Gertrude. A bartender wearing a cowboy hat and boots came over to us. "I'm looking for Mr. Flood. I spoke to him on the phone," Mom said.

"I'll get him," the bartender said. A few minutes later, Mr. Flood came out from the back. He was short but handsome, with blond hair combed straight back. He had shiny skin. His denim shirt was unbuttoned at the top, showing a small gold guitar against his curly chest hair. He wore a gold ring on each finger of each hand, and he moved in so close to Mom, as if he wanted to smell her. He put out his hand. "I'm Bartholomew, but people call me Bart." Mom shook his hand, and then he pushed some of her hair back over her shoulder. "I like your red hair."

"I talked to you on the phone," Mom said.

"I didn't know you have kids."

"They're no trouble. First, I came to see Hank Williams. I told you I'm a singer, but I also do waitress work."

"For the waitressing, I'll need you to fill out an application. But we can talk about that after the show."

"Where should I stay?" Mom asked.

"Lots of girls come through here and they stay next door. You better rent a trailer before they fill up."

We got back in the car, and drove down the road, and turned into the gravel driveway of the combination motel and trailer park. There were some individual bungalows in the front, while the back of the property was filled with trailers of all different sizes parked every which way. Some of the trailers had little lawns in front with awnings on the side. Quite a few older ones were dusty and had black soot in the metal seams and around the windows. There were a few that were shiny with words painted on their sides.

Mom followed the driveway all the way to the back. We passed people in folding chairs alongside their trailers, drinking beer. The driveway made a U-turn and we followed it back to the front. Mom stopped in front of a yellow bungalow with a yard. A bunch of ceramic gnomes stared at us. The sign on the front said, "Office of The Cozy Boot Motel and Trailer Park."

"Here we are," Mom said.

"I don't like this place. I want to go home," I said.

"We're here for the Hank Williams show and then I'll decide what we're doing," Mom said.

"What are you talking about? You said I'd only miss a couple of days of school."

"Everything is up in the air right now. We'll talk about this later," Mom said.

"I want to talk about it now," I said.

"No. Be quiet," Mom said.

A big woman wearing a large hanging flower print dress opened the screen door and walked toward us. Her body stuck out in unexpected places and jiggled when she walked. She had a warm smile above her double chin. "I'm Mama Ruby," she said. She stuck her head in the car window and looked at us. She smelled of popcorn. "Are you looking for accommodations? We're one of the few lodging places around here. It's catch as catch can."

"Right now, we'd like to stay three nights for the show," Mom said.

Mama Ruby kept staring at me, but before I could tell her to keep her eyes to herself, she said, "Since you got kids, I'll put you here in the middle across from me. See, it's fenced in which is good for the kids. It can get pretty rowdy in the back with the regulars, the musicians, and the people comin' fer the show." I looked at the faded pink and white trailer with a sagging metal awning. Around the trailer was a white picket fence that was missing some pieces of wood. On the lawn, there were ceramic ducks watching us. There was a little sign on the front of the trailer that said, "Duck Town."

Mama Ruby got her keys and we followed her across the lawn. She led us up three stairs. Inside, the trailer smelled of mildew and beer. It was clean, but the carpet was stained and the Formica counters were cracked. There were flower decals on the small refrigerator and flower print curtains covering the windows, if you could call those small things windows. It was Texas hot in there. Mama Ruby pulled a cord and turned on the ceiling fan that shook as it turned. She must have seen the expression on Mom's face because she said, "It's safe to leave the door open at night. My Wally sleeps with his guns and nobody'd dare to pull anything."

Mama Ruby pointed to the refrigerator and said, "We always keep ice fer the ice box. It's in the cooler right next to my house. Wally will get it fer you."

There was a small built in bed right behind the kitchen table across from the stove and the icebox. "Your girl can sleep here and you and the little one in the back," Mama Ruby said.

"My name is Tessa," I said.

Mama Ruby ignored me and walked toward the back. We passed a bathroom made for midgets and stood at the door of what was supposed to be a bedroom. "You and the baby can sleep in here," she said.

"We're going to spend most of our time at Floods," Mom said.

Mama Ruby pulled her dress down over some of her fat. "I guess you met Bart. Our hometown celebrity."

"He seemed nice," Mom said.

"Un-huh. I do baby-sitting real reasonable if you want to leave the baby with me during the shows." Mama Ruby took a good look at Mom. "A lot of girls come here wantin' this, or wantin' that. There's a whole lot of wantin' goin' on here." Mom took out money and paid Mama Ruby for three nights.

That evening, Mom got dressed in tight jeans and a red western shirt with white roses and white dangling fringe on it. She put on her new red cowboy boots and danced around a bit to see if they were going to hurt her feet. I put back on my same wrinkled pink dress and pink cowboy boots. We dropped Gertrude off with Mama Ruby and drove to Flood's Saloon.

We got a parking space right in front. The cowboys stared at Mom as we went inside. Even though there was a stage inside, a waitress told us to go out back where there was a much larger stage with seats and tables. The space had a metal roof with many strings of lights. There was a dance floor right in front of the stage with the tables and chairs around it. Mom got us a seat at one of the tables in the front. Other people came in and took seats. The stage was empty except for shiny guitars and one really big guitar, all propped on stands. There was a "Lone Star Beer" sign on the back wall.

A waitress came up, wearing a very short skirt. It would be easy to look up her skirt and see what was underneath. I asked her if that was her "pussy skirt" and the waitress looked surprised. Mom grabbed my arm hard and said, "Don't ruin this for me."

Mom ordered their Famous Enchiladas and a pitcher of beer. Three cowboys sat down at the table next to us. One whistled at Mom and smiled; he had holes where his teeth should be. The place filled up and the lights went down. Bart Flood came onto the stage and told us how lucky we were to have Hank Williams here. Hank Williams came out wearing a white western jacket with black musical notes down the front and down the sleeves. The audience clapped and cheered.

He was skinny, tall, with a square jaw and the bones in his face stood out. His group, the "Drifting Cowboys," came out on stage to back him up. He started playing, *The Honky-Tonk Blues*. People got up from their tables and crowded onto the dance floor. His singing continued with *Your Cheating Heart*. More people crowded onto the dance floor and they danced while holding their glasses of beer. He sang, *Lovesick Blues* and *Hey Good Looking* and the people were dancing and jumping up and down. I climbed up on the table to be able to see over the crowd.

Mom was drinking more beer with each song and she pushed her way to the front right by the stage and sang along with Hank. After he finished a song, he tipped his hat to her. With the next song *Take these Chains from My Heart*, Mom went wild, dancing and singing along. Men stared at her and said, "Go baby." One cowboy put his hand on her rear, but she slapped it away. The men made room for her to dance right in front of the stage. She unbuttoned her shirt, and she had on a black lace bra and she let her breasts bounce. One almost came out of her bra, white and free. The cowboys said, "Let it all hang out." She tucked it back in and kept dancing.

I pushed my way to the stage and found some stairs on the side. Before anyone could stop me, I went to the front by the speakers and started dancing and stomping my feet. The audience watched me until Bart came, and lifted me down, and took me back to my seat.

After awhile, the music stopped and everyone stopped. Hank bowed to the audience, smiled, and left the stage with his group. Mom looked around as if for the first time realizing she was in the front. She noticed her shirt was open and buttoned it up. She pushed her sweaty hair over her shoulders and came back to our table. Some cowboys crowded around her, and one pushed up against her like a stallion, but she told them to go away. She said, "I'm with my daughter."

Mom took my hand and I yelled as Mom dragged me away. Back at the trailer, she made me go to bed on the small foam mattress next to the kitchen table. Even with the side windows open, it was a furnace in there. Mom put on more makeup, fixed her hair, and said, "Don't you dare leave this trailer if you know what's good for you. I'll be back after the show." The screen door slammed as she left. I could still hear the music, but I was tired.

Later, I was awakened by a noise coming from the bedroom. I looked at the clock and it was four in the morning. I got up and put my ear to the thin plywood door. I heard Mom, and then I heard, "I like a feisty lady. You're a handful."

I lay back down on the mattress and pretended I was asleep. The plywood door opened, and in the darkness, I saw a short man. He came toward me. It was Bart, the owner of the saloon. His unbuckled belt clinked as he walked past me carrying his boots. "Buck's Mom's boyfriend, so you better stay away," I said.

He came back and stood over me. "Little lady, you better mind your own business."

He sat on a chair by the door and put on his boots. I heard the sound of his feet on the outside stairs.

CHAPTER-FIFTY-EIGHT

On Sunday, we went to Hank Williams' last show. It was after dark when Mom brought back barbeque, coleslaw, potato salad, and chocolate cake for us. She picked up Gertrude from Mama Ruby. She set up dinner on the little scuffed fold out table and I dripped barbeque sauce on my shirt. I looked at Mom, but she was quiet. "Is everything all right," I asked.

Mom wiped sweat off of her forehead and then wiped her mouth. "I need to talk to you about some important things."

I dished up more coleslaw on my paper plate. I looked at her, and she was just staring at me. "I'm thinking of leaving Buck and moving right in here and working as a waitress at Flood's," she said.

"No." I slammed my hand down on the table, knocking over the cold slaw and barbeque sauce container. BBQ sauce splattered across the table. It reminded me of blood. Something was gripping my stomach and throat. "No. This place is a dump and it smells."

"I can't take the isolation of that ranch, and I have to get you away from that colored boy you spend all your time with." I looked surprised.

"You thought I didn't know you were out with him in the barn every chance you got."

"You just want to be here, so Burt can poke you all the time. All you care about is getting poked just like a horse."

Mom got up and tried to slap me, but I ducked down. "How dare you talk to me like that."

"I'm not leaving Buck. He's going to adopt me."

"He hasn't asked me to marry him," Mom said.

"I'm sure he will. He wants to be my real father." I trembled, but I held back my tears.

"I know this is hard, but part of growing up is realizing we don't always get what we want."

"I'll run away. You have Gertrude, you don't need me."

"The police will come after you. Don't you want me to have a chance with my singing? I'd have that here," Mom said.

"I need a chance for something too."

"Kids adjust to things."

I started slapping my hands on the table. "No. No. You're always saying you're worried about me going crazy like Eunice. Well, there're a lot of things you don't know like what Old Man Henry's spirit is doing to me. I haven't wanted to upset you, but I have to tell you. He followed me here. He comes into my mind and body and he talks to me plain as day. Sometimes I see and feel his hand come over my hand. Then I don't have my own hand anymore," I said. I grabbed the steak knife and cut my hand. Blood oozed out.

She grabbed the knife away from me before I could cut myself again. "Stop this, Tessa. You're frightening me." She tried to look at my hand, but I pulled away.

I started pulling on my hair, hard. "Sometimes when I want to walk, I see his foot come over my foot because he wants to go where I'm going. And when I look in the mirror, I see his body superimposed on mine." Some strands of hair came out in my hands. I started jumping up and down. Mom tried to grab me, but I moved away. "Sometimes I do things to myself to try to make him go away," I said.

"What are you talking about? Come here," Mom said.

I moved around the trailer, staying out of her reach. "You have to help me make him go away!" I yelled. I marched my legs in place, and Mom grabbed my shoulders hard, trying to make me stop moving.

Mom's face twisted. "Stop this. Things are difficult enough. I don't understand all this. You've got me really worried. But it has to be one of your games. It's your imagination. You have to control yourself. I don't know what I can do!" she yelled. Tears mixed with her mascara on her face.

"I feel him coming after me. It will be much worse here. You're my mother and you have to help me," I yelled and twisted out of her grip and got up on one of the big armchairs in the front of the trailer. I jumped up and down. Gertrude cried in the bedroom.

"Stop jumping. You'll damage that chair. Other mothers don't have to deal with this. Do you want me to take you to the hospital? Please, I really need you to cooperate with me right now." I stopped jumping because of the pained look on her face. She grabbed me off the chair and shook me hard and cried, "Whatever you feel, you can act normal if you want to. You have to. Please try for me." She didn't see that I was scratching my arm with my nails, but it wasn't making the horrible feeling go away. She stepped back, pushed her hair over her shoulders, and pulled her blouse down. "I'll get Gertrude and let's go out and watch TV. It will calm us down. I can't think like this."

Mom got Gertrude and we went outside under the awning where there was a big RCA box with a little screen in the middle. The black cord stretched across the cement patio like a snake. She moved the folding chairs close to the TV. She put Gertrude on a couple of pads on the cement and went inside and came back with a beer and sat next to me. I calmed down a bit as we watched *The Tennessee Ernie Ford Show* for awhile, but Mom kept changing her position, trying to get comfortable. "Tessa, you don't understand all the pressure I'm under. Bart Flood is a nice man."

Gertrude started crying and clenching her fists. "She's hungry," Mom said, and stood up.

"Mom, please don't leave me. I'm afraid … afraid to be alone. You have to believe me about Old Man Henry." I trembled.

"I can't listen to any more of this tonight. You wear me out. I have to rest. *I Love Lucy* is coming on and that should cheer you up."

I had a mean awful expression. "Do I look like I can be cheered up? Going back to the ranch and Buck is the only thing that will cheer me up."

Mom turned and went inside, leaving me to watch the little screen.

CHAPTER FIFTY-NINE

A wind whined through the trees and blew against the aluminum sides of the trailer. It blew against my lonely skin and felt as if it entered me, burning me. It was getting cooler, so I went inside. Mom was asleep with Gertrude and I put on a sweater, jacket, cowboy boots, and cowboy hat. I took some money out of Mom's wallet and put it in my white purse, along with my diary.

I walked down the gravel driveway to the road and toward Flood's. I stomped each foot down on the side of the road, imagining that I was stomping on Mom's face. I tried to think of what to do. Headlights came toward me, temporarily blinding me. A car passed close to me and slowed down, and the woman inside motioned for me to move back from the street.

The music was loud at Flood's, but a few people were coming down the stairs and going to their cars. I went to the outside patio and sat at table way in the back. I stuffed leftover French fries in my mouth, and watched a couple at the table in front of me. She pointed her finger at him, and he talked loudly. "You're always saying I don't take you any place and now we're here and you want to leave," he said.

"I want to get back to San Antonio and sleep in my own bed," she said. She grabbed her purse and walked toward the door. I followed behind them as if I was their child. Their voices became louder as they talked to each other. Outside, they both stopped at the driver's side of their pickup truck. Both leaned against the truck to hold themselves up. I pretended I was walking past them, but I snuck back around to the passenger side of the pickup and peeked over the bed of the truck.

She grabbed the keys from the man. "You let me drive. You've had too much to drink."

"Quit telling me what to do," he said. He tried to get the keys from her, but she pushed him away, and he fell to the ground.

She opened the door and got into the driver's seat. The man tried to get up. I put one foot on the footrest sticking out of the side of the truck bed, and quickly lifted myself over and into the truck bed. I lay flat under the window, so the lady couldn't see me. She started the engine and turned on the headlights.

"For such a big man, you can't hold your liquor. Hurry up. Get in," she said.

He went around and opened the passenger door and got in. "Don't think I'm going to fuck you tonight, Miss Bossy."

"Shut up. I take care of myself."

They drove down the highway, and I held my jacket tight around myself, as my hair blew in the wind. I looked toward the back of the truck bed and there was Old Man Henry. "Tessa, you have to go back. Something is not right. I'm having trouble following you."

"Good. I'm leaving everything behind," I said.

I turned away and when I looked back, I could barely see him, but I heard him. "You have to go back to your mother. It's easier to reach you when you're around her … I need my relatives together."

I laughed as his voice sounded weaker. "I hate you. I hope you feel my anger."

After awhile, I saw the lights of San Antonio. Driving into the city, the dark heavy buildings crowded together like a bunch of snobby people.

They reached upward as if to say, "We're growing, and we even own the sky and don't forget it."

The couple in front was still talking loudly to each other. With their mouths grimacing, they looked like cartoon people. In fact, I felt as if I was in a cartoon. I recognized we were on the same road Mom and I had taken when we left.

As we drove right into downtown San Antonio, I peeked over the side of the truck and looked at street signs. After awhile, we turned onto Alamo Plaza. Yes, I know this street, I thought. We drove past the Alamo and then we passed the Menger Hotel all lit up, which was across from the Alamo. I relaxed a little because I knew where I was.

A couple of blocks down the street from the Menger, they stopped at a gas station and the woman rushed to the bathroom. The man was asleep in the front and didn't notice as I climbed out of the back and started walking back toward the Menger Hotel. I was trying to think of what to tell someone if they asked me what I was doing here. I could say, "Mom thought I was in the car. She'd been drinking … I live on a ranch in Boerne … I don't know the address or the phone number … I should have written it down. I have to get back there?" I didn't realize I was talking out loud to myself and I bumped into a woman walking with a man.

The woman put her hand on my shoulder. "Little girl, are you lost?"

"I'm staying at the Menger," I said.

"You better get back to your mama."

"I'm going there right now." I walked away from her.

Even though my hair was uncombed, I stood up straight as I walked into the lobby of the Menger Hotel, the strap from my purse over my arm. I sat on one of the red brocade couches in the lobby. There were only a couple of people by the elevators and a man wearing a green uniform behind the desk. I looked to my side, and Old Man Henry was sitting on the couch next to me. "It's taking lot of effort for me to be here. I can't keep it up. You have to go back to your mother." His voice sounded as if he was under water.

I clenched my jaw. "You need me to believe in you. Lilly Mae told me that someday I'd be strong enough to resist you."

"Don't let me disappear with no one to remember me. I can't fade into that darkness. I have to exist. I won't do anything you don't want me to do," he said. He reached out his arm to me. I swung my purse at him, hitting only air, but a fearful expression came over his face.

"You only care about yourself. See, your voice is becoming weaker. I'm growing up and you don't exist for me anymore," I yelled.

People in the lobby stared at me, and the man behind the desk came over to me. "Where are your parents?" he asked.

"They're upstairs. They told me to wait for them. I'm sorry I yelled. My family yells."

"What's your name?" he asked.

"Bonnie Jane Hubbard."

He went back to his desk. I was so tired I had to lie down, but I didn't put my boots on the couch. My feet stuck over the edge. The next thing I felt was a man's hand on my shoulder shaking me. I opened my eyes and two policemen were standing there. "I didn't put my feet on the couch," I said.

"You need to come with us," one policeman said.

"I'm just a kid. I'm not bothering anybody."

The policeman pulled me up by my arm, and the other one took my other arm, and pulled me toward the door. I let my feet drag across the floor. At the police station, I was led past several men sitting on a bench with their hands handcuffed behind their backs. One smiled at me. They took me into a room with a couch, and a table, and chairs. They told me to sit down and stay there. There were stains on the couch and it smelled of coffee. I kept my purse on my arm and I lay down on the couch. It was late when a woman woke me. Her hair was short and gray, and her face was without makeup, showing a lot of wrinkles. She carried a briefcase and had a bulging black purse over her shoulder. She sat next to me. "I'm Jennifer. Tell me your name," she said.

"Winnie Betty Boop," I said.

"Tell me your real name." I didn't answer. "I want to take you home. I think you've run away and you need to know this isn't a game. Your parents must be worried about you." I looked down and didn't answer. She opened her briefcase and looked through some papers. "You'll have to come with me."

She kept poking me with questions as she drove me to a green house with white shutters and print curtains in the windows. The front door opened and a woman with straight blond hair, old worn jeans, and crooked teeth stood there smiling at me. Behind her was a tall skinny man wearing a plaid shirt. His belt was holding up his pants that were too big. They stepped back so we could step inside. "She says her name is Winnie," Jennifer said.

The blond-haired woman bent down to me and put her hand on my shoulder. I moved back. "My name's Mary Jo, and this is my husband, Clyde."

Jennifer set her briefcase on an end table by the couch and took out a folder and handed it to Mary Jo. Mary Jo looked me up and down. "The bedrooms are in the back. We have to keep our voices down because the other children are sleeping."

I whispered, "I'll do it this one time but …" Then I raised my voice, "I'm not in the habit of keeping my voice down." The man's and the woman's faces both became tense.

Clyde said, "When you're here, you follow our rules. I'll show you where you sleep tonight. We have five other children here."

Mary Jo led me down a hallway past an open bedroom door. I saw kids sleeping in bunk beds. She went in the last bedroom and motioned for me to follow. "You'll sleep in here with Harvey. He's several years younger you. He hasn't talked to anyone since he's been here."

On one side of the room, Harvey was lying in bed, underneath an old blanket with holes in it. He had thick brown hair that stuck out all over the place, a large forehead, and a round face. Mary Jo took a flannel nightgown out of the dresser. "You can change in the bathroom down the hall. Hang your clothes in the closet. Do you want me to hold on to your purse?"

"Don't touch my purse." I held it against my chest.

When I came back from the bathroom wearing the nightgown, Harvey without speaking watched me get into bed. "I don't have a hairbrush or toothbrush," I said. I turned on my side, so I could look at him. "Who are these people?" I asked.

Harvey lifted himself up on his elbows and turned his face toward me, and there was a purple and black color around his swollen eye. "They are foster parents, but temporary ones."

"Do they always act so nice? I can tell they are pretending," I said.

"This is only my second night here. You know they get paid to keep us. I was at another place, but I had to leave."

"What happened?"

"I bit the foster mom and other things. Then she yelled on the phone that I have problems."

"My grandma calls that psycho-mental stuff."

"I don't care what you call it. I don't let people get away with things," he said.

"I don't let people get away with things either."

"Where are you from?" he asked.

"From up north of here. My father has a ranch, but my mother took me away."

"What's your name?"

"Winnie. This is my first time in a place like this."

"I'm Harvey. I've been in several homes. My mom died. I really miss her."

"I don't miss mine."

"She might come here to get you."

"I'll run away again unless she takes me back to the ranch. What happens tomorrow?" I asked.

"We get up and eat breakfast. Maybe we'll go to school, but it won't be a permanent school."

I took out my diary from my purse and sat on the floor by the nightlight and started writing in it.

"What are you doing?" Harvey asked.

"I write down things that have happened to me." I looked at him. "Can we be friends?"

"I've never been friends with a girl. I don't want to be a sissy," he said.

"I'm a strong girl. You won't be a sissy."

"I miss my mom and I have trouble getting to sleep, but don't tell anyone I said that," he said. Tears came to his eyes and he tried to hold them back. I went to his bed.

"Harvey, I understand. Can I sit next to you?"

"Not too close," he said. I sat on the bed next to him.

"Would you like me to tell you a story?"

"Yes."

"Can I hold your hand?" I asked.

"O.K. For a little while."

"Just lie on your back and close your eyes." He turned onto his back and I took his hand. It was warm and sweaty.

"There's a town somewhere south of here off the main highway. It's called *Sky Town*. The land is flat and the town has old buildings that stand next to each other like a bunch of old women gossiping. But the huge sky has the most beautiful clouds. People say the clouds are mysterious. They have their own life and can make themselves into whatever shapes they want to be. And the clouds care about the children. So, if a child is whipped and goes outside, the clouds will come together and take the shape of a lion, a bear, or a dog, to cheer the child up. If the clouds are angry with mean parents, they bring rain and thunder in a matter of minutes."

Harvey opened his eyes. "I don't know if I believe you."

"Pretend. Everything's better when you pretend. In that town, a pretty girl lived with her mother and grandma."

"I don't want to hear no story about a girl," he said.

"O.K. A boy named Clarence lived with his mother and grandma."

Harvey opened his eyes and looked at me. "I lived with just my mom."

"The boy's mother worked as a waitress but wanted to be a country-western singer."

"My mom worked hard in a bar." Harvey rubbed his eye that wasn't swollen, and he yawned.

"The Grandma was strict and used a switch on the boy. She sat in a big chair drinking what she called her "coffee," but it was wine."

"My mother's boyfriend didn't care who saw him drinking and he used his belt on me. Did this boy just stay in the house with his grandma all the time? What a sissy," he said.

"The Grandma had a colored man named Thomas who worked around the place. One day, he saw Clarence sitting on the steps looking sad and he asked him what was wrong. Clarence said, 'I don't have many friends at school. The other kids have fathers who teach them things.'

"The next day, Thomas came to the house and called Clarence into the backyard. He had brought two old gloves and a baseball. He taught him how to play baseball."

Harvey said, "He taught him how to play catch." He hit his hand into an imaginary glove, and said, "Whack."

"Thomas said he was becoming really good at catch and the boys at school noticed and asked him to play ball with them after school. Then Clarence was happy."

"So, what happened?" Harvey asked.

"The problem was that one-day Clarence came home with a note from school that said he used some dirty words that he'd learned from the older boys."

"I got in trouble for using those kinds of words," Harvey said.

"The Grandma became really angry and said she didn't want him playing with those boys. She wanted him to come right home after school. One day, he couldn't stop himself from playing with the boys and stayed out late. When he got home, the Grandma was waiting for him with two switches in her hands. The Mother was at work and didn't know the Grandma was whipping him. There was no one to help him. Then the clouds gathered over his house and started making thunder and lighting. It was so loud that other people in the town came out to see what was going on. They thought it was strange that the sun was out except over the Grandma's house where it was dark, and the lightening was striking. It looked as if it would hit the house. Then rain fell just over the house. The Mother came out of the bar and knew she had to get home. At home, she stopped the Grandma's beating. The Mother decided to take Clarence away. The Mother had a boyfriend who lived on a ranch and the next day she packed their things and left for the ranch."

"The boy had to leave his friends and I had to leave my friends because my mother died," Harvey said.

"But he was going to a ranch where there were cowboys to teach him to ride and other things. The boyfriend was a rodeo cowboy and was going to adopt the boy."

Harvey was having trouble keeping his eyes open. "He was going to have a real father. We can be friends and you'll tell me some more." His eyes were closed, and he was asleep, so I touched his bushy hair.

I wrote in my diary about how I told Harvey a story, and it helped him get to sleep. I also wrote, I won't go back unless it's back to Buck. I'm on my own and I can make friends wherever I go.

www.ingramcontent.com/pod-product-compliance
Lightning Source LLC
Chambersburg PA
CBHW020922110726
47900CB00001B/259